The
Bletchley
Girls

BOOKS BY ANNA STUART

The Berlin Zookeeper
The Secret Diary
A Letter from Pearl Harbor
The Midwife of Auschwitz

The
Bletchley
Girls

ANNA STUART

Bookouture

Published by Bookouture in 2022

An imprint of Storyfire Ltd.
Carmelite House
50 Victoria Embankment
London EC4Y 0DZ

www.bookouture.com

ISBN: 978-1-80314-743-7
eBook ISBN: 978-1-80314-742-0

For Tracey, Francesca and Ptolemy –
top neighbours, fab friends.

PART ONE

1940

ONE

MARCH 1940

Steffie

With a loud whistle and a throaty wheeze, the train pulled into the country station and, gathering up her clutch of matching suitcases with some difficulty, Stefania Carmichael let herself out onto the small platform. As with all train stations, now that the Germans were lurking over the English Channel, the location sign had been removed and, suddenly nervous, she reached for the arm of the guard.

'Is this Bletchley?'

He grinned at her.

'It is, madam. You'll be wanting the Park?'

She nodded.

'Looks like you're not the only one.'

He indicated two other young women alighting a little further up the platform, luggage banging their ankles as they looked uncertainly around in the grey March dusk.

'Right. Yes. Thanks.'

'Good luck.'

And then he was gone, back into the train as it pulled away

through the gloom leaving Steffie stranded. She looked around
the scruffy little station. It had been a long, confusing journey
and, if she was honest, this strange place didn't look entirely
worth the effort. Only three months ago she'd been welcoming
1940 at her engagement party in Rome, and now she was on
some tiny platform in misty England and her fiancé, Matteo,
was... She swallowed. Steffie had no idea where Matteo was,
only that he'd been hurried into the Regia Aeronautica – the
Italian air force – as swiftly as she'd been yanked out of the
British embassy where her father, Major General Anthony
Carmichael, had been the military attaché for six happy years.

It had been a horrific trip across a Europe criss-crossed with
troops and refugees, and a huge relief to see the White Cliffs of
Dover at last, but London had been unbearable. Her mother
had tried to set her up with every British officer who came
through their doors, as if Matteo had been some sort of whim, as
if her engagement was no longer valid because of the war, as if
their love had expired just because a few hundred miles now
separated them. Nonsense!

'I don't want a husband, Mother,' she'd protested after a
particularly painful afternoon tea with some ancient chap from
the Home Office.

Her mother had looked at her aghast. 'But, darling, you're
nearly twenty-one.'

'So? There's a war on.'

'Which will age you terribly. Now, how about Colonel
Thompson? He lost a leg at Gallipoli, but the limp is jolly
rakish, don't you think?'

Steffie had been hugely grateful when her father had
stepped in. The major general had given her an understanding
hug then gone off to his club and come back saying he'd found
her war work 'using her languages'.

'You'll be top-hole at it, old girl,' he'd said, and she'd gone
warm with pride at his belief in her, but looking around this

funny corner of the cold, damp country she was having to get used to calling home again, she wondered if it was some sort of sick joke.

'Chin up,' she told herself firmly. It wasn't as if she was in danger, not like Matteo would be if Italy joined the war.

Italy won't join the war, she promised herself. It's what her father had always said, and he should know. 'He's just bluster, Musso,' he'd tell her. 'He might nick a few colonies in Africa but he won't go all-out against us. Italians prefer love to war.'

God, she hoped he was right because she had certainly found love with *her* Italian and no silly English officer was going to make her forget him. Not that she was likely to even meet one of those out here in the sticks. Fighting for composure, she saw the two other girls were still hovering nearby and looked more closely at the nearest one – a petite young woman with ivory skin and stunning red hair. There was something of the faerie about her, Steffie thought, save that she had never before seen a faerie in the grey-blue uniform of a WAAF.

'You've never seen a faerie at all,' she chided herself, and the girl looked over. Lordy, she'd think Steffie mad if she wasn't careful. She attempted a cheery wave but it only gained her another strange look and, spotting a familiar letter in the girl's hand, she yanked her own out of her handbag and buried herself in it:

> At Bletchley station, take the exit from the arrival platform, go to the station forecourt and report to a hut on the far right-hand side marked RTO and show him but DO NOT GIVE HIM your envelope. He will direct you.

The faerie was standing quite still, reading her own instructions, but the girl on the far side was coming towards them, her tread rapping out confidently on the platform. The first thing Steffie noticed was that she was very tall, her long legs emphasised by elegant flared trousers. She had dark brown hair worn in a smart plait and striking, angular features but she was smiling so Steffie attempted another wave. This time it was returned.

'Hey there. Any idea what an RTO is?' The girl's voice was clipped but not unfriendly.

'None whatsoever,' Steffie said cheerfully, 'but it looks like we might be about to find out. Stefania Carmichael – Steffie.'

She stuck out a hand and the other girl took it and gave it a hearty shake.

'Frances Morgan – Fran. Funny old place this.'

'Very funny. Shall we find this hut then?'

'Let's. And, er...'

Fran turned to the third girl but she was already moving to the exit, a duffel bag almost her own size slung over her slim shoulder. Steffie looked around for a porter but the platform was bare, so she self-consciously hoisted up her hat-box and grabbed a suitcase in each hand. Her mother had urged her to take as many clothes as she could because, 'It's best to be prepared for all social occasions, darling,' but looking at the faerie's simple bag and Fran's single suitcase she thought perhaps she'd overdone it. Ah well, no turning back now.

Trying to look as if she carried her own bags all the time, she marched out to the forecourt and peered around. A small hut sat in the corner with RTO written across the top and an elderly gent inside. He stood up and tipped his cap as she approached.

'Can I help you, miss?'

Gratefully setting her suitcases down, Steffie pointed to the sign.

'RTO?'

'Rail Transport Officer,' he told her proudly.

'Of course. Lovely. We've been told you'll tell us where to go.'

'Have you indeed?' She placed her letter on the counter and

he grinned. 'Ah. The Park!' He pointed a wrinkled finger across the forecourt. 'You want to head down the station approach to the main road there. See?' She nodded obediently. 'Then you turn right and in a few hundred yards you'll come to a country lane. Go up it until you reach a pair of iron gates and one of the sentries will tell you where to go next.'

'Like a treasure hunt,' Steffie suggested.

'Sort of,' he said. 'Only without the treasure.'

'Right.'

'And with a lot of mud. I hope you've got decent shoes on.' He leaned out to peer at the scarlet heels her mother had said were 'just the thing to impress' and shook his head. 'Oh dear. You needed to take a leaf out of your friends' books, love.'

Steffie glanced at Fran's sensible Oxfords and the faerie's sturdy boots and groaned. She should never have listened to her mother.

'We can wait while you change,' Fran suggested. 'You must have another pair among all that lot?'

'Nothing made for mud,' Steffie admitted, feeling stupid, but she'd got halfway across Europe in pretty shoes so she wasn't going to allow an English country lane to stop her. 'It'll brush off, right?'

'Right,' Fran agreed stoutly, and Steffie smiled gratefully and bent to pick up her suitcases once more.

Fran

Fran watched Stefania as she battled with her luggage. She'd been trying not to look her up and down too openly but was glad to have a chance to take her in now, for she'd never seen anyone so immaculately turned out. The other girl's pretty face was expertly made up and her blond hair perfectly waved and set. Her suit had quite clearly been made to measure by a skilled seamstress as it clung to her curves with discreet elegance. Fran, brought up among her parents' Cambridge university set, was used to people looking smart, but rarely this stylish.

She glanced over to the other girl, but she was dressed in WAAF uniform so gave away nothing of her own fashion choices. Fran studied her in the last thin rays of light. She looked young and she had to be a Scot, surely, with that red hair and pale skin dusted with freckles, as if she'd been left out in the rain to rust. Well, there was only one way to find out.

'We haven't been introduced,' she said, sticking out her hand. 'Frances Morgan.'

'Ailsa MacIver,' the girl offered, the soft burr confirming Fran's suspicions.

'Steffie Carmichael,' Steffie put in. 'Sorry I can't shake your hand. Brought far too many bags.'

'You probably had longer than me to pack,' Ailsa said, then turned away with a gruff, 'Shall we get a move on before the light fails?'

Without waiting for an answer, she made off across the fore-court, Steffie struggling manfully after with her armfuls of luggage, and Fran had to grab her own case before she was left behind.

'Lay on, MacDuff!' Fran cried and instantly wished she hadn't as Ailsa frowned over her shoulder and Steffie failed to stifle a giggle. 'I wasn't being rude,' she said, hastening to catch up as they turned onto the main road. 'I just, you know, like Shakespeare. Do you? Like Shakespeare that is?'

'Shakespeare?' the Scots girl asked, frowning as if she'd never even heard of the world's greatest playwright, but then she shook her head. 'Not really. And especially not *Macbeth*. People think all Scots are murdering madmen and women because of that play.'

'Right. I see. That is, *I* don't think that. Just like I don't think all Danes wander around procrastinating or all Romans go about trying to borrow each other's ears.'

This got her another frown but Steffie laughed.

'I confess, a lot of Shakespeare goes over my head,' Steffie said easily. 'I like going to the theatre though – the dressing-up, the cocktails, those miniature boxes of chocolates that keep you going when the third act drags.' Fran stared at her and she grimaced. 'Sorry – I'm not very cultured. I usually prefer the interval to the play.'

Now it was Fran who laughed. At least Steffie was honest, she supposed, and she was probably always in one of those fancy boxes where you couldn't see the play properly, so it was no wonder she didn't get it. Fran fell easily into step with the other two as they headed past a quiet row of houses and a warmly lit pub. A waft of something deliciously meaty drifted out and she looked longingly inside, but supposed they had to press on. Night was falling fast and as they passed the pub, the blackout shutters snapped down over the windows, killing the warm glow and leaving them scarcely able to see ten yards ahead.

'Do you go to the theatre a lot?' she asked Steffie to distract herself from the gathering night.

'More than I deserve, though it was mainly opera in Rome.'

'Rome?'

'Long story. What about you, Ailsa?'

The redhead stopped and pointed up the rough road ahead of them.

'Is this the country lane?'

'It looks appropriately muddy,' Steffie said ruefully, stepping onto the track and sending up an instant splatter of dirt. 'I tell you what, I'd take a theatre right now!'

'Me too,' Fran agreed, fumbling in her gas mask case for her torch and shining the beam up the road. Bare trees cast spiky shadows across the rough tarmac and she shivered.

'I don't think I've ever been to the theatre,' Ailsa said, and Fran swung back, astonished.

'Ever?'

Ailsa shrugged.

'There isn't one on my island and when I go to Skye, I'm always far too busy shopping to waste time in a theatre.'

'Waste...?' Fran spluttered furiously.

This was like her family all over again. Her mother, father and two older brothers were all medics and convinced the only theatre worth entering was an operating one. Two years ago when Fran had said she wanted to do an English Literature degree they'd choked in disgust and told her it was 'pointless self-indulgence'. Last year, when she'd got herself a job in the university library, they'd patted her patronisingly on the head and said they supposed it would keep her busy until she 'came to her senses'. This year, when she'd wanted to sign up for war work, they'd battled to persuade her to join the ambulance service, as if that might somehow bring her back into the medical fold. Thank the Lord for Peter Lucas!

Peter was a brilliant and earnest English don who, before the war, had spent most of his time in the library doing research into the obscure ends of classical literature. He'd embraced Fran's ability to dig out gems from the rarer collections and before long they'd been taking tea together to discuss a plan of attack on the archives. A charming man, shortly to marry his third wife but yet to have any children, he'd taken Fran under his wing and been busily encouraging her to defy her family and study literature when war had broken out and he'd been whipped away. Meeting him on leave last Christmas, she'd bemoaned her family's approach and he'd told her he knew 'just the chaps who could use someone of your skills'. The call to Bletchley had come a week later and she'd been so looking forward to being among like-minded people at last, but already she was meeting opposition.

'I'll have you know—' she started, but Ailsa put up a hand.

'I get to a town once a year,' she said crisply.

'Once a year?' Steffie gasped.

'Exactly. It's a lot of civilisation to catch up on and, besides, the theatre in Portree is awfully wee and mainly shows films and local productions. I listen to radio plays though.'

'Right,' Fran stuttered, thinking of Cambridge, stuffed with arts venues, and trying to picture this curious girl's home. 'Sorry.'

'I tune into ones from all over the world. Recently I listened to a production of *A Streetcar Named Desire* from San Francisco.'

'Really? How?'

Ailsa winked at her in the torchlight and suddenly looked far more human.

'I can sniff out an illegal radio station at a hundred paces. That's why I'm here. You two?'

'Something to do with speaking Italian and German, I think,' Steffie said. 'Fran?'

Fran frowned.

'Honestly, I've no idea. I speak French but hardly fluently. Here, however, it seems I am.'

She gestured to the iron gates looming up in the torchlight before them.

'Who goes there?' a sharp voice demanded, and Fran felt Steffie and Ailsa huddle in on either side of her and was glad of them.

'New recruits,' she stuttered out.

A man stepped from a gatehouse and shone a torch on them, far brighter than Fran's pencil one. He wore a dark uniform and a blue-topped cap and to her horror he was holding a revolver.

'Letters,' he demanded.

Ailsa handed over hers, neatly folded, and Steffie offered up a more crumpled version which the sentry pointedly smoothed out as he checked it. Fran felt her heart thump as she scrabbled in her handbag but finally her fingers closed around the piece of paper and she pulled it out.

'Hmm. This all seems in order.' He handed them back. 'Up there to the mansion – you won't miss it. Report at the door for the OSA.'

'OSA?' Fran asked, her voice squeaking annoyingly.

'Official Secrets Act,' the sentry snapped. 'The most important document you'll ever sign.'

He waved them off and, for the second time, Fran was glad to have Steffie and Ailsa at her side.

'Lay on, MacDuff?' Ailsa suggested and Fran smiled weakly and reached, yet again, for her suitcase.

Ailsa

Ailsa MacIver marched up to the funny-looking 'mansion', trying not to let it show that her duffel bag cord was digging into her shoulder, her eyes were prickling with tiredness, and her stomach was churning with a nauseating mixture of excitement, hunger and – worst of all – homesickness.

You wanted to come, lass, she reminded herself. *You wanted to get off the island. You wanted to see the world.*

It was all true, though she'd imagined more the sparkling waters of the Mediterranean or the elegant streets of Paris than a peculiar Gothic mansion in the dullest countryside she'd ever seen. So many times she'd kicked at the restraints of her tiny village on North Uist, bored with the white beaches, the endless seas, the craggy hills, but right now every bit of her longed to see them again.

If she was still there, she could be running down the beach, or going to see the fishermen in with their catch, or singing around the piano at the Westford Inn just as she had at New

Year. She shuddered at the memory. That had been the night Alasdair had tried to kiss her. They'd escaped the pub to the bothy where he kept his amateur radio station and she'd been tuning his set to find New Year celebrations from around the world when he'd grabbed her.

She'd been so shocked she hadn't resisted at first and when she'd finally pushed him away, he'd gone red as a kestrel's breast and stammered apologies all the way back to her door. She'd put it down to the Hogmanay whisky and gone to sleep but been woken the next morning by Ma whirling into her room like a banshee.

'Aren't you a clever wee lass,' she'd cried, flinging open the curtains. 'We had hopes, of course, Pa and I, 'twas only natural we'd have hopes, but we didn't dare believe it would be so fast. And you only eighteen too! Mrs Murray will be raw with jealousy. Her Lorna's nigh-on twenty and not a whisper, not even from old Jock! Up now, lass. Up! You can't be lazing in bed like an eejit with your groom waiting downstairs, can you?'

'Groom?' Ailsa had stuttered, yelping as her mother had applied a brush to her tangled hair.

'Groom, aye! Isn't it marvellous? Here before the cockerel, he was, cap in hand, asking for your pa. He said yes, of course, dinnae worry about that, and he's off to summon the village. It's a braw New Year, to be sure. Now – this dress, I think, don't ye?'

Ailsa closed her eyes against the picture of her mother trying to wrestle her into her Sunday best with Alasdair in the kitchen below and half the island arriving to celebrate a wedding no one had thought to ask her about.

'Ridiculous,' she muttered.

'Sorry?' Steffie asked.

Ailsa pulled herself out of her reverie and, with a self-conscious cough, gestured to the building before them. It was a curiously lacy mansion house, mainly red brick but with big stone-edged windows sticking out. On one side an ornate green dome, like a colonial officer's hat, perched on top of a jutting wing and the whole effect was somewhere between charming and grotesque.

'This place. It looks a wee bit ridiculous.'

'Doesn't it just,' Steffie agreed. 'Like someone has taken one house and bolted various other ones onto it. Poor ugly old thing.'

Ailsa instantly felt sorry for the building.

'It's not its fault.'

Steffie laughed.

'I suppose not. Maybe it's nicer inside. Shall we?'

Ailsa waved with what she hoped was a polite indicator for her to lead the way. Stefania Carmichael looked as if she was at home in places far smarter than this and she was very glad to step into her shadow as they moved into a wood-panelled hallway.

'Hello there?' Steffie called. 'Anyone at home?'

They looked around. It didn't seem especially intimidating. To one side a sturdy table held a beer barrel, complete with tap, drip tray and glasses, plus a notebook marked in a slanting script with the words 'chit book' which some wag had altered to 'cheat book'. Behind oak doors they could hear the sound of type-writers and voices, but no one came out to meet them.

'Hello?!' Steffie called again.

'Hellooo!' The reply came from above and they all leaned back to see a dapper young man hanging over the balustrade of the large staircase. 'Hang on a sec. I'm coming.' He came tapping down the stairs, hand already outstretched. 'Harry Hinsley. Pleased to meet you. Have you got those letter things they insist on?'

They all produced their battered letters, and he glanced over them.

'Capital. This way. You're in luck. Denniston's off duty but Travis is here. He'll take you through the legals before we find the billeting officer.' He turned to head back up and Ailsa eyed the long run of steps, shifting her duffel bag to her other shoulder with an ill-concealed groan. Harry hit his forehead with his hand. 'Good Lord, sorry. Leave all that clobber there. It'll be quite safe from everything but the odd beer splash. Now, come on – it's getting late and dinner will be on soon.'

'Dinner?' Fran said. 'Why didn't you say! Come on, girls.'

She dumped her suitcase at the bottom of the stairs and bounded up after Mr Hinsley. Steffie was swift to follow, her red shoes shedding mud as she went, and Ailsa had little choice but to go too. Her stomach churned even more as she headed upwards, round-vowelled English voices swirling out of every doorway. What was she doing here?

Not getting married, she reminded herself sternly. Oh, her parents had been furious when she'd turned Alasdair down. Her ma had actually howled, before letting out a stream of curses Ailsa had never heard from her before. The words 'ungrateful bairn', and 'puffed-up wee bantam' stuck in her memory in particular, mainly because they weren't true. She loved her parents and had always been grateful for her safe, happy home. She knew they'd been sad they could have no other children and had done her best to make them proud of her, but this had been too much.

Alasdair was a lovely man but he was nearly forty. He taught the village schoolchildren in the week and played with his home-built wireless set on the weekends and there was nothing wrong with that, but Ailsa wanted more. There was a whole world out there, she'd tried to tell her ma, and she wanted to see a bit of it before she settled down. That had brought on more howling and more curses, and in the end, with the entire village camped on the doorstep to watch the drama, Ailsa had packed the duffel bag that was now sitting at the bottom of some fancy English steps and made for the ferry.

Of course, being New Year's Day, it hadn't been running so

she'd had a humiliating wait in her friend Kelsey's house until it had finally chugged into view two days later. She'd expected her ma to come round, to forgive her, to maybe ask what she meant, but she hadn't even come near. Only her pa had arrived, bumbling around like a nervous bear, asking what she was going to do. She'd told him about the man who'd contacted her on the airwaves before Christmas, the man who'd told her she was skilled as a radio operator and should report to somewhere called Broadway House in London if she wanted to use those skills to help her country defeat the Nazis.

'You?' her father had whispered, looking at her with unflattering incredulity. 'They want you to defeat the Nazis, Ailsa?'

'Not on my own, Pa.'

'Well, no, but even so... You're just a wee slip of a girl.'

'A wee slip of a girl who'd rather give it a try than marry Alasdair.'

'Your ma won't be happy.'

'You'll tell her I love her?'

'I'll try.'

He'd not come again and neither of her parents had been at the tiny pier when the steamer had finally arrived.

'You're away to the mainland, Ailsa MacIver?' the ferryman had asked, staring at her duffel bag.

'Away to London, Fergus.'

'London? In England?'

His horror had made her laugh then, but it echoed through her head now.

'Take a seat, ladies.'

Three chairs sat in a line on one side of a huge desk, three sheaves of paper before them. Ailsa wanted to flee the austere room, run down the stairs, grab her bag and retrace her steps all the way back to the safety of North Uist, but Steffie and Fran were sitting down and, frankly, her legs were shaking too much to stand so she followed their example.

'Thank you.' The man – Travis – was tall and broad-shouldered and looked at them over the top of curiously narrow spectacles. 'Welcome to Bletchley Park. What we do here is top secret. You will be told only what you need to know and you will tell that to no one else unless authorised to do so. Is that understood?'

'Not even each other?' Fran asked.

'Not anyone. Not your friends, not your parents, not your boyfriends. Not the bus driver, not the sentry, not the lady in the canteen.'

'Right,' Fran agreed, and Ailsa was relieved to hear her cultured voice wobble slightly. Clearly she wasn't the only one feeling shaky here.

'I'm sorry if it sounds overly stern,' Travis went on, 'but it is vital. Vital!' They flinched as his voice rose in volume and he visibly pulled himself back. 'I don't want to scare you. Actually, I *do* want to scare you because breaking the Official Secrets Act is treason.'

'Treason?' Steffie whispered.

'And as such, subject to the most severe of punishments.'

'Beheading?'

Ailsa saw a ghost of a smile cross Travis's lips, but it was gone again instantly.

'We don't behead people any more, Stefania.'

'But we do hang them,' another man said behind Travis, and Ailsa felt not just her legs but her whole self shake. This was madness.

'Only if they tell,' Travis said. 'Which they won't, will you, ladies?' They all shook their heads vehemently and finally he smiled. 'Good. So, your choice – are you in, or are you out?'

Out, a voice screamed in Ailsa's head. She stared at the sheets on the desk in front of her, trying to read the words that would bind her to this strange place called Bletchley Park. But then she looked across and saw both Steffie and Fran looking back.

'You will be doing important work,' Travis said softly, 'work that will help your country win this terrible war.'

'Well in that case,' Steffie said, picking up a pen, 'I'm in.'

'Me too,' Fran agreed. 'No one's ever believed I can do important work before, so I'm definitely in.' She signed her name and they both looked to Ailsa.

Ailsa pictured the soft sand of her favourite beach. She pictured the hills and the pub and her mother wrapping her up in bridal white and tying her to North Uist forever. Lord help her, she loved her ma and she loved her homeland but, as she'd said that terrible morning, there was more of the world to see before she settled down. She picked up the pen, pleased to see she wasn't shaking any more.

'I'm in.'

TWO

Steffie

Steffie didn't so much wake up as finally give up pretending to sleep. The bed in her billet was narrow and lumpy and the worn sheets a funny shade of off-cream that she hoped was just age. As she prised her eyes reluctantly open, she looked up at the set of slightly off-focus photos of the local area in home-made wooden frames almost the same colour as the beige walls.

'My Reginald took those with his camera,' her landlady had told her proudly last night as she'd shown her to her room.

'They're lovely,' Steffie had said, getting only a sniff in return. From what she could gather, many of the residents of Bletchley had been coerced into offering accommodation to workers at the Park and, although they were more than ready to take the government's money, they weren't too happy about the inconvenience.

'Course they won't be what the likes of you are used to,' Agnes Jones had grumbled. 'I bet you've got stuff like that Michael-Angel's paintings on your walls. But we're proud of them all the same.'

'They're lovely,' Steffie had repeated. 'And all the more special if your husband took them.'

'They are that.' Agnes had folded her arms across her bosom with a crackle of static from the shiny fabric. 'That's your wardrobe. It won't fit the half of what you've got in them fancy cases but there's space under the bed. Just watch out for the mousetrap. Breakfast is at seven and dinner at six. Reginald doesn't like to eat any later or it sets off his gout something horrible.'

'Of course, thank you. Only, I'm not sure what hours I'll be working yet.'

Mrs Jones had looked askance at her.

'What sort of place would have girls working later than six o'clock? It's not decent. I hope you're not planning on going out *partying*.' She'd drawn out the word with exaggerated horror and Steffie had had to bite hard on the inside of her lip to stop herself giggling. Where on earth would she find a party out here even if she wanted one?

'Of course not, Mrs Jones, but I think it might be shift work.'

'Shift work! Lord help us, what's the world coming to with women doing shift work! Well, if you're not here, I'll leave yours out and you'll just have to take it cold. Right, I'll leave you to settle in. Radio goes on seven till ten in the living room, then I'd appreciate it if we could have lights out and silence. Reginald works hard on the railways all day and needs his sleep.'

Steffie groaned as she remembered last night. It had been lights out at ten but there hadn't been silence. The walls were thin and she'd had to burrow beneath the flimsy pillow to try and escape the sound of Mr Jones claiming his marital rights. She wasn't honestly sure she could bear this. Did that make her a terrible snob? Probably. It wasn't that she required silk sheets or fancy art, though – just a bit of basic comfort and peace.

With a sigh, Steffie got up and opened the door a crack to see if the bathroom was free. An indoor privy was another thing

Agnes had proudly pointed out last night and she supposed she should be grateful for small mercies. The coast looked clear and she darted out but at that moment Reginald emerged from his bedroom, still tucking his shirt into his trousers, and she found herself trapped on the tiny landing.

'Morning, love. Hope you slept well.'

'Very well thanks. Out like a light I was.'

'Yes? Good, good. If you ever struggle to sleep, you let me know, hey? Reg here will tire you out, no problem.'

Steffie pressed herself back against the wall.

'Oh, I'm sure work will do that for me, thank you. Talking of which I, er, better get on.'

He grinned and held open the bathroom door for her, forcing her to slide past. Once inside, she gratefully pushed it shut and fumbled for the lock but found none. Great! She'd take her mother's ridiculous matchmaking over leering Reg any day, and could only pray that the work at Bletchley Park was as good as her father had promised.

'Stefania – welcome.' Harry Hinsley came striding across the lawn to meet her. 'Hope you got your billet sorted. Not too dreadful, is it?' Steffie pulled a face and he rolled his eyes. 'That good, hey?! Hang in there for a bit and maybe the billeting officer can be talked into finding you somewhere else.'

'You think?'

'It has happened – occasionally. Problem is, it's a small town and there are a lot of us. The early bods got all the good rooms in the pubs. There's a few of them at the Shoulder of Mutton down in Old Bletchley and more at the Drunken Arms at Great Brickhill.'

'The Drunken Arms?'

He laughed.

'That's what everyone here calls it. It's something like the

Duncombe Arms really, but it's the place to go for a good
night. Not quite the Ritz, but they serve a decent pint. Oh,
and I'm told their gin isn't half bad either if that's more your
line?'

'I'll drink anything,' Steffie said, thinking of Agnes's shud-
dering reference to partying. Perhaps there *would* be some fun
to be had around here?

'That's the girl. There's a war on after all. Now, let's show
you round Hut 4.'

They'd come to a large, wooden hut to the left of the
mansion and Harry pushed open the door and ushered her in.
A long, narrow corridor ran down the centre, with rooms off to
either side from which Steffie could hear the clatter of type-
writers and a hum of low conversation. Harry led the way into a
big room to the right and chairs scraped noisily back as several
men leaped to their feet.

'New recruit,' Harry told them. 'Stefania Carmichael.'

'Steffie, please,' she said.

A short, balding man leaped forward with surprising agility
and clasped her hand in both of his.

'Frank Birch, fusty academic. And this is William Clarke,
but you can call him Nobby.'

'If you must,' his colleague said with a grin. 'I hear you
speak Italian, Miss Carmichael.'

'Steffie, please, and, yes, I was in Rome for six years before
we had to hotfoot it back to Blighty in the new year.'

'Bad luck. I love Rome.'

'You've been?'

'*Certo, molte volte. Roma è la città più bella del mondo.*'

The words flowed across Steffie's ear like liquid gold.
Nobby's accent was flawless and for a moment she caught an
echo of Matteo in this strange English hut.

'*Amavo vivere lì,*' she said, adding, 'I loved living there,' for
Frank's benefit.

'I figured,' Frank said. 'I may be the German expert but I bashed out plenty of classics at school. Italian's easy.'

'*Deutsch ist auch einfach,*' Steffie threw at him – German is also easy – and he grinned.

'German too. Well, young lady, you *are* going to be useful to Hut 4.'

Now it was Steffie grinning. Swiss finishing school had mostly been dull deportment and etiquette, but it seemed that the German conversational classes might actually pay off.

'Doing what?' she asked eagerly.

'Well, there's a question! This is where all that Official Secrets Act stuff comes in, dear girl. Not a word of it outside our pair of huts, but basically, the clever chaps in Hut 8 are decoding Nazi naval messages and it's down to us here in Hut 4 to translate and make sense of them.'

Steffie felt excitement mount within her. She looked around the room. The men were seated in a sort of semicircle with piles of important-looking messages in wire trays before them, all laid out in five-letter blocks. She could see from the pad in front of Frank Birch that they were turning those blocks into actual German words and working to fill in blanks, presumably where the messages had been corrupted or interrupted. Frank's message said something about troop movements in Poland and she stared at it as she tried to picture the German officer who had sent it blithely off to his superiors without ever dreaming that a load of academics in a funny old park in the dullest bit of middle England were reading it too.

'Don't the Germans have super-clever codes?' she asked.

'They do. Enigma machines. Fiendishly difficult to crack.'

'But we're doing it?' she breathed.

'Giving it a jolly good go, yes. There are all sorts of different keys, some easier to hack into than others. And they change every midnight so then Hut 8 has to start all over again.'

'That sounds impossible.'

Frank Birch grinned at her.

'And yet here we are – listening to the enemy!'

'And, more importantly,' Harry added, 'telling our chaps at the Admiralty what the enemy are saying so that it can be of actual operational use. Which is where you come in, Steffie.'

'Really?'

Steffie was perking up fast. Her heart might be aching but at least she could use her head here. 'Where do I work?'

'This way,' Harry said. 'You can type, right?'

'Type?' she asked uncertainly. 'Well yes, I can, but I don't see—'

'Fantastic. You're down here.' He ushered her past the men with wire trays full of juicy messages and into a smaller room where two girls were sitting at funny old typewriters. A third was set at a blank chair and Steffie felt all her excitement drain out of her.

'You want me to type messages?'

'Outgoing ones, yes, on this baby. It's a Typex machine, set up to encode as it goes along so we can get *their* messages securely out as *our* messages. Good, hey?'

Steffie looked longingly back into the other room where already Frank and Nobby were heads down over their stack of decrypts. After all that talk of her languages and her skills, she was here as nothing more than a secretary.

'Wonderful,' she said dully.

Harry shuffled his feet, then sat on the desk, cutting Steffie off from the other two girls.

'Not what you wanted?'

'I just... *Ich möchte nützlicher sein.*'

'You want to be of more use? Fair enough. Dig in, do this for a bit and I'm sure we can get you learning the other jobs and moving up. Is that all right?'

Steffie sighed.

'That's all right, thanks, Harry.'

What more could she say? But as Harry ambled back to the other room, leaving her to offer a weak smile to the two girls and pick up the first message to type mindlessly into the funny machine, she wasn't sure she was very happy with how this fantastic war work was turning out – a dodgy billet, a leering landlord and a typist's job in a wooden hut! She just hoped she'd get to see Fran and Ailsa at lunchtime or she might go mad here in Bletchley Park.

THREE

Fran

'I mean, really, this is no way to run an index.'

Fran gestured to the shoeboxes stacked on a trestle table at the side of Hut 3 and the four academics sitting at the tables around her hung their heads.

'We're busy, Fran,' Peter Lucas said. 'Enemy messages to read and all that.'

She grinned at her friend, thanking her lucky stars that she was working in his section.

'Then it's a good job you've got me, isn't it?'

'Is that what we employed you for?' asked Malcolm Saunders.

The head of Hut 3 was apparently a lieutenant commander but rarely wore his uniform and kept an informal if intense office. Fran glanced nervously at him, but he was smiling so she relaxed.

'You told me I was here for "general organisational work", Malcolm, and this lot definitely needs organising.'

They all looked again to the shoeboxes. There were around

twelve of them, with categories scrawled on each one in a barely legible script. Fran picked up one marked 'weapons' and threw off the lid. Inside was a pile of cards marked with the names of all the guns, tanks and other German weaponry that the watch had come across in the messages decoded so far, with notes of the time and context of the reference. She lifted several out.

'Look – the cards aren't even the same size.'

'So?' Peter asked.

'So, how will we index them properly? Come on, Peter – where did I meet you?'

'Cambridge University library,' he said promptly.

'And why?'

'Because you helped me with my research.'

'Helped you, to be precise, pinpointing the sources that would be of most use to you in your research.'

'Correct.'

'And how did I do that?'

He groaned.

'With an index, I assume.'

She put the cards triumphantly back into the box.

'Exactly.'

Looking around at the men, she couldn't quite believe her own daring. The team in Hut 3 were linked to the one in Hut 6, who were breaking German army and air force codes, their job being to translate and emend the resultant decrypts. Fran couldn't thank Peter enough for getting her involved in something so vital and was determined to prove worthy of his trust. She'd only been working here for two weeks and was very much the junior member of a team made up almost exclusively of dons and professors. But if there was one thing her work in the university library had taught her, it was that dons and professors were brilliantly clever but terribly disorganised.

'It's like this,' she said carefully. 'Hut 6 are breaking the codes more and more quickly every day, so we're getting more

and more messages to process. Some of them could be of immediate use, yes, and that has to be our top priority, but every
single one contains nuggets of information that, put together in
an easy-to-access form, could offer us a bigger, longer picture.'

Peter leaped up.

'She's right, you know. We started the index so that if something comes up that we think we've seen before, we can find it
to shed light on the current situation.'

'Or give us words to fill in blanks,' Malcolm Saunders said.

'That's right,' Fran agreed, delighted. 'But it will only work
if you can get to that information quickly. You're all far too busy
to be rifling through shoeboxes every time you come across the
name of a German commander or airfield. Which is where I
come in...'

She looked hopefully to Malcolm, who smiled again, more
broadly this time.

'Very well, Miss Morgan – tell me what you need and I'll
see what I can do.'

Fran rubbed her hands together and reached for a requisi-
tion slip. This was going to be fun.

Two hours later, she let herself out of Hut 3 into the sunshine of
a beautiful spring day. Primroses and crocuses were blooming
outside the mansion and the lawns at the centre of Bletchley
Park were green with new growth. She paused a moment to
take in her astonishing workplace.

In front of her, the lawn sloped down to a small pond,
trimmed with rushes and full of frogs and ducks as if this were
nothing more than a village green. But the men and women
throwing crusts of sandwich to the birds were not young
mothers and children, but the cream of the top British universities. Fran recognised many of them from her year in the university library, and even those she didn't know were marked out as

academics by their air of distracted intelligence and their tweedy style.

Now, with the smell of lunch wafting from the mansion kitchens, they were pouring out of the wooden huts around the main building and heading to the dining room inside. Fran looked at the other huts curiously, wondering what went on inside them. Someone, she presumed, was breaking naval codes in the same way that Hut 6 were tackling the army and air force ones, but other than that she had no idea what all these brainboxes were up to. She knew one thing, though – she was delighted to be a part of it.

'Fran!' She turned to see Steffie running across to her and smiled a hello. 'Isn't it a glorious day? Shall we grab sandwiches and eat among the primroses?'

'Sounds good to me.'

Fran let herself be led inside as Steffie chattered away about the flowers and the birds singing in the trees. She looked amazing as always in a cinched-waist dress with matching jacket and coordinating handbag.

'How do you do that?' Fran blurted out.

Steffie stopped her chatter.

'Do what?'

'Look so amazingly stylish all the time?'

Steffie laughed.

'Six years in Italy, darling. Daddy was the military attaché and we had to go to all sorts of dos once we got old enough. Good clothes were more or less part of the job, so Mummy used to take Roseanna and me to Milan twice a year to get stocked up.'

'Milan!' someone breathed enviously behind them. 'I'd love to go to Milan.'

They both swung round. 'Ailsa!'

Steffie let go of Fran to fling her arms around their friend. Fran had no idea how she did that either – her ease with everyone she met. She supposed it was something to do with all those 'dos' she'd been to. Her own upbringing had included dos too, but always in university colleges and always with the same, dry people – medics and scientists, who talked about test tubes and intestines. They probably wouldn't know a primrose if it jumped up and kissed them, and they most certainly wouldn't care about matching handbags.

'Hey, Fran,' Ailsa said, extricating herself from Steffie's hug and giving her a wave.

Their Scottish friend was no more comfortable with Steffie's exuberance than Fran was, and they shared a conspiratorial smile as Steffie started jabbering away to the canteen ladies. Dinner in the mansion was always a sit-down affair, but lunchtimes were more relaxed, and Steffie soon talked the ladies into quite a picnic spread to take out to the lawns.

'Have you had a good morning?' Fran asked Ailsa.

'Aye, thank you. We—' She stopped herself and they grimaced at each other. 'You?'

'Good, yes. I've started, erm... organising.'

'Right. Lovely.'

There was little more to say, or at least little more they *could* say, and they took the food Steffie was holding and tumbled gratefully out to the lawn.

'The grass is damp,' Ailsa said, bending to touch it.

'Oh, it's only a bit of water.' Steffie plonked herself gracefully down.

'Your skirt...'

'Will wash. And I've got more.' Ailsa shrugged and dropped down next to her, and Fran followed their example. Steffie beamed at her. 'I'm so jealous of your marvellous slacks, Fran. Italians still like their women trussed up in dresses, but those look so much easier to wear. I'm going to get some the very first moment I can get up to town.'

'Town?' Ailsa queried.

'London. There's a van goes to the government offices every day. You can hitch a lift if you're quick.'

'London?' Ailsa said, shaking her head uncertainly. 'It's so big. I was only there for a few days for my interview, but I couldn't get over it. I saw more buildings that week than I've seen in my whole life before.'

Fran looked at her curiously.

'You live on an island, right?'

'North Uist, aye. It's pretty wee. Mainly beaches and hills with a handful of villages dotted around. The biggest building is the church, and it only sits about fifty.' She looked around the lawn where people were gathering in small groups. Up near the mansion someone had started a game of rounders and there were raucous cries as they tried to run each other out. 'There are probably more people working in the Park than on the whole of Uist.'

Steffie shook her head incredulously.

'No wonder you wanted out.'

'Exactly!' Ailsa leaned eagerly towards them, her pale skin glowing with sudden passion. 'I want to see the world. I want to go to Rome and Milan. I want to go to Paris and Egypt and, and Australia.'

'Quite right,' Fran told her. 'Why shouldn't you?'

Ailsa looked chastened.

'My parents don't approve. They think I should be satisfied with home. They think wanting to see other places implies criticism of the island and I suppose, therefore, of them.'

'But that's silly—' Fran started and saw Ailsa stiffen. 'I mean, not silly, sorry. Just...'

'Terribly insular?'

'Maybe. But, hey – you've travelled this far now.'

'And isn't it glamorous?'

They all looked around the parochial scene and laughed.

'Especially the accommodation,' Steffie said darkly.

Fran patted her leg.

'Reginald still being bothersome?'

Steffie had told them about her lecherous landlord and Fran thought it sounded dreadful. Not that she'd ever admit it, but she wasn't really sure what other girls saw in men, even the handsome ones, and the thought of some pot-bellied pervert preying on her made her skin physically itch.

'Nothing I can't handle,' Steffie said, with a careless wave that Fran didn't quite believe, 'but it gets pretty wearing. I have no idea what Agnes sees in him, but she follows him around like a lamb, fetching him food and ale and slippers as if he's her damned king. Ridiculous! To be honest, I hate it there.'

Fran thought of her own billet. There was no unpleasant man, but it wasn't very nice. She'd been put into a tiny terrace at the back of Bletchley with Mrs Blenkinsop, an old lady who was kind but fiercely frugal. Despite eagerly taking all Fran's food coupons, she offered meals of turnips, potatoes and slimy barley with little more than the scrag end of a bacon joint for flavour. Fran was allowed one bath a week and the lights went out at nine on the dot.

The house was down by the marshes and horribly damp but Mrs B refused to light the ancient oil stove unless there was actually frost on the ground. Fran's room was on the ground floor behind the kitchen and had brown patches creeping up the walls that she had to scrub at daily to keep fungus from appearing. She regularly woke up with her fingers wrinkled, and the few precious books she read by the light of her torch each night were starting to pucker at the edges.

'I'm thinking of working late, while I'm...' She trailed off.

'Organising?' Ailsa offered.

'Organising, exactly. At least that way I'll get dinner in the hall. Mrs B won't like it cos she's making a handsome profit on my coupons but serves her right for not making me anything decent.'

'I'll join you,' Steffie said instantly. 'Not that I've got anything as exciting as "organising" to do.' She looked unusually downcast and Fran longed to ask more but not with that treason-noose dangling, and besides, her friend was already shaking off her gloom. 'I reckon if I show them what I'm made of, I'll get more, right?'

'Bound to,' Fran agreed. 'Ailsa?'

Ailsa grinned.

'I'm working most evenings, so I'll see you there.'

'You are?'

Fran stared at her. Ailsa had said something on their first night about being a radio operator, so she had to assume she was one of a mystery team plucking the messages out of the airwaves. Then they were fed into Hut 6 and from there to her team at Hut 3 to make it – once Malcolm got her filing cabinets – into her shiny new index. It was curious war work, she reflected, looking round at the mishmash of eccentric colleagues. It wasn't the guns and tanks and uniforms on the posters, but if they did their bit here at Bletchley Park maybe those guns and tanks would be able to aim more effectively at Hitler and his Nazi fiends before they got to British shores. They had to pray so, or idyllic days like this one would be no more.

FOUR

Ailsa

'We're moving?' Ailsa stared in horror at her boss. 'Where to?'

'Not far,' he said. 'Just a few miles up the road to Whaddon Hall. We'll be running a bus from the village, so you'll be able to keep your billet.'

'It's not—'

Ailsa clamped her mouth shut. It wasn't her place to question the top bods and they certainly wouldn't care that moving out of Hut 1 would rob her of the highlight of her day – eating with Steffie and Fran. She and her friends had fallen into a lovely routine in the last two weeks, picnicking on the lawn at lunchtimes and sitting together at dinner in the evenings. Ailsa enjoyed them both, but perhaps liked dinner the best. The room was so gracious, with its high ceilings and wood-panelled walls, and they were served by proper staff. Compared to supper with Ma and Pa around the kitchen table, it made her feel like royalty – and the chatter of a hundred conversations was exciting too.

Here at BP, there was no muttering about weather forecasts

or peat-cutting or ferry schedules. Instead, she would hear people talking about Latin texts and mathematical conundrums, discussing earnest points of philosophy or arguing over historical mysteries. They would chatter about art and theatre and the intricacies of sports and games Ailsa had never even heard of. And the places they mentioned! The other day she'd overheard two men comparing the food in Athens and Istanbul, and had stood there, shamelessly eavesdropping, munching vicariously on dolmades and baklavas and koftes – things she could not picture but that had still tickled her tongue. These people had seen the world and that, above all else, Ailsa was feasting upon. But now her 'Y' wireless station was being moved.

'Will we still eat here?' she asked tentatively.

Her boss frowned.

'I suppose you could. I mean, you'll still have your BP pass, but even with a bike I don't think there'd be time to make it for lunch.' He must have seen her face because he leaned in and said, 'Sorry, Ailsa. Someone special you like to meet?'

She flushed scarlet.

'No! I mean, not like that. Just my friends.'

He patted her hand.

'Friends can be special too, I know, but there's a war on, I'm afraid, and with the section growing we need more space. Plus, Whaddon is up on a hill so reception will be far better. It's all about catching those signals on the airwaves, right?'

'Right,' Ailsa agreed hastily. 'Of course it is. Absolutely.'

'Well done. We move tomorrow.'

'Tomorrow?!'

'Sorry,' he said again. 'Orders just came through. We need to start packing up the sets immediately. All hands on deck, what?'

Ailsa looked around Hut 1 as several young men marched in with large packing crates and suddenly their Y-station in the middle of BP was being dismantled.

'What's the betting half the equipment gets wrecked in the move?' the girl next to Ailsa groaned.

Ailsa nodded grimly.

'They're sensitive wee things. It'll take us ages to tune them back in again.'

'Good job we've got you then!' The girl gave her a nudge and Ailsa looked at her in surprise. 'Oh, come on, Ailsa, you're far and away the best here at finding the tricky frequencies. I don't know how you do it. Scottish magic, perhaps?'

'Away with you!'

Ailsa flapped self-consciously at the air, feeling horribly warm all of a sudden. It was true she'd swiftly learned how to coax coherent messages out of the scramble of traffic flying through the airwaves but to say she was the 'best' was just glaikit. Nice, but glaikit.

'We should get on with it,' she said, bending to her set to cover her confusion but, as she unplugged it, she felt a horrible sadness.

She loved her work but without Steffie and Fran life in Bletchley wouldn't be nearly as much fun. It wasn't that her billet was bad, she thought as she rolled wires into careful loops. She lived with the Johnstones, a jolly family in a nice house in the middle of Bletchley, who offered plain but plentiful food and kind hospitality. She had her own room, tiny but clean and safe, and she didn't dare complain when Steffie talked about Reg lurking on the landing or Fran about her blankets clinging damply to her pyjamas. But when she lay in her bed listening to the family saying their goodnights to each other, she ached for her own parents and would lie awake reliving the horrible argument when she'd left. She'd torture herself speculating about the Germans invading and storming BP, killing her before she could tell them how much she loved them.

They hadn't been the sort of family that went in for shows of affection. A gruff thank you over the porridge or an extra bowl of soup if one of them felt unwell was the extent of the loving gestures in her home, but she'd known how much they cared all the same. They'd always handed her the best portions at dinner, always found time to help her read or to play games, even when they were worn out from their own long days. They'd brought toys and books from the mainland and encouraged her with her interest in the wireless – Alasdair's wireless.

That was another moment she'd turn over in her head on those long nights – that wretched New Year's Eve when she'd escaped with Alasdair to his bothy. She'd been bored of the pub, bored of the same people and the same jokes and the same songs. She'd been enthralled by tuning into other, more thrilling parties around the world and hadn't even noticed the way he'd been looking at her until it had been too late. She'd been naive and stupid, and she'd hurt a kind man who'd been so generous to her.

He'd be glad to know what you are doing with all he taught you, she'd tell herself. She'd been recruited to help communicate with British agents in the field, getting vital operational messages out to them in the face of the German advance, and catching their own transmissions with information on enemy positions and local resistance. It took all the skills in both tuning and Morse that Alasdair had taught her, and she'd like to think he'd be proud of her, but she wasn't sure it was true. He'd be far gladder if she was moving into his house to make his dinners, have his babies and tie herself to North Uist for ever and ever.

Whenever she got to that point in her night-time meanderings, she'd tell her mind to shut up and let her sleep, but then at breakfast there would be the rough-and-tumble of getting the Johnstones' four children out to school and she'd think of her abandoned home all over again. She'd been right to leave, of that she was sure, but she hadn't been right to hurt people in the process and it was only seeing Steffie and Fran that kept those demons at bay. Now that would come to an end.

Ailsa couldn't wait for lunchtime. It was drizzling so she waited in the hallway of the mansion for them to come from their respective huts, remembering the first night they'd arrived. This place had seemed so alien to Ailsa but already it felt like home and for a moment she was tempted to sign her name in the chit book and take a glass of beer.

'Ailsa – why the long face?'

Steffie came bounding up and threw an arm around her shoulders and for once Ailsa leaned into her, grateful for the easy touch she usually found so strange.

'I'm being moved.'

'What? Where?!'

Ailsa panicked; she hadn't been told whether that information was classified or not.

'Not so far away,' she hedged, 'but not close enough to eat with you and Fran.'

'That's awful.'

'I know. War, hey?'

Steffie gave her another squeeze.

'It's rotten bad luck but, look, we can still meet up. Frank Birch – that's my boss – says there are some cracking nights in the Duncombe Arms so we could go there. Would you like that?'

Ailsa swallowed down a lump. It wouldn't do to cry over something so stupid, not when there were men losing their lives out in Europe.

'I'd love that, Steffie, thank you, though it won't be the same as seeing you two every day.'

'What's happened?' Fran was upon them. 'Are you all right, Ailsa? Have you had bad news?'

Ailsa felt touched at her concern and even more dangerously close to tears.

'Ailsa's unit is moving out of BP,' Steffie told Fran.

'No! That's rotten, Ails. Where to? Oh, I bet you can't say, can you?'

'Only a few miles,' Ailsa managed. 'I can stay in my billet.'

'Well, that's something. You like the Johnstones, right?'

'They're lovely,' Ailsa hedged.

'But...?'

'But they're a big, happy family. I feel like a, a spare part – like I'm part of their life, rather than my own.'

'I know what you mean,' Fran agreed. 'I don't even like going "home", and that's not a great feeling.'

'I hate it,' Steffie said vehemently, then shook herself. 'But come on, if this is Ailsa's last lunch here, let's make it a goodie. I'll see what the ladies can whistle up for us.'

A few minutes later they were sitting on the lawn with sandwiches, slices of fruit cake and a glass of beer each. Fran wrinkled her nose at the first taste and Steffie spat hers out.

'That is disgusting!'

Ailsa took a sip. It was rich and malty and tasted strangely of home.

'My dad brews an ale a wee bit like this,' she said, drinking deeper. The other two looked at her in horror. 'What? It's nice when you get used to it.'

Steffie put her glass firmly down in front of Ailsa.

'I, for one, have no intention of getting used to it. All yours, Ailsa girl.'

'I can't have two!' Ailsa protested.

'Three,' Fran corrected, putting her own down next to Steffie's. 'Crack on, lassie – it'll get you through the afternoon.'

In the end, Ailsa donated most of her extra beer to the primroses but her one glassful, along with the loving support of her friends, carried her through the afternoon. She could hardly believe she'd only met Steffie and Fran a month ago; already she felt like she could trust them with her life. They were so different to her too. Fran had grown up among the beautiful buildings of Cambridge, going to garden parties and formal dinners and being educated in the finest schools. And then there was Steffie – until recently she'd led a life of embassy parties, Swiss finishing schools and trips to the boutiques of Milan. She was engaged, for heaven's sake, to apparently the most handsome officer in the whole Italian air force. Steffie had taken to teaching her phrases of Italian over lunch to help her when one day – after this damned war – she got to travel to the Mediterranean. Now that would have to stop.

You'll just have to make an effort in the evenings, Ailsa told herself sternly as she helped to load the packing crates full of wireless equipment into an old Bedford van. Spring was well and truly here, the light was lasting longer, and none of them wanted to be in their billets anyway. This strange new friendship was one that Ailsa treasured and she was going to make sure she held onto it, whatever it took.

FIVE

APRIL 1940

Steffie

'Aaaah!' Harry Hinsley slammed the telephone onto the cradle with a roar and it let out a loud jangle of protest. Steffie looked nervously down the corridor.

'Problem, Harry?'

'Too right. It's those blighters at the Admiralty – they just won't listen.'

The rest of the watch gave sympathetic murmurs but kept their heads down over their decrypts. Harry looked so fed up, though, that Steffie pushed her chair back and went through.

'What won't they listen to?'

'Any bloody thing! Excuse my language.' Steffie waved this away. 'We've been collecting messages indicating the Germans are massing ships around the Baltic, suggesting an invasion of Norway, possibly Denmark too. If the Admiralty would believe us, we could send our ships to counter but instead they mutter platitudes and tell us to "keep up the good work". What's the point in us busting a gut to listen in to the German messages, break their codes, and work out exactly what's going on, if they won't listen?'

He tore at his hair in frustration and Steffie patted his arm. It felt like a pathetically useless gesture, but he smiled gratefully at her and she considered the problem.

'I dare say it's a bit weird for them, getting information from some funny academics – no offence – in a strange house miles from the sea.'

He nodded.

'I guess so, but the Admiralty have been good about intelligence on the whole. They were behind wireless technology when the army and the air force were all for ignoring it, and they understand about interception and its potential value because they've been listening out for broadcasts from enemy ships for years. But you're right, they don't like it coming from a non-naval source. They're very proud, this military lot – especially the navy. If you haven't worked your way up from mopping decks to striding them with your fifty gold stripes, you're not considered worth anything much. And certainly not up to making critical decisions about ship movements.'

'But you're not making critical decisions,' Steffie pointed out. 'You're providing the information to let *them* do so.'

He grimaced.

'Absolutely right, old girl, but they don't see it that way. Cracking the codes is the fiendishly difficult bit. Acting on the information ought to be simple, but...'

'But they don't trust you?'

He cocked his head on one side.

'It would appear not. It's so stupid. What do they think we're doing – sitting around our tables making things up?'

'Probably,' Steffie agreed. 'I mean, they must know how fiendishly difficult cracking the codes is too, so perhaps they think you're just taking stabs in the dark – getting a bit here and a bit there and joining the dots with your foolish civilian brains?'

Harry laughed.

'You know what, Steffie, I think that's exactly what they reckon. How did you know?'

She shrugged.

'I've been around a lot of military types and, from what I've seen, they think they know best about everything. Well, Italian ones do, anyway.'

Harry looked at her curiously.

'You lived in Rome, right?'

'Right. For six years. My sister and I used to walk past Musso's apartment every day on the way to school. He'd often be there, waving, especially once we got to sixth form and grew —' She cut herself off and finished weakly, '...womanly attributes.'

She and Roseanna had often joked about Il Duce looking down their tops from his vantage point on his first-floor balcony, but this was hardly the place to repeat it.

'You met Mussolini?' Harry asked, staring at her.

'Oh yes. He was at all the parties. He tried to hit on me once. Actually, he didn't even try very hard, just said, "Would you like to come and see the Villa Torlonia?" That's his fancy house in Rome. "I have a very fine bed. Very comfortable. Very bouncy."'

Harry stared at her harder. 'He said that to you?'

'Yes. Well, in Italian of course.'

'What did you do?'

'I blushed and hedged and luckily Matteo came up and rescued me.'

'Matteo?'

Steffie bit her lip.

'My fiancé.'

She said the word so fiercely that the rest of the watch looked up. She felt stupid and then cursed herself. She was proud to be engaged to Matteo and she was going to marry him. Indeed, she considered herself already married.

For a moment, she was back in Rome the night before their flight across Europe. It had been all packing and panicking, but at last her parents had gone to bed and she'd been able to sneak out and meet Matteo in the handy nooks of the Borghese park.

'My mother wants me to give your ring back,' she'd told him, snuggling into his arms. 'But I'm not going to – not unless you want me to?'

'Of course not. I'm going to marry you, Stefania Eleanor Carmichael. I'm going to marry you and take you into my home, into my bed, into my whole life – for, if I don't, what will that life be worth?'

She'd kissed him then, pressing her whole self against him as if she could imprint her body on his for the long months ahead.

'Let's get married now,' she'd said. 'Just you and me before God. We don't need a priest, or fancy clothes, or a hundred guests to bear witness. We know what we mean to each other.'

He'd looked at her with awe.

'My Stefania – so full of fire! You are right. Come on.'

He'd grabbed her hand and started running through the park.

'Where are we going?'

'To the Temple, of course, to the altar.'

It had been a beautiful night, the air cold but clear and the stars shining down on them like a million candles. They'd run round the elegant pond and into the mock-Greek Temple of Aesculapius, laughing and breathless. There was no actual altar, but they'd stood between the columns, the breeze on the water as their choir, and the stone Aesculapius as their priest, and they'd spoken their vows to each other. Then Matteo had spun the diamond on her engagement ring so it tucked into her palm and just the plain gold band of a married woman had shown.

'I don't know what this war will bring us, Steffie, or where it will take us, but I promise you this – whatever path it throws us onto, we will tread it bravely and safely and we will make it, one day, back to each other. You will be mine, Stefania Mancini. And we will be happy.'

Steffie sighed now and her lips twitched for Matteo's kiss.

'Steffie? Hello? Are you all right?'

She shook herself, mortified, and came back from her 'wedding' to find herself in a draughty wooden hut with a load of men staring at her.

'God yes, sorry. Just... remembering something.'

'He's a lucky man.'

'He's Italian,' Frank Birch said darkly.

'So?' Harry said. 'They're not fighting anyone.'

'Yet,' was Frank's retort and Steffie shivered. She was so used to loving Matteo that she'd forgotten he might be viewed with suspicion around here and wished she'd kept her mouth shut about him. But now was not the time to be worrying about Italy, not when the Germans were massing around Norway.

'Could Denniston do something about getting through to the Admiralty?' she asked Harry.

'He can try but I reckon they have "Don't listen to this lot" carved into their damned telephone, whoever calls them.'

Steffie considered.

'How do you report to them?'

'What do you mean? I call them up, on this special, dedicated, important-messages-only telephone.'

'Right.'

'And we send copies of all decrypted messages via the courier at the end of every day, though I suspect they put them straight into the bin. Maybe we should pop them in a toy boat and sail them into Admiral Cunningham's office?'

'Or maybe,' Steffie said, 'you should compile a report, a daily resumé of the traffic with important shifts highlighted – something the top bods can read in a minute or two that shows them we really understand the situation at sea.'

Harry nodded slowly.

'That's a really good idea, Steffie. Isn't it, chaps, isn't that a good idea?'

'What admiral would want to wade through a load of scrappy slips when he can have a concise paragraph of summary?' Frank Birch agreed. 'Good thinking, Steffie.'

She flushed with pleasure.

'I could, er, help compile it if you wanted.' They frowned. 'You know, type it up.'

'Right. Yes. Good plan. And in the meantime—'

The door burst open before Harry could finish his sentence and Nobby Clarke ran in.

'Stick on the wireless.'

'What?'

'Stick it on!'

He gestured to the radiogram in the corner and Steffie went over and clicked it on. A crackle of static filled the hut and then the cut-glass voice of the BBC news announcer came through loud and clear: 'News just in that Nazi Germany have invaded Norway. Troops have been parachuted into the airports at Oslo, Kristiansand and Sola, and German ships have been spotted in the Oslofjord.'

The group in Hut 4 looked at each other in horror.

'Maybe now the Admiralty will believe us,' Harry said grimly.

.   .   .

Steffie got back to her billet late that night, exhausted but exhilarated. The news was terrible, of course. Not only had Norway been invaded but Denmark too and the latter had surrendered within two hours, unable to defend their flat land from the Nazi tanks pouring over their border. Norway, however, were resisting and the Allies were sending reinforcements as fast as they could – including a number of the navy's finest ships.

Someone near the top of the Admiralty had said he wished they'd had a way of knowing about the threat sooner and Commander Denniston had been up to London to point out that they had. He'd also taken Steffie's suggestion of a daily report, which had been agreed and, much to her embarrassment, Harry had sent out for wine to toast her at the end of the shift. It had been nice to be appreciated, of course, but hardly right to be celebrating when in Norway people were fighting for their homes, and she'd been glad to escape.

Now she let herself into the house, praying Agnes and Reg were already in bed. She needed to curl up with a hot mug of tea and shake the frantic activity of the day out of her body so she could sleep. All was quiet and she made for the kitchen on tiptoe and filled the stove-top kettle with just enough water for one, standing over it to catch it before the whistle woke the household. Before the first wisps of steam came out of the spout, however, she heard a tell-tale creak on the stairs. She crossed her fingers that it would be Agnes, but as the kitchen door swung open, she saw Reg's slack figure, resplendent in baggy pyjama trousers and an off-white vest.

'You're up late, girl. Been in the pub?'

'No. I've been at work.'

He came further into the room and she pressed herself against the stove.

'Work, my life. I can smell booze.'

'One glass of—'

'And aftershave.' He came round the kitchen table, looming over her. 'You smell of aftershave. What have you been up to? Or should I say, *who* have you been up to.'

Steffie drew herself up tall.

'How dare you? I'm engaged.'

'To this Italian chap? He's off across the other side of Europe, isn't he? I bet you get lonely, right? I bet you like a bit of male company.'

He gave a lewd thrust of his pyjamaed groin and Steffie grabbed a chair, placing it between them.

'I'm quite fine, thank you very much. I just want my cup of tea, and—' He was upon her before she could react, grabbing the chair and tossing it aside with a clatter before clasping her arms. 'Get off me, Reg!'

'I can show you a good time, Steffie. I'm an experienced man of the world. I can soothe your aches—'

'I said get off me.'

Steffie squirmed in his grasp, but he was surprisingly strong and pinned her against the stove, bending down to press his wet lips to her neck.

'Oh God, Steffie, you're so gorgeous. I've wanted you from the moment you walked into my house, your hips swaying in that tight skirt. And you want me too. I know you do. I know — Oww!' He fell back as Steffie brought her knee up into his groin, just as she'd been taught in several of the more unofficial lessons at finishing school. 'What did you do that for?' he squealed, bent over double.

'Because,' she hissed at him, 'I do not "want" you and you have no right to force yourself on me.'

'It's my house.'

'But it's *my* body and I don't want you anywhere near it, thank you very much. Oh.'

She swallowed as Agnes appeared in the doorway, hair

trussed up in curlers, sleepy eyes sharpening as she took in the scene in her kitchen.

'What's going on here?'

'It was her,' Reg said, rushing to his wife's side, still bent over himself. 'She came in and tried to seduce me. I told her no. I told her I was a married man and she attacked me.'

'I did not!' Steffie protested furiously. 'It was him. He—'

'I think,' Agnes interrupted, drawing herself up in front of Steffie in her flannelette nightie, 'that you should get out of my house. Coming in here creating trouble with my Reg when all I've done is offer you a home – you should be ashamed of yourself.'

'But—'

'Out. Now.'

'It's night-time. I could be attacked.'

'Which would be exactly what you deserve, you hussy.'

Steffie gaped at her.

'You're blind. What on earth would I want with him?'

'Oh! Wanton and rude. What have we done to deserve this, Reggie?'

'I don't know, my dear girl. I really don't know.'

Reginald shook his head and put his arm around his wife. Steffie looked from one to the other, furious at the injustice, but they had closed ranks and whatever Agnes truly believed, this was the story that suited her. Well, fine. Steffie hated it here anyway. She stalked to the door.

'I'll be gone in ten minutes.'

'Five,' Agnes snapped and, behind them, the kettle whistled furious agreement.

Steffie made a run for her room, yanking her suitcases from under the bed, grateful now that one of them had never been unpacked. She flung her clothes into the second willy-nilly, thinking ruefully of her mother. Even when they'd been packing to flee Rome, she'd insisted on layering tissue paper between the neatly folded clothes, but tonight Steffie just bundled it all in, jumping on the lid to ram it shut. Five minutes later she was clattering down the stairs and heading out the front door, watched by a furious Agnes and a sly Reg. She gave it a loud slam and headed into the night.

Now where? She thought longingly of Fran and Ailsa. Either one of them would take her in, she knew, but they both had tiny single beds and it was far too late to be knocking up their hosts. There was only one thing for it – Hut 4 had a couple of camp beds for emergency use and this was definitely an emergency. Gathering her luggage, Steffie set her shoulders back and made for the safety of BP.

Two days later and she was fed up with camping out. The billeting officer had not been sympathetic to her story, pursing her lips and offering tart words about the need to 'fit in with your hosts'.

'You think I should have let him take me into his bed?' Steffie had demanded.

'Miss Carmichael, please!'

'What? That was how he wanted me to "fit in".'

'Maybe you led him on, young lady. You wear some very attractive outfits.'

'This is *my* fault? Unbelievable! He could have raped me.'

'Miss Carmichael!' The wretched harridan had gone purple in the face. 'I have no idea where I will find space for a young woman who talks like this.'

'But it's true,' Steffie had protested, to no avail. The woman had decided she was difficult and was making no effort to find her somewhere new to live, which left her sleeping at the back of Hut 4. Harry had offered to report it to the higher-ups, but she didn't want to make trouble or they might throw her out. There were plenty of other typists after all…

On the third day, feeling cooped up, she took herself out for a walk in the fields behind Bletchley Park. Maybe, she thought, this wasn't the life for her after all? Maybe she wasn't cut out for serious work and should just go back to her mother and knit socks for soldiers until it was over and she could be with Matteo once more? She'd written endless letters to his parents' home with the postbox address they were given for correspondence but so far she'd had nothing and she yearned to hear his voice.

'What would you have me do, Matteo?' she asked the blue sky.

What do you want to do, tesoro mio?

She thought about it. Life felt hard at BP, but her father had put himself out to get her the job and she'd been so keen to step up and do it well.

'I want to stay put, Matteo. I want to work to end this damned war and get back into your arms.'

I want that too, cara, *so stand up for yourself. Use all your glorious fire and you'll find a solution.*

Steffie groaned. She should have been getting married at Easter, but Easter had come and gone in a flurry of decrypts and she had no husband and no house. She hated war.

Testa alta, Matteo's imagined voice told her – chin up.

With a sigh, she pushed her chin up and looked out across the fields. There was a hawthorn hedge in front of her, resplendent with white blossoms, and she smiled to see it. Then she noticed something. Behind the hedge, all on its own in a small field at the back of a farmhouse, was a caravan. She went closer, standing on tiptoes to peer over at it. It was neatly kept but empty. Maybe...

'Don't be silly, Steffie,' she told herself and walked on, but at the top of the field she turned back to look down on the caravan, as white and cheery as the hawthorn. Beyond it was the sturdy farmhouse and in the neat yard a well-rounded woman was feeding a flock of chickens, clucking away to them as if she were the very mother-hen.

'Can't harm to ask,' Steffie told herself and, before she could lose her nerve, she marched round to the gate and called out a hello.

The woman spun round.

'Hello, my lovely. Fine weather for a walk.'

'Isn't it,' Steffie agreed. 'And for... for finding accommodation.'

'Sorry?'

Steffie bit her lip.

'You see your caravan.'

'I do.'

A chicken clucked curiously and Steffie forced a smile.

'I don't suppose you'd consider, er, renting it out? To me?'

'To you, my lovely?' Her eyes narrowed. 'Why?'

Oh God, this woman thought she was a hussy too. Steffie felt unaccustomed tears prickle in her eyes.

'Because the man in my billet tried to, to... you know, assault me. And I had to leave. And I'm sleeping in a cupboard at the Park and I just, I just want somewhere safe to call home.'

'Oh! Oh, you poor dear.' Suddenly the woman was there, reaching over the gate and enfolding Steffie against her ample bosom. 'Of course you can have the caravan if you want it. You'll be quite safe here. There's me and my Alfie living on the farm but he's a total gent. Wouldn't dream of hurting you. We've daughters, see, but they've fled the nest now with kiddies of their own, so we'd love to have you. I'd offer you a room in the house, but we've made their bedroom into an apple store so...'

'No, no, the caravan would be perfect, really.'

'Our farmhands used to live in it, before they were called up, Lord bless 'em. It's basic but clean. I see to that. I'm Gloria, by the way.'

'Steffie,' Steffie said.

'Welcome, Steffie. Come on in. Mind the chickens. They're just pleased to see you.'

'And I them,' Steffie said with feeling.

A caravan in a Buckinghamshire field was a long way from her family's beautiful apartment in Rome, but right now, it looked like a palace.

SIX

Ailsa

'Ooh, Ailsa, love, stop a minute.' Mrs Johnstone appeared from a gaggle of children just as Ailsa was reaching the front door.

'Can I help you, Mrs Johnstone?' she asked politely, though with the noise in the cosy house at its usual breakfast level she was keen to get away.

'Can anyone, love?' her landlady asked good-humouredly as her youngest followed her into the hall, wrapping chubby arms around her legs. 'No. It's just that a letter came for you.'

'For me?'

Mrs Johnstone held out a neat white envelope and Ailsa's heart caught as she saw the handwriting. It was round and laboured, with the heavy strokes of someone unused to writing anything down.

'Ma.'

'From your mother? Oh, that's lovely. I bet she's missing you something rotten, the poor dear.'

Ailsa gave Mrs Johnstone a weak smile. She wasn't so sure. She'd written home when she'd first got her address here, trying again to explain that she wanted to do something significant with her life, but she feared that, however kindly she'd tried to express it, it would inevitably be read as a criticism. She'd told them she loved them at least, so if anything bad happened they'd know that much. Maybe this letter was them doing the same? She tucked it into her satchel.

'Aren't you going to open it?' Mrs Johnstone asked.

'No time, I'm afraid. I've got to get the bus.'

She shook her head. 'It's long hours they've got you doing there.'

Ailsa smiled at her kindly host.

'It's fine. I enjoy it. Bye, Mrs Johnstone. See you later.'

She gave her a wave and reached thankfully for the door handle as a fight erupted between two boys in the kitchen. Hurrying down the street she saw the bus coming and ran to join a couple of other BP women at the stop in the middle of the village.

'Ooh, Ailsa,' one of them cried, 'you'll never guess who I went for a drink with last night...'

It was true, she wouldn't. The girl seemed to go for drinks with all and sundry. And why not? But it meant there'd be no chance to read her letter on the bus – and Ailsa had to admit to feeling slightly relieved.

The day was frantically busy. They'd got their Y-station set up well in Whaddon Hall and the powerful antenna on the hill meant that, with careful tuning, they could hear all across Europe. There wasn't much traffic with the agents in France right now so they'd been asked to have a go at picking up the Morse code flashing between German commands in Norway. Ailsa couldn't help but find it exciting.

Hitler's blitzkrieg warfare was scarily fast. He used panzer tanks supported by bombers and fighter planes to blast a way for the artillery, and success relied heavily on radio comms between the units. That meant a lot of messages crowding the airwaves

waiting to be captured by Ailsa and her crew and, with the
advance through poor Norway gaining horrific pace, the day
flashed by glued to her headset.

Thanks to Alasdair's schoolmasterly coaching, her Morse
accuracy was good and her speed was improving every day, but
she was hungry for more knowledge about the radio sets. It frustrated her no end when hers broke and she had to sit waiting for
Tommy Collinson, the technician, to come and repair it, so she'd
talked him into explaining their inner workings in her breaks. It
wasn't as much fun as lunch with Fran and Steffie, but it was
satisfying.

There were ten of them up here now and Mr Gambier-
Perry, their station leader, said new recruits were being trained
to expand the team so they could work around the clock. Ailsa
was due to go onto night shift next week and was already
dreading it. It wasn't only staying awake to listen to the enemy
at two in the morning that concerned her, but trying to get to
sleep in the Johnstones' chaotic home at two in the afternoon.
For the moment, though, she had to focus on plucking Morse
from the air.

The clock seemed to tick around to six before she'd even
looked up, and her mother's letter was still sitting unopened in
her bag. On the bus back down to Bletchley, however, everyone
else was busy chattering away, so Ailsa supposed there was no
avoiding it. Sliding the envelope out, she prised it open and
lifted out the single, carefully written sheet. *Ailsa*, it said baldly
at the top. Not Dear Ailsa, or Our Ailsa – just Ailsa. Swallowing, she forced herself to read on.

Ailsa,

*We got your letter, thank you, and have noted your address.
We will not be writing unless it is urgent as you clearly do not
value us. We are sorry that you feel island life is so limited and*

that the community that raised you is not enough for you. We gave up much to give you a happy childhood and are saddened that we failed. We hope you are having exciting, rewarding adventures far away from us and our dull little lives and won't expect to see you back.

Take care,

Your mother and father

Ailsa's eyes stung. It was so blank, so cold. They hadn't tried to understand her careful explanations. They hadn't listened to her saying that she hoped to learn, hadn't absorbed her protestations of gratitude and love. They'd just seen the offence they'd wanted to see and let that blind them to anything else.

'Well, thank ye,' Ailsa muttered, fighting back tears. She'd been a good daughter. She'd worked hard at school and around the house. She'd made friends on the island and joined in with everything and then simply said she'd like to see a bit of the rest of the world. Was that so very wrong? Immersed in her own misery, she didn't even realise the bus had pulled up in the centre of Bletchley and everyone had got off until the driver gave a loud cough.

'You all right there, love?'

She shook the tears away.

'Fine thanks. Sorry, miles away.'

Shoving the letter into her satchel she jumped up and left the bus, head down.

'Not bad news, I hope?' he said kindly.

She shook her head and with a muttered, 'thank you', hurried away. *Was* it bad news? Her parents hated her and never wanted to see her again. It certainly wasn't good. A glance at her watch told her it was six thirty – prime chaos time in the Johnstone household. She really didn't think she could face the happy tumble of family love with this letter burning a hole in her heart and found her feet turning her automatically in the opposite direction – towards BP.

'Ailsa? What's wrong?'

Steffie came bundling across the lawn towards her.

'Am I that transparent?'

Her friend hugged her.

'Yes. Your shoulders are all hunched and your eyes look red. Have you been crying?'

'Trying not to,' Ailsa said gruffly as the tears threatened again.

'You poor dear. What's happened?'

Ailsa couldn't find the words to explain so instead took out the letter and shoved it at Steffie. She read it in a trice.

'Ouch!' She hugged Ailsa again. 'That's not nice.'

The understatement made Ailsa laugh and once she'd started, she couldn't seem to stop. Steffie wrapped her arms around her as the laughter turned to tears and Ailsa buried her face gratefully in her shoulder.

'Why can't they understand that just because I want to see a few other people and places, it doesn't mean I don't love them?'

'They do understand really – or they will when they think about it more. They're just a bit stunned and lashing out. They'll come round, I promise.'

'You think?'

'Of course. They love you. Mummy was furious when Daddy sorted for me to come here, but she's over it now. I caught the BP van up to town on my day off last week to have lunch with her at the Ritz and she was gabbling away about how good it is that I'm helping with the war effort.'

Ailsa wiped her eyes. A sudden picture of her own mother

taking lunch with her in the Ritz exploded into her mind and the laughter came again. It was an impossible image. She suspected, though, that Steffie's mother was rather more mercurial than her own. Up in the islands a grudge could be nursed for a long time, but she was their bairn, their only bairn, so how could they be so callous?

'What you need,' Steffie pronounced, 'is a stiff drink.'

Ailsa smiled weakly.

'I don't think I've got the money for the Duncombe Arms until my pay cheque comes in.'

'Good job I've got a nice bottle of gin in the caravan then, isn't it?'

That distracted Ailsa. Steffie had told her she'd discovered a vacant caravan the other day, but Ailsa hadn't expected her to actually go through with living there. This fancy-talking debutante had more about her than met the eye.

'You've really moved in?'

'I really have. Gloria's been marvellous. She cleaned the place top to bottom, not that it needed it, and she's brought me all sorts of pots and pans and the prettiest set of crockery. It's quite homely now and will be even more so if you come and toast it with me. Let's find Fran, shall we, and make a party of it?'

'Let's,' Ailsa agreed, cheering up a little. Forget her parents and their insular, closed-off view of the world. She had friends and she was damned well going to make the most of them.

Even so, Ailsa found herself holding her breath as Steffie unlocked the door to the caravan, praying that her friend's new home wasn't too unpleasant. She glanced at Fran and the other girl lifted crossed fingers, but when they took the two steps up and inside, they both gasped with pleasure. The caravan was bigger than Ailsa had pictured and was spotlessly clean. The central table was covered with a red gingham cloth and the bench seats around it padded with soft rugs. The kitchen was small but neat, with a shining stove and dinky cupboards and there was even a 'pantry' – a well-sealed wooden hut out the back. At the rear of the van, Steffie proudly flung open the first of two doors to reveal a tiny bathroom complete with lavatory and miniature plunge-bath.

'There's a boiler for hot water,' she said, 'and this bath barely uses any so it's perfect for wartime.'

Ailsa looked at Fran, who grinned.

'Bet you didn't have luxuries like this in Rome, Stefania.'

Steffie stuck her tongue out at her.

'Make do and mend, Frances. I think it's sweet.'

'It's *very* sweet, Steffie. Really. I love it.'

'Frankly, anything would be magic without Reg prowling around, but I honestly think this place is lovely. And look, here's the bedroom.'

She opened the second door and they all peered in. This room, too, was larger than Ailsa had expected and furnished with two bunks and a long cupboard. Steffie was obviously sleeping in one bed and the other three were covered with her beautiful clothes.

'You should hang those up,' Ailsa told her.

'I will, when I get time. Gloria's found me a load of hangers, bless her, and she says she's going to get me a couple of crates to make drawers under the beds once we've cleared the floor. Oh, look what I found last night.'

She bent and pulled a box from under the right-hand bed. Inside sat a clutch of miniature wooden barns and a set of farm animals. Ailsa had had something similar as a bairn and she reached out a hand to pick up a sheep, tears stinging her eyes again. The animals in her set had been brought in from the mainland one Christmas and her pa had made the buildings himself. Oh, she'd spent hours playing with that farm. She reached for a cow, lost in memories, as Fran bent down beside her to look under the bed.

'There's not much storage space, is there?'

'It was blokes living here before,' Steffie said, 'so they didn't have as many clothes as me.'

'No one has as many clothes as you, Steffie,' Fran told her, and Steffie batted at her arm.

'You can borrow them any time, Fran. Just let me know when you land a hot date and I'm there to provide the finest outfit.'

Fran's cheeks flared. 'I don't date.'

'No? Why not?'

'I'm not keen on men. Loud, smelly beasts, if you ask me.'

Ailsa looked up at her curiously. She was flushed and bothered.

'You've got brothers, right?' Steffie asked and Fran nodded. 'That'll explain it. Brothers are boors; boyfriends are a different thing altogether. My Matteo is just wonderful.' She looked around her cramped bedroom and sighed. 'I should be married by now.'

'So should I,' Ailsa said darkly, 'if my parents and Alasdair had had their way.'

'Then thank goodness they didn't,' Fran told her. 'Come on, Steffie – where's this gin?'

They went back into the living area, Ailsa carrying the box of farm animals and setting them out, one by one, on the table as Steffie produced glasses and a curious-looking bottle.

'What on earth is that?' Fran demanded.

'Gin. Local speciality.'

'You mean...?'

'Gloria's Alfie distils it himself, yes.'

'Isn't that illegal?' Ailsa asked.

Steffie shrugged.

'Probably but it's delicious. Besides, there's a war on. Dig for victory and all that.'

'Distil for victory?' Fran suggested, raising her glass. 'I'll drink to that. Happy housewarming, Steffie.'

She nudged Ailsa, who set down the last of the farm animals and grabbed her glass.

'Happy housewarming.'

She sniffed the home-brew suspiciously but it smelled pleasantly of berries and she took a good swig. The spirit hit the back of her throat hard, making her cough, but it tingled down her throat and into her stomach, filling her with welcome warmth.

'We should eat too, or we'll fall over,' Steffie said. 'Here.' She leaped up again and from her little cupboards produced bread and cheese and a delicious pickle. 'Another local speciality.'

'You mean Gloria made it?'

'Yep.'

Fran grinned.

'You've really landed on your feet here, Stef. It's lovely. Homely.'

She gestured around the room and Ailsa noticed several postcards tacked to the wall. She stood up to get a better look. The first one was of a stunning vista of peaked mountains, a lake shining beneath them.

'Where's that, Steffie?' she asked.

'Switzerland. I have a friend there.'

'A friend in Switzerland? How come?'

Steffie seemed too busy cutting bread to answer and it was Fran who said, 'Finishing school, right?'

'Right,' Steffie agreed gruffly. 'My parents sent me. I didn't have a choice or anything.'

'Tough life.'

'I can't help that.'

Fran put up her hands.

'I didn't say you could. Sorry, Stef. It looks beautiful.'

Ailsa reached out a finger and stroked it across the mountains.

'You're very lucky. I'd love to see places like this.' She sighed. 'That's the sort of thing I had in mind when I left North Uist – mountains, lakes, seas, cities. Now look at me.'

'Stuck in a caravan in Buckinghamshire,' Fran supplied. 'Glamorous!'

'Isn't it? I've upset my parents no end, for this...'

'You've got us,' Steffie said, and Ailsa surprised herself by jumping up and flinging her arms around the girl.

'True. You're far better than any mountains.'

'Get away with you!'

'You are. Now, I'd best have some of that cheese or I'll fall over. This gin is lethal.'

They sat round the table for hours, enjoying Gloria's farm produce. Steffie filled a bowl of water to wash their plates and Ailsa commandeered it to give all the little farm animals a good clean as well. She stood them in a neat circle around the table to watch them laughing their way down the gin and felt her worries subside. She was still unhappy that she'd hurt her ma and pa, but she'd been right to leave North Uist and, somehow, they had to see that.

Eventually, the clock on the wall struck eleven and Fran groaned.

'We'd better get back, Ailsa, or we'll be no use to anyone tomorrow.'

Ailsa knew she was right, but it was with extreme reluctance that she dragged herself to her feet.

'I wish I could sleep here,' she said, glancing fondly around the little caravan.

Steffie looked at her.

'You know, you could do.'

'What?'

Steffie gestured to the bedroom.

'Why don't you move in?'

'Move in?!'

'Yes. Live with me, here. There are four beds, after all.'

Ailsa looked to the open bedroom door and the double-level bunks either side.

'But your clothes...'

'Can go in the cupboard.'

'They won't all fit.'

'Then they can stay in the suitcase. Damn the clothes, Ailsa, they're not important. The bed's there if you want it. You too, Fran.'

'Really?' Fran stuttered. Ailsa looked across and, to her huge surprise, saw tears gleaming in the tall girl's eyes. 'You mean that?'

'Of course I do. It would be wonderful to have us all here. I mean, cramped obviously, but wonderful.'

'No more Mrs Blenkinsop and her damp walls?' Fran whispered.

'No more noisy Johnstones?' Ailsa asked, just as incredulously.

She looked to Fran and then to Steffie and suddenly they were all hugging and squealing and jumping up and down.

'I'll check with Gloria tomorrow,' Steffie said once they were all out of breath and had to calm down, 'but I'm sure she'll be happy. It's income for her, after all, and I bet it will still work out cheaper than your current billets.'

'More money for gin,' Fran giggled.

'And we'll see each other every day,' Ailsa said.

'Like a proper family,' Steffie agreed.

'A proper family!'

Ailsa looked around the caravan, taking in the neat living space, the pretty postcards on the wall and the bright farm animals gazing impassively at them as if they'd known all along that this was going to happen. She shook her head, trying to take it all in. She'd got off the bus from Whaddon Hall feeling rejected by the only home she'd ever known and now she had a new one. And two new sisters besides. It was a feeling headier than any gin and she gave Steffie a last hug and headed into the night with Fran for hopefully the last time, full of plans for their new life together in the caravan at Bletchley Park.

SEVEN

MAY 1940

Fran

The knock sounded out – bang, bang, bang – and all of Hut 3 looked up like children awaiting Santa Claus.

'You get it, Fran,' Peter said, 'it was your idea.'

The others nodded and so, struggling to hide her grin, Fran went to the new hatch installed in the side wall, lifted it up and pulled on the string. With a creak and a jerk, a wooden tray came rattling down the tunnel beyond and Fran was able to grab it and triumphantly lift out a wedge of decrypts. Setting them on the table, she put the tray back and banged. Instantly the tray disappeared down the tunnel, pulled via the string on the other side back into Hut 6.

'It works!' Fran crowed.

'Of course it works,' Peter said, clapping her on the back. 'It was a genius idea.'

Fran waved that away as the nonsense it was. Cracking the German Enigma was genius; building a covered tunnel between Huts 6 and 3 to allow secure passage of the decrypts was just plain common sense. Still, that seemed to be what she was bringing to the team of brilliant academics and she was glad it was helping.

She made a note to seek out the site carpenter and thank him for all his hard work, but right now she had the index to get back to. Two multi-drawer wooden chests had arrived and were standing proudly along the wall to either side of the tunnel entrance. Now, she had to design and implement the system that would store all their information on the enemy forces in an easy-to-access way – and it had never been more critical. Hitler had invaded France last week and the war was starting in earnest. Poor Mr Chamberlain had resigned and Mr Churchill was now in charge, breathing fire and fury.

'He'll be good for us,' Peter had said. 'He's keen on Sigint.'

'Sigint?' Fran had asked, feeing stupid.

'Signals intelligence. Not spies and secret agents and messages dug out of wastebaskets, but high-level eavesdropping. Churchill's been pushing it for years, so he'll have our back.'

'But will he have France's?' Malcolm had asked, and that, sadly, was not looking likely.

The Germans were rampaging towards Paris with their terrible blitzkrieg and the only bonus was the increase in messages, making the codebreakers' job easier. They'd broken 'Red' – the Luftwaffe code for communicating with the ground forces – at the start of the year and it was proving very lucrative. It was still a battle to crack it when the keys changed every midnight but slowly they were processing more and more messages and it was vital they had an efficient way of recording the data. That's where Fran's index came in.

Only last week a partially corrupted message had mentioned a squadron of German fighters heading for some-where in France beginning with J. A check of previously refer-enced airfields produced three possibilities – Jersey, Joigny and Juvincourt. Another check on the records of troop move-ments in the last week suggested it would be Juvincourt, being

in the north-west of France where the Nazis were concentrating their attacks, so they'd sent the decrypt to the Air
Ministry with a comment suggesting they strongly suspected
an attack on this strategic target. A small news bulletin later in
the day had told them that an attack on the key French airfield
of Juvinot had been repelled and Fran had felt the thrill of
seeing the work they were doing here in BP having an effect in
the field.

She'd seen her parents on her next day off, grabbing a seat in
the van up to London to meet them for tea after they'd attended
some lecture on 'treating problems of the mind in soldiers'. Her
brothers were out in France now, working in field hospitals, and
her parents had been both proud and anxious. Fran had longed
to tell them about her own work, but there'd been no way she
was going to blab about BP with the threat of a treason charge
hanging over her, so she'd had to grit her teeth and listen to
them going on and on about medical tents and amputations.

That said, Fran loved her big brothers and the thought of
them so close to danger brought a further urgency to the need to
defeat the Nazis. Plus, of course, if the enemy took France, they
were only a thin strip of sea away from Britain. For a moment
Fran had imagined reading decrypts describing a Nazi advance
through England and right to the door of BP. The soldiers
would shoot them all the minute they discovered their precious
Enigma machines had been levered open in that unassuming
little park. She'd shivered but then pushed the terrible thought
aside and turned the conversation to her new home.

'You're living in a caravan?' her mother had asked, crinkling
her nose up. 'How bohemian.'

Fran had laughed.

'It's not bohemian at all, Mother, just practical. It's at the
back of a farmyard and Gloria, the owner, gives us all sorts of
veg and eggs to supplement our rations. And she makes glorious
chutneys.'

She hadn't mentioned Alfie's gin, or the occasional rabbit from the woods behind the farm – too 'bohemian'.

'We'll have to come and see it,' her father had said, but not with any conviction and that was fine by Fran.

The caravan was her space with her new friends and she had no desire to subject its cosy quirks to her parents' forensic examination. She'd been delighted, mind you, with the delicious chocolates they'd pressed on her as a 'housewarming present' and, given that they'd admitted to getting all sorts of such gifts from grateful patients, she suspected her upright parents weren't immune to the black market either. Who could be? There was a war on and you had to get your treats where you could.

She, Steffie and Ailsa had shared the chocolates that night, savouring the rare sweetness as they'd messed around with the farm animals like kids. Ailsa had cleaned up the two barns that had come with them and, though there was precious little space in the caravan, they all liked the farm's cheery presence and happily ate around it. Every night when Fran went to bed in her bunk across from Steffie and Ailsa, she would snuggle down and listen to their quiet breathing and feel cushioned from harm. The Nazis might be rampaging across France but for the moment, with her new friends, she felt safe. That meant a lot.

'Daydreaming, Fran?'

She jumped guiltily at the sound of Peter's voice.

'Just thinking about the best way to order this lot.'

She gestured to the cards cowering in their shoeboxes.

'Given the way you're ordering all of us, I'd say you'll have it licked in no time. But for now, come and meet our new recruit.'

'New recruit?'

Fran felt herself bristle at the idea of a newcomer to their cosy band and then told herself not to be ridiculous. She'd been new herself a month ago and everyone had been very welcoming. She followed Peter across the hut to find a petite woman in smart civilian skirt and blouse standing inside the door. She had glossy dark hair cut in a stylish bob and artfully rouged lips, and she stepped confidently forward as Peter introduced Fran, holding out a perfectly manicured hand.

'Good morning, Frances. I'm Valérie Rousseau. Delightful to meet you.'

She spoke with a pronounced French accent that drew Fran's eyes to her scarlet lips in instant fascination.

'You're French?' she said, realising too late how gauche that sounded. 'I mean, welcome. *Bienvenue.*'

'*Vous parlez français?*'

'*Oui.* That is... *un peu.*' She felt ridiculously shy suddenly. '*C'est un plaisir de vous avoir ici.*'

'It's lovely to be here,' Valérie agreed easily in English. 'And I am the lucky one. It is not so lovely for all our compatriots, left behind with those bastard Nazis running riot across their homes.'

Fran blinked.

'Well no, quite,' she stuttered. 'It's terrible.'

'It is. This blitzkrieg, Frances, it is not just a smart new noun – it is a scourge. They come with their planes dropping screaming bombs, and their tanks ploughing over everything in sight and then, when you are on your knees in your own blood, they send in the soldiers to round you up.'

Fran felt her breath constricting in her chest and stared at the woman before her.

'It sounds terrifying.'

Valérie gave a curt nod.

'It is, and only de Gaulle is prepared to stand against them.'

'De Gaulle?'

'An officer trying to establish a group of so-called "Free French" in London. You won't have heard of him, nobody has – yet – but he knows, as I know, that we must stop the men stealing our country. That is why I am here – to help get messages to officers in the field and halt the bloody advance.'

'That's certainly what we're trying to do,' Fran agreed, adding, 'Your English is very good.'

'Three years at Cambridge,' Valérie shot back.

'Right. What did you study?'

'English literature.'

Something rippled through Fran – admiration, tinged with envy.

'I wanted to study that, but my parents wouldn't let me.'

Valérie frowned.

'What has it to do with your parents?'

Fran opened her mouth to explain about funding but then closed it again, feeling young and naive before this composed Frenchwoman. Valérie could not be more than three or four years older than her, but she radiated worldly wisdom. Perhaps that's what facing the blitzkrieg did for you? She hoped she never had to find out.

'Nothing,' she said shortly. 'Maybe I'll go back to it after the war.'

'Next year then,' Valérie suggested and then gave a bitter laugh. 'But come on, show me round this hut of yours, will you?'

Fran looked uncertainly to Peter, who nodded her on.

'That would be helpful, Fran. Valérie is here to help us set up a link into France so that we can get urgent decrypts direct to the field with as little delay as possible.'

Fran stared at him.

'The ministries are letting you do that?'

Peter gave a funny grimace. Neither the War Office nor the Air Ministry had, so far, proved amenable to the idea of BP communicating direct with officers, but clearly that was shifting.

'That's where Valérie comes in. We're setting up a Special

Liaison Unit to communicate directly with Lord Gort in the field and Valérie is an expert in telegraphy.'

'Not that it will help much,' Malcolm put in gloomily. 'France is doomed.'

Valérie pulled a face at Fran and Fran suppressed a giggle.

'Not if we can help it,' she assured her. 'Now, let's find you a desk.'

The next two weeks were a whirlwind in Hut 3. Fran battled to get her index in order to accommodate the flood of 'Red' messages full of new locations, squadrons and battalions. Valérie was tracking key personnel to help gain an overall picture of German command and set up a map of France on the wall. Fran was glad to help her with it, but the battalions moved so fast that the map was soon a scrawl of crossings-out and they had to order in a new one and a set of movable pins to better keep pace with the horrifying Nazi advance.

They all worked long hours, staying way after their shifts and often bringing food in from the dining hall. Fran missed her evening meals with Steffie and Ailsa but when she did see them, as they all collapsed into their bunks late at night, she found out that they were as stretched as she. France, their nearest neighbour, was being overrun and whatever the hearty rhetoric of Winston Churchill, it was hard not to feel gloomy when you looked at the picture behind the scenes. Valérie battled to get information out to France, but the German tanks were moving almost as fast as the airwaves and all too often BP's advance warning of attacks arrived in already-flattened areas.

'It's impossible,' Valérie wailed to Fran as the enemy got nearer to Paris. 'Your soldiers are not holding them back.'

'Neither are yours.'

'It's true.' She gave a Gallic shrug but a tear fell from one big, dark eye and Fran felt an unsettling desire to reach out and wipe it away.

And then, as balmy sunshine heralded June, the messages rattling down the tunnel from Hut 6 brought dire news. The Allied troops were being driven back against the sea and Sigint was clear that more German forces were bearing down. Their resistance was going to break, leaving the enemy's path clear to over three hundred thousand men around Dunkirk. The numbers did not lie – the Nazis would trap them and they would massacre them.

'We have to get them out,' Peter said, pacing the hut. 'Half our country's sons are stuck there, and half the French and Belgian ones too. Go to Denniston, Malcolm – this has to get to the top.'

'Churchill?'

'Churchill, yes. It's time to evacuate.'

'You're leaving France?'

Valérie sprang across the hut like a wild cat, looking as if she might attack Peter personally with her manicured nails. He put up his hands.

'I'm so sorry, Valérie, but it's the only option left. Think of it less as leaving, and more as regrouping.'

'Regrouping on the other side of the sea. Pah!'

Valérie spat on the wooden floor and the studious men around the desks looked at each other in horror. Fran rushed over.

'Come on, Valérie, let's get some air.'

'I don't want some air,' Valérie shot back, but when Fran dared to reach out and put an arm around her shoulders, she let herself be led to the door.

Fran felt the French girl's petite frame shaking against her own and her raw emotion seemed to pass between them and course through her own veins. She heard a collective male sigh of relief as she guided Valérie out of Hut 3 and hated them for it. Why shouldn't she be furious? Why shouldn't she feel passionately about the fate of her country? And why shouldn't she show it? Guiding her into the thin passage between Huts 3 and 6, she dared to reach down and smooth the angry tears from Valérie's flushed cheeks. Valérie looked up at her.

'They don't understand, Frances. They don't know what it's like to have their homes taken from them at gunpoint. They don't know what it's like to have an arrogant blond army marching on their capital, threatening all they hold dear.'

'I know,' Fran soothed, trying to ignore the strange sensations rippling through her at Valérie's proximity. 'But they do understand logic and logic says that if we leave the troops there, they will be killed. Every one of them. Is Paris worth that?'

Valérie let out a long sigh and leaned her head against Fran's chest. Fran stroked her glossy hair and fought the urge to pass her hands on down her slim back and pull her even closer.

'It is not,' Valérie said, then she pulled back and looked up at Fran again, her dark eyes swimming with emotion. 'And after all, Frances, *I* left, didn't I? I fled weeks ago. Oh, I told myself I was coming here to help, but I could have done that by picking up a rifle and shooting bastard Nazis in the head.'

'You would have died, Valérie.'

'But at least I would have taken one or two of them with me.'

Fran shook her head.

'No. That's not the way to do it. We have to retreat and regroup and go again when we are ready.'

'When will that be?'

'I don't know. It could be you are stuck here for quite a long time.'

'Stuck here with you?'

Valérie reached up a slender hand and ran her fingers down the line of Fran's jaw.

'Stuck here with me,' Fran agreed hoarsely.

'Well that, at least, is not so bad,' Valérie murmured and pressed herself against Fran again.

Fran held her, her body alive with the feel of her, the scent of her, the almost-taste of her. She could feel Valérie's heart beating against her own and that seemed to increase its strength and send her blood pumping at giddy speeds. What was this feeling? It was both dangerous and wonderful, and she had no idea what to do with it. Turning her face to the scudding clouds above, she prayed for strength; they were all, it seemed, under siege at the moment.

EIGHT

JUNE 1940

Steffie

'That's the Eyeties all over though, isn't it? Cowards, the lot of them.'

Steffie stopped dead on the path around the lake and the two men behind almost ran into her.

'Hey, steady, girl – you almost had me over,' the first one said.

'Good,' Steffie shot back and he threw up his hands in mock surrender.

'What have I done?'

She put her hands on her hips and glared at him.

'I'll have you know the Italians are *not* cowards. They're warm and bold and loving.'

'So how come they've waited until Hitler's troops are swarming all over France and our chaps have evacuated to declare war?'

Steffie's blood froze.

'To, to...?'

'Perhaps it's not cowardice,' he conceded with a mocking tilt of his head. 'Perhaps it's wisdom. I mean, why put your own boys in to fight if you can get someone else's to do it for you?'

Steffie wanted to challenge him again but she was still reeling from the news. Stuck on night shift for the last few days, she'd rather lost sight of the world. She'd been heading home to the caravan for a well-earned rest, but there was no way she'd sleep now.

'When did they declare war?' she demanded.

The two men stared at her.

'Yesterday. Musso stood on his fancy balcony in the evening sunlight and told a roaring crowd of thousands that it was time for Italy to be liberated from the boundaries of her seas – or some such guff. Not that he's deployed any troops yet. They're probably all too busy kissing goodbye to their mistresses!'

The two men laughed heartily and it was all Steffie could do to resist digging her sharp heels into their feet to shut them up. She thought of Mussolini standing on his balcony waving to her and Roseanna when they'd passed on their way to school. She thought of him chatting her up at that party and could, reluctantly, see why the men were making such jokes. But this wasn't funny. If Il Duce had declared war on Britain, then Matteo was officially on the opposing side. She felt the whole world start to spin.

'Hey there, you all right?'

The man caught at her arm but, grateful as she was to be steadied, she pulled away.

'I'm fine. Thank you. I just...'

The second man nudged him.

'Reckon she might be one of those mistresses.'

Red-hot fury shot through Steffie.

'Not mistress,' she snapped, 'wife.'

They stared, then the first one gave a low whistle.

'Married to the enemy? Surprised they let you into this place.'

'Doubt she'll be here long now,' his companion agreed and, with a sideways look, they sidled around her and headed off into the Park, sniggering together.

'*Voi patetici bastardi!*' Steffie shouted after them and they jumped as if she'd uttered a witch's curse. If only!

Instinctively, she turned back to Hut 4, seeking shelter. BP had always been so safe but for the first time it felt hostile, and all because of one innocent love affair. She tumbled into the hut and sank onto a chair.

'Steffie! What are you doing back? Are you not well?'

Nobby Clarke came over and she looked up at him, still trying to take in what she'd just heard.

'*Mussolini dichiarò guerra,*' she shot out – Mussolini has declared war.

She and the older man often talked to each other in Italian and she slipped easily into it now. After all, she'd been in Italy for the last six years and she missed the exuberant patterns of her adopted tongue. Her *enemy* tongue.

'I know,' he agreed. 'Bad news.'

'The worst.'

Nobby crouched down next to her, his old knees creaking.

'You must have many friends out there?'

She nodded.

'Friends and…'

Her eyes went to the diamond on her ring finger and, following them, Nobby gave a little cough.

'Of course. Oh dear.'

It was such a classically English bit of understatement that Steffie felt a ridiculous urge to laugh. It wasn't funny, she reminded herself. Matteo would have to fight and she would have no way of knowing where he was, who he was facing, or if he was still alive. Then there was BP. She grabbed at Nobby's shoulders.

'They won't throw me out, will they?'

'Who?'

'The higher-ups. Denniston and his lot. What if they don't like it, Nobby? What if they think I'm fraternising with the enemy?'

'Are you?'

'No! But I wish I was.' She clapped her hand over her mouth. 'I don't mean that. I just wish I could see Matteo. He's an Italian, yes, but he's not the enemy. At least, he's not *my* enemy. Is he?'

'It's complicated, Steffie, but don't worry – many of us have friends all over Europe. How else would we have learned so many languages?'

'So they won't throw me out?'

'Not unless you do something to deserve it. In fact... Look, Steffie, I've been asked to set up an Italian section here in Hut 4 and I'd really like you to be a part of it.'

She looked up.

'Translating decrypts?'

He gave a small smile.

'Not as such, no. Hut 8 are too busy with important Enigma stuff to worry themselves over simple ciphers like the ones the Italians use, so it wouldn't be so much translating decrypts, as... well, actually decrypting.'

Steffie stared at him incredulously.

'You want me to, to... break codes?'

He nodded firmly.

'I do. You'll be excellent at it. I've watched you working, Steffie. You're rational, logical and clear-thinking, and those are exactly the sort of skills needed.'

Despite the shock of this morning, Steffie felt warmth steal through her whole body. Rational? Logical? Clear-thinking? No one had ever called her any of those things before. Fun, maybe. Jolly, pretty even – but logical...?

'Will you give it a bash?' Nobby asked, and she drew in a deep breath.

'I'd love to. Thank you.'

He smiled and pushed himself stiffly to his feet.

'Good stuff. You can start tomorrow. But for now – home and get some rest.'

'Yes, sir.'

He waved her away with a grin and she stumbled out of Hut 4 and back into the sunshine even more dazed than before. Matteo and his friends were the enemy and she was going to be working to read their codes and defeat them. The world truly had gone mad.

She woke up to the evening sun slanting between the curtains of the caravan and blinked awake, amazed she'd slept so long. She could hear Fran and Ailsa making dinner in the other room and lay there, soothed by the soft domestic noises. Before long, though, her stomach rumbled at the tantalising smells creeping under the bedroom door and she flung back the covers and headed out to join them.

'Hey there, sleepy head,' Ailsa said, waving a wooden spoon in her direction. 'Fancy rabbit stew?'

'Do I ever! You two are the best housemates any girl could hope for.'

'Caravan-mates,' Fran said, gesturing around their unusual home with a vegetable knife. 'And you should thank Alfie for the rabbit. He's been poaching again.'

'Sssh!' Ailsa said, rapping Fran over the knuckles with her spoon. 'It's not poaching, it's "liberating the fruits of the country for the people defending it".'

'Ah yes,' Fran agreed with a grin. 'Alfie the liberator!'

Steffie slid into a seat across the table from Fran and picked up a tiny pond from the toy farm. It was vibrant blue and newly painted with goldfish. Fran, who'd seemed rather agitated since the Dunkirk evacuations last week, had got hold of some paint and been touching up the more battered of the animals so that they gleamed. Steffie turned the pond over in her fingers, thinking how the blue exactly matched the colour of the Mediterranean in July. She groaned.

'Something wrong, Stef?'

'We're at war with Italy.'

'I know! I saw a newsreel of these crazed Eyeties in Rome and... Oh! Your fiancé?'

'Matteo, yes. He's in the air force, Fran. He's just been training until now, but this means he'll have to go into battle.'

'Against our chaps? That's awful. What if he shoots one of them down?'

'Or they him? I swore my marriage vows to him in the Temple of Aesculapius; what if I never get to enjoy the actual marriage?'

'So romantic,' Ailsa sighed from the stove, but Fran, always practical, took the toy pond from Steffie and handed her the vegetable knife instead.

'Don't think about it. What will be will be, and all that. Spuds!'

Steffie picked up a potato and began clumsily peeling it, grateful for something mundane to focus on, but in her mind's eye she could see Matteo, a proud smile on his handsome face as he got into the cockpit of a fighter plane and took off into the skies.

'The worst of it,' she confessed to her friends, 'is that I won't even be able to write to him now. They'll never let letters into an enemy country, will they?'

'Doesn't seem likely,' Fran agreed.

Silence fell, broken only by the bubbling of the rabbit stew. Steffie scraped at another potato, trying to picture where Matteo could be and why his letters weren't getting through. Had he forgotten her? No! She must never think that. This was war, letters got lost, misdirected, held up. He loved her, she was sure of it, and she must keep writing to him – but how? She was pulled out of her reverie by Ailsa tapping loudly on one of the postcards on the wall.

'The friend who sent you this is in Switzerland, right?' Steffie nodded gloomily. 'And Switzerland is neutral?'

Steffie looked over at her, eyes widening.

'So, I could send a letter to Ilka in Switzerland and Ilka could...'

'Send it to Italy. I reckon so, aye.'

Steffie jumped up and hugged Ailsa.

'Ailsa, you're a genius. I'll write immediately.'

'You'll write once the potatoes are finished,' Fran said sternly and, sticking her tongue out at her, Steffie sat down again and applied herself to her peeling.

Fran chopped them up as small as possible to save fuel and set them boiling, so Steffie looked around for her blank airmails, but she was suddenly unsure what to say. With Italy at war, the same babble of chatter and memories she'd been sending felt wrong somehow. Plus, the censors would check even letters to Switzerland and she couldn't afford to risk her words being destroyed at customs.

'This makes it all so complicated,' she wailed. 'It'll be hell in the Med.'

Ailsa frowned and sat down next to her, budging her along the little bench.

'I don't really understand why what happens down there matters to us.'

Steffie sighed, remembering her father's endless lectures on this very subject as war had grown inescapably closer last year.

'It's all about oil. Well, oil and spices and the other goodies that come out of the Far East. They're brought into the Med via the Suez Canal and Egypt, then shipped to Europe from there.

Control of the Med means control of the fuel, and in wartime that's pretty critical.'

'It is.' Fran nodded. 'But Egypt, that's in Africa, right?'

'Right, the bottom side of the Med.'

'Of course! It's a closed-off sea. More of a pond, really?' Fran picked up the clay farm pond and waved it.

'Sort of,' Steffie agreed. 'Look.'

She found one of the circular blue table mats that Gloria had brought in the other day and set it in the middle of the table. 'This is the Med. This big barn' – she picked up the largest of the two toy buildings and set it on Fran's side – 'is Africa. And this little one' – she set the smaller one on her side, angling it into the 'sea' – 'is Italy. This' – she reached for one of the pebbles Fran had been using to prop up the painted animals and set it beneath the little barn – 'is Sicily. And here is Crete.' A second pebble went further over towards the big barn. 'Oh, and this mini patch of grass' – she lifted a luridly green clay tuft – 'is Malta.'

'Malta?' Ailsa queried.

'It's a tiny British island right in the middle of the Med. We used to have a lot of our navy there, though I think Daddy said we moved it to Alexandria at the start of the war, presumably to protect Suez.'

'Here's the navy,' Fran suggested, setting a model duck on the blue mat beside the big barn. 'Oh, and the air force too.' She set a strutting pheasant alongside and, despite herself Steffie laughed.

'I reckon we could do with him on Malta to protect everyone who stops there on their way to the straits of Gibraltar.'

'Why do they stop there?' Ailsa asked.

'To refuel the ships,' Steffie told her, adding with a wink, 'and the men.'

'It's a... a den of vice?' Ailsa stuttered, horror in her green eyes.

Steffie laughed.

'No! Valletta's beautiful. There are a lot of bars and restaurants but it's no wilder than any other port.'

Ailsa pulled a face.

'The only ports I know are single-jetty villages with an alewife if you're lucky.'

'Alewife?' Fran choked out. 'You're joking, right, Ailsa? I know it's remote up in Scotland but it's surely not the eighteenth century?'

'Feels like it at times,' Ailsa said darkly, 'especially when your parents want to shackle you to some bloke's stove instead of letting you make the most of your talents.'

Steffie took her hand.

'Good job you didn't let yourself be shackled then, Ails. You got out and one day you'll be able to see the Med for yourself.'

'It looks lovely,' Ailsa laughed, waving at Steffie's makeshift model.

'It really is,' Steffie assured her, 'although perhaps not once the troops close in on it.'

Ailsa picked up a horse and set it next to the big barn in 'Africa'.

'The British army,' she suggested.

Fran grabbed a sheep.

'And the Italian one,' she said, plonking it down facing the horse. 'It said on the news they're already attacking our battalions in Libya.'

Steffie shivered, but Ailsa was picking up a cow.

'Where are the German army?' she asked, waving it.

'Still up here in Central Europe,' Steffie told her, taking the cow and setting it on the bench-back behind them. 'As are their air force. And their navy are busy in the Atlantic.' She cast around in the box of animals and picked a chicken and a goose to join the horse on the German side of the farm. 'But the Italian navy will be patrolling the Med.' She set the goldfish pond down on the mat. 'And the air force will be on Sicily.'

The last word caught in her throat as she realised that air force could include Matteo. The last animal in the box was a cockerel, very fine with green and orange feathers. With a lump in her throat, she set it on top of the pebble representing the beautiful island. Poor Matteo. And poor Sicily. She'd been there several times on holiday and loved the rugged landscape dotted with citrus trees, the powdery white beaches, and the amazing restaurants. The Sicilian people were as fiery as their volcano, but that fire was every bit as likely to erupt in a party as an argument and she'd spent many happy nights there. Now the restaurants would be full of uniforms, the trees ripped up for runways and the fire poured down the barrels of guns.

'It's all so stupid!' she burst out, looking in dismay at the farm representation of the area she loved. 'Why do we have to have a war, anyway?'

'Because of men fighting over who gets what field,' Fran said, marching the German cow across the mat.

On the stove, the potatoes bubbled over and Ailsa leaped up to rescue them, knocking the creature over as she went.

'May the right cow win,' she said fiercely. 'Now – dinner.'

But Steffie's appetite, even for Alfie's delicious liberated rabbit, was gone. She had no idea which was the right 'cow' these days and hated Adolf Hitler for taking her away from the man who should have been her husband, and Benito Mussolini for setting her inexorably against him. The great men might be playing these games but, whoever ultimately won, it was their people who were truly losing.

NINE

JULY 1940

Fran

'Runway extension at Antwerp,' Peter Lucas said grimly, handing Fran a copy of the latest decrypt to index.

Fran looked at it in horror.

'That's the third one in the last two weeks.'

'Afraid so. And with landing equipment going into the ports in the Low Countries, it can only mean one thing.'

Fran swallowed.

'They're going to invade.'

'Soon,' Peter agreed.

Nausea whisked up the insides of Fran's stomach and she glanced to Valérie, who gave her a sad shrug.

'At least your armies are back over here,' she offered. 'It will make it very hard for the Germans to land.'

'Plus, they don't have air superiority yet,' Peter said.

'And we won't let them get it either,' Humphreys put in, crossing his arms bullishly. 'Our boys will see them off from the home skies, don't you worry.'

Fran looked at Squadron Leader Robert Humphreys, trying

not to smirk at the way his fancy pomade made the grey streaks in his hair shine. He'd joined their team as air adviser two weeks ago, alongside Captain Curtis for the army. Their job was to get information out as fast as possible, though, as far as Fran could see, they were only needed because the ministries didn't trust civilians to truly understand the military situation.

The extra hands were welcome as they scrambled to process the myriad terrifying messages coming in from Northern Europe, but these two self-important men in their uniforms had brought a new bluster into the hut that was not, frankly, welcome. Curtis was quiet enough but Humphreys strode around the place issuing orders, not just down the phone to the Ministry, but to those within the hut too. Malcolm Saunders rarely stood up to him and tension was rising over more than just the imminent attack by the Nazis.

'*Tête de noeud*,' Valérie had muttered the other day when Humphreys had suggested to her that she couldn't understand what it would be like for Britain to be invaded. The insult hadn't been covered in even Fran's higher school certificate lessons, but the tone had been clear.

'Surely, of all of us, Valérie is best placed to understand,' she'd suggested carefully.

Humphreys had snorted.

'Nonsense! The French are used to capitulating but no one has invaded Britain since the Normans.'

'The *French* Normans, who took over the English nobility so thoroughly that most of them are now basically French too,' Valérie had snarled.

He'd looked so taken aback Fran had had to smother a laugh, but he'd recovered himself quickly.

'That was ages ago, woman, which is precisely my point. We're an island, a proud and glorious island.'

'Then I hope your pilots can keep you that way.'

'Oh, they will. They're the best in the world.'

It had been arrogantly said, but it was true that the brave Spitfires duelling in the skies every day and night were the only thing keeping the Nazis away. And if Britain fell, Hitler would have all of Europe in his stranglehold.

Not the only thing, she reminded herself, selecting three index cards to list the airfield, squadron number and commanding officer mentioned in the message. BP was working hard too, processing every enemy communication as fast as humanly possible to give those fighters an edge. With Hut 3's help, pilots could be scrambled into the skies at the right time and place to inflict the maximum damage and, to be fair to Humphreys, annoying as he was, he had got those at the top listening to Sigint. The question was – would it be enough?

At lunchtime, when Fran escaped to the canteen, the once pretty lawn was filled with men doing home guard drills. All males of fighting age at BP had been made to join and at first there had been something comic about seeing them running around in their cardigans and tweed jackets brandishing rifles, but with every new message this shabby defence became a horrifying reality.

As Valérie had rightly said, much of the army was on British shores again after the brave Dunkirk evacuations, but many soldiers had been recruited in the last year and there wasn't going to be time to truly get them up to speed. If the Nazis came marching up the road to BP, were they going to have to rely on the likes of Turing and Twinn seeing them off? Fran had heard mutterings about their brilliance and assumed they were two of the men tasked with breaking the Enigma codes, but they had no agility and their brilliant brains would be blown out in a failing heartbeat by any half-trained Nazi.

Fran stood watching the drill. She'd volunteered herself but had been politely turned down because 'women don't fight'. It was a nonsense; she'd be far more capable than half of these greying boffins.

'Penny for them.'

Fran jumped as Valérie came up next to her, so close that she caught the delicious waft of the delicate French perfume she always wore. Her head spun.

'Sorry?'

'Is that not what you English say? A penny for your thoughts?'

Fran smiled.

'It is, yes. Sorry, Valérie, I was miles away.'

'Imagining German soldiers mowing down your bold British ones?'

She gestured to the men attempting to crawl under a net fastened across the croquet lawn. Fran groaned and turned more fully to Valérie.

'What's it like?'

'Being invaded?'

Fran bit her lip but nodded. Valérie threaded an arm into hers and Fran felt the heat of her.

'It is awful, Frances. Your home, it is sacred. You don't realise how much until someone comes storming in to take it from you. My family live mainly down south in the Ardèche but we have a base in the outskirts of Paris for, you know, business. If I ever stayed in the apartment, I would moan about how small it was, but once the Nazis were close it felt like the most precious, beautiful place in the world. Everything – the photos on the wall, the plates we ate off, the cushions on the armchairs – they all felt like gold and I hated leaving them to those pigs.'

Fran heard the suffering in her voice as she remembered and squeezed the arm hooked gently in her own.

'*Je suis désolée*, Valérie.'

'*Merci*. It is why I came here, to keep on fighting. Oh, it is a poor way to do it, perhaps, but it is the only way I have. I am better with words than guns.'

She looked up at Fran, who felt the rest of BP blur around the edges of the Frenchwoman's passionate face.

'Me too,' was all she could manage.

Valérie smiled.

'Ah well, words are better weapons in the long run. Look at Shakespeare – he is the best ever ambassador for your glorious island, is he not?'

'He is,' Fran agreed, but she couldn't help thinking that Shakespeare was safe in his grave and would not be facing the Wehrmacht if they made it onto British shores.

'Ah, come on!' Valérie tugged her towards the dining hall. 'The Germans are not here yet and it is lunchtime. We cannot make war on empty stomachs, *n'est-ce pas?*'

Fran's own stomach rumbled its agreement and, with a sigh, she let herself be pulled away from the poor men scrambling around on the grass. She was delighted to see that Steffie was already in the mansion and rushed across to her friend. She loved being with Valérie but never felt as relaxed as with Steffie or Ailsa. She wasn't sure if it was because Valérie was French, or because of the unsettling way she looked at her with her beautiful dark eyes, but something about her always made Fran feel like she'd put her finger in a plug socket.

'Stef, have you met Valérie?'

'Only heard about her – until now. Lovely to meet you, Valérie. Isn't your hair just divine? How do you get it so glossy?'

Fran listened to them chattering about washing hair in lavender water and, again, envied Steffie her ease with people. She stood shyly to one side, trying to ignore the uncomfortable feeling inside her as Valérie laughed at something Steffie said, and was almost glad when someone else called her name – until, that is, she saw that it was Commander Denniston, head of the whole of Bletchley Park.

'Yes, sir?' she stuttered, feeling as if every eye in the dining hall had turned her way.

'Sorry to take you from your luncheon, Miss Morgan, but I wonder if I could have a word?'

Everyone was definitely staring. Fran's cheeks flared and she didn't dare look at either Steffie or Valérie. What had she done? She'd said nothing to anyone, not even her parents, and she'd been careful in her work, she was sure she had. She'd be mortified if she was sent away. Mortified and sad. She thought of the caravan, of her friends, of her half-completed index, of Valérie...

'Don't worry,' Denniston said, 'you've done nothing wrong. This way, please.'

It was some comfort, she supposed, but she could still only look at the patterned carpet as the commander led her from the crowded dining hall and through to his office.

'Take a seat, Miss Morgan, please.'

'Thank you, sir.' Fran sank into the proffered chair and folded her fingers nervously in her lap. 'Is there a problem?'

'No, no. Quite the reverse. Peter Lucas tells me you're doing marvellous work with the indexing in Hut 3.'

'He does? Oh. Er, that's good to hear. Thank you.'

'Absolutely vital, he says. Cross-referencing is the key, apparently?'

'It's important to be able to access information quickly, sir. It's proved useful a few times already.'

'Invaluable, Peter says.'

'That's very kind of him.'

Fran felt her cheeks flush and had to force herself not to fidget in her seat. Invaluable! She wasn't sure anyone had ever described her that way before.

Commander Denniston leaned towards her.

'So invaluable, in fact, that I'd like to invite you to join a new team. It's a team that we very much hope will never have to actually exist but if it does, I'd like you to be part of it.'

Fran frowned, desperately trying to work out what this

earnest man was on about. Denniston rapped a hand on the desk.

'Listen to me! You must think I'm mad. What it is, Frances – may I call you Frances? Thank you. What it is, is Column BQ.' He paused, as if this explained things. Fran bit her lip but then, thankfully, he spoke again. 'It's a terrible thing, to have to think the worst – and I don't think it, let me assure you that I don't, but I do have to plan for it.'

'The worst?' Fran dared to ask.

'Invasion, Frances.'

'Ah, yes.' Her stomach tightened.

'Obviously our boys are doing all they can to stop the Germans. We're strengthening the beaches, training the army, sending up our amazing pilots, and, of course, reading their nasty plans right here at BP – and recording them in your excellent index, right, Frances?'

'Right, sir. But…?'

'But, if – and it's a very big if, you understand – if the worst happened and they did land, we need to be ready. This operation here at BP is vital to the Allied effort and if it came under threat there would be serious consequences for the nation. We are therefore planning Column BQ.'

'That seems very wise, sir,' Frances said cautiously. 'But what exactly is it?'

Again he rapped his hand on the desk.

'Apologies. I go round the houses at times. It's age, Frances. Terrible thing. To the point – Column BQ is a group of around five hundred key personnel from BP who, in the event of the Germans landing on British soil, will be evacuated to America.'

Fran sucked in a breath.

'America, sir? And you want me…?'

'To be part of that group, yes. Obviously, there will be a lot of the senior staff going but we need people to organise us,

Frances, and Peter assures me that you are the best organiser in the Park. So – will you come?'

'To America?' Fran repeated, still unable to believe it.

'That's right. Washington, to be precise. Churchill's been plotting it all with Roosevelt. We've got four of the billet buses on alert ready to hotfoot it to Liverpool and from there...'

'Washington?'

'Yes. Well, New York first, obviously. But then Washington.'

Fran could hardly believe it. A moment ago she'd been watching men training on the lawn and trying to picture Nazis hammering down the gates of BP and now it appeared that if that should happen – and pray God it didn't – she'd already be gone, sneaking out the back door of Britain and across the Atlantic. The Atlantic where the wolfpacks of Nazi U-boats patrolled... But, then, with Nazi infantry running up England, nowhere would be safe, so better to take your chances at sea than cower in your home.

She remembered Valérie's words just a few minutes ago: *Your home, it is sacred. You don't realise how much until someone comes storming in to take it from you.*

She prayed the Nazis weren't coming for her home but if they were, she wanted to be part of a team that might be able to strike back. She sat up straight, looking Commander Denniston in the eye.

'I'd be honoured to be a part of Column BQ, sir, thank you.'

'Excellent. Have a bag ready to go at the drop of a hat. You can't tell anyone, I'm afraid – bad for morale and all that – but the office have complete files on the team and will let the relevant relatives know if we have to, to...'

'Regroup, sir?'

He smiled at her.

'Regroup, Frances, exactly. Thank you for your time and I do hope there's some luncheon left.'

She was dismissed. Rising, she made for the door feeling rather unsteady. It was an honour to be picked as a key team member, of course, and it would be amazing to see Washington under any other circumstances, but having an escape plan made the invasion feel even more plausible and her hand, as she reached for the door handle, was shaking.

'Oh, and Frances...' She looked back and Commander Denniston smiled at her. 'Don't worry too much. It's just a contingency plan. I'm sure we won't drop the bat.'

'I'm sure we won't, sir,' she agreed, but as she headed back to Hut 3 to file yet more messages about troops and equipment gathering just over the Channel, it was getting increasingly hard to see how on earth they were going to hold onto it.

TEN

Ailsa

Charlie Acton, one of the noisiest radio operators at Whaddon, stomped dramatically across the Y-station and Ailsa looked up, irritated. She was trying to tune into a remote signal from up in the Arctic lair of Hitler's U-boats and could hear nothing with Charlie making all this fuss. She yanked off her headset.

'What's wrong, Charlie?'

'Malta!' was the cryptic reply, accompanied by the scornful wave of an official-looking letter.

'What about Malta?'

'They only want me to go there.'

Ailsa stared at him enviously, picturing the tuft of grass on the toy farm back in the caravan.

'That's amazing.'

'Is it?' He frowned at her. 'Where even is Malta? The boss said it's in the Mediterranean, but I ain't ever heard of it before.'

'It's an island,' Ailsa told him.

'An island? Why would I want to live on an island?'

Ailsa squinted at him. Charlie was a whizz with a radio but

he hadn't the sharpest brain. Even so, this was particularly stupid.

'*This* is an island, Charlie.'

'What is? Whaddon?'

'No! Great Britain.'

'What?'

'Great Britain is an island – surrounded by sea.'

He thought about it for a while.

'True,' he agreed in the end, 'but it's so big that you don't notice.'

'Hitler's noticed,' one of the other girls pointed out, taking off her own headset, 'because he can't just stomp his jackboots across our borders.'

'Even if he could, he'd get a good kicking here,' was Charlie's instant answer. 'We wouldn't take no invasion in England.'

Ailsa prayed for patience.

'The Poles said the same, Charlie, the French too, but blitzkrieg is merciless. They come at you on all fronts. You've heard the messages – all that Morse between tanks and planes and armoured divisions.'

'Well, yeah, but it's just dots and dashes, ain't it? How am I meant to know what they're saying?'

'You're not,' Ailsa agreed. 'But you can tell who's saying it and where they're saying it from. That's enough to build up a picture, right?'

Charlie frowned, as if this hadn't occurred to him, and Ailsa exchanged an eye roll with the other girl. It didn't matter, she supposed. Charlie could take down Morse at twenty words per minute – a speed she was still battling towards – but perhaps he did that because he didn't look beyond the symbols to what they might mean. Lucky him.

'So,' Charlie pushed, sitting down on the side of her table and tipping her radio set so she had to put out a hand to steady it. 'Where is this Malta island then, clever clogs?'

Ailsa flushed. She wouldn't have known herself until she'd met Steffie, but now she could see it clearly, if only as a tuft of grass on a blue table mat.

'It's just below Sicily – which is just below Italy.'

'Italy? Holy Lord, we're at war with Italy!'

'Well, aye. I imagine that's why they want you there – to listen in to their messages from close up.'

'But I could get bombed.'

'You could get bombed here, mate,' the other girl put in. 'Especially if the White Cliffs crumble.'

Ailsa shivered. Yesterday over dinner Steffie had been reading out some journalist's gory predictions of what an invasion would be like.

'Surely they won't really be able to land here?' Ailsa had said, and Fran had muttered something like 'They're getting ready to give it a damn good try', then clapped her hand over her mouth and hurriedly added, 'I mean – that's what that article is suggesting.'

She and Steffie had let it go but Ailsa had lain awake that night wondering what Fran, sleeping in the bunk below her, knew about Hitler's invasion plans. The Cambridge girl had pulled a bag out of storage in Gloria's shed the other day and stashed it under her bed with some basic clothing in, and to Ailsa it looked horribly like she was packing for an emergency departure. An *imminent* emergency departure.

Up until recently Ailsa had been enjoying the summer. The weather here in protected Buckinghamshire was far balmier than she'd ever known in windswept North Uist and her only concern had been protecting her annoyingly peely-wally skin. She'd got used to having bare arms and had let Steffie take her shopping for a light summer dress that she loved, but these days even the sun-filled skies seemed dark.

There were horrible tales from the south coast of people gathering to watch dog fights in the air above the cliffs, cheering if a Messerschmitt was shot down and crying if it was a Spitfire. To Ailsa it seemed wrong to treat such bitter battles as sport, and wrong, too, to feel so differently about two young men plunging to their deaths. The German pilots were young, apparently, kids signing up to the air force because it was exciting and because girls love a flying jacket. They had sweethearts and mothers and sisters who would mourn them if they were sent, burning, into the sea.

'The difference is that they're attacking us and we're just defending ourselves,' Fran had told her – and she was right, Ailsa knew, but she still didn't like it and was glad they'd seen little of it over BP. She was glad, too, that her parents and friends back home would be unlikely to see it. Even if Germany invaded, it would take any Nazi a long time to get out to North Uist, so hopefully they were safe.

She was the worry; she knew too much to be safe. Back in the spring, one of the lads had been trying to leave Whaddon Hall to go and fight in France but had been told no one from BP and its satellites would be allowed near the front line.

'Why not?' he'd demanded.

The answer had been a chilling: 'Because we can't afford to have you fold under interrogation.'

Would Ailsa 'fold' before Nazi torturers? Almost certainly. She wasn't bold or brave. The most courageous thing she'd ever done was walk away from a proposal, and even that still gave her nightmares. Kelsey had written her a letter the other day saying that Alasdair was 'moping around like an old seal' and, although her friend's jokey imagery had made her smile, she'd felt bad all the same.

'It's not your problem,' Steffie had told her. 'You did the right thing – who'd want to be married to an old seal, for heaven's sake?'

Ailsa had giggled.

'He wouldn't be moping if I was marrying him,' she'd protested, but Steffie had been having none of that.

'He'd still have been an old seal, and you, Ailsa MacIver, deserve more than that.'

'What animal *do* I deserve then?' she'd asked.

They'd been at Alfie's gin again, if she remembered rightly. It had been a rare wet evening and the three of them had sat around the table with the rain drumming on the roof of the caravan and the animals getting on with life in their Mediterranean farm between the gin glasses.

'You deserve a giraffe,' Steffie had decided. 'Sleek and elegant and a bit unusual.'

'Or a lion,' Fran had suggested, 'with a great mane of hair and lithe limbs.'

They'd all giggled at that and Ailsa had counted herself blessed to have friends who thought so highly of her. Not that she wanted a lion, or a giraffe, or even a seal. There would be time for men after the war and she had to focus on herself.

Now, she stood up and faced Charlie.

'I'd love to go to Malta. I hear Valletta is beautiful.'

'Valletta?' he asked. 'Aren't the Italians bombing that? I'm sure I saw something about it on the news the other day.'

Ailsa shivered. Steffie's fiancé could be one of the pilots dropping the bombs – imagine if Matteo killed poor Charlie.

'I'm not going,' he said, scotching that worry, 'and they can't make me.'

Ailsa wasn't so sure about that. Charlie was a signalman employed by the RAF so didn't that mean he had to obey orders? Still, if he didn't want the posting...

'I'll go.'

'What?'

She reached out and took the letter from him.

'I said, I'll go. To Malta.'

If Fran was packing her bag because the Germans were

coming then it would be no more dangerous out there than here in England. Before she could lose her nerve, she marched across and tapped on the door of the boss, Mr Gambier-Perry.

'Come in.' Ailsa felt momentarily dizzied by her own daring, but there was no point stopping now, so she grabbed the door handle. 'Ailsa! My number one operator, what can I do for you?'

Richard Gambier-Perry rose as she came in and swept her a small bow. She flushed.

'I'd like to go to Malta, sir.'

'You'd like to do what?'

Ailsa placed the letter down on the desk.

'Charlie's had a letter asking him to go to the Y-Station on Malta but he doesn't want to go so I was thinking I could go instead.'

Gambier-Perry blinked.

'To Malta?'

'What's so strange about that?'

He shook himself.

'Nothing, I suppose. Sorry. It's just... Haven't you come from some tiny island in Scotland?'

'Aye, so surely that makes me a good fit for some tiny island in the Mediterranean?'

'Can't fault your logic, but it's a bit different. Malta is under fire.'

'I know that, sir, but it's close to Italy so perfect for listening in to their messages. And the ones in Africa too. They're vital, are they not?'

'They are, Ailsa. We need to protect—'

'Our oil reserves coming through the Suez Canal,' she said eagerly.

'Yes. You're very well informed for—'

He cut himself off and Ailsa frowned.

'For a Scot?'

He laughed.

'I was going to say for a girl.'

Ailsa's frown deepened.

'That's no better. Girls read newspapers too, you know.'

'Of course. I'm sorry, Ailsa. You're absolutely right. All my girls are proving themselves to be exceptionally capable. But what girls don't do is go into war zones.'

Ailsa felt frustration building within her.

'Why not? Why is it less dangerous for Charlie than for me?'

'Well, it isn't, I suppose. But he's a chap so...'

'So?'

Gambier-Perry was foundering. Ailsa pressed her advantage.

'I'm good with the radios, you know I am. I can find all the frequencies and my Morse is fast now. I'd do a good job.'

Her boss slid around the table and took her hand.

'I don't doubt that, Ailsa. But even so – girls don't go into war zones.'

'Why on earth not?'

He shuddered.

'Because at that point we would kiss goodbye to all civilisation.'

Ailsa wanted to scream but that would hardly be appropriate.

'So, sir, I can't go to Malta to protect Britain because I'm a symbol of the sort of Britain that we want to protect?'

His eyes lit up.

'Exactly!'

That made her want to scream even more and it was only through superhuman effort that she held it in all the way back to the caravan. Once there, though, she let rip with such a roar of rage that all the farm animals rattled in their warzone pastures.

'Why can't the eejits see what we're capable of?' she demanded of her two friends.

'Because,' Steffie said, hands on curvy hips, 'it would mean facing that we're as capable as them!'

Ailsa supposed she was right but that didn't stop it being annoying. Picking up the tuft of Malta grass, she stroked the spiky clay blades.

'One day, Malta,' she murmured to them. 'One day I'll see you, I swear it.'

ELEVEN

AUGUST 1940

Steffie

Steffie rubbed fiercely at her eyes and wriggled on her wooden chair, trying to keep herself awake. Night shifts were hell. This was her third night in, but her body definitely hadn't got used to it yet and her stinging eyes drifted longingly to the camp beds at the back of the office. She remembered sleeping here back in April after Reg had made his disgusting advances; that had been an unpleasant time but it had led her to the caravan and to sharing it with Fran and Ailsa so, in the end, Reg had done her a favour. Not that she'd ever forgive him.

The stir of anger at her one-time landlord got her blood pumping again and she picked up her pencil, determined to crack the latest set of weather reports. The Germans, orderly by nature, sent up weather planes over the Mediterranean at the same times every day to report back to Central Command. The reports were then radioed to their Italian allies in a low-grade cipher that Hut 4 had levered their way into a while back and it was Steffie's job to find the day's key and translate the reports. It wasn't very exciting codebreaking, and certainly not as glamorous as cracking Enigma, but it was quietly satisfying and Harry assured her that every message contributed to the overall picture.

Sometimes, if the weather was especially important to an operation, the Axis forces sent the weather messages through Enigma to their commanding officers, and if Steffie had already cracked them, they could provide a vital way into the main traffic. Once, Alan Turing had come to Hut 4 to thank them for providing a critical crib and, briefly, Steffie had felt like the most important person in the world. If she looked back on the girl she'd been this time last year, expert only in what shoes went with what dresses, she felt as if the war had turned not just her world, but her very self upside down. And she liked it.

Unbelievably, she seemed to fit in at this funny park full of academics, and she was slowly working out how it all came together. The high-ups at BP liked to keep everyone in their separate cubbyholes for security, but if you were part of the processing of Sigint it was easy to figure out what had to be happening in other units. She knew that the messages came in from Y-stations all around the country and, indeed, from several remote ones across the empire. She knew, for example, that Ailsa had been furious the other day because one of her male colleagues was being sent to Malta and they'd refused to let her go, so Ailsa must be part of the Y radio service.

She knew that the naval Enigma codes were being broken in their own Hut 8 and that Huts 6 and 3 worked as a similar pairing, presumably on the army and air force traffic. She knew that there was an additional crack team working in the old cottages in the stable yard under the eccentric Dilly Knox, and that he liked working with women. There were lots of inevitable jokes about why that was, but Steffie had got talking to someone called Mavis at dinner the other day and she'd said that Dilly, an older man and devoted to his wife, believed that women's brains were excellent for 'the sort of work we do here' – by which Steffie assumed she'd meant codebreaking.

She could understand it. Women, it seemed to her, were more patient than men and happier to get on with the repetition of the codebreaking, which was less about genius and more about plain old-fashioned graft. They were clever too. So many of the women here had been to university and had degrees in complex things like mathematics and classics, and Steffie worried they'd look down on a debutante with little more than a flair for fashion and a suspicious Italian fiancé, but so far everyone seemed to accept her at face value and let her get on with her work. It was all rather exciting.

Last week, Harry had told them to clear their desks of anything secret because they were having an 'indexing expert' in. Steffie had been expecting some dry old gent with rheumy eyes, so imagine her surprise when Fran had walked in. Their eyes had locked and Harry, who knew they were friends from evenings in the Duncombe Arms, had given them both a wry smile before they'd all got on with what they were doing.

It had been fascinating seeing Fran in a work environment, her long legs striding up and down the office, explaining the best way to organise an efficient indexing system. Steffie had felt a tingle of a feeling she'd struggled to name until it had suddenly come to her – pride. Pride that such a competent, clever woman was her friend. Yes, life was certainly different now and Steffie was enjoying it – though not, perhaps, at two in the morning.

Pushing back her chair, she went over to the small stove on which they made the strange hickory concoction that passed for coffee these days. Steffie, accustomed to Italian fresh-ground nectar, had found it as unpalatable as that strange beer Ailsa claimed to enjoy, but these days she was as used to it as she was

to walking up muddy paths, cooking root vegetables and
sleeping in a tiny bunk bed. She bent to light the ring and set
the kettle on top, then turned back to her fellow sufferers.

'Coffee anyone?'

She got a chorus of 'pleases' from the five others on shift and
went to gather tin mugs from desks but as she was heading back
to the stove, there was a loud knock at the door. They looked
nervously at each other. Steffie was pretty sure she wasn't the
only one to fear that it was the Germans, but she shook it away.
A parachute invasion would surely come with more noise? And
what self-respecting Nazi would *knock*?!

She put down the mugs with a clatter and went to the door.

'Mavis?' The woman from the dinner hall was standing
outside in the darkness, stamping her feet against the chill
creeping into the late August air. 'Are you well?'

'Quite well.' Mavis had a curious light in her eyes and she
looked over Steffie's shoulder. 'Who's in charge here?'

It was Walter Ettinghausen tonight and he was already
striding across. With a nod of thanks to Steffie, he went outside
to join Mavis. Steffie looked to the others, all staring keenly at
the wooden door, but then the kettle boiled and there seemed
little else to do but make the coffee. She ladled it out, adding
water carefully and trying not to look as if she were straining to
hear the conversation outside. It was too hushed to catch any
words, but it sounded exciting.

At last Walter was back and everyone turned his way. He
took the coffee Steffie was proffering and smiled around at
them.

'It seems,' he said, 'that the cottage have secured a break in
Hagelin.'

Steffie gasped. Hagelin was the machine used for the main
Italian naval code and it had been eluding them. If Mavis had
found a way in, it could vastly improve the intel they provided

to Admiral Cunningham and his fleet out in the Mediterranean. Steffie pictured the toy farm back in the caravan. She saw the goldfish Fran had selected to represent the Regia Marina and the ducks, positioned squarely by the 'big barn', representing the British navy. It was silly, really, to imagine ducks and fish fighting – but, then, a year ago it had felt silly to imagine herself and Matteo doing so and now it seemed, by dint of their respective countries of birth, they were.

Steffie shivered and wrapped her hands around her tin mug, craving warmth. Also on the farm was the sleek green and gold cockerel of the Regia Aeronautica, stationed on Sicily, and suddenly Mavis's 'break' felt like a personal threat to her own happiness. What if a message that they passed on to the Admiralty led to Matteo's plane being shot out of the sky? Oh, she hated war. Whatever opportunities it was bringing her, it wasn't worth the horrible loss of life – especially if that loss included her dear fiancé.

Walter was digging a bottle of whisky out of his desk drawer and liberally topping up everyone's coffee to celebrate the breakthrough, but Steffie refused her tot and went back to her desk to wrangle with weather reports and pray for dawn.

A week later and work in the Italian section had gone mad, with the new decrypts coming through at pace. Steffie had been switched from weather reports to operational messages and was relishing the linguistic challenge of filling in the gaps to make sense of the enemy instructions, while trying not to worry what they might mean for Matteo. She didn't dare even mention his name now that she was actively working against him and she hated that her once easy love had been tainted this way.

The only consolation was that Nobby was pleased with her work and Harry delighted with how much trust was finally being put in their intel thanks to their daily reports. The Admiralty were even sharing their own operational plans to help Hut 4 put their messages in context, and Fran's indexing system was up and running to collate the information. Steffie was starting to dream in ships and ports, and felt she was getting to know the Mediterranean in a whole new way. In part, it kept her sane as the rest of BP fretted over Hitler's plans just across the Channel, and in part it drove her mad with fear.

The other day a British destroyer had torpedoed an Italian ship thanks to Bletchley Sigint and the whole hut had cheered at the news – bar Steffie. She'd felt a little like the time she'd watched a touring England team play football in Rome and been left in her seat as everyone around her had leaped up at an Italian goal. Several people in the hut had looked at her suspiciously and she'd had to cheer in an over-hearty way to make up. She wasn't sure it had been convincing and worried every day that she might be summoned to Denniston and told she was too much of a security risk to work here any longer.

At least her work was critical. Churchill had big plans to ship planes to Malta to take on the Italians based in Sicily and Steffie had spent much of the afternoon working with Nobby to pin down where the 'enemy' squadrons were stationed. The thought that one of those bases could be Matteo's sent her head spinning and she was grateful when the end of her shift came. Fran was working evenings this week but hopefully Ailsa would be back at the caravan and they could eat together. It felt, these days, as if her two caravan-mates were the only people she could talk to about her enemy fiancé and she all but ran home.

The caravan was empty. Slumping on one of the steps, Steffie stared gloomily into the grass.

'Steffie? Cooee, Steffie!'

Looking up, she saw Gloria waving and forced herself to smile at her kindly landlady. Perhaps she was bringing gin? She looked hopefully at Gloria's hands but they were empty of enticing bottles, though was that...?

'Letter for you. Looks like it's been all over the place. Lots of fancy stamps on it.'

Gloria thrust the airmail at Steffie and it was, indeed, marked with several border stamps – notable among them the clear red mark of Switzerland. Steffie looked to the handwriting and gasped in joy. Matteo! She stroked the envelope, wanting to prolong the precious moment before she opened it. The looped letters instantly evoked memories of the love notes he used to leave in her bike basket, or her bag or, if he could sweet-talk the maid into helping, under her pillow.

She'd always loved finding those after he'd gone home from a visit, especially if they'd been closely chaperoned. It had always been all right if Mama had been in charge, as she would wander away, content to let the relationship with the handsome, well-connected young man develop. But if Mama had left Signora Alberta, the forbidding housekeeper, in charge, there'd been no hope of anything more than a stilted chat from opposite ends of the couch. It had made them giggle, all the same, and then, when Matteo had been chased away, she would find one of his notes and luxuriate in it.

She could still remember the first time he'd mentioned marriage. It had been just before she'd been sent off to Switzerland to be 'finished', and he'd been invited to dinner with the family. There had been far too many guests for them to get any time alone but when she'd gone up to bed that night, she'd found a rose on her pillow, a note wrapped tightly around its stem.

My most beautiful Stefania,

You are the only light I need to see, the only scent I wish to inhale, the only taste I long for. One day, my darling girl, if you will have me, I will marry you and we can feast on each other forever.

Yours, Matteo

It had made her blush terribly, with its deliciously improper suggestiveness, though it had been written in Italian, of course, the extravagant romance of it flowing freely in that more naturally sinuous language. She had it still, stashed with the others in a silk bag in her underwear drawer (underwear crate now), but this – a new letter – was precious indeed.

'Thank you!' she cried, plucking it from Gloria's hand and giving her surprised landlady a smacking kiss on her soft cheek. 'Thank you so much.'

Gloria grinned.

'Sweetheart, is it?'

'The sweetest heart in the world,' Steffie agreed gaily, and waltzed up into the caravan to grab a knife and slice the flimsy paper apart with all the gentleness she could muster.

She folded the sheet out and stared at it, her heart sinking at the sight of the heavy crossings out. They were in two different pens and she felt sick at the thought of complete strangers pawing through Matteo's words, but it was yet another privation of war and there were a few left for her. He had written in English, presuming that no letter in Italian would be allowed through, and she perused it eagerly, her recent work emending Italian decodes heightening her ability to guess quickly at the gaps created by the censors' cruel pens.

My darling girl,

It was so clever of you to write to me from a neutral country and I hope that, somehow, this finds you by the same route. The Italian postal service was disorganised before, as you know, but it's chaos now. My letters may take time to reach you, but rest assured that even if they had to go to the moon and back, my love for you would not be one bit diminished by the journey. I hate that the world has forced us onto opposite sides and want you to know that, however much our countries stand against each other, I could only ever be at your side.

Would that we could be as neutral as Switzerland and stand as our own country, with our own borders and own rules. They would be few, my love – just that we care for each other and listen to each other and never have to be apart. But until we can build that idyll, we must remain in separate lands. I will do my duty here and send you greetings from myself, my company and our adopted cat, Ra.

Stay safe, my love, and I will be with you on the other side of this madness,

Matteo

She clutched it to her chest. His adopted cat, Ra! So – they were in Egypt. Ra was the sun god, worshipped by the ancient Egyptians from a centre at Heliopolis, the City of the Sun. Matteo had loved Egyptology and once told her that she was Hathor to his Ra. She had looked Hathor up and found her to be goddess of love, beauty, music, dancing, fertility and pleasure. Back then she'd thought that sounded glorious. Now, a sneaking part of Steffie wondered what Hathor would make of slogging over dull old messages in a creaking wooden hut, but she dismissed the miserable thought instantly. No one got much in the way of dancing or beauty with a war on and receiving this letter was the greatest pleasure she could have.

Matteo was safe and stationed somewhere in Egypt. The navy could deliver planes to Malta without her having to worry about them shooting him out of the sky – for the moment. A glance at the postmark told her that Matteo had posted this over a month ago, so of course there was no guarantee he was still in Egypt, or even still alive, but for tonight it was enough to hold his words against her cheek and pray that her own private sun god could stay in the skies until their rulers came to their senses and let them be together once more.

TWELVE

SEPTEMBER 1940

Fran

Fran paced Hut 3, trying to peel her mind away from the south coast and her imagined pictures of great German warships disgorging wave after wave of soldiers onto British shores. It had started as a nightmare that would wake her in her bunk, her breath coming fast and sweat prickling at her brow, and these days the same images would creep into her head in the spaces in the day too. The newspapers were full of the threat of invasion and it was discussed in every pub in England, but working at BP and hearing the mass of messages flying around Northern Europe made it so much more real.

On the wall, Valérie had a chart tracking the positions of all the battalions, squadrons, airfields, boats and pieces of key equipment that they knew about. Fran's index was central to keeping this information updated and she had two girls working on the other shifts to keep pace and free her up to help plot the enemy in starkly clear detail. It made a terrifying map of Hitler's intentions. They had so many pins dotted around Northern France and the Low Countries that there wasn't enough space to fit new ones in and they were left crowding ominously into the sea. Soon they would be at the White Cliffs and not just as brass tacks but real men, with real guns.

Fran had been to several Column BQ planning meetings and had stood at the back looking at the important people the government was paying to evacuate and wondering how on earth she was a part of this. To be fair, more than half of the five hundred people seemed to be admin staff like herself (though her method of distinguishing was entirely based on whether they were cowering like her, or sitting confidently at the front), but there were many dons, distinguished in their fields. So few in the country would ever know, but these tweedy eccentrics were a vital element of Britain's front line and she was honoured to be a part of the team to keep them working. Honoured and terrified.

She paced again, the pictures all too vivid. At the start of September, messages on the 'Red' Luftwaffe code had started referring to Tag des Adlers – Eagle Day. It hadn't taken a genius to work out it would involve an aerial attack, but further information had told them almost every German plane would be pointed at Britain in an attempt to win air superiority for invasion. For the last two weeks they had upped their efforts, with everyone working overtime to get as much information as possible to the RAF in the heated Battle of Britain.

Humphreys, for all his irritating pomposity, had been a bundle of energy and encouragement, feeding information constantly to the Air Ministry and reporting back to Hut 3 when he was told of successful British defence, scrambled with unerring accuracy thanks to BP's Sigint. Despite the Luftwaffe flying well over three thousand sorties across the Channel in the last two days and nights, British Spitfires had kept them at bay, so air superiority was not yet won by Hitler. The question was, what would he do next?

'Here, Fran.'

Fran blinked out of her reverie to see Valérie at her side, holding out a mug of tea.

'Thank you.'

She took the tea, trying not to notice the tingle that ran across her skin when their fingers touched. Something about this petite Frenchwoman made her come alive and it was both exciting and confusing. Occasionally, when she wasn't tormented by pictures of German invaders, she remembered the way the girls had talked about boyfriends at school:

'Ooh, it's like electricity when we touch!'

'It makes me prickle all over when he's near.'

'I literally cannot breathe if he's in the room.'

Fran had dismissed their exclamations as wild exaggerations but finally she was starting to understand what they meant. If she and Valérie were on shift together, the stuffy hut felt charged, as if something exciting might happen in it at any moment. And if Valérie got close, Fran's whole body seemed to pay attention, including parts of her she hadn't realised even knew *how* to pay attention before. She'd had aches from playing hockey, and aches from being ill, but never aches from being too close to someone, and she had no idea what to do about them.

'Is something troubling you, Frances?' Valérie asked, putting a soft hand on her arm.

Fran felt as if she was physically trembling but it must just be inside as her arm was, thankfully, steady. She even loved the way Valérie said her name, always in full and with the 's' on the end drawn out on a soft sigh. Oh Lord – listen to her!

'I'm worried about the invasion,' she managed, though right at this moment it felt as if a hundred German soldiers could hammer into Hut 4 and it would be the least of her problems.

'Me too,' Valérie agreed, 'because if the Germans come, you will go and I will miss you.'

Fran swallowed. The shorter girl was looking openly up into her face, her lips slightly parted so that Fran felt a sudden urge to bend down and kiss her. Why did she feel like this? Yes, Valérie was sparky and intelligent and fun, not to mention very pretty, but she wasn't a boy so it didn't make sense.

'You'll miss me?' she stuttered.

They were the only ones in the corridor and Valérie took a step closer, so that she was almost up against Frances.

'With every part of me.'

Fran swallowed again. It seemed maybe Valérie was feeling the tingles between them as well – and was quite happy with it. Was that how things were in France? Fran felt suddenly desperately naive. She leaned down.

'Valérie, you're a... a girl. *Une fille.*'

Valérie let out a bell-chime of a laugh.

'I am a person, Frances, that is all.'

'But...'

Valérie stood on tiptoes and brushed a kiss across Fran's lips, so fast and so faint that it was barely there at all, save for the rush of sensations it set loose inside her.

'The world is a more complex place than any of us realise, Frances. You should—'

But at that moment there was a banging on the main hut door and they both froze and looked down the corridor towards it.

'Let me in. It's important.'

Fran ran to the door and pulled it back to see Stuart Milner-Barry, one of the leading lights of Hut 6, standing there.

'Is there a problem, Mr Milner-Barry? Is the tunnel not working?'

She glanced guiltily through to the office. She'd been so caught up with Valérie that she must have missed the bang on the wall that signified a new pile of decrypts.

'No, no, the tunnel's fine. This is just way too important for a wooden tray and a bit of string.'

He strode into the main office where everyone was rising at

the commotion. Hut 3 and Hut 6 personnel were allowed into each other's areas because they worked so intimately together, but although the Hut 3 watchkeepers often went next door to check messages, it was unusual for it to happen the other way round. Stuart Milner-Barry waved a decrypt.

'I need someone to check this. Immediately. My German's not exactly top notch but if it says what I think, it's crucial.'

Malcolm Saunders took it.

'No problem, Stuart. Give me a minute.'

He sat at his desk, frowning in concentration as Stuart hovered over him and everyone gathered around, magnetised by his energy. After what felt like forever, Malcolm looked up with a wide grin.

'I'd say, old chap, that this says exactly what you think. And you're right – it's crucial. Crucial and amazing and, and... Oh God!'

He leaped up and, to the astonishment of everyone in Hut 3, hugged his Hut 6 counterpart, who happily lifted him off his feet and spun him round like a couple in a ballroom dance.

'What is it?' Peter demanded, grabbing the decrypt as it whirled through the air still in Malcolm's hand. 'No way!' He turned to the rest of them. 'Hitler is dismantling his lifting equipment in Holland. He's given up on the invasion!'

Frances felt the hut swirl around her as her colleagues joined Stuart and Malcolm's mad dance. Hitler was retreating. They'd seen off his famed Luftwaffe with their Spitfires – and a bit of help from BP – and now it seemed they'd seen off his army too. The soldiers of her nightmares would not stamp onto Britain's shores, her family and friends would be safe, and she would not have to escape across the Atlantic away from all she knew and cared about.

She felt Valérie wrap her arms around her waist and, in the general confusion, took the chance to pull her close and dance her around Hut 3 in their own, personal celebration. She had no idea what this meant but it felt amazing and she gave in to it with joy.

That night, a party kicked off in the Duncombe Arms. Further messages throughout the day had confirmed troop movements southwards and it was clear from the bouncy presence of half the naval department that Hut 8 had picked up something similar, so the mood was ebullient.

'Your lot have heard then?' Steffie whispered to Fran when she came into the pub with a few colleagues to find Fran and her team already at the bar.

'We believe so – unless it's an elaborate bluff.'

That was still a possibility but, if so, it was an astonishingly good one as the tone of the messages was sharp even by German standards. There had been positive terms like 'reassessing strategy' and 'new targets', plus careful use of 'advance south' instead of 'retreat' but there was no hiding the truth of it and the commanders' terse replies had made their displeasure clear. The Battle of Britain was a defeat for Germany and the landlord of the Drunken Arms was hastily pulling in bar staff as more and more BP workers clamoured for a well-earned drink.

Tables were pushed back and Hugh Fosse, a Japanese expert and talented Scottish dancer, performed an impressive jig for the cheering crowd, before pulling people into an impromptu reel. Fran found herself dancing with Valérie, opposite Alan Turing and Angus Wilson, a large man with an extravagant, mincing manner who flung his tiny partner around to the music with such abandon that Fran feared the skinny academic would crack against the pub walls. Somehow, though, Angus kept him safe until the song changed and they made way for new dancers.

Fran sank against a table and watched as Ailsa, newly arrived, was swept into the reel by Hugh and proved herself surprisingly adept. A delighted Hugh upped the complexity of his steps, with Ailsa following his lead easily. Fran supposed they must get taught it in schools in Scotland but was pleased to see her usually quiet friend letting her wilder side out and clapped with the rest as the pair's feet flashed across the sticky pub carpet.

'What on earth is this all about?' Ailsa asked when she was finally released and could join Steffie and Fran. They exchanged glances and Ailsa groaned. 'You can't tell me, right?'

'Right. Let's just say it's good news.'

Ailsa nodded.

'No doubt something to do with the wealth of messages pouring in from Northern Europe today.'

They didn't need to reply. They all had a rough idea what their caravan-mates did without having to discuss it openly and today their various operations had come together in the best possible way. It was a night to relax, and they made the most of it.

Much later, when the landlord reluctantly rang time on his eager punters, the three of them walked home to the caravan beneath the stars. There was an autumnal chill in the air but at least it would not bring the Nazis descending with the leaves. Steffie linked arms with Fran and pulled Ailsa in on her other side and together they turned, just a little unsteadily, up the lane to the farm.

Fran felt giddy, perhaps from the three gins she had drunk, perhaps from the news, or the dancing or the noise of happy chatter, or perhaps from having Valérie at her side all evening long, pressed close by the unusual crowd in the pub. She listened to Steffie and Ailsa laughing at how Angus had flung poor Alan Turing around to the music and felt a sudden, desperate urge to speak.

'Do you think it matters if they, you know, dance together?'

Steffie glanced over, an eyebrow arched in the moonlight.

'*Dance* together, Fran?'

'Well, yes, and, you know...'

'A bit more? Matter to whom?'

Fran considered.

'To the world, I suppose. I mean, it doesn't seem to matter to them, but—'

'Isn't that what counts? If they're happy, I don't see that they're doing anyone any harm.'

'Really?'

'Of course. Certainly, far less harm than those macho idiots stamping into other people's countries waving their big guns. Make love, not war, that's what I say.'

'But they're both men.'

Steffie gave her arm a squeeze.

'They're both people.'

It was exactly what Valérie had said earlier in the corridor of Hut 3 and Fran felt her heart squeeze excitedly, but it still seemed confusing.

'What do you think, Ailsa?' she asked.

'What? Sorry, I'm trying not to fall over on these ruts. Not sure what size that whisky Hugh bought me was but it's making my head spin like a whirligig. What do you want to know?'

It was Steffie who answered. 'Fran wants to know if you think it's wrong for men to be with men – or women with women.'

'I didn't say...' Fran started but shut herself up. Steffie could be annoyingly perceptive.

Ailsa danced ahead of them.

'I've never really thought about it much, but I don't care. Seals are always at it.' Fran and Steffie exchanged curious looks. 'They are! The girl seals roll all over each other and you should see the boys when the wind's up – they go at each other like, well, like they're mating.'

'They do?' Steffie asked. 'Well, I never! You learn something every day.'

Ailsa shrugged and gave a happy skip that nearly sent her into the hedge.

'As long as they're not hurting anyone else, people should just, you know, dance with whoever makes them happy, shouldn't they?'

'But is it right?' Fran pushed. 'Is it, you know, legal?'

Steffie grimaced.

'I think there might be laws against it for men.'

'But not women?'

'Nope. Finally – we get something better than them! And who says it won't change. Laws do, you know, and now seems as good as time as any with everything up in the air.'

'Exactly,' Ailsa agreed, sobering. 'Look at me. Not so long ago my father would have been able to force me to marry Alasdair, but that law got changed. The sign of an advanced society is the ability to adapt, right?'

'Right,' Steffie agreed firmly.

And as the three of them turned into the farm and helped each other, giggling, up the steps, Fran prayed that their simple wisdom was right. The world was changing and it was unsettling for sure, but as she let herself into the caravan with her friends, she felt the electricity of today coalescing into something quieter and warmer deep inside her – something that felt very like happiness.

THIRTEEN

DECEMBER 1940

Ailsa

Ailsa sat on a bench, wrapped up in the woollies that had seen her through so many island winters, and watched her colleagues having the time of their lives on the iced-up pond at the centre of the Park. There was a huge variety of skill level on show, from a couple with immaculate white boots zipping around doing jumps and tricks, to those who spent more time on their behinds than their feet, but all were enjoying themselves.

Stuart Milner-Barry had come over and offered her a go with his blades a few minutes ago, but his feet were far bigger than hers so they wouldn't strap onto her boots. She'd been relieved, if she was honest, but sad too. It had been a miserable Christmastime so far and at least ice-skating might have pulled her out of her funk.

Ailsa tugged her scarf closer around her neck, trying to ignore the hole unravelling in the wool and trying even harder not to think about the many scarves her ma had knitted her over the years. There'd been the succession of lilac ones as a bairn, she remembered. She'd been as keen as the next little girl on pink, but the colour had not found a happy home next to her red hair and her ma had worked hard to find acceptable alternatives. She'd moved onto rainbow ones at the back end of primary school and one with much-envied sparkles in it for her first year in high school. Then the muted teenage shades in black and olive green that she knew her mother had disliked but that she had knitted her anyway, spiriting the colourful ones to the back of the cupboard until she came to her senses again around seventeen.

There had been no scarf this winter.

In fact, there had been nothing at all bar a card with a picture of North Uist in the snow and a terse note wishing her a 'purposeful Christmas'. She had braved a trip to London with Steffie and Fran and gone around the crowded shops searching for the perfect tobacco for her father and prettiest hankies for her mother, wrapping them with care and sending them north from a post office within sight of Buckingham Palace. She had no idea if they'd got there and these last few days she'd vacillated wildly between anger at her parents for being so cold with her, and sorrow at having made them feel that way.

It didn't help that Steffie and Fran had gone to their own families for the festive period. Fran had returned to the spires of Cambridge with half of BP, and Steffie had lived it up in London – not that Ailsa envied her with the Blitz tearing the capital apart. The Luftwaffe, robbed of glory in the Battle of Britain, had taken to bombing her cities in the dead of night instead, especially poor London. Every morning reports came into the Park of the number of bombs that the Germans had dropped the night before, and they made horrific reading. The Londoners, so Steffie assured her, were battling bravely on, but this was a war against civilians now and why Steffie wanted to risk herself in the capital, Ailsa had no idea.

'Can't let the Hun steal our parties, darling,' Steffie had

said, all blasé, but they'd stolen Ailsa's, hadn't they? She was
never going to get home on just one week's leave.

Ailsa, as a Scot, had been given her leave for Hogmanay
rather than Christmas, so today, 30 December, was her first day
off. She'd spent Christmas on shift up in Whaddon Hall but
even the agents in the field had taken time off from radioing in,
too busy undercover enjoying themselves, and there'd been
precious little to do bar mope. She had, at least, made it to
dinner in the hall and been spoiled rotten with amazing food,
flowing wine and an impromptu sing-song, but when Hugh
Fosse had whisked her into a reel, it had been all she could do
not to cry at the sounds of home. Honestly! This time last year
she'd been moaning about how samey it was every year, and
now that she'd actually got out of North Uist she was moping
around missing it. There was no pleasing her.

Ailsa stood up crossly. It was being alone in the caravan,
that was all. And perhaps coming down from her two-week
adventure last month. She'd nearly burst with pride when
Travis had called her in and said they needed her skills to help
set up a new Y-station. Beaumanor Hall in leafy Leicestershire
hadn't, perhaps, been much more of a challenge than bucolic
Buckinghamshire, but it had been obliging enough to feature on
postcards in the local shop so she'd sent one to Steffie and Fran.
It was on the wall of the caravan now and if the view wasn't
quite as grand as Switzerland, it was a start. She'd nearly sent
one to her parents too, but, unable to think what to write
without offending them, had chickened out.

She thought again of their Christmas card: 'We hope you
have a purposeful Christmas'. Ridiculous! But at least they had
sent something, and she knew that between those stiff words
was an acre of hurt, so maybe it was down to her to try and
mend that. Neither of her parents had been any further south
than Glasgow in their entire lives, so they were hardly going to
turn up in Buckinghamshire, but she could go back. It would be

a long trip, aye, but perhaps it would convince them that leaving the island wasn't leaving them too.

She glanced at her watch. If she was quick, she could catch the afternoon train to London and get the sleeper north to Glasgow and a train on to Skye tomorrow. The last ferry went across at four o'clock on New Year's Eve and, with a following wind, she should get forty-eight hours on the island before she had to come back to start work again. It would be tight and almost certainly exhausting, but worth it.

She leaped up and, with a last look at the happy skaters, turned her steps out of BP and back to the caravan. It was time to see home again. She'd take the time-honoured first-footing gifts of a piece of coal, a loaf of bread and a handful of salt and knock on the door as the New Year struck. Tradition dictated they'd have to take her in and all would be well once more.

Twelve hours later, at a standstill somewhere just north of Birmingham, Ailsa's mood was as stuck as the train. A stray Luftwaffe bomb had hit the track and there would be no mending it until daytime. The stewards had brought round the bad news with drams of whisky, as if that would soften the blow, and assured all passengers that the train was quite safe and they could sleep easy in their beds. It wasn't sleeping that was Ailsa's problem, though; it was time. Even if the damage was repairable, the delay into Glasgow would mean she'd never make the train to Skye tomorrow and if she didn't make the train to Skye, she wouldn't make the ferry before it stopped for Hogmanay. She would be within sight of North Uist but unable to reach it before she had to turn round and go back to BP.

'Can't we back up and take a different track?' she asked the steward.

'Back up and take a, a...'

The rest of his words were lost in uproarious laugher that

was, apparently, all the answer she needed. So here she was, stranded among the chimneys of Birmingham while her precious leave drained away.

'Ooooh!' She kicked at the wall of her sleeping compartment in frustration but it was little use.

'Patience, dear,' counselled the old lady who had the misfortune to be sharing with her, and it was all Ailsa could do not to kick her too.

'All my plans are spoiled,' she wailed, feeling every inch a bairn in a sparkly lilac scarf.

The old lady patted her leg.

'There, there, dear. It's hard, I know, but there is a war on.'

Ailsa contented herself with glaring at her companion in the gloom, but inside she was kicking every damned wall in the useless train. She lay there, waiting for dawn, but daylight brought nothing more than a clear sight of the gaping wound in the tracks.

'That could have been us,' the old lady gasped, and Ailsa supposed she had to be grateful for small mercies but as the train puffed back into Birmingham and she was disgorged to join a queue at the ticket office, it was hard to feel anything other than cross. Was this why her parents never left the island? On North Uist the worst delay you ever suffered was having to wait for a sheep to cross the road.

You could be married by now, she told herself as she listened to a woman squabbling with the harassed ticket officer about her tickets to a gala ball in Manchester that evening. *You could be married to Alasdair and living in his lovely cottage overlooking the sea and exploring the world via his radio with nothing more troublesome than a few tricky frequencies to get in the way. You could be pregnant with his bairn and...*

But at that thought she stopped. Picturing herself, belly bulging beneath a floral pinny, she laughed out loud and everyone in the queue turned to stare at her.

'Sorry,' she said. 'It's just... A baby!' She laughed again. 'Suddenly Birmingham doesn't look quite so gloomy after all. Ticket to Bletchley, please – I've got friends to catch up with.'

The ticket officer was delighted to give up his tussle with the tricky customer to serve her and, with a train going ten minutes later, Ailsa hurried across the grimy station and jumped on. It was almost twenty-four hours since she'd made her decision by the BP pond and she'd got exactly nowhere but at least she knew where she was going now. Steffie and Fran would be back and there was a fresh bottle of Alfie's finest blackberry gin awaiting them. It wasn't home but it was the closest thing she had, and she turned her face to the window, looking eagerly for the funny little station that would welcome her back.

'Ten, nine, eight...' Angus Wilson led the countdown to midnight at the top of his reedy voice and the rest of the crowd in the Duncombe Arms joined in enthusiastically. Ailsa draped her arms around Steffie's shoulders on one side and Fran's on the other, bellowing out the numbers as if they might be the countdown to the end of this wretched war.

She saw tears shine on Steffie's cheeks and impetuously leaned in to kiss them away. She knew her friend fretted constantly for her fiancé and hated seeing her suffer. After a strong initial Italian attack in the desert, the British had been pushing them back all December and the cinemas had been full of newsreels of our glorious army marching through empty tracts of sand, driving Italian POWs before them like cattle. Poor Steffie was very brave about being parted from her fiancé most of the time, so it was a shock to see her in tears and Ailsa was glad to hold her tight as she bawled out the countdown.

'Seven, six...'

On the other side, Fran's eyes were alight as she shouted

along. Valérie was in London for a few days and Fran seemed
more relaxed without her here, though perhaps also less happy.
That was love for you, Ailsa reckoned – endless trouble. Look at
Alasdair. They'd had such happy times working with his radio
set and then he'd kissed her and it had all gone wrong. She
tutted at herself. That wasn't fair. If she'd felt the same way as
Alasdair, then it could have been a match made in heaven – or
at least in the airwaves. But she hadn't.

'Five, four, three...'

Ailsa held on tight to her friends as all eyes in the pub fixed
on the big clock on the wall, waiting for it to chime in 1941.
This time last year was when she'd run away from home and
she should have been back there now if it wasn't for that
damned bomb in Birmingham. She was sorry to miss the oppor-
tunity to try and make up with her parents but, as she jumped
up and down with Steffie and Fran and half of the crazy crowd
at the funny 'Park' that was fighting the enemy with the
sharpest of brain-bayonets, she felt a momentary stirring of gratitude to the German pilot who'd taken out that train line.

'Two, one – Happy New Year!!!'

The pub went wild and Ailsa with it. She was kissed by
virtually every man and woman in the place and, face stinging
joyously, she could only surrender. She would write to her
family again assuring them of her love, but it seemed that the
war did not want her back in North Uist. It was time to look
forward, not back, and, as 1941 was born, she wondered where
on earth it might send them all before this time next year.

PART TWO

1941

FOURTEEN

FEBRUARY 1941

Steffie

'Rommel!' Harry Hinsley banged a folded newspaper on the table in frustration. 'Bloody Rommel – we told them. Didn't we tell them?'

'We did,' Steffie agreed when no one else in Hut 4 looked inclined to reply. 'Well, *you* did.'

'I did!' he agreed. 'How often was I on that phone, Steffie? "Our messages indicate a massing of shipping in the Tripoli area, sir." "We're picking up movement of troops around the Italian ports that we strongly believe suggests new battalions are going to Africa, sir." We've given them their nice, concise daily reports and they send us stupid pats on the head and murmur, "very interesting", but when it comes to something really important, they still don't actually *do* anything!'

'I know,' Steffie agreed. 'The arrival of the Germans is disastrous.'

Up until now, the British had continued to romp across Northern Africa, driving the Italian forces before them like sheep. They'd triumphantly taken the vital port at Tobruk, about five hundred miles east of Cairo, but now Rommel had arrived and things were going to get much, much harder. Harry hit out at the wall.

'We even told them that Hut 3 were picking up aircraft and troop movements suggesting the Wehrmacht were heading over to help out the Italians, but did they care? The damned Admiralty's internal, all-knowing operational gurus did not believe that Hitler would bother entering the African theatre, so they didn't want to hear. And now look.' He waved the newspaper with its bold headline: *Rommel lands Afrika Korps in Tripoli*. 'Honestly – I could scream!'

'It is frustrating,' Steffie agreed, trying to be diplomatic, but Harry was building himself into a real fury.

'Frustrating? It's a bloody disaster! What on earth is the point of us flogging ourselves to get the sort of valuable Sigint that could win a war if the men with the fancy braiding on their posh uniforms still won't listen?'

Steffie went across and put a hand on his arm.

'No point at all, Harry, and I'm sure that, when you take this to Denniston, that's exactly what he'll say to the PM.'

'Hmm.' Harry looked at her. 'The thing is though, Steffie, I don't want them to tell me I was right; I just want them to listen so it doesn't happen again.'

'What do you think would help?'

'Sorry?'

'Well, if we're going to send Denniston in to complain, then what do we suggest for next time?'

'That they bloody well believe me when I tell them what's going to happen?'

'Who's "they"?'

'The stuffed shirts in the Admiralty, sitting around in their St James's clubs with their cigars and brandy, twenty years from the last time they saw a front line and with no idea at all what it's like out there.'

Steffie nodded.

'It's like going to the lady of the house if you're peckish mid-afternoon.'

'What?' Harry squinted at her. 'What on earth are you going on about, Stefania?'

Steffie swallowed. It did sound rather foolish but she'd started, so she'd better explain.

'If you go to a weekend house party with, you know, everything laid on according to well-mannered plans, but you get hungry way before dinner, you can't go and tell your hostess, can you? Because she'd be offended. And, besides, she'd be far too busy having her hair done for the evening and wouldn't have any idea where to get food from. Not her job.'

Harry eyed her sideways.

'Right. So – who would you go to?'

'Oh, come on, Harry, you know this.'

'The cook.'

'Exactly. The cook or, at least your maid, or a friendly butler. Everyone knows that the first rule of a house party is to cosy up to the staff, the people on the—'

'Front line!' Harry cried triumphantly. 'By God, Steffie, you're dead right. Your daily reports are splendid but we shouldn't be talking to the Admiralty at all if we truly want anything done. We can report in afterwards, when we've alerted the commanders of the danger and they've taken action to counter it, but we can't expect them to, to...'

'Find us a nice chicken sandwich in the pantry.'

He grinned at her.

'You're a genius, Steffie. We need our own operators in the field to get messages across fast. We'll have military advisers, of course – God forbid us woolly-pully civilians could make actual decisions – but we won't go through head office.'

Nobby Clarke came over.

'We tried it in France, remember. We set up a Special

Liaison Unit over there. The only problem there was that by the time we got it operational, the Germans were blitzkrieging so fast it could only really aid the retreat. But in Africa...'

'In Africa, it could be of real value!' Harry agreed. 'I'll get in with Denniston this afternoon and he can take it to the top, but first we need a solid proposal. We need to talk to the comms experts. Steffie – can you drive?'

'Drive? Er, yes, sir.'

'Good stuff. With me.'

Steffie looked to the pile of decrypts on her desk.

'But...'

'They can wait. No point in us unravelling enemy messages if we can't get them to those who need them most. Come on.'

He was striding to the door, so Steffie had little choice but to grab her bag and hurry after him.

'Where are we going, Harry?'

'Oh, just up to the SIS unit a few miles away. I need Richard Gambier-Perry to tell me what's possible before I go for the jugular with the high-ups and there's no time like the present. Right – which car do you fancy?'

He'd led her round to the stable yard where various cars were kept in low garages. An overalled man came running out and looked Steffie nervously up and down.

'Do you have a licence, miss?'

'Of course,' Steffie said. 'I used to drive all the diplomatic cars at the embassy.'

'Embassy?'

'Rome,' she said imperiously. 'And let me tell you, if you can drive there, you can drive anywhere!'

'You're Italian?' The man looked horrified.

'As English as the next girl,' Steffie rushed to reassure him. 'I just grew up in Rome.'

He still looked uncertain and it took Harry rapping at him to 'grow up and get the keys' to send him scurrying into his office. Harry winked at Steffie and she tried to smile back but in truth the man's suspicious looks had dug into her. She loved Italy and she loved Italians – one in particular – so to have people looking at her as if they were somehow evil felt very uncomfortable.

'You don't drive?' she asked Harry, trying to distract herself.

'Nope. Prefer horses. Stupid really. I did try to take my test last year, but they've suspended them. Apparently, there's a war on!'

He laughed and swung himself into the passenger seat of a rather nice Rolls as the garage man came back and reluctantly held the keys out to Steffie. She gave him her sweetest smile, sat in, and revved the engine purposefully.

'It'll do,' she told him and then put her foot down and shot out of the garage at speed, making Harry bobble up and down over the cobbles and the poor man wave furiously.

'I bet he wouldn't have grilled me if I was a man,' she said crossly as she turned down the path to the gateway.

'Probably not,' Harry agreed, clutching the door handle 'Does everyone drive this fast in Italy?'

'You think this is fast? I can—'

'It's fine. Really. Right here – follow the signs to Whaddon Hall.'

'Whaddon?' Steffie's ears pricked up and she slowed down to look over at her passenger and be sure of what he'd said. Whaddon Hall was where Ailsa worked. Was she finally going to get to see her caravan-mate in action?

'That's the one. Nice place. Massive aerials. They can get messages out to undercover agents cowering under bushes in Provence with a half-baked carry-case of a radio, so surely they can reach a full unit in Africa? Ah, here we are. Up this driveway.'

Steffie pulled up at the gates and eyed the hall as Harry showed his authorisation to the guards. It was smaller and neater than the mansion in BP but also had huts going up all around it. Where was Ailsa? she wondered, feeling curiously voyeuristic. Ten minutes later and she found out when she and Harry were ushered into a large room filled with wooden tables bearing complex-looking radio sets. Dead centre, headphones over her red hair and finger tapping away at a Morse key at quite ridiculous speed, was her friend.

Ailsa was deep in concentration and didn't spot Steffie, so she was able to watch her at work. Message completed, Ailsa reached out to a big dial on the front of the radio and fiddled with it, wrinkling her nose as she switched to listening in to some secret signal coming across the airwaves, then she grabbed a pencil and wrote urgently on a message slip. Steffie was fascinated. She'd seen the decrypts coming in from Hut 6, but never the raw messages arriving, and it felt like a very visceral link with the war.

When Ailsa had finally finished taking down her message, she looked up to put it onto a wire tray and, catching sight of Steffie, gave a shocked gasp and dropped it. It fluttered to the ground and Steffie stepped forward and picked it up.

'Yours, I believe, radio operator.'

'Thank you kindly, mysterious visitor.'

Steffie grinned and opened her mouth to reply but Harry was calling her over so, with a quick wink to her friend, she went to join him. Most of the conversation, full of wires and cables and high-frequency somethings, went over her head, but she got the gist – there was already a BP outpost in Cairo and it would be a simple matter, with the right kit, to run an SLU out of it. Indeed, Richard Gambier-Perry, a livewire of a man, was already talking about putting receivers into 'desert-ready vans' to get right to the core commanders.

'We could beam messages to the front line itself,' he assured Harry. 'If they stuck us on loudspeaker we could shout "sod off" in Italian right at them.'

'*Levati dalle palle!*' Steffie said automatically. The two men stared at her and she shrugged. 'It's "sod off" in Italian.'

Gambier-Perry looked at her suspiciously.

'How do you know?'

'She's in the Italian department,' Harry snapped at him. 'It's her job to know.'

'Course. Yes. Sorry.'

He gave her a tight little bow but now Harry was talking him into coming to see Denniston at BP and Steffie found herself driving them both back down the hill. It was a sunny day and reminded her painfully of drives into the hills around Rome with Matteo back when the Italians had been their friends and there'd been nothing more pressing to reach than a nice picnic spot. Where was her fiancé now? she wondered, as the men discussed strategy for approaching the commander. Was Matteo even still alive? And was everyone here going to treat her like a possible traitor if she dared to mention him?

Remembering how Gambier-Perry's eyes had narrowed at her Italian, she bumped him into the yard at speed and felt not a shred of remorse when he scrambled gratefully out of the Rolls. Tossing the keys to the equally suspicious garage man, she stomped back to Hut 4, feeling bruised. However hard she worked around here, people seemed to judge her on the nationality of her fiancé. How was that fair?

She hadn't much time to simmer, however, before Harry was back, bouncing eagerly around.

'Listen up, everyone. New initiative. We're setting up an SLU in Cairo.'

'Already?' Steffie gasped.

'Yep. That's to say, we're going to get a team out there to set it up. It'll need the right kit and people, obviously, but Richard's confident he can help with the kit and I... I said I could find the people.'

The Hut 4 workers looked around at each other and back at Harry.

'Us?' someone asked.

'Just one of you for now,' Harry said. 'I'm looking for a volunteer.'

'To go to Cairo?' Walter asked. 'As in Cairo in Africa, next to the desert and the last line of British defence before the Suez Canal?'

'That's the place.'

'The Suez Canal that Hitler so desperately wants access to that he's sent one of his best generals out there with an army of tanks and infantry?'

'And Luftwaffe support,' Harry agreed cheerfully, 'that's right. The closer we are to the action, the faster we can process messages of actual operational use. And it's not so bad out there, you know. Cairo's been a colonial city for years and is very cosmopolitan.'

Still the Hut 4 workers looked sceptical. Steffie tutted furiously. She wouldn't mind heading somewhere else right now – some nice cosmopolitan city that didn't look at you sideways because you could say spaghetti with the proper accent. And where Italian airmen might, possibly take their leave...

The thought was thrilling. What if she walked into a bar to find Matteo sipping a cocktail with his dark hair slicked back and that gorgeous sideways smile on his face and... She cut off her own daydream. Surely no Italian would take his leave in a British-held city? Even so...

She shot her hand into the air.

'I'll go.'

Everyone stared at her.

'You?' Walter Ettinghausen said.

She glared at him.

'Why not?'

'Well, you're a... a...'

'Trusted and hardworking member of the team?' Steffie suggested.

'A woman,' he blurted out.

'*And* a trusted and hardworking member of the team,' Harry said. 'I'm told the Foreign Office are relaxing their rules on women serving abroad, so I can't see why not.'

'But it could be dangerous,' Walter protested.

'As is Steffie,' Harry said with feeling. 'You should go in a car with her.'

'Seriously – we can't be sending females into a war zone.'

Harry considered.

'Technically, Cairo isn't a warzone. The front line is a thousand miles west at Beda Fomm. And there are women in Cairo, you know. Plenty of them.'

'But still...'

That did it. Steffie wasn't sure quite what had made her put her hand up for this assignment, or if she even wanted to go to Cairo, but she didn't see why being a woman should stop her.

'Oh, I wouldn't worry on that score,' she said, drawing herself up tall and stepping up to Walter. 'It seems to me that, given I'm prepared to volunteer, I have far more balls than you do.'

Hut 4 let out a collective chuckle, Walter went scarlet, and Harry clapped Steffie on the back.

'It certainly does. Thank you, Steffie. Report to Denniston and we'll get the ball rolling.'

'Right. Er, now?'

'No time like the present!'

He held the door open and Steffie found herself heading into the soft frost of a British February and across the lawn, next stop Egypt. It turned out she was going to have rather more to discuss with Ailsa at dinner than travelling the airwaves, and her head was spinning as if she were already in a desert storm.

March 1941

The heat of Egypt was intense. Steffie had been used to stifling summers in Italy but this was something else. The Egyptian air was so dry it seemed to burn your lungs, and winds constantly whipped up the sand so that every breath felt thick with it. She was parched within minutes of clambering down from the plane and her head was spinning with all the new sights and sounds. It seemed just yesterday that she'd been in Hut 4, defiantly putting her hand up for this posting, and now she was here, with no turning back. She swallowed and tasted grit.

Her journey had been eventful. She'd been flown to South Africa in a big old bomber that had been pretty scary, especially when they'd spotted enemy planes on the horizon. Steffie had pressed her face to the tiny window, wondering if it had been Matteo, but the plane had been German and had, besides, been plunging into the sea, wing on fire. It had been her first true sight of a plane going down and had churned agonisingly in her stomach so that she'd been very glad to land at Cape Town.

This morning, things had looked up when she'd been put on a flying boat to Cairo, following the golden line of the Nile in the morning light. Steffie had seen men working the verdant fields either side, exotic feluccas fishing and children bathing with happy cries, and she'd felt very pleased with herself indeed. Now, though, with the heat slapping her around the face, her stomach was churning once more.

'Stefania Carmichael? So glad you're here. Major Frederick Jacobs at your service but, please, call me Freddie.'

The major, a tall man with a mop of hair the colour of the desert sand, shook her hand enthusiastically and she felt herself relax slightly.

'Delighted to be here, Freddie.'

'I knew your father, actually. Served with him in the Great

War. Top man. Honoured to have his daughter working with me.'

Steffie blinked. She was used to people knowing her father but had never before had a chance to prove herself as his child.

'I can't wait to get stuck in,' she said, and meant it.

Already the heat of Egypt seemed to be settling around her and she could breathe more easily. She followed Freddie to his jeep, looking excitedly around as he drove them at pace into Cairo – a city brimming with life, just as Harry had promised.

'There's the Gezira Club,' Freddie said, waving at an incredible-looking complex on an island in the middle of the river. 'And there's Shepheard's Hotel.' He indicated a stunning colonial building. 'And Groppi's café – divine spot if you get an hour off – and the KitKat Club. Quite the place for a fun Saturday night, I can tell you.'

Steffie was beginning to think perhaps she'd been flown into heaven, but they drove on, right through the city, into the sprawling suburb of Heliopolis and to the very edge of the built-up area until it seemed all that was before them was sand.

'This is us, Stefania – the Museum.'

Freddie indicated a grand white building that seemed to be rising up out of the very desert. It was almost perfectly square and metal struts were still poking out of the flat roof. A large porchway was leaning precariously across the main door, elegant Doric columns on one side and wooden posts on the other, and two very small palm trees were wilting in front of them.

'It's a fright, isn't it?' he said with an apologetic grimace. 'It was all set to be a flora and fauna museum but then the war broke out. Now the flora is dying and the only fauna the poor thing has is us lot. Come on in.'

He offered Steffie a hand down and she headed curiously inside. The atrium was nice enough, with marble floors and a grand staircase leading up to several galleried levels, but as

Steffie followed Freddie up two floors, she saw, through every open door, banks of trestle tables laden with radio sets, Typex machines and wire trays of raw messages and decrypts. It was as if she was right back in Hut 4, only now the floors were sand-covered white tiles, the view out of the window was of endless dunes, and in the back garden was a sprawling army camp of taupe tents and intimidating tanks. There was no park, no lawns, no happy dining hall and no caravan. Steffie thought of Ailsa and Fran back home and felt a stupid tear leak out of her eye and collect sand against her cheek.

'This is your desk, Stefania. Is that all right?'

'Lovely,' she managed and slid into it, wiping the tear furiously away.

This nice major was expecting her to do as good a job as her father and, however hard it might feel right now, she was damned well going to do it.

FIFTEEN

Fran

'Postcard!'

Fran blinked awake at the shrieked word from Ailsa and sat up as the Scottish girl came flying into the bedroom brandishing the card. On the front was a picture of the Sphinx and Fran pulled her legs up to let Ailsa bundle into her bed next to her.

'It's from Steffie,' she said delightedly, pointing to the signature at the bottom of the closely written message.

'Of course it's from Steffie,' Ailsa scoffed. 'Who else do we know in Egypt?'

'Matteo,' Fran suggested, and Ailsa groaned.

'Matteo – good point. Honestly, there's no way the poor girl is going to meet him out there and, even if she did, they wouldn't exactly be allowed to date, would they? It's just not the done thing to step out with the enemy!'

Fran shook her head, remembering Steffie that night, over a month ago, when she'd come home to the caravan to say she was being posted to Cairo. Neither of them had believed it but when her orders had come through and she'd started packing they'd had to accept it was real. Within the week she'd been gone and they'd been left to care for her caravan without her.

It felt very strange. Steffie was the lively one – the one who could throw a meal together without worrying about a recipe, the one who could charm gin out of Alfie, the one who'd get them up and dancing at ten o'clock at night so that they all fell giggling into bed and slept like logs whatever traumatic messages they'd been dealing with earlier in the day. Fran knew that she had a tendency towards the serious, and Ailsa was quite quiet, so it was a very different feel in the caravan these days. They were happy still but missed their friend's exuberance and pored over her words.

Girls,

Cairo is crazy. I'm stationed in a very grand building but it was sadly requisitioned by the forces before it was finished, so there are very few doors and no windows and the sand blows in whenever there's the slightest wind – which, incidentally, is all the time. Thank heavens for strong knicker elastic, that's all I can say!

The journey was pretty good, though we did spot an enemy aircraft and I thought for a moment it might be Matteo. Imagine the irony if he'd shot us down! But it was just a stray German, wounded and weaving around like a drunkard. Sometimes I think I might never see Matteo again, but then I tell myself to stop moping and get on. Thank heavens for work!

It's strange being with a new crowd. My boss knows Daddy and I'm told there's a few people in the city I might know from my embassy days. I've got leave next weekend so maybe I'll sniff out a party but, Lordy, I miss you two. This farm of ours doesn't look half so cute from right inside the big barn. Take good care of yourselves.

All my love, Steffie

Fran read it over and over, trying to swallow a nasty lump in her throat, but when she finally dared to look across to Ailsa, she saw a tear on her pale cheek and reached out to give her a hug.

'Darling Steffie.'

'I hope she's safe. I'd hate for anything to—'

'Don't, Ailsa! Anyway, I've been reading up on Africa and there's nothing much happening bar troops lining up and that's absolutely miles away from Cairo in El Agheila.'

'How many miles?'

'Over eight hundred.'

'Right.' Ailsa gave her a small smile. 'Quite a lot of miles then.'

'About the length of Great Britain, I'm told. I reckon Steffie was in more danger shopping for summer dresses in Knightsbridge than she is wearing them out in Egypt.'

Ailsa grinned and jumped up.

'Come on then, let's put her into the farm.'

'What?'

Fran reluctantly got out from under her warm covers and grabbed her dressing gown to follow Ailsa. The caravan had a paraffin heater in the main room but nothing in the bedroom and Fran was permanently cold. It didn't seem to bother Ailsa so much but, then, she had an array of Highland undergarments that looked amusingly rustic to Fran but certainly seemed to insulate her. They'd teased Steffie that she'd only taken this commission to get to the sunshine and right now Fran had to admit to feeling pretty jealous. She swore her feet might actually ice to the caravan floor if she stood still. Ailsa laughed.

'Try these.'

She threw Fran some socks that looked as if they might have been knitted from purest yak. Fran caught them and, putting her hand tentatively inside, was surprised to feel how soft they were – and how marvellously warm over her toes.

'These are fantastic.'

'Arran wool lined with silk. It gets pretty chilly up north so we've learned a few tricks over the years.'

She looked sad and Fran gave her shoulders a quick squeeze.

'Not heard from your mother?'

Ailsa shook her head.

'I sent them a long New Year's letter explaining I'd tried to visit, but got nothing more than a 'thank you for our gifts' telegram back. Stupid, isn't it? It would be unheard of not to say thank you for silly little objects, but it's fine to say nothing at all about messages of love. Honestly! My Aunty Morag did write the other day, saying everyone is well and telling me to "have a little patience with your stubborn parents", but it all seems so stupid. I'm doing war work, for heaven's sake – they should be proud of me.'

'I'm sure they are, underneath,' Fran reassured her. 'They'll just not be very good at saying it. My family are like that. At Christmas, all I got was "Doing your bit then, Fran?" Course, the problem is that we can't tell them *what* we're doing so the conversation stops there but at least you're in uniform.'

'That's only clothing.'

'You reckon? My parents would be delighted if I had a uniform – especially if it said Medical Corps.'

Ailsa laughed but it wasn't funny to Fran, not really.

'Are you sure you wouldn't like to drive an ambulance, Frances?' her mother had asked her more than once in the five days she'd spent back in Cambridge. 'Professor Shrimpton's wife is running a marvellous service in the East End and she's desperate for people. Think what value you could be. Think of the poor injured people you could save.'

'Isn't it better to work to stop people being injured at all, Mother, than to drag them out of the rubble covered in blood?'

Her mother had frowned at her.

'What are you talking about, Frances?'

She said 'Frances' in a clipped way, the 's' a sharp sigh of reproach and not at all like the silky caress of Valérie's pronunciation.

'Never mind, Mother.'

Her family wouldn't ever get it, wouldn't ever think there was more than one way to save lives, or that not every hero had to wave a scalpel.

'My parents think I'm just a secretary for some War Office bods,' she sighed.

Ailsa cocked an eyebrow at her. 'Aren't you?'

Fran laughed.

'Course I am! Now – let's get Steffie in the farm, shall we?'

Ailsa took the postcard, found some tape, and stuck it to the side of the big barn. The Sphinx smiled serenely at them and instinctively Fran blew it a kiss. Her parents might still believe she was wasting her life on non-medical pursuits, but she knew differently. Seeing the Cairo postmark on Steffie's postcard had made her think about the Mediterranean as a real place with real people fighting a real war and, although she might be sitting safely in Buckinghamshire, she could make a difference. She glanced at the clock – time to get to work.

Hut 3 was abuzz when she arrived.

'What is it?' Fran asked Peter. 'Has something happened?'

'More like something is about to happen. The cottage have broken a message that tells us that today is "X minus 3" in the Med. We need all hands on deck to work out what X is so we can get our boys onto it. Hut 6 are running all the overtime they can and I've got a full watch on.'

'I think you'll find,' Humphreys said, cutting self-impor-
tantly between them, 'that it is Curtis and I who have the full
watch on. You run the research department, Peter, not the
whole hut.'

'I'm aware of that,' Peter said mildly. 'Malcolm runs Hut 3
but he's not on shift right now and as long as the work is done,
does it even matter?'

Humphreys tutted and looked conspiratorially over to
Curtis. 'Bloody civilians, no sense of order.'

Fran stepped past the pair of them and pointedly opened
one of her highly ordered index cards. Humphreys, too
wrapped up in his own importance, did not even notice but
Peter gave her a wink.

'Glad to see you ready to go, Fran. We're going to need to
link into the index to bring the whole picture together, so stand
by your cards!'

'Cards!' Humphreys shook his head and went off to dial
through to the Air Ministry and loudly announce the breakthrough as if it were his own.

'Minus 3, sir, yes. Critical, I agree. Thank you. Sorry? Er,
no, no we're not sure what X is yet but we're working on it.'

Peter and Fran exchanged a wry smile. *They* were certainly
working on it, though neither of them was in doubt about who
would claim the credit. No matter. If a major attack was
planned, uncovering it would be a big concrete victory for BP's
Sigint. Fran looked at her long run of card index drawers and
rubbed her hands. Bring it on!

Four hours later, having not once found time for a cup of
tea, a bite to eat or even a sit down, she was exhausted. Everyone, even Humphreys and Curtis, had been poring through all
available intel and the atmosphere in the hut was charged. The
messages appeared to centre around Alexandria and another
place whose code name they couldn't identify. It wasn't directly
listed in the index, but Fran was sure she'd heard it somewhere

before and was scouring her cross-referencing. She rubbed at her temples, willing her brain to fire underneath, then felt soft hands go over her own and gently push them aside. Clever fingers massaged her skin and, closing her eyes, she leaned back with a soft sigh.

'You can do it, Frances,' a French voice whispered confidently into her ear. 'You're brilliant.'

'I'm efficient.'

'*Brilliant.* Just think – it's in there somewhere, I know it is.'

Fran felt Valérie's fingertips probing deep into her mind, her body soft against her own. Everyone else was busy about their tasks and, drawing in a deep breath she relaxed against her and let her mind drift across the myriad foreign terms and places alive within her index.

'Yes!' She spun round, clasping Valérie's hands and pulling her into a hug. '*You're* the brilliant one, Valérie. *T'est le génie!* You've teased it out of my mind with your clever hands.'

Valérie arched an eyebrow suggestively and Fran flushed as strange tendrils of purest pleasure shot across her body, but now was not the time. Within a few hours X would be minus 2 and she'd remembered where the reference was. It had come in yesterday on a weather report from Greece, where the Italians were battling to take the capital. Giving Valérie's hands a squeeze she reluctantly let go and ran across to the weather index, flicking through it at speed.

'Piraeus!' she cried. 'The codename is for Piraeus.'

Peter came bounding over.

'Are you sure?'

'Ninety per cent. This came in yesterday and tallied with other Athens references.'

Peter rushed back to his own desk, leafing through a set of maps and plans, then he froze.

'If you're right, Fran – and I'd say you probably are – then that suggests that the Italians are planning to attack a convoy scheduled to take supplies from Alexandria to Piraeus in...'

'Three days' time,' Nobby cried triumphantly. 'That's it! That's the target. I have to get this to Denniston, and Hut 4 need to know too. If we get this right, we could turn *their* attack into *our* ambush. Admiral Cunningham will be delighted!'

Humphreys leaped forward.

'I'll call the Air Ministry immediately. They'll need to know.'

'Know what?' Fran muttered. 'How clever you've been?'

Humphreys' eyes narrowed.

'How clever we've *all* been,' he said piously. 'Great work, team.'

The words sounded hollow on his lips but that made them no less true and as he turned excitedly to his telephone, Peter went round shaking hands with everyone in the hut. Fran sank into her chair, exhausted, but was instantly revived when Valérie came up behind her, close enough for her glossy hair to brush across the top of her head.

'Fancy a trip to the cinema?'

'Sorry?'

She looked up and saw Valérie's lovely face very close to her own.

'The cinema, Frances. I was thinking in, perhaps four days' time? I've heard the newsreels alone might be worth a watch.'

Fran looked at her, eyes wide.

'I most certainly do.'

They sat together in the darkened County Cinema in Fenny Stratford as the newsreel came on, showing grainy black-and-white images of pale ships on a dark sea while a reporter excitedly hailed a great victory at the 'Battle of Cape Matapan'. Admiral Cunningham's fleet had snuck out of Alexandria under cover of darkness and intercepted the Italian attack on its way from Sicily, breaking it up and chasing it ruthlessly around the seas with the ultimate loss of four destroyers and four cruisers. Badly stung, the entire Italian navy had, so the reporter gleefully said, retreated to the safety of their home ports and the British could claim naval superiority in the Mediterranean. There was much talk of the heroism of the sailors, of the power of the ships and the cunning of the plotters – and not a single breath about the codebreakers, translators and indexers of Bletchley Park. And that was exactly as it should be.

Fran sat there feeling Valérie's hand sneak into her own and folding it tight in her fingers as a glow of pride spread through her. She might not be pulling the injured from the rubble of the East End, but she and her team had protected a whole convoy carrying much-needed supplies to Greece and that was surely every bit as important. Now they had to find a way to stop Rommel marching across Africa, towards Cairo – and Steffie. Never had Fran's work, monotonous and secret as it might be, felt more vital.

SIXTEEN

APRIL 1941

Steffie

Steffie twisted and turned, trying to see herself in the rough scrap of mirror. It was only about two inches wide and barely twenty long, but it was still good to see even half of herself in an evening gown once more. And what a place to be wearing it – an army camp in the middle of the desert!

Steffie glanced around the square tent in which she was billeted with seven other girls, all members of the 11th Convoy of Motorised Transport. They'd arrived in Cairo just a few days after her, setting up a female corner of the vast Hilmiya army camp into which Steffie had been conveniently slotted. It was hot, sandy and hectic but the company was very lively.

'Come on, Stef – get a shift on or we'll never cadge a lift! Nice dress by the way.'

Betty Lampson, niece of Sir Miles, the British ambassador in Cairo, gave Steffie a nod of approval and she smiled. Betty had borrowed it off one of the other girls for her and it *was* a nice dress. In figure-hugging gold silk with appliqué details, it made her feel like a sand goddess, which was appropriate as she lived coated in the stuff these days.

'You look amazing, Betty,' she said, pulling on strappy sandals and hurrying after her new friend.

Betty was well over six foot with piles of blond hair and made a striking figure in her day uniform but tonight, in extravagant scarlet, she shone. Her uncle had known Steffie's father and Betty had announced she was taking Steffie under her wing – a wing that had turned out to have a considerable span. Betty knew everyone important and had access to all the best bars and clubs in the city, and every Saturday night Steffie found herself thrust into the height of a social whirl she'd thought a thing of the past. Who'd have imagined that being posted out to the desert could have ended up so much fun!

A jeep was passing, driven by none other than Steffie's boss, Freddie, and she felt suddenly aware of the incongruous picture they made standing in the centre of an army camp in evening gowns. Betty, however, was completely unfazed and leaped into the road to flag him down.

'Are you going into the city, Freds?'

'Freds' looked a little uncomfortable but nodded obligingly and Betty swung herself into the seat beside him, leaving Steffie with little choice but to climb into the back with a second officer. Freddie looked back and grinned.

'You look... different, Steffie.'

'She looks gorgeous, Freds,' Betty corrected him firmly.

'She does,' he agreed gallantly, giving in to Betty's incorrigible spirit. 'Where to, ladies?'

'Shepheard's,' Betty said. 'I'm desperate for some pretty decor after all this damned khaki – not to mention one of their divine Martinis. And I hope you'll join us?'

'Why not,' the officer at Steffie's side said eagerly, and Freddie gave an easy nod and drove off across the sandy camp before, thankfully, whipping them onto the main road into

Cairo. Pretty soon he had to slow down as they hit the city proper and the streets became rammed with the clutter of local traffic. Battered trams and buses, largely built last century, vied for space with even more battered carts and donkeys, all piled high with goods. Sheep and goats were herded between them and people weaved in and out in one huge melee.

From her vantage point in the jeep, Steffie could look down on them all and was struck by the mass of different headgear – from the turbans and tarbooshes of the locals to the myriad hats of the international battalions stationed around Egypt's capital. Britain had reached out to its empire for help here, at its heart, and Australians in their funny 'wide-awake hats' stood shoulder to shoulder with Indians in pugrees, Canadians in peak caps and South Africans with their sola topis. There were Polish soldiers in diamond-shaped *czapkas*, Greek ones in green, white and blue caps and Free French in elegant kepis, looking very at home in a city that based its entire top-level culture on Paris. Steffie shook her head, struggling again to believe she was truly here. Her mother had been delighted when she'd told her.

'Say hello to Jacqueline Lampson for me, will you, darling? Such a sweet woman. So elegant. She's half-Italian, you know.'

That, in her mother's world, was high recommendation. She kept getting herself into trouble in London for singing the praises of her Italian friends, but out here no one paid them much note.

'It's the Germans,' everyone would say. 'It's the Germans that started it and the Germans that we need to stop from finishing it off.'

Everyone was afraid of Rommel. Already his troops had advanced far further than was comfortable, exploding out of the Italians' stronghold at Beda Fomm last month and blitzing west across the top of Africa with brutal panzer tanks and ruthless infantry. To compound the problem, Hitler had also sent the Wehrmacht storming into both Yugoslavia and Greece, and

many of Egypt's forces had been shipped out to help, leaving
the lines here rather thin.

Last week the terrible news had come in that Rommel was
besieging the vital port of Tobruk that the British had so
triumphantly taken from the Italians two months ago. A valiant
Australian garrison was keeping him at bay, but it was a huge
concern. Suddenly Steffie felt foolish for heading out dancing
when the enemy could be on their doorstep within weeks. But
on the other hand, when better to get on and live life...

I wish you were with me, Matteo, she thought for about the
hundredth time that day. Her fiancé had loved a party and he'd
looked so delicious in his dress uniform. If only the Italians had
come in on the Allied side, they could be working together to
fight the Nazis, instead of being stuck on opposing lines.

'Penny for them?' the officer next to Steffie said jovially and,
jerked out of her thoughts, she glared at him.

'Oh, I don't know – I was mainly reflecting on the way that
we are caught in a pincer between the German forces marching
inexorably down the Greek peninsula and those storming across
the top of Africa.'

He looked startled.

'Steady on, old girl. It's Saturday night!'

'Tell that to the civilians fleeing for their lives,' she retorted,
and was unsurprised when he leaned forward to talk to Betty
instead.

That was unnecessary, she told herself, but some of these
men were such vacuous asses. No wonder the Egyptians hated
the British if this was all they'd seen of them. Everywhere you
went there were posters and speakers shouting about indepen-
dence and the war wasn't helping. In theory Egypt had been
granted freedom from British rule back in 1936 but the agreement had included Britain's obligation to defend Egypt in the
event of war so here they still were. The alliance was an uneasy
one and Steffie sometimes feared the locals would welcome the

Germans – and with idiot British officers running roughshod over their country, who could blame them?

This chap and his ilk thought that strutting around the camp drilling men with pointy guns and fancy cannons meant they were part of the war. Of course, if it came to it, they would be but for now, it was only Steffie and the others in the offices at the one-time flora and fauna museum who were tuned in. Every day they listened to messages, decoded them, translated them and battled to work out what they meant. The officers on the ground saw nothing but the empty desert in front of them; the workers in the SLU, with their direct link to BP and their network across the multiplying battlefronts around the Med, saw the enemy creeping ever closer. It was terrifying.

'It's Saturday night,' she mumbled sternly. There was nothing she could do as she was off duty and all dressed up, so she should just relax and enjoy herself, as Matteo would.

I wish you were with me, Matteo, she thought again. She felt so frustratingly close to him out here and yet still so far away. It had been over a year since they'd sworn their vows in the Temple of Aesculapius and she had to admit that she struggled to picture him in as much detail as she would like, to feel him against her skin, to imagine his lips on hers...

'Phew – here at last!'

Steffie looked around to see that they'd pulled up outside the imposing facade of Shepheard's Hotel, the colonial master-piece at the centre of the city. She leaped down from the jeep and went eagerly into the vast Moorish hall, pausing to let the muted elegance of the room seep into her after the chaos of the city. The light, shining down from a dome of coloured glass in the ceiling, was soft and refreshingly dim, and the grand stair-case swept upwards, assured in its exquisite taste.

Mind you, there was already raucous chatter coming from the Long Bar on the far side and, as Betty joined her, two young officers ran past, jackets undone and shirts askew. They raced up the stairs to swing themselves onto the ebony caryatids supporting the upper gallery, placing their hands firmly around the women's proudly sculpted breasts as a gang spilling out of the bar cheered them.

'Dead heat!' someone proclaimed as both men proceeded to enthusiastically rub their motionless dates.

Betty stepped forward, hands on hips.

'Get yourself a real woman, hey, lads!' she called.

'You offering, gorgeous?' one of them called back.

'You must be joking! If you stroked *my* breasts like that, I'd have you shot!'

The men roared approval and Steffie glanced to Freddie, who rolled his eyes.

'That girl will get herself into trouble one of these days,' he said, but as Steffie looked at stately Betty standing at the bottom of the stairs to watch the racing officers clamber sheepishly down from the ebony women, it seemed unlikely. The woman was a force of nature and Steffie was grateful to be at her side as they crossed the hall towards the terrace at the back.

'Why don't we ever go in there?' she asked, glancing to the Long Bar as the men retreated into it.

'Women aren't allowed,' Betty said. 'That's why the men get so damned badly behaved in there. Best avoided, it's far nicer on the terrace. Besides...' she leaned in, 'I'm told it's a hotbed of spies.'

'Shepheard's Hotel?'

'Oh yes. The best places are always the ripest. Officers are famously loose-lipped, especially the top ones. Far too important to watch their tongues! There's a barman in there, Swiss Joe, who knows everything there is to know about everything.'

'And who does he tell?'

'No one, as far as we know – but he *could*.'

Steffie shivered, aware again of the network of enemy forces gathering, waiting to catch them out, and was grateful to make it onto the terrace and accept a Martini as she was drawn into a crowd of Cairo's elite. Oh, it was nice to be out again and, if a tiny part of her thought longingly of Fran and Ailsa and Saturday nights on the beer-soaked boards of the Drunken Arms, she suppressed it. She'd send them another postcard tomorrow but, for tonight, she should get on and enjoy herself.

Two hours and considerably more Martinis later, she rolled happily down to the Nile with the rest of their party to head into the glamorous KitKat Club, housed in a beautiful old steamer moored up at the water's edge. The air here was blissfully fresh, the music excellent and, best of all, there wasn't a grain of sand to be found. Betty dragged Freddie onto the floor in a lively jive and many others followed. Steffie received several invitations to dance and enjoyed kicking up her heels again, but when one rather louche Australian officer tried for a kiss, she shoved him firmly away. She was happy to dance, but that was where it stopped and she was grateful when she was hailed by Jacqueline Lampson, wife of the British ambassador and her mother's friend.

'Stefania, so lovely to see you here. How are you settling in?'

'Very well, thank you. I'm glad I've seen you, Jacqueline – Mother was keen for me to say hello.'

'Ah, dear Julianna. That's very kind of her. How is she?'

'Bored and restless and missing Rome. She hates being set against our friends – we all do.'

Steffie felt a tear tug at her eye and wiped it hastily away but Jacqueline was sharp.

'You had a fiancé, did you not? Matteo Mancini?'

Steffie looked eagerly at her.

'That's right. I'm told he's stationed out here somewhere. You haven't heard anything, have you?'

Jacqueline gave her a sad smile.

'I'm afraid we don't get a rundown of enemy officers.' Steffie flinched and Jacqueline put a slim hand on her arm. 'Don't worry, this will all be over at some point, one way or another.'

Steffie frowned at her insouciance.

'If it's one way – the Nazi way – then we're all in trouble.'

Jacqueline waved a hand.

'Leaders have come and gone for centuries, my dear, and the world has not changed much. Look at us here, drinking and talking and dancing just as our ancestors would have done hundreds of years ago.'

'Well yes, but the Nazis—'

'Look at the pyramids,' Jacqueline went on, her voice mild but firm. She indicated the tips of the great monuments, visible on the horizon. 'They've stood for thousands of years, through much change.'

'Yes, and one direct hit from a German bomber could blow them apart. This is an enemy like no other, Jacqueline. They have the weapons to tear into the world and the ideology to tear it apart. Take Lord and Lady Rolo over there – they're Jewish, are they not?'

'Well yes, but...'

'Dead.'

'Sorry?'

'If Hitler gets to Cairo, they will be dead, they and all their fellows. Their riches and titles won't save them from the Nazis, who only care about their "tainted" blood.'

'Stefania – please. The poor Rolos are wonderful people.'

'I know! That's why we must defeat the Nazis.'

Jacqueline looked at her, clearly annoyed she was being so irritatingly real, and Steffie was relieved when someone stepped up at her side with a, 'Well said, young lady.'

The voice was American and Steffie turned curiously to the newcomer.

'Bonner Fellers at your service, ma'am. I'm the American

military attaché here in Cairo, sent by Roosevelt to try and neutralise these horrific Nazis before their poison reaches all the way across the Atlantic. Pleased to meet you.' Steffie took his proffered hand and tried not to wobble on her delicate heels at the hearty shake he gave it. 'What do you do here?'

She was grateful for the question, not that she could answer it fully.

'I'm working with SOE out in Heliopolis.'

'Ah!' He gave her a sideways smile that suggested he knew anyway. 'Say no more. Sterling work going on out there. Sterling. I have a great admiration for those fighting, shall we say, behind the scenes and it's excellent to see all you British girls doing your bit. I hope my daughter gets such chances – though ideally not in war, of course.'

'How old is she?'

'Jane? Just turned eleven, bless her. She's a livewire all right – keeps my lovely wife on her toes dawn till dusk.'

'Are they out here with you?'

'I'm afraid they're back home in DC. Doris used to travel everywhere with me when we were younger. Jane too. She was born in the Philippines, you know. Lovely nurses. So kind. But she's growing up and we wanted her stable for high school so they're back in the good old US and I'm out here with all of yous.'

'That's very good of you.'

He laughed and gestured around the beautiful bar.

'I can't claim it's a hardship. I miss them, of course, but life has to go on, right?'

'Right,' Steffie agreed firmly.

She did not agree with Jacqueline that they could just let the war ripple over them – the Nazis were far too evil for that – but life had to be enjoyed where it could be and she clapped with the rest as the lights went down and a sultry woman draped in silks appeared on the stage.

'Hekmet,' Bonner told her. 'Finest belly dancer in all of Egypt, or so she claims. Her show is certainly... involving. You might want this.'

He waved a barman over and procured her a large glass of champagne and, as Hekmet started up the sort of sultry routine that looked as if it belonged far more in a bedroom than on stage, Steffie gulped gratefully at it. She was no innocent. The Italians were a sensuous race and affairs of the heart – or at least the body – were always top of the gossip chain around Rome but, heavens, these Easterners didn't do things by halves! The dance went by in something of a haze and it wasn't until Betty strung an arm over her shoulders and told her they should 'probably grab a lift back to base' that she realised it was almost 2 a.m.

'Where's Freddie?' she asked.

'Went home ages ago, the old darling. But Teddy's car is going any minute and he says we can jump in.'

'Teddy?'

Betty took her arm, pulling her to her feet.

'Air Marshal Tedder, if you want to get formal, but I always call him Teddy cos he's such a sweetie. And his driver... Divine! Come on, we don't want to miss him.'

With that Steffie certainly agreed. She was suddenly feeling horribly tired and she let Betty lead her down the gangplank of the emptying KitKat Club to where a very smart staff car was sitting waiting.

'Cooee, Teddy! Here we are.'

A suave man in his fifties gave Betty an easy wave from the back seat and Betty waved back then slid into the front alongside the handsome Egyptian at the wheel. Steffie climbed in next to the air marshal and smiled awkwardly at him.

'This is dashed kind of you, sir.'

'Can't have ladies stranded in Cairo, can we? And it's Arthur, please.'

'Not Teddy?'

'Not if you want me to talk to you.'

Steffie smiled more easily now. He spoke with a soft brogue that reminded her of Ailsa and suddenly she missed her friend.

'Are you from Scotland, Arthur?'

'I am. The Campsie hills, to be precise. Do you know them?'

'No, sorry, but I have a friend from North Uist.'

'Do you indeed?' He whistled. 'And how on earth did you meet an island girl? They don't tend to come onshore much.'

Steffie laughed.

'No. Ailsa said that. I, er, worked with her in Bletchley.'

'Bletchley?' Steffie flushed, terrified she'd been indiscreet, but he put a hand on her arm. 'Say no more. I'm guessing you're working at the Museum then?'

She nodded. 'And you?'

'Oh, all over the place. I'm commander of the air forces in the Middle East, you see, so although I'm based in Cairo, I'm not actually here all that much.'

Steffie flushed. She should have realised that an 'air marshal' would be something important but this was another level and here she was, dishevelled and Martini-headed, chatting to him like a moron.

'You're doing amazing work,' she stuttered.

He looked amused.

'Thank you, but I'm not sure that's true. I'm desperately trying to get planes to Malta but every damned convoy gets hit by the Axis. They come out of nowhere.'

Steffie looked at him in surprise.

'Aren't you listening to them?' she blurted, then clapped a hand over her mouth and looked guiltily to the driver. Luckily, he was deep in flirty conversation with Betty but that was no excuse and she bit her lip, not daring to look at Tedder.

He leaned in and she waited for the tongue-lashing she surely deserved but instead he said, 'We'd like to.' She glanced at him and saw his lean face ravaged with worry in the pale light of the moon. 'We don't have enough radio operators,' he went on in a low voice. 'There's a handful on Malta, but they're inexperienced and don't fully understand the kit. We need better people to let us listen in to the enemy and find a way past.'

Steffie nodded, sober now. She remembered her visit to Whaddon Hall and how impressed she'd been with the speed at which the radio operators had plucked signals out of the air. One in particular. With startling clarity, she recalled Ailsa standing in the caravan, telling them how her colleague Charlie was being sent to Malta instead of her because he was a man. She'd been furious.

'You should get hold of my friend,' she told Arthur Tedder confidently.

'The Scottish one? She's a radio operator?'

'A top one. A WAAF. Very skilled. I think she learned all about it on the island – only way to communicate with the world, or something like that. She can tune into the tiniest frequencies, apparently, and she knows how to mend the sets too. She licked Beau— a new unit in England into shape in a couple of weeks, and I bet she'd get your folks out on Malta sorted too.'

'Would she indeed. Ailsa, did you say?'

'Ailsa MacIver, yes. Oh but...'

They were bumping into camp now and heading for the fenced-off female quarter at the far side. Even in the beautiful staff car, the sand was already coming in and the desert stretched out past the tents, an empty expanse with Nazis somewhere on the other side of it. After the bright lights of Cairo, war suddenly seemed close again. 'Is it not very dangerous in Malta?'

Air Marshal Tedder looked at her solemnly.

'Not half as dangerous as it will be if the Nazis take it. Good night, Stefania. Lovely meeting you.'

'But...'

Steffie was already regretting what she'd said. She'd given this powerful man Ailsa's name and suggested he send her to Malta – a beleaguered island that was, by all reports, taking more Nazi bombs than London. It seemed she wasn't sober at all. The driver was opening the door for her and she dutifully clambered out but then turned to lean back in again.

'I didn't mean...'

Arthur Tedder smiled.

'Don't fret, Steffie. No woman, even in the forces, can be sent abroad without her open consent. Good night.'

He waved merrily as he was driven off in his shiny car and Steffie stood there, in the heart of an army camp on the edge of the desert, and shivered in the warm Eastern air. What on earth had she said? And what would it mean for her dear friend back in the safety of England?

SEVENTEEN

Ailsa

'Ailsa MacIver – you're wanted down at BP.'

'Me? Why?'

Her boss shrugged.

'No idea but it's a summons from Commander Denniston himself. What on earth have you been up to, girl?'

Ailsa scanned her brain but could come up with nothing. There'd been that incident when she and Fran had gone paddling the other evening and a load of frogs had leaped out of the rushes making several of the new WRENS scream like banshees, but surely that wasn't something for the top man to deal with?

'Now?' she asked nervously.

'Now! There's a car waiting.'

A car! Ailsa's heart pounded. There was no way she was important enough for a car, which meant this had to be bad news. Had she broken the Official Secrets Act? She couldn't remember doing so, but it was so hard to know what you could and couldn't say. Or was it perhaps her parents? Her heart pounded harder. Had something happened to them? But wouldn't that fall to someone in staff care rather than the commander himself? No, she had to have done something wrong.

Pulling off her headset, she fumbled her way into her coat and made for the door. A smart car was waiting outside with a uniformed driver who leaped to open the back door. Did they do that for miscreants? Surely not. Even so, as she was swept down the hill and into the Park, Ailsa felt herself shaking and had to press both hands onto her knees to steady them. She was going to be sacked, she knew it. She was going to be sacked and then she'd have to go home to her parents' crowing and Alasdair's courtship, assuming he still wanted her. Not that she wanted him, but...

'Miss? You can get out now.'

The driver had stopped in front of the mansion. Commander Denniston's office was just inside the door – ten steps and she would know her fate.

'Thank you,' she managed squeakily and scrambled out, catching her skirt on the door frame and having to free herself in a messy tangle.

Setting her chin high, she pushed open the big door with an ominous creak, feeling like something out of the Boris Karloff films they'd showed on a rattling projector in the village hall back home.

'Miss MacIver?' a voice called, as softly Scottish as her own.

Ailsa's heart sank. Commander Denniston must have seen her undignified arrival out of his window; just what she needed.

'Yes, sir,' she managed, creeping to the door.

'Good, good. Come on in, lass.'

The sound of home was warming but she still felt terrified as she moved into the big office and perched on the edge of a chair. Denniston had to be in his sixties and had the look of a man who would be more comfortable in pipe and slippers than uniform but his eyes were disturbingly sharp.

'Have I done something wrong, sir?' Ailsa stuttered.

'Wrong? Good Lord, no, Miss MacIver. Quite the reverse. You have done something right. Many things, in fact. I am told by Gambier-Perry that you are our finest radio operator and news of your skills has spread rather wider than just Whaddon Hall.'

'I beg your pardon, sir?'

He smiled at her.

'I have had a request from Air Marshal Arthur Tedder, commander of the air forces in the Middle East. He wants you, lass.'

'Air Marshal Tedder wants *me*? For, for what?'

'For your radio skills, of course. He has a struggling Y-station on Malta and needs someone to whip it into shape. I'm told you were recommended to him.'

'Malta?' Ailsa stuttered, picturing the funny clay tuft of grass in the middle of Steffie's table-mat sea. She'd said at the time that her friend had laid the Mediterranean out on their dining table that she'd love to see it, and she'd been furious when Richard had refused to send her instead of Charlie. But now...? 'Is it not being bombed?'

Denniston nodded gravely.

'It is, my dear, and I will quite understand if you wish to turn this position down. No one wants to send any of our people into danger, and least of all our women.'

'But women are allowed to go now?'

'So I'm told. New directive. You girls are proving yourself well worth re-writing the rule book for.'

She smiled.

'That's good. Sensible too. I'm in no more or less danger because of my sex, am I, sir?'

'No,' he agreed, 'though it goes against civilised instincts to send the fairer sex out of the protection of the home.'

'And yet so many women in Britain are finding their homes sorely without protection until we beat the Germans.'

'Indeed. Well put, Miss MacIver. Even so, Malta is perhaps a bigger leap than the East End and I would caution you to think carefully.'

Ailsa was already thinking carefully. This was madness, wasn't it? And yet, she'd left North Uist wanting adventure and here was Commander Denniston offering it to her.

'It would be a long way from home,' he said kindly, as if reading her mind. 'You're from the islands, right?'

'North Uist, sir, aye.'

'I've been there several times. Stunning. Air Marshal Tedder is a Scot too, you know – making quite a name for ourselves, are we not?' He winked at her and, surprised, she smiled back. 'Malta is an island too, of course, if a very different one. It's a beautiful place.'

'You want me to go, sir?'

'I want the best person to go.'

'And you think that's me?' She felt herself swell with pride and swiftly told herself not to be so arrogant. *Puffed-up bantam*, she could almost hear her mother scoffing.

'Who recommended me to the air marshal?' she asked. 'Was it Charlie?'

Denniston frowned.

'Charlie? I don't think it was a Charlie. I was told it was someone in Cairo.'

Ailsa felt a smile break across her face.

'Steffie! The wee devil.'

'Sorry, lass?'

Ailsa shook herself, feeling foolish but nothing would take away the warmth that the thought of her friend had sent running through her. If Steffie could cope in 'big barn' Egypt, then surely she could manage a tuft of an island?

'I'll go!'

Denniston blinked.

'Are you sure? Would you not like some time to—'

'I'll go. It will be my honour. And I'll do a good job for you, sir, I swear it. Those radios will pluck the best available messages out of every last bit of sea air by the time I'm done with them.'

Denniston leaped up, smiling broadly, and reached a hand across the desk.

'In that case, I'm certain you're the right man – sorry, woman – for the job. Pack your bags and say your goodbyes and I'll be in touch about transport.'

'Yes, sir.'

Ailsa left the mansion feeling as if she'd stepped on a mine and all the old bits of herself had been blown apart to make way for a new girl – one who apparently caught military transport out to a beleaguered island to help them listen in to the enemy. If her parents could see her now!

The thought made her sad but not, in truth, as sad as the sudden realisation that she was going to have to say goodbye to Fran, and leave her alone in the caravan. The car had gone and no one seemed to expect her to go back to Whaddon, so she turned her steps towards Bletchley, feeling in her bag for her purse and ration book. She'd find something nice in the grocer's for supper, because who knew when they might be able to eat together again.

May 1941

A week later, Ailsa crouched in the vast bay of what she had been told was a Blenheim bomber, clutching a terrifyingly thin strap attached to the metal wall. The crew of a Blenheim was normally three but on Malta they would fly it in rotation so there were six of them plus her crammed into the aeroplane. There were no bombs in the bay but there were machine guns positioned beneath it, manned from the cockpit, and one man was on alert through the glass dome of a gun turret. Ailsa focused on not being sick – less from the motion of the plane, which was no greater than a fishing schooner, than from nerves – and was, for once, grateful for her ivory skin which could not go much paler however scared she was.

'Not far now,' one kind-faced lad said, leaning over to pat her foot.

Ailsa offered him a wan smile. Above her, through the dome, she could see that the sky was a cerulean blue but it was hard to focus on its beauty with the gunner spinning to all sides. Plus, someone had very kindly told her that the most dangerous part of a flight was landing and she clung tightly to the flimsy strap as the pilot cheerfully called out 'cleared to land' and the plane began to dive downwards.

Dear Lord God, please save and protect me, Ailsa said in her head, imagining herself as a bairn on her knees in the tiny chapel back home. To be honest she'd neglected God of late, but she sure as hell needed him right now. There was a loud judder and the whole floor of the plane seemed to groan.

'What's that?' Ailsa shrieked.

The men laughed.

'Don't worry, girlie, it's just the landing gear going down. Believe me, you really want to feel that.'

'Right. Good. Thank you.'

'Cos if we have to skid across the runway on our belly, it's sure as hell going to get hot in here.'

Ailsa gaped at him and the man at his side gave him a nudge.

'Don't, mate, can't you see she's scared?'

'If you can't take the heat...'

'Get out of the plane,' Ailsa finished for him. 'Believe you me, I can't wait.'

The big bomber was tipping alarmingly and when Ailsa looked to her left, she suddenly saw land out of the cockpit cover. Valletta stretched before her, a city of beautiful pale stone, curving around an elegant port. They were close – she could see the ships in the water, people in the streets, even the detailing around the tops of the many buildings.

'Oh!' she gasped. 'It's stunning.'

And in that moment, with a bump and a grind of brakes, the plane touched down, the engines roared and they came to a swift halt. Silence filled the warm air and then the men cheered.

'Nice one, Skip! Perfect landing as always. Never in doubt.'

Ailsa wasn't quite so sure about that. She saw a couple of the younger men surreptitiously wiping sweat from their brows, relieved now they were here. They were safe. Someone pulled the switch to release the cockpit lid and, once the pilot and navigator had scrambled out of the top, Ailsa was gallantly ushered to take her turn. It was quite a feat climbing out of the small opening in a WAAF skirt and for once Ailsa was grateful for the ridiculously large standard-issue bloomers.

Once out, she paused on the wing, looking around. She could feel the sun on her face and wondered if the Ambre Solaire lotion Fran had pressed on her would help stop her pale Scottish skin from burning. A glance down the runway to the hangar, however, told her that sunburn was the least of her worries. The metal building was ripped in two and there was a large bomb crater in the ground, over which an aircraft worker was cheerfully leaping, spanner aloft. She swallowed and looked nervously at the five-foot jump down to the ground.

'Can I offer you a hand, miss?'

Ailsa squinted into the sun and saw a young man standing below her, hand held out.

'Thank you. That would be very kind.'

She sat down on the wing, feeling the heat of it beneath her legs, and reached for the proffered hand. It was warm and dry and the long fingers clasped hers tightly as she drew in a deep breath and jumped. Her legs, wobbly from crouching in the plane all the way from Gibraltar, crumpled on landing but the young man held her solid.

'Welcome to Malta. You're a brave girl to come.'

His voice was warm and his smile open and, as she looked into his brown eyes, she saw a different sort of man to the teasing pilots she'd flown out with.

'I don't feel very brave,' she confessed, and his hand, still holding hers, gave it a reassuring squeeze.

'Most of us don't. It's less about bravery and more about getting on with things.'

Ailsa smiled.

'Now *that* I can do.'

'So I've heard. I'm Ned Robinson, chief radio operator here on Malta. Or, rather, I was until you arrived.'

Ailsa looked at him aghast.

'Goodness, I'm not here to replace you.'

Ned grinned.

'I very much hope you are. I've got barely any experience and, if I'm honest, I'm winging it. That's why we're not getting all the messages we need. I can't wait for a bit of guidance.'

Ailsa blinked, not sure she'd ever heard such humble words from a man before. In her, admittedly limited, experience, men believed themselves experts at everything. She could still remember a temporary teacher on the island one summer who'd said he'd teach the children hockey – not a game any of them had ever played. Little Jock Kinsey had stood up, chest puffed out, and assured the man that he was 'the best at hockey on the whole island.' That might have been a reasonable claim but he went on to add, 'probably the best in all Scotland.' He had, in fact, been useless. Ailsa could still recall running rings around him – and still recall that had not in any way dented his belief in his own superiority.

'Miss MacIver?'

'Sorry. Miles away. And it's Ailsa, please.'

'Ailsa. That's a beautiful name. This way please, Ailsa, and I'll take you to your new office.' Ned led her across the airfield and, seeing her sideways glance at the bomb crater, shot her an apologetic look. 'You'll find Valletta... let's just say, not quite as beautiful as it was a year ago.'

Ten minutes later, as they drove into the outskirts of the city, Ailsa found out just what an understatement that was. The first impression was stunning. They drove round the curve of the harbour and everywhere Ailsa looked she saw gracious buildings, many seeming carved out of the pale cliffs behind. Domes and spires pointed upwards into the deep blue sky, secret alleyways climbed between buildings, and the ancient walls ringing the whole place seemed dipped in gold as the sun started to drop.

Ailsa drank it all in but as they moved closer she started to see cracks in the beautiful architecture – cracks and holes and huge tears that enemy bombs had riven in houses and apartments, churches and halls, shops and bars. Their driver steered blithely around craters in the road and, coming up against a block of apartments that seemed to have collapsed wholesale, gave a quiet tut and reversed to try a different route, taking care not to run over any of the myriad people clambering over the rubble trying to rescue goods and people trapped beneath. Ailsa looked across to Ned and saw him eyeing her with concern.

'It's awful,' she breathed.

He grimaced.

'You're right, it is. You get sort of used to it, but looking at it through fresh eyes...'

He trailed off, clearly struggling to find the words to pin

down the horror. Ailsa looked back as they drove away and saw a mother staggering out of the carnage, clutching a bairn in her arms. It was limp, a little leg dangling uselessly down, and Ailsa bit back tears as the poor woman fell to her knees, keening for her baby.

'You're wondering why you came?' Ned suggested tentatively.

Ailsa swung back.

'No.' She shook her head. 'No, I'm thinking that the sooner I get working to stop these... these...'

'Bastards?'

She nodded grimly.

'Bastards, aye – the better.'

He smiled.

'Fantastic. And just in time because here we are. Welcome to the offices.'

Ailsa looked around, confused. They'd pulled up in an old square dominated by a castle. Surely they weren't working out of there?

'This way.'

Ned took her bag from the boot and ushered her across the square to a discreet corner where a small door was tucked into the curve of the rock. Ailsa felt her eyes widen. This was like something out of a children's book – Ailsa in Wonderland, perhaps, only with more bombs. A man in army uniform materialised out of a side booth and checked Ned's pass, then saluted and opened up the door.

'After you,' Ned said, ushering her into the darkness.

Ailsa took a few tentative steps and found herself in a tunnel, carved from the very rock of the island and winding downwards. She glanced back and Ned nodded her on.

'It's quite secure, I promise you. These are the Lascaris caves and they're probably the safest place on the island. In fact...' he checked his watch, 'we got here just in time.'

'For what?'

'For the evening raid.'

Sure enough, a siren wailed out from speakers both within the cave and out on the street, echoing down the tunnel like some ancient cry for help. Suddenly this was less like a children's book than a horror film and Ailsa pressed herself against the stone wall, trying not to cry and suddenly – ridiculously – wishing that her mother were here to fold her into her arms as she used to do if she'd had a nightmare. It had been the only time she'd really cuddled Ailsa, rocking her gently and pushing the hair back from her face to drop a kiss on her forehead, saying it was a 'blessing from the faeries to send the demon dreams away'. But she was a bairn no longer and she wasn't on North Uist but on a rock in the middle of the Mediterranean, and the demons that she could hear flying in above them would not go away with the kisses of a thousand faeries.

'Luftwaffe?' she breathed.

'That's right,' Ned agreed. 'They come at least twice a day and far too often in the night as well. Did, er, did no one tell you?'

Ailsa thought of Commander Denniston telling her that it would be 'dangerous' and that she should think carefully about it, but it had been hard to truly imagine danger sat in an elegant mansion house in the middle of the English countryside.

'They told me,' she said. 'I just didn't listen carefully enough. But come on, I'm here now. Show me to the radios.'

Ned's fingers closed around hers once more and she held his hand gratefully as he led her down and down, until the sound of the bombers thankfully faded into a dull drone. At the bottom the tunnel flattened out into a corridor with rooms either side. Ned took her further along, then stopped and self-consciously let go of her hand.

'This is radio ops.'

He flung open a door and Ailsa gasped. There were the

usual trestle tables and radio sets but they were in a cave of a room, rock on three sides, with windows along the front looking right out over the harbour, some fifty feet below. At either end, doors stood open to a balcony and two people were standing on it, watching with apparent calm as a Nazi plane flew past, not much above them, and released a silver bomb on the city.

Ned flinched.

'Welcome to Lascaris, Ailsa MacIver,' he offered sheepishly.

Ailsa attempted a weak smile and turned to the nearest radio set. She'd been dropped in a mad, mad world, but radios she knew. Sitting down, she picked up the headset and began tuning into the enemy who were now right on her doorstep.

Later that night, heading to her accommodation in a nearby women's hostel, she passed a stunning building. It was a vast rectangular structure with archways and columns reaching up level after level to an ornate roof. The tattered remains of a poster for *La Traviata* told her that this must be the opera house and Ailsa stood, imagining the parade of elegant men and women who, in happier times, must have climbed the dual stairways in all their finery. Not now. The streets of the beautiful capital were blacked out and deserted and only the moon was brave enough to look on their glory.

Ailsa turned wearily away and that's when she noticed a rusty old slot machine, selling postcards for tuppence. It was clear no tourists had been here to buy one for some time but Ailsa drew out her purse, found a coin and pushed it into the slot. The machine gave a chink of surprise and the handle groaned slightly but clicked round. A remarkably shiny card fell into the slot at the bottom and Ailsa plucked it out and put in another coin for a second.

This wee machine seemed, in that moment, to embody the astonishing resilience she had seen in the people of this beautiful city today and, tucking the cards into her bag, she hurried to her lodgings to write to Fran in the caravan at BP and Steffie somewhere across the water in Egypt. Their tiny farm was a stretching reality now and Ailsa could only pray they would all keep safe in their scattered positions around it until their cruel attackers were defeated.

EIGHTEEN

JULY 1941

Fran

Fran heaved herself out of bed feeling as if she'd only collapsed into it ten minutes ago. Last month Hitler had surprised everyone in Britain (except Huts 3 and 4, but no one had been listening to them) by invading Russia and work had been crazy ever since. Even Valérie, who apparently had family in Russia selling caviar, had been assigned to track the campaign and for a while all eyes had been drawn away from the Mediterranean – all eyes, that is, apart from Fran's.

She glanced through to the farm, the little animals her only dinner companions these days. She missed her friends so much. Steffie had been gone five months and Ailsa three but she still wasn't used to having the caravan to herself. Gloria often came bustling over to bring her a treat from the farm, but it wasn't the same as having the girls living here. All she had of them these days was Steffie's Sphinx postcard taped to the 'big barn' and Ailsa's opera house one, stuck into the tuft of Malta on an improvised stand.

They wrote regularly, both postcards and airmail, and she wrote back, but if their letters were as censored as hers, they wouldn't be a very satisfying read. It wasn't nice, seeing your intimate correspondence scrawled through with a stranger's pen. It felt akin to having your underwear drawer rifled through, and Fran had taken to writing stilted, stupid missives about new shoes and picnics, as if she was the sort of frivolous girlie that she'd always worked hard not to be. The only way that they could write anything sensible was using their farm as a form of code – a ridiculously simple, childish code but it seemed to be avoiding the censors and allowed Fran to know something about her friends' lives out in the Mediterranean.

Steffie talked gaily of parties and soirees with the elite of Cairo but her letters were run through with tension about the cows proving troublesome in the main field and wanting to get into the big barn. The censors apparently saw nothing strange in a society girl fretting about cows and it took only a cursory glance at the endless news reports to know that she was referring to Rommel's continuing siege at Tobruk and fears that he might, at any moment, launch an attack into the Nile Delta. Steffie wrote that the farmhands were on regular watch for strange behaviour in the cows and that they were 'trying to improve the supports in the barn' and Fran, remembering the nervous tension in Britain last year as they'd faced the very real prospect of invasion, felt her friend's fear through the lightly written lines.

As for Ailsa, her letters reported that she was enjoying her work but that 'the poor grass in our little field is perpetually torn up by the ravenous chickens'. She feared, she wrote, that there would soon be no grass left at all with so much poultry around and that she worried that their only hope was if the ducks could get the geese off the pond. Fran often sat at the table alone, moving the wooden animals around, willing the British ducks to chase away the German geese, but news reports suggested that the ducks were struggling and that German convoys to Africa were getting through far more easily than British ones. The war in the Med had become a battle of supplies. Whoever could replenish their troops in Africa most successfully was likely to win and, right now, the Germans were on top.

Fran sighed, made herself toast for one, and set out for BP. They needed a break or the Mediterranean would be lost, and quite possibly her friends with it. She took the now familiar track up to BP, flashed her pass at the sentry who had once felt so intimidating, and marched around the lake to Hut 3. She could hear an unusual racket inside and feared Squadron Leader Humphreys was up to his usual attempts to dominate. The man clearly felt that he should be leading, but he had no idea how to work with a team and all his pompous blustering did was to tear people apart. It was making them far less effi-cient and Fran was beginning to tense up every time she heard his grating voice. Steeling herself, she stepped through the door but was pleasantly surprised when Peter leaped up to greet her.

'Fran! Welcome, welcome. Breakfast?'

She looked around in a daze as he ushered her to a trestle table stacked with jam sandwiches, iced buns and, if she wasn't mistaken, champagne. She remembered that both the air and army advisers were up in London today for meetings with the ministries and the mood in the hut was as jolly as it had always used to be before their arrival. Even so, champagne was a bit over the top.

'What the...?'

'C38m!' Peter cried, doing a funny little jig.

'What about it, Peter?'

C38m was the Italian naval cipher, brought into wide-spread use last December. It had been eluding the codebreakers ever since, but did this extravagant breakfast mean...?

'They've broken it,' Valérie burst out from the far side of the table. 'The cottage have broken it, Fran. Decrypts are flooding through to Hut 4, but it's the code the Regia Marina use to communicate with the other Axis units so we need to all work together.'

'Exactly,' Peter agreed. 'Put C38m together with our own decrypts from the Light Blue Wehrmacht traffic in Africa, the Red Luftwaffe messages and some of the minor codes, and we can build an unparalleled picture of the convoy routes. Hut 4 have asked if our research department can take on the overall coordination and I'm game.'

Fran smiled. 'Humphreys won't like it.'

'Humphreys is busy kowtowing to the top dogs so there's nothing he can do about it. Look, I've got some kit...' He gestured to a fresh map of the Med, a box of drawing pins and a large ball of string, 'but I need someone good at organising to help me do the tracking.'

'Valérie?' Fran asked, confused.

'Not Valérie, no. She'll help where she can, but most of the time she'll be busy on the Russian campaign.'

'You mean...?'

Peter cocked an eyebrow and it was Valérie who bounced up and hugged her.

'He means you, Fran. You're the top coordinator around here. You're the one who can bring all sorts of different information together into a coherent picture.'

'So, what do you say?' Peter asked. 'Fancy a promotion to head of convoy research?'

'Are you allowed to do that?' she asked.

Peter laughed.

'I may not be head of hut, Fran, as good old Humphreys constantly likes to remind us, but I'm head of research and this is research. So...?'

'So, yes please,' Fran said eagerly, lifting up the map and

looking around Hut 3. There was the perfect stretch of wall above her line of index cabinets with room on top to keep the string and pins. It wasn't exactly cutting edge. She'd heard on the rumour mill that elsewhere in BP machines were being brought in that could count a thousand times faster than any human, even Alan Turing. More and more WRENS were arriving to work them and you could hear their clattering whir through the walls of Hut 1 if you listened carefully. Fran's string-and-pins mapping wasn't going to revolutionise anything like these mysterious machines might, but if they could stop just one convoy being bombed then they'd be worth their weight in gold.

'Let's get started,' she said, reaching for her scissors and cutting her first length of string.

By the end of the day, her enthusiasm was faltering. She'd spent hours going through the index and charting every port around the Mediterranean with all they knew about it in terms of defences, garrisons and ship movements, then she'd done the same with the airfields. Even as she'd written a squadron number onto the airfield outside Tobruk, however, a message had come in suggesting they were being moved to El Adem and it was clear that they were going to need as many erasers as pencils to keep this primitive system up to date.

She and Peter had, however, made a start on plotting their first convoys – an Italian one from Naples to Tripoli, and a British one from Alexandria to Malta – and Valérie had tracked down some green gardening twine from one of the old sheds to differentiate Allied routes from Axis ones.

As the shift ground to a halt at 4 p.m., the three of them stood back and admired their map, littered with information. A white Allied line stretched from Egypt to Malta, as if connecting Fran's two friends, and, perhaps more critically, a

180

green Axis one reached halfway into the sea from Italy. Hopefully tomorrow the messages would come in to pinpoint the rest of the planned route and then they just needed to strike lucky with someone broadcasting clear dates and times of shipping and aerial strikes. That would put them in a position to strike at the green enemy lines and defend the white home ones. Fran's eyes itched with tiredness and her legs ached from being on her feet all day. She looked to the others.

'Will this work, do you think?'

Peter slung a fatherly arm around her shoulders.

'It stands a chance, Fran. It won't be easy and it won't be quick, but it stands a chance.'

That simple statement summed up so much of what went on here in BP – the daily grind of chasing down information and matching it up with other information to find a way to worm into the enemy plans.

'I'll take that. And now, I'm ready to collapse.'

'You must be hungry, Frances,' Valérie said, as Peter gave her a quick squeeze and ambled back to his own desk.

Fran considered. Had she even had lunch today? Her stomach rumbled out the answer.

'I'm starving.'

'I'm a good cook,' Valérie said, unusually shy. 'If you want, I could bring a few things over to this caravan of yours and whip us up a nice supper. I even have a bottle of wine my uncle sent me the other day.'

Fran stared at her.

'You have an uncle that sends you wine?'

'Crates of it. He knows someone who runs fishing boats out of Brittany and drops supplies into Cornish coves.'

'Seriously? There's a war on and your family are smuggling wine?'

Valérie gave a cute shrug.

'What can I say? We're French. And that beer stuff you lot brew is disgusting!'

Fran laughed. A bottle of wine would be very welcome tonight, as would someone cooking for her, and she had to admit that the thought of lively Valérie bouncing around the caravan was enticing. Their friendship had grown in the last six months but Valérie hadn't kissed her again and Fran didn't dare take the lead herself. Hut 3 still lit up like a searchlight whenever Valérie was in it, however, and with Steffie and Ailsa so far away she needed the company.

'You're on,' she agreed. 'Let's go via your place and fetch whatever you need, then we can call into the grocer's on the way home.'

'Perfect!'

Valérie tucked an arm through Fran's and they left Hut 3 together and headed out of the Park. Fran had never been to Valérie's digs before and her steps faltered as the French girl led her through a twist of streets to a clutch of rundown cottages at the bottom.

'You live here?'

Valérie pulled a face.

''Fraid so. Nearly as disgusting as the beer, yes? My mother would be horrified. Last week I woke up to find a rat sitting next to my bed, staring right up at me as he chewed on the edge of my boot.'

'Your boot?'

She gave another shrug.

'What can I say? I have very tasty sweet.'

'Sweet? Oh – you mean sweat!'

'I do? Right. You English with your stupid spellings that never match your pronunciations.'

'Like you French with your words all running into each other so you can never tell when one stops and another one starts.'

'Sorry?'

'All those l' things. They used to drive me mad in lessons. You even do it with names. How are you meant to say L'Aigle, for example? And how does anyone know it's not just Laigle? And why does Aigle need to be a "the" anyway?'

Fran had a feeling she was getting her point rather tangled up and certainly Valérie laughed.

'You do it too.'

'Do what?'

'Change "the".'

'We do not!' Fran said indignantly. 'The is just the – no genders, no funny apostrophes, just a good, solid word.'

'What, then, about when it is thee?'

Fran stared at her.

'Thee?'

'As in "thee umbrella" or "thee ankle".'

'But, but...' Fran battled to think about it – this was, frankly, blowing her mind.

'Whenever your noun starts with a vowel you change "the" to "thee". Did you not know?'

Fran groaned.

'No, Valérie, it seems I didn't know.'

Valérie smiled triumphantly.

'So, you see – our languages are every bit as silly as each other! Now, wait here and I will be out again shortly.'

She skipped through the rickety front door and reappeared before Fran had got through even ten more nouns to test the 'thee' theory. She had a bag slung over her shoulder and was carrying a dead rat in the other hand, which she flung nonchalantly into the hedge. Fran watched it arc over the leaves and shuddered.

'This place is awful.'

'It is,' Valérie agreed cheerfully. 'It is *thee* awful place.'

Fran groaned and nudged at her and, arms linked once

more, they headed back up the maze of streets. The caravan, when they reached it, had never looked cleaner or more homely and Fran let Valérie inside, proud of the bright main room with its gingham curtains and scrubbed units. Valérie gave a happy sigh and sank onto the bench.

'This is lovely, Frances. You were very lucky to find it.'

'Steffie found it. Ailsa and I just got to move in with her.'

'And now they are both gone.'

'Afraid so.'

'And it is just you...'

'Just me.'

'And now me.' Valérie held Fran's eyes for a fraction of a second longer than was truly comfortable, then leaped up again. 'So – I cook for you. It is my mother's finest cassoulet. Well, a version of it. She would put in ham hock and pork fillet as well as saucisson and Basque chorizo. I have only your English bacon and a little dried saucisson sent from my uncle.'

'The uncle that gets you wine?'

'Another uncle.'

'How many do you have?'

Valérie considered.

'As many as I need. My father is an influential man and has many brothers. But talking of wine...'

She pulled a bottle out of her bag and Fran went to pass her a corkscrew. She had to squeeze past her in the tiny kitchen and felt her breath quicken at the other girl's touch. Was this meal really wise? Then she glanced at the farm model and saw Steffie's Sphinx staring implacably back at her and gave a Gallic shrug of her own. Who needed wisdom? This was wartime and happiness had to be seized wherever it could be found.

'Is your father still influential?' she asked, as Valérie opened the wine with a rich pop and she fetched glasses out of the tiny top cupboard.

'You mean does he run a big Resistance ring in the hills...?'

'No, I—'

'Because, yes, he does.'

'Oh. Is that... is that safe?'

Valérie stroked a hand down her cheek.

'No, Frances, it is not safe, but it is necessary. If de Gaulle has the balls to muster troops beyond our borders, we must do our bit within them or we will never be truly "Free French" again. And do not worry. I come from the hills of the Ardèche. There are many, many places to hide and my father knows them all from his poaching days.'

'Poaching?'

Valérie huffed.

'Why not? He does not do it full time, you understand. He is a lawyer, a good one, but the land rules in France are very unfair. Much to the aristocracy, little to the rest. We simply... redress the imbalance.'

'Right.'

'And now we redress the imbalance in our country between those who have their roots, lives and very blood in its soil, and those who have marched in and stolen it.'

Fran felt the quake of Valérie's passion and moved closer.

'I'm so sorry, Valérie. It must be very hard.'

'Hard? *Oui*. It is hard, but not as hard as it will be for them when we win. I am learning to kill rats, Frances, and rats, let's face it, have done nothing wrong save try and live in a space too close to my own. Wait until I get my hands on Nazis...'

Her face was flushed with fury, her eyes sparkling with it and her lips parted as her breathing came in angry little puffs. Her pain was more than Fran could bear and, cupping Valérie's face in both hands, she leaned down, pressed her lips against the other girl's, and kissed her.

Valérie's response was immediate. Her arms went around Fran's neck and she pulled her close, kissing her back fiercely and clutching at her so tightly that Fran felt the dig of her nails in her back and knew, with startling clarity, that she wanted this strong, fierce, wounded Frenchwoman to hold onto her forever more. It was strange and scary and dizzying, but it felt so right. Steffie and Ailsa might be off travelling the wide world, but it seemed that Fran was getting her own adventure right here in Bletchley and she was determined to make the very most of it while she could.

NINETEEN

NOVEMBER 1941

Ailsa

Ailsa stretched out her back, stiff from hours hunched over her radio set, and, pulling her headset off, stood up and went out onto the balcony to clear her head. It would take more than the five minutes of her break to do that, mind you, as the chatter of Morse was filling her brain. She'd got herself up to twenty words a minute now, the best speed on the island, but that came at a price. Sometimes these days Morse filled her dreams too and she feared she might be in danger of starting to actually talk in dots and dashes if she wasn't careful.

She leaned on the balcony and turned her face to the sun, weaker now that winter was upon them but still hotter than most summer days back home. Her heart squeezed. She'd heard nothing from her parents in all her six months on Malta. She'd had not one letter, postcard or telegram to let her know that they'd received her note about her overseas posting. Her own missive had been pretty curt, she knew – she'd been short on time in the mad scramble after Denniston calling her into his office – but at least she'd tried. They, it seemed, no longer wanted to know her and she had to admit that without their solid if undemonstrative care, she felt slightly adrift.

'All right there?'

She turned to see Ned leaning on the balcony at her side and smiled. He'd been such a support to her in these first months on Malta and she found herself looking out for him on her breaks and at the end of her shifts. She wasn't looking for a suitor, not after the fiasco with Alasdair, but Ned was so easy to talk to and there was nothing wrong with being friends, right?

'I was just thinking how different this is to home,' she said carefully.

'Isn't it? You don't get fancy buildings like this where I come from. Or sunshine. D'you know, it rains more in Manchester than in any other part of England?'

Ailsa laughed.

'But not Scotland. North Uist could definitely give that record a run for its money.'

'Is it pretty?'

Ailsa jumped, surprised by the question, though she should be used to it by now. Ned wasn't like any man she'd known before. He was always asking questions, drawing things out of people, wanting to know their opinions.

'It's pretty, aye. Totally different colours to here – all greens and purples and blues where this is whites and yellows and browns.'

'Except for the sea. And the sky.'

Ailsa looked into the harbour and then up above.

'Both of those seem to be filled with darkness,' she said, and Ned gave a quiet sigh.

The raids never stopped but Ailsa had been thankfully occupied getting her Maltese Y-station up and running to inter-cept as many messages as possible from across the Mediter-ranean theatre. It hadn't been hard. Charlie was gone – taking shrapnel in his leg as a ready excuse to be sent back to

Whaddon – but there were plenty of more resilient workers.
The mixture of young RAF officers, locals, and wives and
daughters of service personnel on the island were sharp and
keen and had only needed some basic training and a more
coherent comms system to up their efficiency. Their proximity
to the fields of battle in Greece, Africa and Russia made the
enemy messages terrifyingly clear and BP was always clam-
ouring for more. As well as their base in the Lascaris tunnels,
Ailsa had helped set up outposts in St Paul's Bay in the west of
the island and on the Dingli cliffs in the east.

She ran the Morse section, listening in to German and
Italian signals, leaving Ned – who spoke excellent German – to
lead the monitoring of the 'en clair' broadcasts from enemy
pilots to their control. Often, over a swelteringly hot summer,
Ailsa had found him upset over triumphant shouts as enemy
pilots had shot down their boys, as well as over distressing cries
for 'Mamma' and 'Mutti' as Italian and German lads had been
taken out. When a plane fell from the sky with a young man on
board, it mattered little who he'd been fighting for and more
who would miss him, and it upset Ned every time. Ailsa's
Morse, at least, was blank in its communication – no one
screamed for their mother in dots and dashes.

The only relief on Malta had been when the Luftwaffe had
flown off to help the Wehrmacht in their assault on Greece,
leaving the Italians in charge. The bombardments of Valletta
had continued but the 'cockerels' of the Regia Aeronautica
were not as ruthless as their German counterparts. They did
not have the dive bombers to screech in and hit targets with
deadly accuracy, and more bombs fell in the sea than on land,
as if the pilots couldn't quite bring themselves to destroy the
beauty of the ancient port. Often, Ailsa wondered if one of
those dashing Italians up in the sky was Steffie's Matteo and
tried to send him telepathic messages not to hurt her – or
himself. Ridiculous, really, but when the streets around you

were perpetually shaken with bombs it could be hard to think straight.

In the end, sadly, all the messages they'd picked out of the airwaves had suggested horrible German strength in Greece and BP decrypts had offered the troops on the ground only the time to retreat before too many lives were lost. Seventeen thousand men had been shipped off the island of Crete in a 'mini-Dunkirk' that had had the Germans crowing on their radios. Not only that, but the poor boys had been plunged back into North Africa where the Wehrmacht were still besieging Tobruk.

Ailsa thought daily of Steffie and wrote letters to both her and Fran every week. Sometimes she got letters back, often in batches of two or three where they'd been held up in transports. Steffie's were full of tales of parties and galas and polo matches that made her assignment in Egypt sound like one big social engagement. Quiet references to the fact that 'the big barn needs a lot of looking after', however, told Ailsa that her friend was also working very hard in scary conditions.

Fran's letters were quieter. She said the caravan felt very empty without them there and she was glad work was so busy. It sounded as if things in Hut 3 were rather tense but from little snippets she shyly let drop, Valérie was at her side and Ailsa was glad of it. It helped to know both her friends were well and she tried to keep her own letters positive, but it was hard.

The island was getting increasingly cut off and it was only the 'magic carpet' deliveries of old submarines between Alexandria and Valletta that were keeping vital food and weapons coming into the island. Several ship-based convoys had been sunk by the enemy recently and Malta was beginning to feel every bit as under siege as Tobruk. The governor, Lieutenant General Sir William Dobbie, made lots of morale-boosting speeches via the old Rediffusion system running through speakers on the streets and in bars and shops, but even his bluster could not hide the seriousness of the situation. Rationing was ruthlessly tight, and the other day Ailsa had had to drive another hole into her WAAF belt to hold her skirt up.

Every day there were more casualties, more deaths. The cemeteries were bursting at the seams and there always seemed to be a dark-clad funeral procession weeping down the main street. At least their base in the ancient Lascaris tunnels was solid. The occasional bullet might ricochet into the office but other than that, it was the safest place on the island and, in some of the worst raids, Ailsa had joined others in sleeping here. It had been a curious form of sleepover with everyone bedded down between the desks. One night, someone had brought two bottles of local spirit to what had rapidly become a party. Ailsa had found herself sleeping barely two feet from Ned and, if she was honest, the awareness of his closeness had been more disturbing than the bombs overhead.

Now she looked surreptitiously at him as she scanned the sky for the dark shapes that would presage yet another bombardment. He was a lovely man – kind, caring and so interested in the world. Although a proud Manchester lad, he'd spent much of his childhood in Europe with his parents, who'd run some sort of textile trading business, and spoke not just German but Italian, French and a smattering of Russian. Ailsa was always asking him to tell her about the places he'd seen, and they'd spent many happy hours discussing where they'd like to visit once the war was over.

The other day, they'd been chatting about Italy and Ned had said, 'I'd like to take you to Rome,' and then they'd both looked at each other, discomfited, and neither of them had been able to find anything else to add. Answers had run through Ailsa's head like wildfire: 'When will we go?'; 'How would we travel together?'; and the uncomfortably intriguing, 'Where would we stay?'

She'd spoken none of them aloud but they'd hung between

them all the same and she'd known that if she were as confident as Steffie, or as bold as Fran, she would probably have stepped up and kissed him. But she wasn't. She was just little Ailsa MacIver from North Uist who'd only ever been kissed once, and that by a man she'd not wanted. Finding someone she might truly like was as scary as watching planes zoom in out of the blue, so she'd stuttered and muttered and dived back under her headsets where she felt safe. They hadn't talked much about travelling since and she was sad about that so she steeled herself and turned towards him.

'Have you ever been to Turkey, Ned?'

He looked at her eagerly.

'No, but I'd like to. I hear Istanbul is the most glorious city. It faces onto two seas, you know, and it has buildings that stretch back centuries. The Hagia Sophia was first built in the 500s and turned from a church into a mosque sometime in the fifteenth century. Isn't that peculiar?'

Ailsa nodded. 'Just proves, I suppose, that God is the same whatever your faith.'

He cocked his head on one side.

'You know what, Ailsa, I think maybe it does – though most wars have been fought over that very point.'

'But not this one.'

'No. Or maybe yes – the Nazis believe themselves to be gods and that is perhaps the most dangerous belief of all — Oh no!'

The cry came out of him on a strangled yelp and Ailsa turned to where he was pointing just in time to see a single plane swooping round from behind the Lascaris cliffs. It dipped daringly close to the buildings, and opened fire while they stood there, transfixed.

'Get down!'

Ned was first to react. He dived, wrapping his arms around her and pulling her to the ground just before a line of bullets fired directly into the office, cracking several panes of glass where their heads had been a moment before. Ailsa lay on the stone of the balcony, staring up at the spider's web death patterns and feeling Ned's heart beating loud and strong against her own. She reached out and touched a hand to his cheek.

'You saved me.'

'Of course,' he said simply.

For a moment, the soft November air shimmered between them but then the rest of the unit were tumbling out of the doors and pulling them to their feet with exclamations of horror and the moment was gone. Gone, but not forgotten. Ailsa could not wipe the sensations of being close to Ned from her skin and neither did she want to. It had felt so different to the time Alasdair had pulled her into his arms and she longed to feel it again, but she had read Alasdair wrong back then so was she, now, doing the same with Ned? Conversely to Alasdair, was he just being friendly? And did it really matter, with enemy planes firing on them?

One thing she knew – there was serious work to be done. Either that plane had taken a lucky potshot, or the enemy had worked out where their offices were. They would have to board up the windows, losing their glorious view but safeguarding their lives, and they would have to redouble their efforts to break this growing siege. Brushing off her colleagues' concern with the balcony dust from her uniform, Ailsa sat down at her workstation once more. Pulling on her headset, she picked up her pencil and began listening to the dots and dashes of enemy plans on the blue Mediterranean air. Before she could even take down a full message, however, Ned waved her over, his eyes wild.

'What is it?' she asked. 'What's going on?'

'It's the Luftwaffe. They're crowing. Something's been hit. Something big.'

Ailsa looked around the Y-station.

'Anyone picking up distress signals?' she demanded.

The navy ran their own comms but any radio operator worth their salt could find their frequencies. Marcia, a reliable army-wife, put up a hand.

'Here. It's an SOS from...' She listened carefully, 'HMS *Barham*.'

They all stared at her, aghast. HMS *Barham* was a prized battleship with a crew of over a thousand men.

'They're scrambling boats to rescue the crew,' Marcia went on, one ear glued to her headset, 'but it's going down fast. U-boat, by the sounds of it.'

Ailsa cringed at the thought of all those poor men fighting for their life in the sea with the dark, predatory submarine gliding away beneath them.

'How did the damned wolf catch her?' Marcia was asking. 'She was part of a fleet out hunting Italian convoys. There should have been no way of plotting her route.'

'Luck?' someone suggested dully, but Ailsa wasn't so sure.

Only last week they'd lost HMS *Ark Royal* in similar circumstances and that, alongside an increasingly accurate targeting of their supply convoys, implied insider knowledge. She looked at Ned, but he was glued to his headset, frantically taking notes on a pad.

'What is it?' she demanded when he'd finished taking it all down. 'What can you hear?'

He looked at her.

'They're laughing. The bastards are laughing because the ship is going down too fast for the men to get out. And they're proposing a toast.'

'A toast? To who?'

Ned bit his lip.

'To Gute Quelle.'

Ailsa looked at him. 'Gute Quelle?'

'It means "good source". The Germans are toasting their "good source".'

'You mean...?'

'They may have a spy, yes. Somewhere across the Med, or even as far away as England, the enemy may have a spy who's targeting our ships with horrible accuracy.'

Ailsa gripped the edge of her trestle table, feeling weaker than when she'd been wrestled out of range of a Messerschmitt gun just a few minutes ago. It was all very well congratulating themselves on listening in to the enemy, but if the enemy were listening in to them too then the gloves were well and truly off.

TWENTY

DECEMBER 1941

Steffie

Steffie turned Ailsa's postcard over and over in her hands before forcing herself to put it down and get on with her work. Still, though, her friends' words seemed to glare out like some enemy searchlight: *The farm is in a right mess. It looks like we might have a chicken and cockerel in with the pheasants, and geese creating havoc among the ducks.* It was a suitably oblique message but Steffie understood – a German had infiltrated their ranks in one way or another and she needed to be on alert. It made sense of a new tension among the high-ups but, with Operation Crusader, a huge Allied offensive, in full swing against Rommel at Tobruk, and all hands on deck to get signal intercepts out to the front line, there was no time to focus on anything else.

A new SLU had been set up in a rough desert-van to follow the main commanders and Steffie was working all the hours to get the intercepts teleprinted across Europe to the codebreakers in BP and the decrypts back and out to the boys in the van. Alongside that, she was working with her team to break lower-grade ciphers on site and she was worn out. All leave had been cancelled for the last month but today they'd intercepted messages from Rommel, bewailing his lack of supplies and indicating he was ready to pull back.

'That's it!' Freddie Jacobs cried, punching the air. 'That's the retreat. He's ordered the retreat. Tobruk is relieved. Tobruk is bloody well relieved.'

'I bet it is,' Steffie said, happiness rippling through her tense shoulders. She glanced at the clock. 'Does that mean we're free to go out this evening?'

Freddie shook his head in admiration.

'If you think you can last the course, Steffie, then it's fine by me.'

'It's Sunday, Freddie – and the first one not spent hunched over our desks. You bet I can last the course!'

He patted her back.

'The joys of youth. I shall be tucked up in the mess with a large whisky and one of the Bedouin's finest tagines, but you go for it, you deserve it. You've done a fantastic job for us in the last month. Really fantastic.'

'I... I have?'

'Of course. Don't think I haven't noticed. Your energy is impressive but, more than that, you're sharp, Steffie. You see connections where others don't. You take in the whole picture and make deductions accordingly, and that's a skill even some of the top generals out there don't have. Good work.'

Steffie blinked ferociously; she must have some of the ever-present desert sand in her eye.

'Thank you, sir,' she managed.

'Credit where credit's due, woman. Now – go find your party shoes and get yourself a lift into town!'

Steffie needed no second urging and, grabbing her bag, she made a dash for the exit. It was only 3 p.m. but there would be afternoon tea at the Gezira Club if she was quick and the thought of their green lawns, flower-draped terraces, and lush lido was desperately tempting. Plus, perhaps, at last, she would have time to make a few discreet enquiries around Ailsa's warning. If there was a spy, it could damage them all and there was no place like a cocktail lounge to find out more.

The Gezira Club, set on a lush island in the centre of the Nile, was a showcase of colonial opulence. The grand cream and brown art deco building looked more like a temple than a club and inside it was indeed a temple – to leisure pursuits of all kinds. Opening out at the back to a large terrace, shaded with flowered vines, it sported a sparkling pool, croquet lawns and tennis courts. Beyond, a vast polo pitch stretched out, vibrantly green and, as Steffie stepped onto the terrace, the pounding of horses' hooves filled the air.

She drew her silk robe more tightly over her bathing suit and threaded her way between the tables towards the pool. It had been unusually hot for autumn and even today, 7 December, the temperature was in the sixties. She could see Maria and Francine Endozzi, two lively Italian sisters, playing with a brightly coloured beach ball in the shallow end and picked up her pace, anticipating the glorious rush of cool water across her desert-parched skin.

'Stefania, *ma chérie*! I haven't seen you for ages.'

Steffie looked round to see Momo Marriott waving and headed reluctantly her way. She was dying to get in the pool but Momo was the wife of Major General Marriott and it wouldn't do to be rude to this doyenne of the Cairo scene.

'Soo lovely to see you,' she gushed, inclining her head in thanks as a waiter rushed forward to pour her tea though, frankly, the last thing she wanted was a hot drink. 'Apologies I've not been around much. Work, you know.'

A frown dimpled Momo's elegant forehead and Steffie hid

a smile. Of course she didn't know – she hadn't done a day's work in her life, unless you counted organising social events. Steffie didn't mind. Her own mother was the same and she might well have become so herself if it hadn't been for the war taking her over to her father's line of work – thank heavens. She thought of her sandy, dusty, fly-infested offices with sudden fondness. Oh, she missed Matteo so much, but she did enjoy being useful.

'You poor dear, how awful for you,' Momo soothed. 'You'll be needing something stronger. Waiter – champagne!'

The Egyptian raced off and Steffie sat up in her seat – champagne was more like it.

'It's only apt,' Momo said, leaning in. 'Have you heard?'

'What?' Steffie asked obligingly.

'Rommel is retreating. Tobruk is free!'

'No!' Steffie said, again battling to hide her amusement.

Not that it was funny. If top generals were leaking information to their wives, and via them to half the Gezira Club, then it was no wonder information was getting out. The Germans didn't need a trained spy, just a pretty girl in a bathing costume.

'Isn't it wonderful? Totally hush-hush, of course. Keep it to yourself, darling.'

'Oh, I will,' Steffie agreed, meaning it.

A delicious pop behind her indicated the opening of the champagne and she accepted a glass, forcing herself to wait for Momo to propose a terribly discreet toast, 'to our boys in the desert', before taking the first wonderful sip. As the cool liquid slid down her throat and the bubbles burst on her tongue, she contemplated her next question carefully.

'Do you think there are, then, people around here that aren't to be trusted?'

'Oh yes! Why do you think Major Sansom is always around?'

'Who?'

'Major Sansom. Sammy. Short, tubby chap, bald head, whizz with languages. He can even chat in Arabic.'

'And his job is...?'

'Spy-hunter,' she said confidently, then put a finger to her lip and giggled.

It was all Steffie could do not to shake her head. How stupid were these people? If everyone knew this Sansom chap was a spy-hunter then the spies were going to avoid him like the plague.

'The poor man has a terrible life,' Momo was going on. 'Has to hang out with prostitutes and belly dancers every night.'

'They're spies?'

'So he says,' she agreed with a wicked wink, then shook her head at herself. 'That's not fair. Sammy's not long married. And he spends plenty of time with the Bedouin too. There's always someone shady-looking heading into his offices.'

'Poor man,' Steffie said. 'And, er, where are his offices?'

'Oh, in Grey Towers with everyone else, but he's more often around here. In fact...' Momo cast her eyes across the terrace and clapped her hands. 'There he is, smoking a pipe by the croquet lawn. Shall I introduce you?'

'Please,' Steffie agreed. She wasn't inspired by what she'd heard of 'Sammy' Sansom but she was prepared to give him a chance to surprise her.

Thankfully he did.

'Double bluff,' he said when Momo had retreated and she'd asked him about his rather public role as 'spy-hunter'. 'It makes people very aware of me and then they will tend to get nervous, or to go out of their way to make things up. The key, you see, isn't in what people tell you but in the way they do it.'

'Have you caught many spies?'

'Plenty.'

Steffie's heart sank.

'Really?'

'Lord, yes. Cairo's stuffed to the ginnels with them. Mind you, half of them are ours.' He gave her a wink. 'Most are just locals seeking to make a quick penny for information. They'll as readily sell it to the enemy as to us – often do.'

'But then...'

'But then we feed them what we want them to hear.'

'And they do the same to you?'

'Of course. And somewhere in the middle lies the truth.'

'It sounds exhausting.'

He smiled and drew deeply on his pipe.

'Exhausting and perhaps a little farcical, like so much of life, but important all the same. The nation that can best keep its secrets will be victorious.'

'*That* I agree with,' Steffie said, adjusting her robe self-consciously and looking around. 'Major Sansom, I work in the Museum.'

'Ah. Say no more, say no more. I understand.'

'Good. But, you see, I've had it on strong intelligence that we may have a spy listening in to us. I think it might be to do with ducks. That is, sorry, shipping – convoys.'

'Convoys?' He straightened. 'That's serious stuff.'

'Yes, sir.'

He looked at her with new eyes.

'You've come to the right man. I'll look into it, my dear. Top priority, I assure you.'

'Thank you.'

'No problem. No problem at all. Don't you worry your pretty little head about it. Look – your friends are waving.'

Steffie glanced round to see the Endozzi girls calling her name. Maria threw the beach ball, forcing her to scramble after it before it bounced into someone's cream tea, and when she looked back to Major Sansom he just gave her a benevolent smile and waved her towards the pool. Steffie ground her teeth. She was pretty sure the wretched man hadn't taken her seriously. She'd have to pursue her own enquiries but, for now, the pool beckoned and, draining her champagne glass and returning it with a smile of thanks to Momo's table, she flung off her robe and jumped happily into the water at last.

The afternoon merged into the evening. Maria and Francine ordered mint juleps to the poolside and it wasn't until dusk started to fall, bringing a wintery chill with it, that Steffie thought to dress. She hurried into the changing room to slide into an evening gown, piling her still-damp hair into a loose chignon, and dabbing on lipstick and mascara. Already she could feel her eyelids starting to droop and feared Freddie had been right to doubt her ability to 'stay the course', but surely it was nothing a Martini and a bite of supper wouldn't sort out?

She headed back to the foyer, delighted to bump into Betty making for the main bar and linked arms to join her but, to their surprise, they found the room unusually sombre, with many people pressed around a large radiogram.

'What's going on?' Betty demanded and was roundly hushed.

Exchanging nervous glances, they crept forward and that's when Steffie spotted Bonner Fellers fanning himself by the bar and looking decidedly green about the gills. She headed across.

'What's happened?' she asked.

'They've attacked us,' Bonner moaned.

'Who've attacked? Where?'

'The Japanese. The Japanese have attacked the United States.'

'No!' Steffie's hands flew to her mouth. 'Where?'

'Pearl Harbor.' Steffie looked at him blankly. 'Hawaii. It's a group of islands in the middle of the Pacific where we base our fleet. It's important, sure, but it's miles from anywhere – including Japan.'

'Then how did they…?'

'Lawd knows. Crept up on us in aircraft carriers and let rip at dawn. Evil little devils.'

Steffie looked sideways at Bonner. She knew enough about naval craft these days to be pretty sure that you couldn't 'creep up' on anyone in a giant aircraft carrier, but the details weren't important right now.

'Is anyone hurt?'

'Hundreds. Maybe thousands. Whole boats are on fire in the port and there might be more attacks yet. It's not even 9 a.m. in the Pacific.' His usually amiable eyes narrowed. 'This is it for the US, Steffie, this is us in the war – properly in, not hovering on the edges.'

Steffie fought to grasp this. She'd seen Bonner out at Heliopolis a few times recently, liaising with the British troops, and knew he found his observer role frustrating. Churchill wanted the Americans involved to draw them into a fuller role in the Med, but it was slow going. Or it had been until now. Bonner looked dazedly at her.

'Roosevelt will have to declare war, Steffie. I won't be reporting back to Washington as a bystander any more, but as a full participant.'

'We'll certainly be glad to have you.'

He gave her a wry grimace.

'That's very generous, after all I've said about your lot.'

Steffie grimaced. Bonner hadn't always been complimentary about British tactics but today, with the US navy under attack in their own backyard, he was swallowing his criticism graciously.

'Drink?' she suggested as the barman hovered hopefully. 'To toast the fact we're truly on the same side now?'

'Why not,' he agreed morosely.

Looking at his long face, Steffie opted for whisky and asked for it with ice, the way the Yanks liked it, even though such sacrilege would have made her father blow a gasket. She ordered one for herself too, wishing she could be toasting the Italians joining them rather than the Americans. If that was the case, she might be able to ride up to an Italian airfield next week, wave her 'Allied forces' pass and ask for Sottotenente Mancini and then just step right into his arms...

'Your whiskies, madam.'

Steffie paid and handed one over to her American friend.

'As allies go, you're not a bad one, Bonner.'

'Praise indeed.'

The room was still quiet, the main sound the BBC announcer talking about sinking ships, and a sea on fire, and an island – indeed a whole nation – in shock. Steffie could well believe it if the mood in the usually irrepressible Gezira Club was anything to go by.

'Looks like 1942 will be a heck of a year,' Bonner muttered.

He could say that again, Steffie thought, as she sipped her whisky (really quite nice with ice, though she'd never tell Daddy) and reminded herself to go looking for postcards in the souks tomorrow. There was bound to be one with a bison on it somewhere and Ailsa and Fran would understand immediately – there was a new animal on the farm and they had to hope it was big and lairy enough to chase off the rest.

PART THREE

1942

TWENTY-ONE

NEW YEAR'S EVE 1941-2

Ailsa

Ailsa looked around the laughing room and had to admire the spirit of the Maltese. Some of the people in the Sliema Club for tonight's celebrations were living permanently in bunkers and yet here they were, hair done and finery on, dancing in the New Year.

'They're not going to destroy us,' one young woman had told Ailsa as she'd stood in the Ladies, shaking dust from her pretty dress and drawing scarlet lipstick across her lips. 'They can destroy our homes and our offices, our churches and our shops. They can even destroy our loved ones, but they're not having our heart. These' – she'd held up a pair of sparkly shoes – 'are my weapon against the Nazis.' Then she'd put them on and marched out to the dance floor, head high. Ailsa had watched her with awe.

'Would you like to dance, Ailsa?'

She turned to see Ned at her side, hand outstretched and cheeks flushed sweetly pink.

'I'd love to.'

She put her hand in his and he grasped it and smiled.

'Can you jive?'

'Jive? I'm not sure. I can jig – is that the same thing?'

It was not, it rapidly turned out, the same thing at all, but Ned was a proficient partner and Ailsa's years of training in reels stood her in good stead as she applied herself to following his lead. The dance was faster and livelier and more thrillingly close up than she'd ever had the luck to enjoy before and she was soon flushed and laughing.

'That's amazing!' she said, hugging Ned as the music faded out and they finally came to a stop.

'I'm so glad you like it, Ailsa. You're a quick learner!'

'I'll have to teach you Scottish reels in return.'

'I'd like that.'

She looked up at him, ready to tell him that he might not find the Gay Gordons as much fun as jiving, but her words died as she realised how very close he was. Ailsa felt heat flood her body and had no idea whether to step into him or back off. He seemed to be making no move and, once again, she feared she was reading the situation all wrong. Why were men so complicated?

Up on stage the compère was babbling away about it being nearly midnight and the crowd were pressing in around them, but she could hear nothing coherent over the pounding of her own blood. She remembered Alasdair kissing her – the unpleasant press of his body, the rubberiness of his lips, the prickle of his beard – and knew already that kissing Ned would be a hundred times better. Instinctively she pushed herself up onto her toes and saw Ned's eyes darken. Oh Lord, was she embarrassing him?

'Ten, nine...!'

She sprang away, grateful for the interruption of the count-down to 1942 to spare her blushes. As she looked around at the crowd of Maltese locals and Allied service people shouting the countdown around the Sliema Club, a new memory flooded into her. This time last year she'd been seeing in 1941 in the Duncombe Arms with Steffie, Fran and half of BP, and look at her now – halfway across the Mediterranean. And with a lovely man at her side, even if he was a lovely man who just wanted to be friends. Friends was good, right? Friends was a nice thing?

'Two, One. Happy—'

The siren cut across the cheers, shrieking malevolently through the happy crowd.

'No,' Ailsa moaned. 'Not now.'

'Get down!'

The people nearest the window flung themselves to the floor and Ailsa glimpsed a plane fly past, silver in the moonlight, bullets spraying as it thundered towards the harbour.

'Messerschmitt!' Ned gasped. 'It's the Luftwaffe. The Luft-waffe are back.'

'Happy New Year,' Ailsa said darkly and then she was stumbling, with Ned, towards the stairs.

'Shelter in the basement, folks,' the compère was calling over the microphone. 'Plenty of shelter in the basement.'

They all ran down the stairs as another plane rumbled past. Someone in the ballroom screamed and Ailsa twisted round to see the girl from the Ladies fall against her dance partner. Blood bloomed from her chest as she choked out a last breath in the distraught man's arms and he collapsed to the floor with her, her sparkly shoes forever stilled.

'Bastards!' Ailsa cried. She'd been brought up never to use bad language but, really, some things were beyond bearing without it.

'At least she died happy,' Ned said grimly. 'Come on, this way. It's going to take ages to get everyone into the basement and there's a public shelter round the corner.'

She nodded and let him lead her across the lobby to the doors. Outside, the cold air bit into her bare shoulders but there was another plane coming in, low and fast, and there was no time to go back for a coat. Clutching Ned's hand, she ran for the relative shelter of the building across the road, feeling as exposed as a mouse beneath a hawk's stare as the plane dived. It was so close she could see the detailing of the guns on the underside and pressed herself tight against the stone. Ned shielded her with his own body and for a second heat flared again at his touch, but this was no time for romance. A stream of bullets ripped up the pavement in front of them and she heard a sob escape from her own chest.

'Round here,' Ned urged.

The plane gone, they darted round the corner to where, thank God, steps led into a shelter. An older couple were making their way unsteadily downwards and Ailsa and Ned rushed to take their arms and guide them.

'Thank you, dear,' the lady said, clutching at Ailsa. 'Oh, and what a pretty frock.'

Ailsa could have cried at her matter-of-fact attitude.

'Thank you,' she said. 'Though it's a bit wasted down here.'

She gestured around the dank shelter, a far cry from the sparkling ballroom she'd been standing in just minutes ago.

'Oh, I don't know. A pretty frock is never wasted and I'd say yours is getting its fair share of admiration.'

She nodded knowingly to Ned who had settled her husband and was coming back to help them. Ailsa flushed.

'Oh, we're just friends,' she said quickly.

'For now, maybe.' The woman gave her a broad wink that made her flush even more. Was she right? Might Ned like her too? And if so, why didn't he kiss her? Ailsa shivered and the woman squeezed her arm. 'You poor dear, you must be horribly chilly.' She dug in her bag and drew out a warm blanket. 'Take this.'

'I couldn't possibly,' Ailsa protested, but the woman was

already pushing it at her and digging in her bag again, producing some sort of fruit wine.

'And this! We'll have our own little party, hey? Away from bloody Fritz!'

Ailsa shook her head, amazed anew at the plucky Maltese, and settled down with them in a small alcove at the back of the shelter. More people arrived, white-faced and panting. The planes roared overhead and the bombs fell, shaking the ground beneath them, but the older couple calmly introduced themselves as Filomena and Ruzar, and Filomena dug into her bag once more. It seemed a magical vessel, producing glasses, bread, cheese and even a tiny bar of chocolate, all of which she selflessly shared out.

Ailsa began to relax. Ned was sitting deliciously close to her and she let the cherry wine, the rich cheese and, above all, the goodwill of her companions flood through her.

'They're terrible things, these bombs,' Ruzar muttered, as one landed scarily close and the whole shelter shook. 'Poor Malta. It's not like the Great War. Back then, we had casualties aplenty but few of them were our own.'

Ailsa looked at him, fascinated.

'Where were they from?'

'Gallipoli mainly. So many poor men brought to the island with terrible injuries. Australians and New Zealanders, most of them. We treated them and, if they were unlucky, we sent the poor buggers back.'

'You were a medic?'

'Oh yes,' Filomena said. 'Ruzar was the best doctor in St Elmo's hospital.'

'And Filly was the best matron – and the bossiest.' Ruzar grinned as his wife batted at his arm. 'Our two children worked there too. Endless, it was, but at least we weren't under attack right here on the island. Not like—'

But at that moment, a new plane arrived in a vicious rattle

of bullets. A horrible squeal rent the air, a loud boom shook the ground, and rocks and plaster began to rain down. The thirty or so people in the shelter leaped up, crying out as a long crack appeared in the roof. A teenage boy had been hit and lay groaning on the floor, his temple bleeding terribly while his mother gathered him into her arms.

'We have to get out,' Ned said loudly over the chaos. 'It's not safe. Don't panic – just make for the exit as calmly as possible.'

He stood up, guiding Filomena and Ruzar out of the alcove. Ailsa rose to follow him, telling herself to keep calm, but more rubble was falling from the roof and a large rock landed on her foot. She gasped as pain shot up her leg, knife sharp, but there was no time to hang around and, bending, she shoved the rock off. Pain rolled in anew, making her cry out.

'Ailsa!' Ned turned back but he had a hand through each of Filomena and Ruzar's arms and, in the time it took him to extricate himself, more rocks fell.

Ailsa backed up into the alcove. It was still intact but, as the crack in the main ceiling widened, dropping more rock, she was shut off from everyone else.

'Ailsa, you have to get out!' Ned shouted.

She looked at the pile of rubble growing before her and knew he was right but, as she forced herself to hop forward on her good foot, another shower of rocks came down, catching her shoulder, and she cowered back.

'I can't, Ned. I can't.'

'I'm coming.'

Ned almost shoved his elderly charges towards the exit. Through the terrible dust filling the shelter, Ailsa could see them asking to help but was glad Ned prevailed on them to leave. What was the point in more people dying down here? The thought cut into her, sharper than the pain in her foot. Was she going to die? Was the ceiling of the alcove going to cave in and bury her?

'Ma,' she moaned. 'Pa.'

Her mouth filled with dust and it clagged in her tears, turning them to grit. She put her arms around her face to try and protect it, realising what a futile gesture it would be if the whole shelter collapsed. Through the dust she could see the others heading up the stairs. Even the injured boy was being carried away, leaving her alone down here.

'Ailsa!' Ned's voice was the only thing that penetrated the fug. 'Ailsa, hold on. I'm here. I'm going to get you out. I'm going to keep you safe. Just hold on.'

'Ned!' she cried, but it was so dark, and so painful and still the rubble was falling so all she could do was curl up into the smallest possible ball and pray the alcove held. And then there was another loud bang and everything went black.

Ailsa came round to darkness, dust and a terrible sense of constriction. Slowly she moved one leg then the other, and then her arms. Piles of stones fell away and she was relieved to feel everything moving as it should. Her foot throbbed and there was an unpleasant dampness down her arm where she must have been cut, but she was still breathing and still whole.

She blinked furiously, trying to wipe the dust from her eyes, but realised that she could blink until Domesday and still not clear a view because it was pitch black. Feeling tentatively around, she found the back of the alcove, still solid, and then a vast wall of collapsed rubble before her. Oh God, she was trapped. She was trapped in what might become her tomb.

'Help!' It came out as a poor rasp and she spat and swallowed, trying to clear her throat. 'Help!' she shouted again, louder this time.

'Ailsa?'

'Ned! Ned, are you there? Where are you?'

'I'm right here, Ailsa. I'm right here, my darling girl.'

A tiny part of her brain registered the endearment and went slightly squishy at it. Darling girl? People didn't say that to their friends, did they? But then a cloud of dust made her cough and she realised the ridiculousness of her thoughts – what use was being someone's darling girl if you were stuck in a tomb?

'I can't get out, Ned. I can't see anything and I can't get out.'

'One minute.' She heard the sound of a match striking and made out the faintest of lights flickering through gaps in the rubble.

'I can see that! I can see it faintly.'

'That's good. That means the rubble is loose. You'll be able to breathe and we'll be able to get to you. Filomena and Ruzar have gone to fetch spades and there's plenty of people to help. You just have to stay calm, Ailsa – calm and still.'

'Why? Might it collapse more?'

'Of course not,' he said but his initial pause told her all she needed to know.

She felt panic rising inside her and had to resist the urge to fling herself bodily at the rubble and bust out. She couldn't stay in here. She couldn't stay in here and be crushed to death.

'Ma,' she gasped again, cursing herself for her stubbornness.

So what if her mother hadn't written? *She* was the one who had left, *she* was the one who had changed everything between them.

'I want to write home,' she gasped out.

'Now?' Ned sounded almost amused.

'Now, aye. Before I die.'

His laughter stopped instantly.

'You're not going to die, Ailsa. I promise you. I'm so, so sorry I brought you down here but I'm going to get you out if it's the last— I'm going to get you out. It will take patience, that's all. Look – tell me what you want to say and I'll write it down.'

'On what?'

'On my arm if I have to. The shovels are here so talk to me, Ailsa. Tell me what you want to say.'

Ailsa clutched her knees tight against her chest as she heard the tentative scrape of a shovel towards the top of the rubble wall holding her prisoner. She pushed herself as far against the solid rock of the alcove as she could, closed her eyes against the darkness, and thought of home.

'I want to say how much I love them, Ned. I want them to know what a happy childhood they gave me and how grateful I am for all the sacrifices they made. I want them to know that North Uist is in my bones and in my blood and just because I want to travel, it doesn't mean I won't ever return. I want to— Oh!'

A large rock was pulled away and suddenly there was Ned's face, flickering in the light of a storm lamp. He smiled gently.

'I think you'll be able to write it yourself, Ailsa. Hang on – I'm coming.'

The shovel angled into the hole and Ned carefully pulled more of the rocks away. Ailsa could see two other men behind, fixing large wooden props either side of the horrible crack. It was right over Ned's head but he seemed oblivious to the danger as he worked on to dig her out, tongue caught between his teeth in concentration. The hole grew and now there was enough light coming in for Ailsa to see the gash on her arm, the immodest rips in her party dress, and the blue bruise blooming on her foot.

'I'm a mess,' she said and was rewarded by a low laugh from Ned.

'You're alive, Ailsa, and that makes you the most beautiful thing in the world to me.'

He cleared another shovelful of rubble and suddenly the lower level was falling away, pouring out across the floor, and Ned was stepping through the gap and lifting her bodily into his arms.

'Ned!' She batted self-consciously at him but felt so weak and shaky that it was easier to wrap her arms around his neck and cling to him as he lifted her over the wall and strode towards the exit. The other two men had headed back up and he paused at the bottom of the steps.

'Am I too heavy?' she asked nervously.

'No,' he said. 'I just wanted a moment.'

'For what?'

She looked up at him, his face as close to hers as it had been before the countdown had begun, but both of them now coated in sweat and dust and blood.

'To ask you something.'

'Oh. What?'

He bit at his lip.

'May I kiss you?'

She laughed as all the tension drained away.

'Oh Ned, I thought you'd never ask!'

She looked into his eyes as he bent his head and felt his lips, feather-light, against her own. Her heart, so nearly robbed of more beats, started pounding in double time and she kissed him back.

'I thought I'd lost you,' he murmured into her tangled hair.

She pressed herself into his shoulder, too shy to respond, but then one of the props shifted and he quickly took the steps up into the icy fresh air where an anxious crowd cheered loudly. The Luftwaffe had, it seemed, gone for the night and all that was left were the stars and the moon and the brave love of the Maltese people.

'We're going to take you to the hospital with this lad here,' Filomena said, ushering them towards a jeep in which the teenage boy was lying weakly with his mother.

'I'm fine,' Ailsa protested, but Filomena tutted maternally.

'You are not fine. You have a veritable crevice of blood down your arm and your foot is the size of a ball.' Ailsa blinked at the vivid descriptions of her injuries and let herself be lowered into the jeep next to the others, though she held tight onto Ned to be sure he came with them. 'You *will* be fine, though,' Filomena said. 'All you need is cleaning up.'

'And some writing paper,' Ailsa muttered.

'Some what?' she asked.

'I'll get you some straight away,' Ned said. 'Now rest.'

Ailsa curled gratefully up in his arms but as they bumped down the bomb-ravaged street, with flames roaring from buildings, people crying for help from every corner, and the boy at her side moaning pitifully, it was impossible to rest. When would they be rescued from this hell?

TWENTY-TWO

JANUARY 1942

Fran

Fran pinned the last section of a German convoy route onto the map and looked at the green string in satisfaction.

'Naples to Tripoli via Marsala, Pantelleria and Monastir, leaving tomorrow at dawn with, I think, two cargos of weapons, one of food and sundries, and one oil tanker.'

'Great work, Fran.' Peter clapped her on the back. 'I'll get this to Air Marshal Tedder and Admiral Cunningham and, between them, they'll blow those supplies out of the water. Not one drop of that fuel will get to Rommel's bloody panzers and then we'll see how far he can advance.'

Fran smiled shyly and looked across the hut to Valérie, who gave her a broad smile and a mock clap. Fran stuck her tongue out and she threw back a cheeky wink that made Fran feel even giddier. But now Humphreys was striding across the room and plucking the paper from a surprised Peter's hands.

'I think you'll find, Peter, that this is air force intelligence, so it's up to the Air Ministry what to do with it.'

Peter's eyes narrowed.

'I think *you'll* find, Robert, that this is *BP* intelligence, so it is up to BP what to do with it.'

Fran groaned as the two men squared up to each other. Too often these days Hut 3 rang with petty power struggles and they were getting in the way of work. Back in January, they'd missed critical messages warning that Rommel was about to launch a new attack in North Africa and who knew what else was getting through the net while everyone was bickering. Frankly, she'd had enough.

'Gentleman, please.' She stepped between them, hands on hips, feeling uncomfortably like her old headmistress, but someone had to make them see sense. 'What on earth is the point of squabbling about whose damned information it is? The important thing is that it gets out to whoever needs it as soon as possible.'

'But who decides who needs it?' Humphreys demanded.

'We do,' Fran said. 'All of us here in Hut 3. That's our job.'

'It's not *your* job, Frances. You're just a bloody collator, providing the information. It's up to the ministries to disseminate it appropriately.'

'Not any more,' Fran said, mustering her patience. 'The principle underpinning the establishment of the SLUs is that information goes direct from BP to the field where the commanding officers can make the relevant decisions.'

Humphreys glared at her.

'Don't be ridiculous, girl. You have no idea how hard it is commanding in the field. These men are under huge pressure from front-line attack and do not need to be spending their valuable time deciding which messages are of significance.'

'Which,' Fran countered, waving to the maps, charts and indexing along the wall, 'is why we have such a rigorous system to determine exactly that.'

'You think that you, a slip of a librarian, can tell an experienced wing commander which messages matter?'

Fran stared into his bulging eyes and set her hands on her hips.

'I do.'

Humphreys threw his own hands in the air.

'Then Lord help us all!'

'Enough,' Peter said, his voice low but run through with quiet authority. 'Fran is absolutely right. We have a proven system to test the importance of any messages within the overall picture of the Mediterranean theatre. It's not perfect – this is war, after all – but it is an adequate filter to get the messages down to a manageable number for those on the front line. Then it's up to them to prioritise based on what they know of the on-the-ground situation.'

'But, but...' Humphreys looked furiously around the Hut but the only man standing with him was Captain Curtis and no one paid him much attention. 'But you're civilians,' he finished on an indignant squeak.

'Intelligence officers,' Peter correctly him calmly. 'And we have a job to do, so if you don't mind...'

'I do mind.'

'Then perhaps you should leave.'

Humphreys stood there, his hands clenching into furious fists, and for a moment Fran thought he was going to hit the quiet academic, but then he turned on his heel with a loud tut and strode over to his chair, throwing himself into it like a tantrumming toddler. Fran and Peter exchanged a look but things were quiet for now and they both retreated to their own workstations.

As Fran sat down opposite Valérie, she felt the French girl edge herself forward so that their knees touched and smiled gratefully. Valérie came to the caravan several evenings a week these days. They would cook then curl up together to read or flick through magazines, or, more often, to talk. Fran's French was improving rapidly and, if Valérie teased her about her pronunciation, she just kissed her quiet. Valérie had told her all about her home in the Ardèche and what she knew of her father's dangerous resistance work. In return, Fran had told her about her parents, doing many additional hours in the convalescent hospitals around Cambridge, and her brothers, both now stationed in a fixed field hospital in Algiers. She told her how much she admired them but how their preoccupation with the medical profession drove her mad.

'They just want you to be secure,' Valérie had said when she'd complained that her mother had, yet again, been sending her clippings of advertisements for ambulance drivers, 'and that's the only security they understand.'

'Then they need to open their minds.'

'I'm sure they will once they learn about the amazing work you're doing here.'

'Which they won't, because I'm sworn to secrecy.'

'True. I know – why don't you tell them that you're working with an organisation providing medical aid to the troops.' She'd stroked Fran's hair gently. 'It's not exactly untrue – every bit of information we provide to those men out there could save lives as effectively as any bandage.'

'I suppose,' Fran had agreed, though she didn't like the idea of lying and liked, even less, the fact that she felt tempted. Why couldn't they just trust her to be doing something decent?

She put her head down over the latest run of messages but it was hard to concentrate with the arguments ringing in her brain. It infuriated her. Poor Malta was being bombarded by the Luftwaffe again, and messages on the Red Luftwaffe code suggested strongly that Generalfeldmarschall Kesselring, head of German operations in the Med, was pushing for an invasion. Churchill had issued direct orders to ship more planes over to intercept aerial attacks before they hit the beleaguered island and a convoy of nimble Spitfires had recently set out, but would it be enough? Would they get through? And why couldn't the men in Hut 3 see how much more that mattered than their own petty power struggles?

Fran glanced nervously to her convoy map, noting the line that represented the aircraft carrier with the critical Spitfires and praying it got through. She'd had no letters from Ailsa for ages and the other day she'd broken protocol and asked a girl from personnel to check she was still on the books and therefore, hopefully, alive. She was, though there'd been a mark by her name that the girl had thought might mean injured and that had turned Fran's stomach. The Scottish girl may have been keen to see the world, but the world was a dangerous place right now and she was still very young.

Steffie, at least, seemed well. A postcard had arrived from her at the start of the year, bearing a picture of a bison and the comment, *Let's hope things change now there are new animals in the farm.* There had certainly been grand hopes around BP for what the entry of the Americans would mean to the war effort but so far there had been little concrete effect and they battled on alone. Last October, Alan Turing and a handful of his codebreaking friends had gone over Denniston's head to write direct to Churchill for more resources. The result had been an instant release of funds from the prime minster but, unfortunately, the release of Denniston as well. He'd been gently moved sideways into diplomatic codebreaking in White-hall, leaving Edward Travis in charge and the Park expanding at pace.

Everyone now knew about the 'bombe' machines that crunched the endless permutations of German codes, and WRENS were being recruited in their hundreds to run them. Everywhere you went you found girls in smart, navy-blue uniforms, arms linked and happy laughs tinkling in the deli-cately scented air around them. They were billeted at places like Woburn Abbey and various tales floated back of parties on the roof, apple-pie beds and shopping trolley races – as if, Fran thought scornfully, they were school kids, not workers in the most important intelligence unit in the country.

Dinner was no longer served with waiting staff in the dining room of the mansion but in a 24-hour canteen in a purpose-built building down near the gates. On the far side of the pond, massive concrete blocks were going up to rehouse sections that were straining at the seams of the wooden huts and, while Fran had to admit that more space would be good for her rapidly growing index system, she hated the impersonality of the larger staff and strict shift rotation.

'You British,' Valérie had tutted when she'd complained. 'You like things, how you say – amateur? Like your sports, yes? It is more noble, you all think, if it is done a bit wonky and improvised, rather than with efficiency and order.'

Fran had had to laugh at the embarrassingly accurate observation, but it didn't stop her missing the old days when it had been just a few of them battling with paper and pens, building tunnels for wooden trays, and playing rounders in their breaks.

She jumped, jerked out of her grumpy reverie as Humphreys slammed a new set of decrypts on her desk. Thanking him as sweetly as she could manage, she read the first message carefully, scanning as always for locations, names and any key references that could potentially be cross-linked with existing sources for a fuller picture. She picked out a few and put them onto cards, but slowly the overall sense of the Luft-waffe message began to penetrate and, putting down her pen, she read it carefully through.

47 ORKAN TO BE DELIVERED TO HERKULES. FX STANDBY.

She leaped up and ran to the index but she didn't need to check it to understand.

'Peter,' she called. 'Peter, the Luftwaffe are going to hit the new planes being sent to Malta.'

'What? How do you know?'

She showed him the message.

'Orkan is their codeword for our Spitfires. And Herkules is the airfield at Takali. FX is Fliegerkorps X, the Luftwaffe squadron based on Sicily. Look!' She tapped at a white line on the convoy map. 'We have a delivery scheduled for Malta from the USS *Wasp* tomorrow. This is an instruction to take out our planes before they even land.'

Peter read it over.

'It is,' he agreed. 'Humph!'

'What is it now?' Humphreys demanded.

'This message. Have you read it?'

'Of course. It's a simple instruction for a supply unit.'

'No, it isn't. This is a high-level operational command to attack. And you missed it.'

Humphrey's eyes narrowed.

'Could happen to anyone.'

'Anyone who's too busy blowing his own trumpet to listen to any other tune, yes. I'm taking this to the top.'

'You're going to tell on me?'

Peter shook his head.

'This isn't prep school, Squadron Leader Humphreys. I'm going to *report* you. Fran – get this to the teleprinters immediately and out to the SLU in Lascaris. Air Vice Marshal Lloyd needs to know.'

Humphreys looked flustered.

'I can tell Lloyd.'

'That's fine, thank you.'

'But I have a direct line—'

'Oh, we know. That's half the problem. Fran, please. I'll be back shortly.'

Peter nodded her towards the teleprinter room at the back

of the Hut and marched out of the door. Fran swallowed as Humphreys stepped across the passageway and folded his arms. Captain Curtis was at his back and suddenly, without Peter here, Hut 3 felt horribly volatile.

'I'll take that, thank you, Miss Morgan.'

Humphreys tried to pluck the message from her hands but Fran held on and it tore across one corner, leaving him with a pathetic triangle in his grasp.

'Peter asked *me* to teleprint it,' Fran said.

'And now I'm asking you to hand it to me.'

'With all due respect, sir, I don't report to you.'

Valérie stood up at her side and Fran gave her a grateful smile. Humph laughed coarsely.

'Ooh, look – is this your tame French poodle come to protect you? How sweet.'

'This is my colleague, come to help me do my job. Move aside please, Squadron Leader Humphreys, and let us through.'

'No.'

'No?! Why, pray?'

'Because you, missy, are a meddling girlie with ideas way above your station.'

For a moment, he sounded so exactly like her parents that Fran was blindsided and could find no appropriate retort. Valérie, however, had no trouble.

'On the contrary,' she snapped. 'Frances is a very intelligent woman who is – unlike you – working to defeat the Nazis rather than to further her own career.'

Humphreys squared his shoulders.

'I'm glad you think so, but we all know that your judgement, Mademoiselle Rousseau, is impaired by the fact that you lust after Miss Morgan.'

A gasp ran around the other workers in Hut 3 and Fran felt her face flare.

'How dare you?' she demanded, but Valérie was standing

between her and Humphreys, her tiny frame bristling with purpose.

'I do actually,' she agreed. 'Why would I not? A woman who knows her job and does it with skill and integrity is very attractive.'

Humphreys gave a boyish snigger.

'So you *do* have a crush on her?'

Valérie gave her Gallic shrug, the one that usually sent Fran squiggly inside but right now just made her squirm with mortification.

'Don't be ridiculous,' Fran said to Humphreys.

'I've heard about these French and their filthy habits. They'll go to bed with anything.'

'That's horrible,' Fran said. 'Take that back.'

She could feel all eyes in the hut upon them, the brightest, most intense ones being Valérie's.

'What about you, Frances?' Humphreys taunted. 'Maybe you have a crush on Valérie here. Maybe you want to kiss our French firecracker. Maybe you—'

'Of course I don't,' she snapped. 'Why on earth would I? Let us past this instant.'

Humphreys stepped slowly aside but his grin was sly as Fran marched past him and when she got to the teleprinter room she could see why. Valérie was still in the corridor, staring after her, hurt in every line of her petite body.

'Valérie,' she started, but before the word was even out of her mouth, Valérie had turned and run from Hut 3, slamming the door furiously against the wall in her haste to leave.

'Valérie!' Fran called again but now Peter was re-entering, looking confused by the whirlwind that had just passed him, and Travis was at his back.

'I think we have some serious discussions to hold,' the new commander said sternly, looking around at the gaping Hut 3 staff. 'To your desks please.'

Fran swallowed and caught Peter's eye.

'I still have this message to teleprint.'

'Go!' He nodded her to the teleprinter room and she fled thankfully.

There were several girls working the Typex machines and she asked one of them if she could slip hers to the front of the queue.

'Of course, Fran,' she agreed instantly, adding, 'What's going on back there?'

Fran rolled her eyes.

'Battle of egos.'

The girl tossed her head.

'Why don't they just get their dicks out and fence with them – that's what they want to do really.' Fran gave a snort of laughter at the unexpected suggestion and the girl grinned up at her and whipped the encrypted message off the Typex. 'D'you want me to teleprint it?'

'It's fine. I'll do it.'

Fran had been trained on the teleprinters with everyone else in the Hut so that any message could be got out by whoever was on duty. It was a curiously satisfying piece of kit and she checked the list of lines, dialled Lascaris, and began transmitting the critical information, every letter feeling like a stab at the Nazi regime.

'We're coming for you,' she muttered, glad to focus on this and ignore the heated discussions in the other room, not to mention the hurt look on Valérie's face as she'd slammed out of the hut.

She understood, she really did. It wasn't fair that Steffie could brag to everyone about her gorgeous fiancé – her gorgeous *enemy* fiancé – and they had to keep their own blossoming love quiet, but it was just how it was. She wasn't going to give the likes of Humphreys the chance to sully their relationship with his snide remarks and surely Valérie didn't want that either? As she slid back into her seat, however, all she could focus on was the empty space against her knees where Valérie should be.

She only half listened to Travis as he read the riot act to the warring hut and was glad to get back to her work when he'd finally finished. The commander took both Humphreys and Curtis away with him and Fran prayed they'd never come back. Already, the atmosphere felt calmer and, picking up the first message, she applied herself to the routine. It was a list of Italian POWs sent to hospital in Alexandria and the names would all need recording and cross-referencing to pick out any senior figures. She began to work her way steadily through and that's when she saw it – a name that wasn't especially senior but was very, very important, especially to one person: *Matteo Mancini.*

Leaping up, Fran made for the teleprinter machine once more. They were expressly forbidden to use it for personal messages but this was far too crucial for a damned postcard and, with a quick glance around, she sat back down at the teleprinter and dialled up Heliopolis.

TWENTY-THREE

Steffie

'There's a message coming through here looks a bit unusual. Says it's for SC. Do we have an SC?'

Steffie looked up as a young signals officer came into the office, waving a teleprinter slip. She'd been doing battle over a low-level code that seemed to mainly carry messages about the stockings and cosmetics the Italian officers' wives needed sending to them and was glad of the distraction.

'I'm SC,' she said, 'but I don't suppose it's for me.'

'I guess that depends on whether you know a Matteo Mancini?'

Heat shot through Steffie – joy mixed with fear – but she forced herself to stay calm. People were more relaxed out here but Matteo was still the enemy.

'Rings a vague bell,' she said casually. 'I'll take a look.'

The lad handed it over and, legs shaking violently, Steffie sank back against the nearest desk, not quite daring to read it. What if it said he was dead? She didn't know how she'd bear it. Not knowing where or how Matteo was was bad enough but she'd take that uncertainty for the whole rest of the damned war over finding out he was gone. Slowly she lifted the message and looked down, her eyes seeking the preamble – FAO SC. How strange. She read on for the sender's initials and saw it had come from England, operator FM.

'Fran?' she breathed.

Surely Fran wouldn't send her bad news? But even as she told herself that, she thought of her down-to-earth friend and wasn't so sure. Fran would probably take a 'she needs to know' attitude and... She tutted at herself to stop speculating and, taking a deep breath, read the message. It was short and to the point: *Matteo Mancini listed as POW. Alexandria Hospital.*

She swallowed, her throat suddenly as dry as if half the desert had blown into it.

'All well, Steffie?' Freddie asked, coming over.

Was it? Matteo was alive. But not well. If he was in hospital he was not well. Though, on the other hand, he might not be that ill. He might just have a small wound or a slight fever or... She stopped herself. The important thing was that he was close so if she could just get to Alexandria, she could see him, hold him, talk to him.

'It's my fiancé, Freddie,' she said. 'He's in hospital in Alexandria and I haven't seen him for two years. Could I possibly get permission to go?'

Freddie took the slip from her and raised an eyebrow.

'Matteo Mancini? Your fiancé is an Italian, Steffie?'

Steffie squirmed.

'Yes. That's why I haven't seen him. I met him before the war – before everyone had to take sides. He's not a bad man, I promise.'

'But he's still the enemy.'

'Not to me!'

She felt pathetic tears come and turned away to hide them. Where was a sandstorm when you needed it? But then she felt a fatherly arm around her shoulders and looked up to see Freddie smiling kindly at her.

'I understand that. Look, Steffie, if you can find a way to get to Alex, you can go. You're one of my best workers, so I'd say you've earned a little time off. Just, you know, don't talk to him about any of this.'

She pulled back, shocked.

'I wouldn't, Freddie! No way. Never.'

'Then off you go.'

'Thank you. Thank you so much.'

She flung her arms around him, kissing him heartily on his cheek so that he flushed and muttered 'get away with you' and 'there, there' in a way that made her want to hug him again. Sparing him, she grabbed her handbag and rushed out to find someone in transport and see how on earth she could get up the Nile Delta to the great port. She'd been hoping to see Alexandria for a while, but right now it wasn't the renowned Corniche walkway, or the ancient Catacombs of Kom el Shoqafa that were drawing her, just the city's simple military hospital and a treasure far greater than any pharaoh's gold.

An hour later and she was tearing her hair out in frustration. There were no staff cars or supply lorries going north for days. She could pay an Egyptian to take her up the river, but she'd been warned too many times about stepping into a vehicle alone with the locals to risk it. Then she remembered – Betty worked for the transport corps so surely she could get her a lift? Running out of the office, she made for their barracks.

The area had been extended and improved in the last six months and although they still lived in square tents, they now had a decent shower and lavatory block and the transport corps had a workshop where the women mended their vehicles between trips. Steffie threaded her way across the camp towards it but was stopped by a jaunty toot and turned to see Bonner Fellers coming towards her in his smart American jeep.

'Stefania! You're a sight for sore eyes this fine morning.'

Steffie forced a smile, though any delay felt like agony.

'Thanks, Bonner, but I'm in a bit of a rush. I've just found out my fiancé is in hospital in Alex and I'm looking for a lift to get to him.'

Bonner clutched his chest dramatically.

'Such romance! It will be my honour to carry you on my not-so-noble steed.'

He gestured to the jeep and Steffie's brain fought to catch up.

'You mean it?'

'Hop in, my lady. It's been ages since I went to Alexandria and I bet Washington would appreciate a report on the situation in port, especially now they might be getting involved over here.'

'They might?'

Bonner put a finger to his lips and winked at her.

'Anything is possible. Shall we go?'

Steffie stared at him, stunned. You had to hand it to Americans – their positivity and enthusiasm was second to none.

'Thank you,' she said, swinging herself into the passenger seat. 'That's so kind of you.'

He winked again.

'Hey, a guy gets a bit bored of reporting on men sitting around in tents in the sand. A trip to the seaside will do us both good, right?'

'Right,' Steffie agreed, already itching to get there. Three hours was going to feel like forever.

In the event, though, there was so much to see as they headed up the increasingly lush Nile Delta, that it passed surprisingly quickly. Bonner was an entertaining companion, though his opinion of the British had not improved much.

'It's not so much your guys on the ground,' he told her as they bounced past endless fields of corn. 'It's the top men. They're tactically poor. It's no wonder Rommel decided to attack; the positions your men were taking were far too weak.'

'But how did Rommel know that?' Steffie asked, startled.

'Reconnaissance, of course. You've seen the planes.'

Steffie had – it was always a relief when one went over with only a camera pointing out of the cockpit, but in truth they were every bit as dangerous as the guns, perhaps more so.

'I've reported back on it a number of times,' Bonner went on. 'There are too many of your officers sat on their arses in the Gezira Club when they should be out drilling the troops. If Churchill wants to convince Roosevelt to put American forces into Africa, then he needs to get his own house in order first. The embassy thinks I'm a defeatist, but I'm just a realist. The Allies can win in Africa but only if they sharpen up.'

'And get supplies.'

'That too,' he conceded. 'I hear Churchill wants to borrow US ships to get supplies to Malta but should we...?'

'Yes!' Steffie said.

'When virtually every convoy is being bombed by the Luftwaffe with unerring accuracy?'

'Someone has to get through or Malta will be starved into submission.' Steffie thought of Ailsa and her heart broke at the idea of her friend wasting away on some foreign shore. 'If Malta submits,' she went on determinedly, 'then the Luftwaffe will have a lethal base from which to control air and sea in the Med. And then we've all had it.'

Bonner nodded solemnly.

'That much is true. I'll try and impress on Washington how urgent it is.'

'You can do that?'

'I'm the military attaché, Steffie, that's my job.'

She gave him a sheepish smile.

'Of course. Sorry.'

'That and driving damsels in distress around,' he said graciously. 'I believe we're coming into Alexandria.'

He indicated the buildings ahead and Steffie looked around, distracted by her first sight of the ancient port. The outskirts were the usual scruffy mix of slums and warehouses but as they got closer to the centre, the roads opened out into great avenues and suddenly there were ancient temples and monuments at every turn. As they reached the harbour front and she saw the glorious blue shimmer of the sea, her spirits lifted. The air was the freshest she'd known since coming to Egypt, with a tang of salt that tickled at her dry lips. Sea birds squawked overhead and the chink of sail on mast marked out a pretty tune.

'And here we are.' Bonner pulled up in front of a large, white building and, as two orderlies rushed out and drew a moaning man from an ambulance, Steffie was pulled back into the reason for her visit and felt a new rush of panic.

'Will they let me in, Bonner?'

'To see the enemy?' She flinched but nodded. 'Hmm. Could be tricky. What you need is a senior officer with a shiny uniform and a few fancy braids.'

He puffed out his already large chest with a grin.

'Would you?'

'It would be my pleasure.'

With Bonner at her side, bristling with American confidence, she was swept through the hospital and into a secure unit at the back where men lay, as clean and well cared-for as the others, save that their hands were cuffed to the iron bedsteads. Steffie's stomach churned and she had to order herself to breathe. She put a hand to the door frame and Bonner gave her a friendly pat on the back.

'I'll go off to visit the naval lot and be back for you later.'

'Right. Thank you, Bonner.'

She watched him go, feeling lost, and then turned back into the ward.

'Can I help you?' a brashly pretty nurse asked.

'I'm here to see Matteo Mancini?'

'Lucky girl! This way.'

Steffie followed the nurse up the ward, jealously taking in the sway of her hips in her smart uniform and wondering what her words had meant – hopefully that Matteo wasn't too badly injured. Hopefully...

'Oh!'

He was asleep in the white bed, his hair dark against the pillow, his face handsome in repose and the lines of it achingly familiar. Steffie stilled, not wanting to wake him, not wanting to do anything but drink him in and take herself back to a time when he had been hers every day.

'What's wrong with him?' she whispered to the nurse.

'Bullet in the leg. Nasty wound but he'll recover.'

'Thank God.'

She looked sideways at her.

'What is Matteo to you?' Steffie lifted her hand and flashed her diamond and the girl frowned. 'Is that allowed?' she snapped and then she'd turned on her heel and was gone.

Apparently Steffie wasn't a 'lucky girl' any longer, but now Matteo was stirring and she ran to his side, taking his hand in hers. His eyes flickered open and she looked into their gorgeous chocolate-brown depths and saw disbelief morph into delight.

'Stefania?' Her name came out of him on a moan. 'Stefania, is that really you?'

He squeezed at her hand, as if checking she was real, and tried to push himself up on his pillows but winced in pain. Steffie smiled and leaned over, pressing a kiss onto his lips, soft and slow. He responded instantly and suddenly there was no hospital, no Egypt, no enemies, no war – there was just Matteo and she lost herself willingly in him.

TWENTY-FOUR

APRIL 1942

Ailsa

Ailsa turned her tuning dial with studied concentration, trying not to flinch when a bomb dropped onto the harbour below. It was hard. Since that terrible night in the shelter, she found it impossible not to imagine every bomb was coming straight for her, and given that Kesselring's skilled pilots were dropping them ten times a day, that was a lot of flinching. So far the Lascaris caves, deep in the ancient limestone cliffs, had held, but in her nightmares Ailsa often saw the cleft opening up in the ceiling of the shelter and it was hard not to imagine it happening again.

She fought to find a clear frequency but with the Luftwaffe back, the dive-bombers came in so low and so loud that it was almost impossible to hear anything over the drone and boom of endless death. Last week they'd had the terrible news that the boy who'd ridden to hospital with them had succumbed to his injuries after weeks of desperate fighting, and it had made her realise all over again how close to death she'd come – and might still come. Valletta was hit daily and the poor city was a mess –

more rubble than walls, with some streets totally blocked. Most of the Rediffusion system's speakers were blown apart or hung by threads and even the sirens sounded weary.

The opera house had taken a direct hit, a bomb ripping a gaping hole across its main facade, sending the funny wee post-card machine so high into the air that it was now lodged on top. Ailsa had stood beneath it, thinking of the day she'd put her tuppences in the slot to send pictures to Steffie and Fran, so proud of herself for getting to this glamorous location; it would be a dark irony indeed if she never got out again.

Not that the opera house mattered as much as the myriad homes that were being lost every day. This morning Ailsa had gone past a bombed-out hotel and seen a whole set of rooms exposed to the air. On the very top floor, a woman's chest of drawers had teetered on the edge, a vase of flowers still intact upon it. A young soldier had been valiantly climbing up the open wall to throw down the woman's clothes, making minia-ture parachutes in the dust-rich air. The crowd below had managed a cheer for the rescued items but it had been muted and they would all be cowering underground again now.

A bomb landed somewhere close by, making the wood across the once panoramic windows shake, and Ailsa with them. Sometimes, when she thought of that terrible New Year's Eve four months ago, she remembered how impressed she'd been by the resilience of the Maltese people, but that resilience was truly being called on now. The raids were so relentless that there was barely time to clear the bodies from the streets before the Luftwaffe were shrieking in over the harbour once more. And even if you weren't hit by bombs, you were starving – a slower but equally lethal death.

Last month a large convoy had set out across the Mediter-ranean with vital weapons and foodstuffs, but the Luftwaffe had been onto it immediately, forcing half the ships back to Alexandria and bombing the rest. Two ships had limped into harbour, but shockingly slow unloading had meant that the Luftwaffe had had time to come back with more bombs. All Malta's desperately needed supplies had been sunk in front of the hungry people they'd come to save and although divers had dredged the seas for weeks, little of real use had been brought to the surface.

Shops were empty and even black marketeers were struggling to find goods to sell. Bread was rationed at just ten ounces a day and even pasta, rice and tomato paste – the staples of the Maltese diet – required coupons now. The governor's wife had set up the optimistically named 'Victory Kitchens' where people could get a main meal for sixpence or a bowl of something like minestrone soup for three. It wasn't haute cuisine but it was hot and nutritious and helped out those who no longer had a home of their own in which to cook. The Maltese were a proud people, though, fierce in their hospitality, and while being fed in a communal kitchen was filling their stomachs, it was breaking their hearts.

At last the planes dropped their final loads and the skies outside the offices were clear once more. In their place, the wails of ambulances filled the streets and Ailsa fought not to picture all the people digging their loved ones out of the piles of destruction, as Ned had dug her out. She looked across to where he sat at the next radio set and he reached out a quiet hand to place over her own. She smiled. Ned was the bright spot in the darkness of this bedevilled spring. Steadfastly at her side, he knew when to prop her up and when to push her on. Without him here, she might have accepted Commander Hugh Lloyd's nervous suggestion that she was flown back to Britain after her 'nasty accident'.

'It wasn't an accident,' she'd told him crisply. 'It was a calculated attack and we're not going to stop there being more by heading home to hide.'

He'd patted her on the head, like a schoolgirl, and said no

more of it, but Ailsa had to admit that she wasn't feeling so bullishly brave with the whole of Valletta as much of a prison as
that dark alcove beneath the ground. She'd dispatched her letter
to her parents, written from the hospital on New Year's Day,
but could expect no reply, for no post came any more and there
was no going home. If they couldn't get supplies in, they sure as
hell couldn't get people out. And now the Germans were going
to invade.

The other day she'd picked up high-frequency signals transmitting furious messages. Direction-finding had pinned them
down to Rome at one end and the mountains of Bavaria at the
other – almost certainly Hitler's retreat in Berchtesgaden.
They'd teleprinted the whole set to BP and received the
decrypts some twelve hours later.

In theory, it wasn't in Ailsa's remit to hear the plain text, but
with the island under siege, most news spread around the
Lascaris operations centre freely – and this hadn't just been
'most news'. The messages had confirmed that Hitler and
Mussolini had approved plans for the invasion of Malta. Kesselring had signalled delighted confirmation from Sicily and their
only hope was protest from Rommel, who wanted all air power
to aid his planned assault on the Gazala line in North Africa.

Ailsa had sat there, absorbing the implications of these
wretched men's casual decisions as they sipped schnapps in the
mountains, far from the true hurt and suffering of the front
lines. For her, it was far more personal. If Kesselring got his way,
the Nazis could be knocking on their doors within the month; if
Rommel did, they would be knocking on Steffie's. It was hard to
see how the Allies could get out of this one.

'What can we do to stop them?' she asked Ned now.

'Make it impossible for them to land in any serious
numbers. The Spitfires should help.'

Twenty-five of the renowned fighter planes had finally
made it to Malta last month – somehow avoiding an attempted

attack by the Germans – and had made their first sortie just two days after arriving. Ailsa could still remember Ned's excited face as he'd thrust his headphones at her.

'Listen to this!'

Ailsa's German was still poor but even she had been able to recognise the frantic call of 'Spitfeuer! Spitfeuer!' and hear rare panic in the Luftwaffe pilot's voice. It had given everyone hope for a week or two, but without fuel or weaponry even the magical Spitfires weren't much use.

'The Spitfires need supplies – and so do we.'

Ned nodded grimly.

'There's a convoy due in a couple of weeks. We can hold out till then.'

Ailsa hoped he was right but now there was a new commotion down the corridor in Central Command. She waited nervously for the air-raid sirens but they didn't come. A whisper was passing round the office, buzzing as loudly as any Morse, and Ailsa grabbed at Marcia's arm as she passed by.

'What's happening?'

'Haven't you heard?'

Ailsa tutted.

'Obviously not or I wouldn't be asking, would I?'

'Oooh, grumpy! It's good news for once. You'll never believe it but we've got the George Cross.'

'Who has?' Ned demanded.

Marcia spread her arms wide.

'*We* have. All of us. The whole island is getting a gallantry medal – isn't it wonderful?'

'Wonderful,' Ailsa agreed, stunned, although a nasty, cynical bit of her wondered what use a medal was going to be. On balance, she'd rather have more bread.

The island, however, did not seem to agree. The happy news was blared out of every still-working speaker on the Rediffusion system and the next morning a picture of the medal was plastered across the front page of the *Times of Malta* alongside King George's speech in praise of the courage and strength of her people. The Maltese gathered around the harbour, singing and waving flags, and only the inevitable arrival of the Luftwaffe dispersed them.

The island's governor, Lieutenant General Sir William Dobbie, toured around telling everyone how proud he was of them and finally, after enforced stops in three air-raid shelters around Valletta during raids, he made it to Lascaris.

'Amazing work,' he kept saying, shaking any hand he could get to. 'Amazing work, amazing work.'

'If only those working to supply the island could do amazing work too,' Ailsa couldn't stop herself responding.

He looked at her sharply but then nodded.

'If only. Sadly, though, I received news this morning that May's convoy is going to be put back to June.'

'June?' Ailsa gasped. 'Can we last until June?'

'Just about,' the governor said, tapping the floor with his foot. 'On the current projections, capitulation is set at ten weeks.'

Ailsa gaped at him.

'We have ten weeks before we have to, to…'

'Surrender. Correct. We need a convoy, young lady, but it seems they are rarer, these days, than miracles. I am asking everyone to pray for us.'

Do we think God is listening any more? Ailsa wanted to ask but she'd said more than enough already and Lloyd was tugging the governor away. Ailsa watched him retreat and turned to Ned.

'If the Germans come, what will happen to us?' she dared to ask.

He didn't patronise her by dismissing her fears, or promising her the governor's miracle.

'I suppose we'll become prisoners of war.' Her stomach

clenched. 'But it's not happened yet, my darling girl, and we must fight on while we can.'

'How, Ned, without weapons and food?'

He tapped his headset.

'With information, of course. The more we know of enemy plans, the better.'

Ailsa wasn't so sure about that any more, but she dutifully put on her headset and began scrolling through the frequencies, looking for something – anything – that might get them a hook into Germany's seemingly impenetrable skin.

And that's when she heard it.

Not the tap-tap of Morse but a German voice, clear as day across the airwaves, and laughing. The sound chilled her to the core and she could not pull herself away. The words meant nothing to her, just a collection of consonants and vowels, seemingly all jumbled up, but there was no mistaking the triumphant tone.

'Bastards,' she muttered – a word she was using all too often. She heard her mother tut and half-smiled but then two words came out of the melee and she froze.

'Gute Quelle,' the far-off German said and instantly she remembered Ned translating that for her last year – good source. The man on the line gave a rippling laugh and another run of German and then it came again, clear and proud and unbearably smug: *'Unsere sehr Gute Quelle.'*

TWENTY-FIVE

Fran

Fran stared at the message coming out of the teleprinter down the secure line from Lascaris: *Alert. Suspected leak. Reference Gute Quelle in German comms. Serious implications on Convoy security in the Med.* As the words unscrolled before her, she felt them fit together all too neatly and glanced across to her convoy-plotting map. They had every Allied and Axis ship they knew about carefully plotted with string and pins, but presumably somewhere in Germany a girl not dissimilar to herself was doing exactly the same. And perhaps with even better intel.

'A totally *dis*similar girl,' she chided herself crossly, 'because she'll be a Nazi who believes that the German people are the only ones genuinely worthy of a place on God's earth.'

She ripped the print off the machine and was about to take it through to Peter when she spotted the operator initials in the preamble. AMI. Could it be? First Steffie and now Ailsa. She wasn't missing this chance.

Quick as a flash she typed out: *FM to AMI – how are you?*

There was an agonising pause then the teleprinter leapt

into life: *Hungry.* Fran smiled as she almost heard the word in Ailsa's soft brogue. *But safe. Got someone to look after me.*

Who? Fran shot back.

Tell you when I see you. Just get these convoys sorted. We really need them, Fran.

Fran's heart stung.

I'll do all I can. Chickens among the pheasants?

And geese with the ducks. Gute Quelle is dangerous. This is second reference to good source.

A shiver ran down Fran's spine at the thought.

Any other clues?

We hear him en clair. They all know. He's a joke to them. Find Gute Quelle. Please. Before he finds us.

Fran glanced to her index drawers, running the full length of the side wall.

If he's there, I'll find him. I promise.

Thank you. Got to go. Air raid siren. I miss you.

I miss you too.

Fran stood staring at the teleprinter for a long time, the spool of precious words clutched in her hand, but no more messages came.

Got to go. Air raid siren, she read again. She couldn't begin to imagine what life was like on Malta. She'd seen the news-reels, of course, and read all about how the 'plucky island' had been awarded the George Cross, but Ailsa's terse messages told the real story – shortages, danger, fear. Fran clutched the teleprinter spool to her chest, tears stinging her eyes, and wished with all her heart that it was her friend she was hugging. She'd only lived with those two girls for a few months but they'd been some of the best of her life and she hated the thought of either of them in trouble.

'Gute Quelle,' she said determinedly and buried herself in her index cards.

It wasn't easy. They were not words they'd automatically

sort out, so had no card of their own. She had to think laterally. She tried the 'technical terms' index and the 'topographical' index but no joy.

'Come on, Fran,' she urged herself.

Across the hut Valérie looked up but did not rise. Things had been horribly frosty since Fran had refused to admit their relationship to Humphreys. Against all her hopes, both Humphreys and Curtis had been removed from Hut 3, with Malcolm Saunders also resigning. The place was now being run with relative calm by Peter but, despite Fran's repeated advances, Valérie had refused to thaw.

Fran had tried to explain, tried bringing little gifts and writing notes in both English and French, but Valérie had just blocked her out. It made Fran's whole body ache with sadness and she swore she'd never felt so lonely as she did now, with Ailsa and Steffie gone and Valérie refusing to even speak to her. Whenever they were in the hut together, she felt as if every nerve ending in her body was wide open and right now it took all her effort not to cross the room and beg her to make up.

'Everything all right, Fran?' Peter asked, and she turned gratefully to him.

'There's a message come in from Ail— from the Y-station on Malta. They've picked up a reference to Gute Quelle.'

'Good source?'

'Yes. Apparently the Germans are laughing at us.'

She saw Peter's jaw clench and knew how he felt.

'Right then, let's show them just how funny we can be, shall we? Look up spies, agents, collaborators. Anything flagged as suspicious.'

Fran began flicking through cards again, trying to make connections. They had the heads-up on a few shady characters, especially in Cairo, but nothing she could make fit.

'It has to be someone with high-up connections,' Peter was saying, going through his own notes. Every week he did round-up reports on the longer-term trends and patterns in the decrypts and he was reading through as fast as Fran was checking her cards. 'So, an established agent. I'll check our pre-war records.'

Fran nodded but she wasn't really paying attention. Up above her was the map of the convoy routes, meticulously constructed from decrypts.

'Peter...'

He looked over but she hardly dared say it.

'What?' he demanded impatiently.

She took a deep breath.

'What if it isn't an agent? What if they're reading our codes?'

The small gasp that ran round Hut 3 told her just how many people were listening in to their exchange.

'Impossible,' Peter said crossly.

'Why is it?'

'Because our Typex machines are state of the art.'

'As are their Enigmas.' Peter gaped at her and she felt a sudden sting of fury. 'Oh, come on – surely it's the height of codebreaking naivety to believe your own codes are secure but your enemy's are not?'

Valérie stood up.

'She has a point, Peter. And "Gute Quelle" – good source. That doesn't sound like an agent, does it?' Fran gaped at this surprise support. 'What?' Valérie snapped. 'I know sharp thinking when I hear it.'

'Right. Yes. Thank you, Valérie.'

'Don't thank me – find this source. It could be the reason why they can jump on our convoys without any warning.'

'I know!' Fran agreed and turned with even greater urgency back to her indexing.

.   .   .

'Ever come across Gute Quelle?' she asked the evening shift indexer when she came in at four o'clock.

The girl frowned, thinking. She was a quiet, earnest youngster who spoke little but worked hard, which suited Fran fine.

'It does ring a bit of a bell. I think I might have lodged a query on Quelle with the codename boys.'

Fran spun round to Peter.

'Codenames, Peter! That's your area.'

He looked sheepish.

'We've got horribly behind since I shifted to convoy plotting. We've been promised more staff, but they have to have official training these days and it all takes time.'

Fran remembered her own 'training' – Peter pointing her to a pile of shoeboxes and telling her to sort them out as best she could.

'Is there a list waiting to be checked?'

He crossed the hut and pulled a large box file out of the corner cupboard.

'Less a list; more a pile. Give me some.'

Fran handed him a sheaf and took the rest back to her own desk.

'Here,' Valérie grunted, 'I'll do some too.'

'Really?'

'You look worn out.'

Briefly a knee nudged her own and the touch of it jolted through Fran like electricity.

'Thank you, Valérie.'

'Yeah, well – we work together, don't we?'

'Not as well as we used to,' Fran said quietly.

Valérie bit her lip and for a moment Fran thought she was going to respond but then she just buried herself in her share of the codename queries and silence fell. The clock ticked on. Their shift was officially long over but Fran, Valérie and Peter stuck at it until, at around eight o'clock, Valérie leaped up.

'Here – Gute Quelle! I've got it. I've got it, Frances!'

Fran leaped up and ran round to Valérie's desk and Valérie pulled her close to read the message. The familiar touch of her made Fran's head spin but she forced herself to concentrate.

HMS Galatea – direct hit. Strike 4 for Pilot Muller. Strike 1000 for Gute Quelle.

'Strike 1000?' she gasped.

'I think it might be German humour,' Valérie said.

Peter crowded in on Fran's other side, forcing her closer to the French girl, and she let her nose dip into Valérie's shiny hair, drinking in her heady scent.

'I think you're right, Valérie,' Peter was agreeing. 'When's this from?'

'That will be in the ship lists.'

'Right. Fran? Hello – earth to Fran!'

Fran jumped.

'Sorry. Miles away.'

'So I see. When was HMS *Galatea* sunk?'

It was all Fran could do to pull herself away from Valérie, but there was more at stake than her romantic mess-ups and she shot across to the index, finding *Galatea* with ease.

'Fifteenth December 1941.'

'Five months ago! And what comms did we send her route out on?'

Fran scanned the card.

'We didn't.'

'What?'

'She'd only just set out from port and was operating under radio silence when she was hit by a U-boat.'

'From what port?'

'Alexandria.'

Peter swallowed.

'So we're saying that the only people that would have known about this were navy command in Alexandria.'

'And anyone they'd reported to on the ground, yes. They use landline comms in Egypt wherever possible for security.'

'So the one thing we think we can say for sure is that this "Gute Quelle", whoever or whatever it is, is operating out of Egypt?'

Fran, Peter and Valérie looked at one another.

'That's about the size of it,' Fran agreed.

'Well, it's a start. I'll raise the alert with the higher-ups immediately. Great work, Fran. Can I fetch you something lovely from the canteen in recompense?'

'I doubt it,' Valérie said sardonically. 'Everything in there tastes like dog food.'

Fran snorted with laughter.

'Dog food would be good for me, Peter. I'm starving.'

Peter tipped an imaginary hat at them both and made for the door, leaving a sudden quiet behind him.

'You coming to do the teleprint?' Fran asked Valérie.

She got a small shrug but it was enough and she led the way down to the comms room at the back with a fleck of hope in her heart. There was one girl in there, nodding over her machine, and Fran sent her off for her break and took her place. Valérie swung herself up onto the table at her side and watched as Fran dialled Alexandria, GHQ in Cairo and then the outpost at Heliopolis. When she'd finally done, Fran looked up at her.

'I'm glad you're here, Valérie.'

'Hmm. Why did you send the last message with FAO SC at the top?'

Fran bit her lip.

'SC – Stefania Carmichael. I thought, perhaps, she'd pay the most attention.'

'Because?'

'Because it's come from me, I suppose.'

'And she's special to you?'

'She's my *friend*, Valérie. *Mon amie.*'

The French girl pouted and Fran stood up and moved towards her.

'There are friends who are special,' she said softly, 'and then there are friends who are so, so much more.'

Their faces were on a level and as Fran looked into Valérie's eyes, she could see a swirl of hurt and longing within them that made hope bloom. She dipped her head slowly downwards and felt Valérie tip her lips towards her for a kiss.

'Corned beef hash!'

She leaped back as the main door slammed open and Peter bounded in, waving a foil package triumphantly.

'Coming, Peter,' she called, turning back to Valérie.

But the prickly French girl had slid off the table and was pounding down the corridor and out into the night, with a muttered, 'Bloody English and their bloody dog food,' as she went.

Fran sighed.

'What's up with her?' Peter asked.

'Long story,' she groaned, and took the corned beef, though her appetite was gone and it was all she could do to force it down.

She'd thought it was boys she was useless with, she reflected darkly as she chewed on a strange piece of gristle in the hash, but it seemed it was anyone. Maybe the only relationship she'd truly get to enjoy was with her index cards. She grimaced at them. It wasn't their fault but, fascinating as she found them, they didn't warm her heart like Valérie did. Or carve it up like her either.

TWENTY-SIX

MAY 1942

Steffie

Steffie sat as close to Matteo as she dared, clutching at his hand and trying to ignore the fact that the other one was handcuffed to the bed. He'd tried to persuade the nurses to let him have time 'free to hold my fiancée', but they had not budged. Steffie supposed they were only doing their job but, oh, it would have been nice to cuddle.

Matteo's leg wound was nearly mended and he was due to be sent to a POW camp any day so she'd been very grateful when Bonner Fellers had offered her another lift up to Alexandria to see him. Already Steffie could feel his loss and cursed that she hadn't been able to spend more time here. With Rommel threatening the Gazala line and shipping in the Med under constant threat, even sympathetic Freddie had been unable to issue her much leave. Plus, of course, the man she was visiting was the enemy.

She wasn't alone. Plenty of people turned up in the prisoners' ward. Sometimes British airmen would arrive to see the pilots they had shot down, drawn by a bond with their fellow fliers, even enemy ones. Steffie had watched the gruff exchanges, like teams shaking hands after a rugger match, and wondered if it was all a game to some of these boys. No wonder the war was dragging on.

'It's noble, *tesoro*,' Matteo told her after she'd queried one young airman who'd sat for some time with the man he'd shot out of the sky. 'We wish to defeat the plane, not the man.'

'But the soldiers on the ground have to shoot each other.'

'Pah! Army – they are different.'

'It's still killing,' she'd said dully, and he'd stroked her cheek, told her she was beautiful and changed the subject.

It was hard, though, finding things to talk about without straying into dangerous waters. She longed to tell him about her work, about the men and women who shared her unique office and the vital intelligence they were gathering, but of course she could not. When he'd asked, she'd said – as instructed – that she was a secretary for the War Office, but it had stuck in her craw almost as much as the easy way in which he'd accepted it.

'Don't let them work you too hard, *tesoro*.'

'Oh, I enjoy it. I like having a purpose.'

'Ah, Stefania,' he'd said, pulling her close. 'Your purpose is to be with me, as mine is to be with you. We are merely marking time until our real life can begin together.'

Then he'd kissed her and she'd given in gladly, burying what she'd truly wanted to say in their embraces, though she'd tried again later.

'I think, maybe, even when we are married, I would like to work.'

'Work?' he'd gasped. 'You won't need to work, *tesoro*. I will keep you in style, I promise it. I may not look like much chained to this bed in stupid, cheap pyjamas, but once I am recovered, I will be a man again.'

'I don't doubt it, Matteo. That's not the point. What I'm saying is that I would *like* to work.'

He'd tapped gently at the side of her head.

'Has the war got to you, my beauty?'

'It hasn't got to me at all, Matteo. Sometimes I feel guilty because, although I hate all the horrid killing and I hate being apart from you, the war has treated me rather well. Look at me, here, in Egypt, doing, doing...'

'A secretarial job? Is that what your parents would want for you?'

'My father got it for me, actually, and I'm good at it, Matteo.'

'That I don't doubt, *cara*. You are a smart, sassy, brilliant woman. You have fire and can turn your glorious flame to whatever you wish, so don't waste it on typing.'

Oh, it had been so hard not to say more.

'Not on typing, no – but I'd like to do something.'

'Charity work?' he'd suggested. 'Running balls and gala days and the like. You'd be amazing at that.'

'Thank you,' she'd managed.

He was probably right, she would be quite good at that and she'd even enjoy it, but did she want to be a society hostess? She had done before the war. If it wasn't for Hitler, she'd no doubt be holding salons and parties and dinners while Matteo climbed his way up military ladders just like her father. And what was wrong with that?

'What about when we have children?' Matteo had gone on and the thought of the miniature Steffie and Matteos they would produce to run around their pretty marital home had banished her worries. They'd spent the rest of that visit discussing names and places they'd like to take their future brood, and she'd been happy, but now, with Matteo close to being sent off to POW camp, she felt a renewed rush of fear that these dreams would never become a reality.

'I don't want you to go,' she said, pressing his hand.

He looked furtively around then leaned in and said, 'At least I won't be flying again.'

She looked at him in surprise.

'I thought you loved flying?'

'I do, but I don't like shooting at people and I hate dropping bombs. It's awful, Steffie. All I have to do is press a button on my shiny dashboard and seconds later, boom – people are being blown out of the homes below me. It's not right, not...'

'Noble?'

'Exactly. Do you think that's silly?'

She kissed him, long and slow.

'I think it's admirable, Matteo. Why would I want a husband who enjoys killing people?'

Matteo gave a sigh of relief.

'I don't even feel as if they are my enemy,' he whispered. 'Why do I want to bomb the Maltese? They are our neighbours, our friends.'

'The Maltese?' Steffie sat up straighter. 'You've been bombing Malta, Matteo?'

'Sssh!' He gestured around the ward and she bit her lip. They were talking in Italian but there were plenty here who could understand.

'Sorry, but Malta?'

'I had to bomb somewhere, Steffie, and that's where they've been sending me. Does it matter?'

'I have a friend on Malta.'

'Really? Who? Someone I know?' She shook her head. 'Someone from finishing school?'

'No.'

He stared at her.

'A man or a woman?'

'A woman, of course. Someone I trained with.'

'Who's now on Malta?'

'Yes.'

'Being a secretary?'

'Yes!'

He shrugged.

'You British are very strange, sending your women into such dangerous places. Italian women are not doing that.'

'They must be working at home?'

'At home, yes. They are running the factories and the shops and the offices, of course. Italian women are amazing. But we are not sending them out of Italy.'

'I don't see the difference,' Steffie said, pulling away from him. 'If I can work in an office at home, why not in Cairo?'

'I am sure you can, *tresoro*, but you cannot be cherished in the same way.'

'Nonsense! And why would I want to be "cherished" when I can be useful?'

Matteo looked hurt.

'I cherish you, *cara*.'

She drew in a deep breath. This could be their last time together for too long; they should not be fighting.

'Thank you, Matteo. You know, I mainly came to Cairo in the hope of being near you – and it worked.'

'It did, my bold beauty. I love you.'

She kissed him. Kissing was easier than talking sometimes. There were so many things they couldn't tell each other and it created gaps. Maybe if Matteo knew what she was actually doing he would understand better, but she couldn't tell him. She pictured the Official Secrets Act displayed on the desk in front of her, Fran and Ailsa that very first night in Bletchley Park, and shook her head. It felt so long ago. She'd come so far and she wasn't sure she could ever truly go back again. Her work was vital, which reminded her...

'Matteo,' she said, low-voiced, 'have you ever heard the Germans talking about a Gute Quelle?'

'A what?' He frowned. 'What does that mean?'

She looked at him curiously. She'd thought his German was reasonable but clearly not. Still, that might help her.

'Something like 'good... good egg,' she fudged.

'Good egg? Heavens – the Germans have expressions as strange as you English. Gute Quelle...?'

'Sssh!'

She looked nervously around. She really shouldn't be talking about this but ever since she'd received the teleprinter message from Fran she'd been worried. No one else seemed to be taking it seriously. General Sansom had got nowhere, despite his assurances, and others out here seemed to share his attitude that you had to play the game and hope your lot got more information than theirs. But what if the Germans were reading their codes? Everyone at BP knew what golden treasure decrypts were to the Allies; they would be just as valuable to the Axis. Every spare moment she had, Steffie was making enquiries, but she'd got nowhere and maybe, just maybe, her fiancé – her 'enemy' fiancé – might know something.

'It does ring a bell,' Matteo said, considering. 'I think I've maybe heard my squadron leader mention it when setting the coordinates for a strike. Why?'

'Setting the coordinates?'

'Yes, you know – telling you where to fly to before you, you know...'

'Drop the bombs?'

'Exactly.'

'So this, er, good egg tells them where the ships will be?'

He frowned at her.

'Should we be talking about this, Steffie?'

She bit her lip.

'Probably not. Forget it.'

'Funny thing for a secretary to be asking about.'

'Oh, you know secretaries, we hear all sorts. And I was just interested in the, er, the German. It wasn't a phrase I knew from finishing school.'

'Because they only taught you to say "what a lovely dress" and "aren't these canapés divine", right?'

'Right,' Steffie agreed with a horribly fake-sounding laugh, but Matteo didn't seem to notice.

'I wish we could go back to Rome,' he said wistfully.

'Me too.'

'Really?'

'Yes. Back to Rome, back to before the war, back to everyone being friends.'

'Ah, yes.'

'Is that not what you meant?'

'Sort of.'

Silence fell between them and Steffie shifted awkwardly.

'When will they take you away, Matteo?'

He grimaced.

'I'm due to be "assessed" tomorrow, so it could be any time after that.'

'Where will you go?'

'I don't know. The man across the way says it will be to a camp near something called the Great Bitter Lake. Have you heard of it?'

'Yes!' Steffie was delighted. 'It's just above Suez, about two hours from Cairo. Maybe I'll be able to visit you.'

'Maybe,' he agreed but there was a catch in his voice and he looked suddenly furtive.

'Matteo? Do you know something about the camps?'

'Sssh.' He pulled her down as close as his chained wrist would allow. 'I know only, my darling, that I might not even get there.'

'Why? What will they do to you?'

'Nothing. Sssh, *cara*. It is simply that I have a plan.'

'A plan?'

'To escape.' He put a hand over her mouth to keep her quiet. 'It is a good plan.'

'This is a high-security ward, Matteo.'

'I am aware,' he said drily, rattling the chain of his hand-cuffs. 'But don't worry – I know people.'

'Matteo, I don't think—'

'You don't need to think, *cara*, or to know more of it, save that it stands a fine chance of working.'

'And if it doesn't?'

'If it doesn't, I will go the camp.'

'But if they catch you—'

'They will discipline me, but this is British territory. The British idea of discipline is a "damned good thrashing", right?'

'Well...'

'I am not, thank the Lord, captured by the cruel Nazis.'

'Your *allies*.'

He put a dramatic hand to his heart.

'Not mine, *cara*.'

'But Italy's.'

'I know, I know. Musso has got himself in a bind. All he really wanted was Suez and now he has a bloody great big war on his hands.'

'As do we all,' Steffie hissed furiously.

'Which is why, if you listen, *mio tresoro*, I want to escape. And I want you, Stefania, my girl, my fiancée, my wife, to come with me.' Again his hand went over her mouth but it did little to smother her gasp. 'It will be very romantic. We will get a boat out of the harbour and back to Italy.'

'How?'

'I told you – I know people. Sssh. We will get the boat and we will get to Italy and we will go to my grandfather's villa in the farthest corner of the Lepini hills and be happy together.'

He made it sound so simple but Steffie wasn't fooled.

'What would we live on, Matteo?'

'Local produce.'

'You know how to grow things, do you?'

'Grandfather has a farm run by a marvellous old couple.'

'And they will be happy to feed you, you think?'

Matteo frowned.

'Why would they not?'

'Perhaps because you are hiding instead of fighting?'

He gasped.

'You said you loved that I did not like killing people.'

'I *do*.'

'And if I was in a POW camp, I would not be fighting.'

'True.'

'But this way we can be together, be happy, not be at war.'

It was an attractive idea, but it just didn't feel right.

'*I* would be hiding though, Matteo.'

'You?'

'I would be hiding instead of doing my job.'

'Your secretarial job? I'm sure the Brits will find someone else to type their messages.'

Steffie ground her teeth and Matteo pulled her closer. 'Come with me, Stefania. Marry me for real. Why should we wait for our future just because some stupid men want to take parts of the world that do not belong to them?'

It was an excellent point and the picture of them living as man and wife in the hills was an idyllic one but...

'I can't, Matteo. It sounds lovely but the locals wouldn't want a Brit in the area.'

He tossed his head.

'Your Italian is perfect, *cara* – they'd never know.'

She sighed. He had an answer for everything – bar the one critical point.

'I'd be letting people down.'

His eyes narrowed.

'And letting "people" down matters more to you than letting *me* down?'

'No! Matteo, please. It's wartime. Fascism is a terrible, terrible force and has to be defeated. I would love to hide from it all with you but if I can do even one thing to help stop the Nazis, then I have to stay.'

He drew himself away.

'It seems you are the noble one now,' he said stiffly.

'It's not because I don't love you, Matteo.'

'Just that you don't love me enough.'

'No! You're not seeing this right. This is war and I want to do my bit.'

'You think your little letters will stop Hitler?'

'No, but I think that everyone doing their own tiny part just might. If we all run away, then he *will* win. It's different for you, Matteo. I understand that you don't want to go to a camp but I'm not a prisoner and I have to keep on working.'

He yanked his hand away.

'So you won't come with me?'

She drew in a deep breath. Pain was tangling in her stomach at seeing the hurt in his gorgeous eyes but this was important.

'No. Not now. But after the war—'

'You won't be my wife and stand at my side, as you swore to do in the Temple of Aesculapius?'

That was a low blow. Steffie remembered that night so vividly – their earnest vows, whispered to the stars.

'I *will* be your wife and, in my heart, I will be standing at your side.'

'But in reality, you will be a thousand miles away?'

'Yes.'

He shook his head.

'I don't want a wife like that.'

'What?' Pain stabbed through Steffie. 'Matteo, you don't mean that.'

'I do.' He backed up against the bed frame he was shackled to, pushing her away with his feet. 'You've changed, Steffie. You're not as much fun now.'

'Fun?! You're in hospital with a war injury, Matteo, and you want me to be fun?'

'Why not? A wife should cheer her husband up.'

'And a husband his wife.'

'Which is why I suggested you come—' He cut himself off. 'Just go, Steffie. I'm glad I've found out how little you value me. It hurts. It hurts more than being shot out of the sky, but my leg has mended and maybe, one day, my heart will mend too.'

Steffie fought for breath.

'You're... you're finishing with me?'

'It's for the best. I would hate to shackle you to my cowardly ways when you are clearly so important.'

'Matteo, you are being petty, you—'

'My *petty*, cowardly ways.' He drew himself up as tall as he could on the bed. 'My ring, please, Stefania, if you don't mind. It was my grandmother's and she would hate for it to go to waste on someone who is not fully committed to the family.'

Tears ran down Steffie's cheeks.

'I *am* committed, Matteo. You're not being fair. There's a war on.'

'Not in Lepini. My ring. Please.'

Steffie looked down at him. He looked small suddenly, cowed by his pride and fury, and she felt her own anger rise.

'Fine. If that's how you feel, here's your precious ring.'

She tried to yank it dramatically off her finger but it had been there for nearly three years and was reluctant to relinquish its grip on her skin. For an agonisingly long time she stood, working it over her knuckle as Matteo watched, hand still outstretched, and the nurses whispered in the corner of the ward. Eventually it was free but the drama had gone and she stepped forward and placed it gently into his hand. His own fingers wavered but then closed around it.

'Goodbye, Stefania.'

'Goodbye, Matteo. And good luck.'

Then she spun on her heel and, head held high, stalked out of the ward. The nurse who'd first shown her in sniggered as she passed but she forced herself to keep on looking forward and it was not until she left the hospital and stumbled down the steps to a waiting Bonner Fellers that she collapsed.

'Oh dear,' the American said. 'Not gone so well with your fiancé?'

'He's not my fiancé any more,' Steffie said darkly. 'Can we go home please?'

Three days later, head low over the weather reports to hide her red eyes, Steffie was finding it hard to concentrate on anything but that bitter conversation with her fiancé – ex-fiancé. She'd gone over and over it, tossing and turning in her bunk, trying to remember every nuance of the debate and where it had gone wrong. Should she have said yes? Should she have agreed to meet Matteo and flee to the hills? It would have been lovely in theory but she'd have felt so guilty leaving everyone in Heliopolis in the lurch. And would it not have made her a traitor? Would she even be safe in Italy? Why had Matteo thought it reasonable to ask that of her?

Because he's a romantic, had come back the answer in her head but if so, what did that make her? A realist? A pessimist? A grumpy woman who didn't love him as much as she should?

'No,' she muttered, pressing so hard with her pencil that it snapped. She had loved him, she *did* love him. But she had her job. Freddie said she was good at it, that she was a valuable member of the team, and that had to count for something.

She rose to fetch a pencil sharpener and caught sight of two men in Freddie's office talking intently. They wore the white chest band and red cap of the military police and were carrying rifles, not something usually seen in the cerebral Heliopolis office. Freddie glanced over, his eyes met hers, and she saw a disturbing mix of horror and confusion in them.

'Miss Carmichael, could you come here please?'

She gaped. Her boss never called her by her surname.

'Of course.'

Self-consciously adjusting her hair and praying her eyes weren't too swollen, she went through to Freddie's office.

'Miss Carmichael?' the elder of the two policemen asked.

'Yes.'

'You are under arrest.'

'Arrest?! Why?'

'I ask that you come quietly to avoid unnecessary use of force.'

He reached out to take her arm but she yanked back.

'I will if you tell me what I'm supposed to have done?'

'I was going to keep this discreet but if you insist...' He puffed out his chest. 'You are arrested, Miss Carmichael, on charges of aiding and abetting an enemy spy.'

'A spy?'

'A potentially dangerous spy – Matteo Mancini.'

'No!'

Steffie's legs gave way and she was almost grateful when the two policemen stepped up and took her arms.

'I've done nothing,' she said. 'He was my fiancé, that's all, and we aren't even engaged any more. I was visiting him in hospital because I... I love him. But we didn't talk of the war. Ask him.'

'We would,' the policeman said grimly, 'if he hadn't escaped.'

'He did it?' The words were out before she could think, but she knew instantly that they would damn her.

'You knew?'

'He told me he had a plan. He asked me to go with him but I refused. He's aiming to get a boat to Italy, I know that much. He's going to hide in his grandfather's house in the Lepini hills.'

'A much-discussed plan, it seems, Miss Carmichael, and one that needed someone on the outside.'

'Yes, but not me. He said he knew people.'

'Oh, he knows people. He's intimate with Mussolini.'

'Well of course. They used to go to the same parties. We all...'

She bit back the end of the last sentence but the policemen were exchanging smug glances and even Freddie was looking at her askance.

'Please,' she said, looking desperately to her boss. 'It's no secret that I lived in Rome before the war. My father was the military attaché, I moved in all the diplomatic circles.'

'Making you exceptionally useful to the enemy,' the policeman said, 'especially now you work in intelligence. We've been to your tent, Stefania. We've seen your personal goods. You're communicating regularly with people in both Malta and Bletchley Park.'

'My friends.'

'Your *contacts*. Tell me about the farm, Miss Carmichael.'

Steffie felt the world close in on her; what on earth was going on?

'The farm?'

'We've seen your messages. It's clearly code. How big is the network? How far have you penetrated?'

'It's not like that!'

'Oh, come on. We're hunting a spy, Stefania – a spy operating out of Cairo and known to the Germans as Gute Quelle.'

'I know! I've—'

'And we think *you* are it.'

This time Steffie's knees did give way and she had no strength left to protest as Freddie slowly opened his office door and the military police marched her out of the building and down the steps to a blacked-out van.

TWENTY-SEVEN

Ailsa

Ailsa pulled her headset off and shook out her hair, massaging her ears where they ached from the metal edges. The cushioning had long since crumbled away but there was no chance of getting more shipped to poor, besieged Malta so they had to make do and mend. She'd attempted a repair with fabric from a pair of stockings worn so thin they looked more risqué than bare legs, but it was impossible to get the improvised padding to stick properly and these days she'd learned to tolerate having ears as red as her hair.

'Ice?' Ned suggested and she looked over and smiled.

'Good idea. I'll fetch it.'

The lowest of the Lascaris caves were so cold that ice could be stored there and, with the weather hotting up, they'd all taken to fetching cubes up for their drinks, and to cool their sore ears. Iced water was a small luxury but in this time of extreme deprivation they made the most of it and Ailsa pushed her chair back, grabbed a miniature bucket, and headed down the corridor.

There was some sort of commotion in the main ops room and she glanced curiously in as she passed. Two men in brown uniforms with white bands and scarlet caps were talking earnestly to the air commodore, who seemed most agitated. Wondering who was in trouble, she crept past.

Down below it was blissfully cool and Ailsa took her time easing the ice cubes out of their metal trays, refilling the trays with the water from the bucket, then scooping up the precious blocks in their place. Her stomach rumbled with ever-present hunger and she popped a cube into her mouth to fool it into thinking she was providing some sustenance. It didn't work.

The convoy they so desperately needed had been put back again to August and everyone on the island was on their knees. Fuel for the valiant Spitfires was coming through on the subs, but that meant no room for food. Sometimes Ailsa felt so giddy with hunger that the Morse code seemed to swim around her brain. She had to battle to separate out the dots and dashes, praying that some of them would form into something magical to break this horrible siege. The Luftwaffe attacks had dropped off since April had turned into May but everyone said that was because they were gearing up for invasion and every morning Ailsa woke up expecting to hear German shouts from the beaches.

Malta wasn't easy to invade. The only beaches not over-looked by steep cliffs were in the north, and a line of hills just inland would make any beachhead almost impossible to break out of. The only clear line of entry was the harbour right here in Valletta, strongly defended by the ancient walls lined with anti-aircraft guns that could be pointed just as effectively at advancing ships as planes. The island's natural defences had kept it safe until now, but guns were no use without bullets and defenders no use if they hadn't enough food to stand, let alone fight. Malta was ripe for the picking and they all knew it; the only question was when they would come.

Ailsa leaned back against the cool wall and closed her eyes. Her brief exchange with Fran on the teleprinter two weeks ago had been a wonderful contact with a world beyond Malta's ravaged shores and she could still remember those precious words coming off the loop: *FM to AMI – how are you?* For a moment, she'd been back in the caravan at the end of a shift, chatting to Fran over a cup of tea, or a glass of Alfie's illicit gin, and the world had felt halfway normal again. But then the air-raid sirens had blared their constant, vicious warning and she'd been torn away.

'Ailsa?'

She opened her eyes to see Ned looking at her in concern.

'Ned! Sorry. Was I ages? It's so cool and quiet down here, and I'm so tired.'

He stepped forward, pushing her hair back off her face and kissing her tenderly.

'It's not that. There's, er, some people here to see you.'

'People?'

'Some policemen.'

Ailsa remembered the strange uniforms she'd seen talking to Hugh Lloyd in the ops room.

'To see *me*? Why?'

'I don't know but they look very serious. They came asking for you and when you weren't in the office they went a bit mad. One of them said "Don't let her escape!"'

Ailsa stared at him, trying to process what on earth he was going on about.

'Are you sure they want *me*?'

'They seem pretty certain.'

'Well, we'd better go and find them then.'

She turned for the ice bucket but Ned was still holding her and staring deep into her eyes.

'They don't look very nice men, Ailsa.'

'Probably for the best in their line of work, but I've done nothing wrong.'

'I know! Oh God, Ailsa, I know that. But things can get twisted, can't they?'

'What things? This is obviously just some misunderstanding. Don't worry.'

He smiled weakly.

'But I do worry, Ailsa – I worry because I, I love you.'

Ailsa blinked. She and Ned had been spending a lot of time together and, although she hadn't examined her feelings too closely, she knew he was important to her. This, though, felt like more. She looked into his eyes, seeing his warmth, his care, his clear concern, and she realised he wasn't just important; he was everything. Without Ned, she would have fallen apart on this beleaguered island, but with him, despite the bombs and the hunger and the endless grind of spending half your days underground, she could honestly say it had been the happiest time of her life.

'I love you too,' she said simply.

She leaned in to kiss him back, but they sprang apart as boots rapped down the stairs.

'Here you are, Miss MacIver – you can't hide from us.'

'I wasn't trying to,' she said, stepping forward so that Ned had to let go of her. 'I was just fetching ice.'

She reached for the bucket but the closest of the policemen knocked it out of her hand as if it were a grenade and the cubes went smashing across the rock floor.

'Was that really necessary?' she asked mildly.

'We can't be too careful with suspects,' was the sharp retort. 'Miss MacIver, I am arresting you for aiding and abetting a spy.'

'A spy?!'

'I suggest you come quietly.'

'Of course,' she agreed. 'I wouldn't dream of anything else

and I'm sure this is all a misunderstanding. I'm a simple radio operator.'

'Not so simple,' the policeman growled, ushering her up the stairs. 'You, Miss MacIver, look to be coordinating the comms on an operation codenamed "The Farm".'

'The Farm?' Ailsa stopped so suddenly that the man ran into the back of her. She turned to look down on his scarlet cap and his equally scarlet face beneath. 'The Farm is just a joke, a game I play with two friends.'

'It may be a game to you, girlie,' was the dark reply, 'but it's deadly serious to us. Now – move!'

TWENTY-EIGHT

Fran

The knock at the door was so hard that it shook the whole caravan. Fran looked up, terrified. The sun was going down outside the windows and for the first time since moving here she felt isolated.

'Who is it?' she demanded, grabbing a kitchen knife.

'Police! Open up.'

She glanced out the window and, sure enough, standing on the steps in the red caps of the military police, were two burly men. Gloria and Alfie were huddled in the farmyard, openly staring, and Fran went to the door feeling her simple baked-bean supper curdling in her stomach.

'Can I help you?'

'We very much hope so. Can we come in please, miss?'

'Of course.'

She stood back to let them enter and gave Gloria and Alfie what she hoped was a reassuring wave.

'You need me, our Fran, and you just shout,' Alfie called across and Fran's heart melted with gratitude. She'd never been 'our Fran' before and the sound of it calmed her stomach.

'Thank you, Alfie, but I'm sure it will be fine,' she managed.

Even so, the men seemed to loom large in the caravan and she chose to leave the door open as they set about poking around the cupboards, their heavy hands rattling Gloria's pretty crockery.

'Is something the matter?'

They turned back to her, having the grace to look sheepish as they closed the cupboard doors.

'We have orders to arrest you, miss.'

'Arrest me?'

'On suspicion of aiding and abetting an enemy spy. What do you have to say?'

Fran looked them up and down.

'I have to say that's total nonsense,' she told them crisply. 'Who on earth sent you?'

'Classified information, I'm afraid, but let me assure you it's from the highest possible level. We are hunting down a "Gute Quelle"—'

'Yes,' Fran agreed eagerly. 'So am I. Ask Peter Lucas. Ask anyone in Hut 3. My friend, Ailsa, radioed the term in from Malta and we've been combing our indexing for clues.'

'Clever of you.'

'Not clever, just a lot of diligent—'

'Clever of you to cover your tracks that way.'

'What? No! I—'

'Tell me about The Farm, Miss Morgan.'

'The farm? What farm?'

'We believe it to be an elaborate code system for a potential network of spies working to undermine Allied positions in the Mediterranean.'

'Do you?' Fran looked from one man to the other, fighting a dangerous urge to laugh. 'Do you really?'

'And we believe you to be at the heart of it.'

Fran nodded.

'I suppose I am.'

'You admit it?'

They both stood up straighter, as if unable to believe their luck, and she shook her head.

'Oh, I admit it all right, if what I'm admitting is to sending messages to my friends about ducks and chickens and geese.'

'Your "friends" Stefania Carmichael and Ailsa MacIver?'

'Those *friends*, yes. We created it together.'

'The network?'

'The farm. Would you like to see it?'

'See it?'

Confusion cut across their complacency.

'Yes. See it.'

She gave her finest tourist-guide wave to the little table on which sat the blue table mat, the barns, pebbles, grassy tuft and freshly painted collection of children's animals.

'But this, this...'

'Is a toy,' Fran agreed calmly. 'Correct. It is a toy farm that we found under the bed when Ailsa and I moved in with Stefania and that she used to explain the situation in the Mediterranean to us. She'd been living in Rome for years before the war, you see, so knew the area. Ailsa and I were not so well-travelled, so were grateful for the education. We used the animals to represent German, Italian and British forces in order to further our understanding of the Allied and Axis positions and, because it amused us, we continued to use those terms in our postcards.' The two men were shifting uncomfortably. 'Just girls' stuff,' Fran added, going for the jugular. 'Silliness really, but it helped us.'

'Girls' stuff?' the first officer repeated gruffly.

'Silliness?' the second one said.

'Exactly,' Fran agreed.

'We'll have to take this as evidence,' the first one decided.

'Please do. Would you like the box?'

'Erm, yes. Thank you.'

Fran bent down and pulled the original box from beneath the bunks. It was painted in bright, primary colours with a lovely picture of two children playing with the metal animals and she tried not to smile as the two men fumbled the toys inside.

But then the first one turned to her and said, 'Right, Miss Morgan – what about Gute Quelle?'

'It means good source in German.'

'Oh, we know.'

'And we've been picking it up on messages surrounding troop movements in Africa and shipping in the Mediterranean.'

'We know that too – the question is, who is it?'

'Well, exactly.'

'Do you know Matteo Mancini, Miss Morgan?'

Fran's heart stopped.

'Matteo Mancini, Steffie's fiancé?'

'Matteo Mancini, the Italian spy.'

All amusement drained out of Fran. Had she inadvertently been giving BP secrets to the enemy? What on earth would her parents say? This would prove her as useless as they'd always thought. Sinking back down onto the bench, she looked desperately around the caravan as its bright walls seemed to close right in on her.

TWENTY-NINE

Steffie

'*Sag mir was du weißt!*'

The man stood over Steffie, so close that spittle flew into her face as he fired out the words – tell me what you know. He'd been shouting at her in German all morning and she'd done her best to understand and reply. She wasn't going to hide her knowledge of the language. They had her file. They knew she'd been to finishing school in Switzerland, just as they knew she'd grown up in Rome. BP had employed her for her language skills and now they were using them against her.

'*Ich weiß nichts,*' she insisted – I know nothing. 'Actually, that's not true,' she said, switching to English. 'I know that the Germans have a "Gute Quelle" telling them more than we would like about our movements and I've been working to try and find out who it is. Ask Major Sansom, I spoke to him a while back about my concerns. Why would I do that if Gute Quelle was me?'

'Double bluff,' the man said scornfully. 'Do you think we're stupid?'

'Do you think *I* am? Why would I be talking to BP about it? Why would I be encouraging their finest indexer to search out the term if it was likely to lead to me? Hut 3 identified that the leak was coming from Cairo.'

'How do you know?'

'Because I saw the teleprinted message. Look, I've told officers all this already. I'm sorry Matteo escaped and I should have alerted the hospital of his intentions but he'd just broken off our engagement and all I wanted to do was get out of there. I told you where he said he was going – surely it's up to you to chase him down?'

'Oh, we will,' she was assured. 'We already have your contacts in Malta and Bletchley under arrest.'

'You have Ailsa and Fran?'

'We do. Does that worry you, Miss Carmichael?'

'Of course it worries me. They're my friends.'

'And one of them will crack very soon.'

'Crack?! What are you doing to them? The Geneva Convention means that—'

'We know all about the Geneva Convention, thank you, Miss Carmichael. And we know all about your fancy contacts. Daddy has been in touch and it's been explained to him that you are under serious suspicion and cannot be granted any special treatment.'

Steffie rubbed at her weary eyes, hating the fact that her father knew about this. He'd be very concerned for her, and her mother would be having fits. She'd be weeping and wailing and berating herself to all her friends for not getting Steffie married off to a nice Englishman who'd keep her out of trouble. That was nonsense, but it hurt terribly that Major General Carmichael might feel she'd let him down. She'd been so happy in BP, so proud of herself for getting onto the codebreaking team, and so pleased when Freddie Jacobs had praised her work. Now all that was ruined. She should have damned well run away with Matteo after all.

'Are you hungry, Miss Carmichael?'

She was. The rations in the military prison were thin and unpleasant and maybe this man could bring her something halfway edible. But then she thought of Fran and Ailsa imprisoned because of her damned fiancé and all appetite left her.

'No. Thank you.'

'I'll fetch food anyway.'

He slid out of the room, locking it noisily behind him and leaving Steffie willing herself to come up with something that would convince the authorities of their innocence. Nothing came, however, and a little time later the door ground open and a tray laden with cold meats and cheeses came into the room, carried by a new officer. Despite herself, her mouth watered.

'Help yourself, Steffie.'

The man placed the tray in front of her and sat down, one leg crossed casually over the other as she dug into the prosciutto. It tasted of her Italian home and she saw the irony of that but ate anyway. She'd need all her strength if this was to be another interrogation, but the man's first question surprised her.

'How well do you know Francine and Maria Endozzi, Steffie?'

'Well enough, I suppose. I've been to a few parties with them.'

'You've often been seen together at the Gezira Club.'

'Hardly often. Do you know my shift pattern, sir?'

He ignored her.

'You swim with them.'

'Of a fashion.'

'Talk?'

'Well, yes, as girls do.'

'All dresses and shoes and lipsticks, is it?'

'Pretty much. They like their fashion. Why? What has this to do with anything?'

He leaned in suddenly.

'Have you seen their list, Stefania?'

'What list?'

'Oh, come on – their *list*. Perhaps you helped them make it? Suggested names, tested people out?'

Steffie looked at him blankly.

'Truly, I know nothing about a list. What's on it?'

'Just the names of every Italian or proto-Italian in Cairo and whether they could be trusted to "sympathise" if Rommel makes it "into town".'

Steffie gulped down air; this looked bad, even she could see that.

'Am I on it?' she asked.

'You are.'

'And what does it say about me?'

'You don't know?'

'Would I be asking if I did?'

'If you had any sense, yes. And I think you do, Stefania. I think you're very sharp indeed.'

Somehow it didn't sound as much of a compliment as when Freddie had said it to her.

'So – what does it say about me?'

'It says you are highly unlikely to collaborate,' he admitted.

'There you are then!'

He frowned at her.

'We're hardly taking the word of two known spies.'

'And yet you *are* taking their word on those who they say are likely to collaborate? Isn't that a bit... inconsistent?'

He acknowledged this with a tip of his head.

'We have been to the houses of everyone on the list. Many of them have Nazi flags in their drawers.'

'As do almost all the locals. The shopkeepers have been

churning them out because everyone wants to curry favour if
the Germans take Cairo. It's not support of the Nazis that
drives those flags but fear of them.' She thought of something.
'Did you find one in my belongings?'

'No. But we have not ruled out the possibility of you having
another stash somewhere.'

'Stash?!'

This was getting ridiculous. Steffie didn't know whether to
laugh or cry. One thing she did know though – the authorities
were getting themselves in a mess over Gute Quelle and the
only way she and the others were going to clear their names was
if they, somehow, found out who he really was. Quite how she
did that from a cell beneath Cairo's teeming streets, however,
she had no idea.

THIRTY

Ailsa

'Why a farm?'

Ailsa groaned.

'I've told you already – we found the toy set in the caravan and it just appealed to us. Can I have some water please?'

'Soon. You "found" the toy set?'

'We did, aye. We found it under a bunk in its box. I believe it belonged to Gloria and Alfie's grandson, but you'd have to check that with them.'

'Oh, we will. They are helping us with our enquiries.'

'Gloria and Alfie are?'

She hated the thought of the kindly farmers being drawn into this.

'They have some very... robust views, especially about you girls. Very protective they are.'

'They've been good to us.'

'An unusual set-up though, isn't it? I'm not aware of anyone else in Bletchley Park living in a caravan.'

'Perhaps because ours is the only one available?'

'Perhaps. Or perhaps it was all set up very carefully. A farm within a farm – neat.'

Ailsa shifted in the hard chair and licked at her dry lips.

'I don't know what you want me to say. None of us liked our digs. Mine was very crowded, Fran's was very damp, and Steffie's landlord was a lecherous goat. In the caravan, we felt safe.'

'I bet you did. Alfie has an unusual collection of guns.'

'He's a farmer!'

'And a poacher.'

'So? There's a war on – people have to eat. At least in England there are still rabbits to track down. Now, please, can I have that water?'

Her interrogator got up and went to the door and Ailsa closed her eyes against the dank, cold cell they'd had her locked in for the last week. She pictured herself gaily collecting ice to rub on her sore ears before they'd come and wanted to cry, save that she'd done more than enough of that already, especially at night.

The first night had been the worst. She'd huddled beneath scratchy blankets, hearing the creaks of the rock and the far-off roar of an air raid as the walls had closed in on her and she'd been there again – New Year's Eve in the shelter. Every part of her body had been lost in a very physical memory of the alcove and she'd even reached out to brush off rubble, her hands panicking as much as the rest of her until, like a visit from the faeries – had she believed in such things – she'd heard the song.

It had lilted into her head in Ma's voice, a little croaky and definitely not as perfectly as an actual faerie would have sung it, but all the better for that. And suddenly she'd been able to see, not a collapsing roof and a cloud of lung-clogging dust, but her old bedroom and her mother pottering up and down in the tiny hallway beyond. Ma hadn't ever sat down and sung her a lullaby – that would have been 'indulgent' – but she'd always found jobs to do just outside Ailsa's door and she'd always sung this same old song, of seas and selkies and souls on the air. The story, as with all stories on the island, had been a tragic one but it wasn't the words that had soothed young Ailsa to sleep as much as the sharp sweetness of the tune and it had been the same that first night locked in the Lascaris caves – and every night since.

'Tiring you, are we, Miss MacIver?'

The voice was crisp and impatient and her eyes shot open to see Lieutenant General Sir William Dobbie, Governor of Malta and the man she'd last met on the day the island had been awarded the George Cross.

'I'm sorry, sir,' she stuttered. 'I'm not sleeping well.'

'An uneasy conscience can do that.'

She sat up straighter.

'As can being locked in a room that reminds you of the collapsed air-raid shelter you had to be dug out of.'

For a moment she saw something soften in his grey eyes but then he snapped himself back to attention.

'You shouldn't have got yourself into trouble then.'

Now she was angry.

'I did not "get myself into trouble", sir. I have been wrongly arrested on foolish charges and am having to suffer the consequences.'

He looked taken aback.

'Did you, or did you not, make up a code with your colleagues in secret intelligence?'

'I did not.'

'Think carefully.'

'I – we – did not make up a code. We used a set of toy animals to understand the situation in the Mediterranean and continued to reference that when communicating with each other so as to avoid writing anything that might compromise international security.'

'You wrote in code.'

Ailsa fought for the words to explain, wishing her tiny village school had provided the sort of vocabulary Fran's Cambridge grammar had given her. She drew herself up and tried to channel her friend.

'We wrote about references only ourselves understood. That is neither, strictly speaking, a code nor a cipher.'

'Don't get smart with me, young lady.'

Ailsa wanted to howl with frustration.

'I am not being "smart", sir. I am simply trying to explain my situation which, from where I'm sitting, feels dire. My colleague, Ned Robinson, was the one who first picked up a reference to Gute Quelle and I raised the alarm with BP. I have had contact with my friends directly about it because (a) I was worried for their safety, (b) I believed they had the skills to find the leak and (c) they were the only people truly listening.'

Dobbie paced in front of her, hands clasped behind his back and bushy moustache twitching.

'Edward Robinson is also being held for questioning.'

'What?'

She looked to the walls as if she might see through them to whatever cell poor Ned was in, but they were quite literally rock solid. She was sorry he'd got dragged into this mess but it felt a little better knowing that he was down here with her. Dobbie was back in front of her now, though, bending down to peer into her face.

'Why were you worried for your friends' safety?'

'Not so much Fran, but Steffie is in Cairo. If Rommel advances, she could be in the direct firing line.'

'As could we if Kesselring gets the green light to invade Malta.'

'I know! And that's far more likely to happen if they have a source telling them the positions of our convoys so that they can starve us into submission.'

'I'm aware of the military implications, thank you, Miss MacIver. These skills your friends have...?'

Ailsa licked again at her lips. Her glass of water hadn't arrived but she didn't dare ask the governor.

'I admit I don't know exactly what they do. We never talked about it – as instructed. But Steffie must be good if they chose her to go out to Heliopolis and Fran has been promoted twice in Hut 3, so I assume the same. She's very organised. Very thorough.'

'A useful quality in a spy.'

Ailsa sighed. They were going round and round in circles and it was starting to feel dangerously like a sick joke. Perhaps that was just the hunger and the thirst and the fear of her tiny room, but this was becoming a permanent, swirling nightmare.

'We are *not* spies. We are *not* giving information to the enemy. Quite the reverse, we are the ones who have been battling to get to Gute Quelle and no one has been listening to us. Many lives must have been lost on his intel, many convoy ships sunk, and now all anyone seems to care about is a stupid wee farm. You're wasting time interrogating us – you should be out there, finding Gute Quelle before we all live – or don't live – to regret it.'

Dobbie had gone a strange shade of purple beneath his grey moustache.

'That's quite enough, thank you, Miss MacIver,' he growled. 'Either you are part of a dangerous spy network, or you and your girlie chums with your boarding-school games are proving a serious distraction to an important operation.'

'Girlie chums?!'

Oh, Ailsa could scream! When Dobbie had stalked out, slamming the door behind him, she picked up her stupid, uncomfortable chair and flung it at the rock wall. It smashed satisfyingly, two legs coming off and rolling across the floor. Ailsa felt better but, as her anger subsided into a mix of frustration and fear, she realised that all she'd achieved was robbing herself of somewhere to sit. Leaning against the cold wall, she wondered what was happening to Steffie and Fran in their respective cells – and what sort of miracle it was going to take to get them all out.

THIRTY-ONE

JUNE 1942

Fran

'Frances? Frances, are you in there?'

Fran's heart leaped at the sound of the soft, French voice.

'Of course I'm in here,' she called through the caravan window. 'I'm not allowed to go anywhere else.'

She'd undergone round after round of questioning from first the policemen, then their superiors, and then Edward Travis himself. She'd been frogmarched into BP under escort, drawing delightedly scandalised whispers from the gaggles of WRENS. Not that she'd cared about them but when she'd passed Hut 3, she'd almost broken down at the sight of Valérie in the doorway, dark eyes wide with horror.

She'd not been terribly coherent at first and had had to give herself a stern talking-to. She refused to be a hysterical woman about this. She had been charged, wrongly and unfairly, with being the very leak that she had alerted everyone to, and she was not going to go down weeping.

'This is a grave misunderstanding, sir,' she'd insisted to

Travis. 'I've been working in Hut 3 for two years and have done my utmost to ensure the success of our enemy decrypts and the security of our own encryptions. It was me, along with Peter Lucas and Valérie Rousseau, who tracked Gute Quelle down to Cairo. Ask them. Please. Ask Peter.'

'I already have,' Travis had said, 'and he insists on your hard work and integrity. Mademoiselle Rousseau has also vouched for you, but we have been led to believe that you and she were... intimate friends.'

'We were,' she'd agreed defiantly. Valérie might not have been there to hear her stand up for whatever it was they'd had, but it had been the right thing to do all the same.

'So, we can hardly trust her judgement on your character.'

'On the contrary, I would say she would be the most ruthlessly honest about it.'

He'd grunted and picked up a document.

'Do you know what this is?'

'The Official Secrets Act, sir.'

'To be more precise, it is the Official Secrets Act that you signed, Frances, on the very first day you arrived here in Bletchley Park. Do you remember?'

'Of course.' How could she forget that sombre moment – she, Steffie and Ailsa sat in a line, wondering what on earth they'd got themselves into. Little had they known it would lead to this. 'I remember you impressing the vital importance of secrecy upon us and I remember taking that very much to heart – as I still do. When we were living together, we never spoke of what we did. Even when I went into Hut 4 to help with their indexing and Steffie was there doing whatever she was doing, we didn't speak of it. I'm not stupid, sir.'

'No, Frances, I don't believe you are, which is precisely why we have to take these accusations so seriously. Either you are an active part of some sort of enemy network, you have unwittingly facilitated one, or you may know something, whether you realise it or not, that could unlock one.'

'Or, I am as baffled by this as everyone else. Sir.'

'Hmm, well, we can't take that risk. Rommel is closing in on Tobruk again, Churchill has gone to Washington to try and talk Roosevelt into helping us, and we have a damned spy on the loose. How do you think that looks?'

'About as poor as it did when I first alerted the authorities to it in April, sir.'

'Yes, well, with the Americans in the loop it's diplomatically very sensitive.'

'I imagine it's pretty sensitive for the men facing panzers across the desert too.'

He hadn't liked that and there had followed another endless run of questions, looping in and out and back, as if they might catch her in a lie. Finally, he'd told her he didn't believe the police had sufficient evidence to keep her under arrest but he was suspending her from duties until the investigation was complete and would like her to stay in the caravan for her 'own safety'. The policeman on permanent duty outside her door was apparently also for safety, but Fran knew surveillance when she saw it and hated the invasion of her privacy.

She didn't blame the young men put on the tedious duty of standing guard. She even felt sorry for them sometimes, if it was raining or if Alfie chose to parade up and down with his shotgun pretending to look for rabbits. But she still hated it. Now, she opened the door to find Valérie staring down a cowering guard on the doorstep.

'Get a kick out of this, do you, boy?' she was asking him. 'I bet you look through the windows when she's undressing, don't you? I bet you tell all your mates about the gorgeous woman you've been set over. I bet you think about that when you're in bed at night and—'

'Come in, Valérie,' Fran interrupted her before the poor lad melted of mortification.

'No guests allowed, miss,' he stuttered.

'I'm not a guest, boy, I'm her lover.'

His mouth fell open and Valérie pushed past him and gave Fran a kiss, square on her lips. It was so warm, and confident and empowering that Fran clasped her tight and kissed her right back. When she finally stepped away, Valérie was looking up at her with something suspiciously like tears in her eyes, but she pulled herself together enough to snap, 'Hope that's given you something to fantasise about,' at the young man standing help-lessly in the doorway.

'Don't worry,' Fran said to him. 'I'll leave the door open so you can hear everything we say.'

'But it'll be very dirty,' Valérie warned.

'Valérie! Do you want me arrested again?'

Valérie looked contrite at that.

'No. No I do not, though I have to say you did look gorgeous marching through BP with your escort.'

'I looked like a criminal.'

'But a gorgeous criminal.'

Fran laughed, the sound alien after nearly two weeks stuck in here alone.

'Thank you, Valérie,' she said.

'For what?'

'For making me laugh, for standing up for me, just for being here.'

'Oh, Frances.' Her voice was soft and a tear fell from her dark eyes. 'You should be berating me for walking away. I was a fool, a cruel fool. I knew that this – us – was new for you. I knew how odd that can feel. I was the same at first. I was with an older girl at school but I refused to walk anywhere near her, talk to her, or acknowledge her in any way. I don't know why she put up with it, perhaps she was just nicer than I am. So, I am the one thanking you for taking me back.' She looked uncertain suddenly. 'That is, if you are? Taking me back?'

Fran laughed again and, leaning forward, kissed Valérie once more.

'I am.'

'*Hourra!* This is good news. This is the best news. No!' She hit herself comically over the head. 'This is *not* the best news. The best news would be that you are free of these ridiculous charges and *that*, my lovely Frances, is why I am here.'

'It is?'

'Well, that and hoping that you would kiss me. But you *have* kissed me, so, to business.'

Fran shook her head. Lord, she'd missed Valérie.

'What do you have?'

The French girl gave her a slow, deliberate wink.

'Last night a new message came into Hut 3 on Red, and guess what it referenced.'

'Gute Quelle?' Fran gasped.

'The very same. And with you under arrest...'

'And Steffie and Ailsa too...'

'Then surely you cannot be operating your supposed spy network?'

'Can I see?' Fran asked eagerly.

'Not see,' Valérie told her. 'You know we're not allowed to take any papers out of the Park. Up here, however...' She tapped at her head, then grabbed paper and a pen and wrote in fast, hard strokes. She pushed the message across to Fran.

Gute Quelle reports British in over-extended positions along the Gazala line. Gaps south of Bir Hacheim and poor use of available infantry. Buffalo-style drives would penetrate the Italian Trieste and Ariete divisions and offer far greater

chance of breaking up Axis lines ahead of an attempted
assault

'Well remembered.'

'Thank you.'

'But are you sure this is right – "Buffalo-style drives"?'

'Quite sure. It stuck with me.'

'As it would.'

Fran looked up at the faded spaces on the wall where her postcards from Steffie had been taped before the police had taken them away with the blinking farm. She remembered the bison one and Steffie's gleeful comment: *Let's hope things change now there are new animals in the farm.*

She leaped up.

'It's American. It has to be. Gute Quelle is talking about American tactics so surely it stands to reason that he – or she – is American.'

'But the Americans haven't been deployed to Africa yet.'

They stared at each other, confused, then Fran remembered Steffie's letters from Cairo, about parties and dinners, about British drivers and half-Italian ambassador's wives and about a friendly American military attaché reporting back to Washington...

She gasped.

Churchill is with Roosevelt, right?' she asked Valérie.

'On his way,' she agreed.

'Then we need to get to Travis fast. Come on.'

She grabbed Valérie's hand and made for the door of the caravan, almost knocking the poor guard over as they tumbled out.

'Oi! Where d'you think you're going?' he demanded, reaching for his gun.

'Bletchley Park,' Fran retorted. 'Immediately. I'm happy to

go under armed guard. In fact, you can handcuff me if you want...'

'Ooh, please do,' Valérie said.

'...but let's just go – now!'

The bewildered young man could only manage a muttered, 'Yes, miss,' and then they were off, up the track to BP to untangle this mess once and for all.

THIRTY-TWO

Steffie

'I believe we owe you an apology, Miss Carmichael.'

Steffie looked blankly at Major Sansom, his short frame rigid before her, and it wasn't until he repeated the unexpected statement that she could really take it in. She was tired. Her hair was matted, her skin was prickling with heat, and she felt pathetically close to tears most of the time. All she could think about was Ailsa and Fran, hating that they would be in a similar situation because of her, and now she looked blearily up at the man.

'For what?'

'You understand, of course, that we had to follow due process.'

'Sorry?'

'If you *had* turned out to be the source of the leak, we would have been most negligent if we had not kept you under lock and key. You do see that?'

'*If?*' Steffie asked, a spec of something that might just be hope taking seed in her heart. 'What do you mean if? Have you found Gute Quelle?'

Major Sansom coughed.

'We believe so. Further enquires are needed to verify it fully, and it's a bit, er, sensitive, but we have enough to prove your innocence, Miss Carmichael.'

'Innocence?' All Steffie seemed to be able to do was repeat his words like a dumb echo. 'My innocence?'

'Yes, miss.'

'Finally!' She stood up and faced the little man, anger coursing in on the back of her relief. 'You know, Major Sansom, that if you had taken me seriously when I alerted you to the possibility of a German source at the Gezira Club last December, we would not be in this situation now.'

'I *did* take you seriously.'

'Really? Well, in that case, if you had done your job correctly last December, we would not be in this situation now.'

Sansom cleared his throat.

'I work for GHQ, Miss Carmichael, in charge of agents and spies. Sigint is not my responsibility.'

'Oh well, as long as it wasn't your responsibility!'

'I am really very sorry.'

'Right. Marvellous. That's all tickety-boo then. Can I go?'

He seized on this.

'Of course. You're free to go whenever you wish. I believe Jacobs has booked you into Shepheard's Hotel for the night as way of an, er...'

'Apology?'

'Recompense for your discomfort in the cells.'

Steffie put a hand to her filthy hair and allowed herself a glimmer of a smile at the thought of a suite in opulent Shepheard's.

'Will there be a Martini?'

'There will be everything you wish, miss.'

Then there would definitely be a Martini. God, she needed a drink. The only bright side of the whole being-imprisoned-in-a-filthy-cell-suspected-of-hanging-level-treachery thing, was that it had distracted her from Matteo leaving, but already she could feel that hurt resurfacing. She'd really thought she loved him. Maybe she was as stupid as everyone had suspected after all.

'Is there any news of Matteo Mancini?'

It was hard saying his name out loud, especially the surname – the one that should have been hers: Stefania Mancini. She'd loved the sound of her would-be married name but that woman would never exist now.

'Sottotenente Mancini has been recaptured.'

'Where?'

'In a fishing trawler off Sicily.'

He'd nearly made it then. He'd be furious. Would he know that she'd told the authorities where to look? Should she have done so? She still loved him, after all, however much she wished she didn't, and the thought of him suffering tore at her heart.

He deserves to be caught, she told herself sternly. He'd always told her that he liked her 'fire', but it seemed he'd only liked it contained within his own hearth.

'Is he really a spy?'

'He is, but not, perhaps, in the way you are imagining. It would seem that Mancini has been spying on the Germans for Mussolini.'

'Are Germany and Italy not allies?'

'Not, it would seem, easy ones. Mussolini has been using your fiancé—'

'He's not my fiancé.'

'Apologies. Again. Mussolini has been using Mr Mancini to keep tabs on what Kesselring was up to on Sicily. We are in discussion with him about how that might be of use to us. Major General Carmichael has been sent out to talk to him.'

'Daddy? He knows I'm innocent then?'

'I'm told he never doubted it, Miss Carmichael.'

Relief coursed through her; she'd so wanted to do a good job to make her father proud. And now he was with Matteo. That thought made her head spin.

'Is Matteo going to work for us?'

'He does not seem averse. He says he hates the Germans. Something to do with their rigid manners and lack of wine at dinner...?'

A smile flickered through Steffie – that sounded so like Matteo – but then she remembered that he wasn't hers to smile about any more and wiped it from her face. He might be with her father, but he wasn't with her and never would be.

'If I may, I'd like to go now.'

She stood up but Sansom gave another cough.

'Might I, perhaps, prevail on your time slightly longer, Miss Carmichael? We have a few questions.'

'*More* questions?'

'If you don't mind. I could order you a Martini here...'

'Done!'

She sat down again as he slipped out, amazed at how much cheerier the room already looked just from knowing she could leave it whenever she wished. Her head began to clear and she straightened her skirt and dabbed a touch of her fast-dwindling gloss on her parched lips. By the time Sansom returned with a Martini, elegant in the proper glass and complete with olive, she was feeling almost human.

'What do you want to know?' she asked.

He handed over her cocktail and coughed.

'It's not so much me, miss, as the air marshal.'

He gestured as Arthur Tedder strode into the room.

'Stefania. Good to see you again.'

'Air Marshal,' Steffie stuttered.

'Arthur, please. Sorry about all this bother, but tell me, my girl, what do you know about the American military attaché here in Cairo?'

'Bonner Fellers?' Steffie gasped. 'Bonner is Gute Quelle?'

Sansom put up a hand.

'We cannot say for sure, but it seems likely that, yes, he has unwittingly been a source for Hitler. His job, as you know, is to report to Washington on British activity in Africa to foster Anglo-American cooperation and he does so almost daily, using the Black Code.'

'The Black Code?'

'It's a book cipher. The Americans believe it to be completely secure.'

'But?'

'But BP cracked it six months ago. Not that they're meant to read friendly communications, you understand, but someone in Hut 6 got bored. And, thank God, because if we can read it...'

'The Germans can read it,' Steffie finished. 'So they've been getting near-daily updates on everything we've been doing in Africa? The Italians too.'

Tedder's eyes narrowed.

'How do you know that?'

'Matteo told me Gute Quelle was referenced in the Regia Aeronautica's briefings,' Steffie said. 'So they must have broken the code too.'

'Which is more surprising,' Tedder said.

'Are you saying Italians can't apply themselves to code-breaking?'

'I wouldn't want to generalise so sweepingly.'

'But...'

'But we've seen little evidence of it to date.'

'You'd seen little evidence of the American codes being broken either,' Steffie pointed out tartly.

'A fair point.'

She sipped at her Martini, revelling in the fresh tang and

feeling the alcohol – Sansom had not been stingy in his ordering – hit her bloodstream.

'So,' she said, thinking it through, 'if the Italians haven't broken the code, they must have got hold of a codebook.'

Tedder stared at her.

'How do you think they might have done that?'

Steffie laughed.

'Easily. Musso was at it all the time in Rome. He used to send people into the embassies at night to look for useful stuff.'

'Mussolini raided foreign embassies?'

'That surprises you?'

'Maybe not. How did he get in?'

'Oh, he had keys to them all.'

'Keys? To foreign embassies?'

Tedder looked to Sansom, who spread his hands wide and Steffie stifled a smile at their British naivety.

'Did he have one to ours?' Sansom asked.

'We suspected so. My father was certainly very rigorous in monitoring the quality of the night watch in the British embassy, but you know Italy – a bottle of finest olive oil or prim-itivo wine and anything can change hands, especially if the man asking is Mussolini.'

Tedder buried his head in his hands.

'So his men could have purloined the Black Code book out of the American embassy at any point and been merrily reading along with us every time Bonner sent one of his damned updates?'

'Correct. I'm not saying that's what happened, you under-stand – just that it's possible. They may even have passed it on to the Germans once they were official allies.'

Tedder took his hands away from his face and looked straight at her.

'You're a sharp woman, Miss Carmichael. I have to say, if you had been Gute Quelle, I doubt we'd have found you.'

As compliments went, it was a peculiar one, but Steffie thanked him and took the last blissful sip of her Martini.

'I'm assuming the Black Code has been stopped?' Both men looked uncomfortable and she stared at them in horror. 'Tell me it has. We have thousands of men strung out along the Gazala line. All comms suggest Rommel is poised to strike at Tobruk at any minute – and no wonder if he's getting high-level intel from America. Those soldiers' lives are in our hands, Air Marshal, and Rommel won't stop at Tobruk. He'll be marching on us all here in Cairo if he succeeds. We need to shut this down. We need to shut it down *now*.'

'We know,' Tedder said darkly. 'But it's tricky telling your most important ally that they've messed up.'

'You had no problem telling *me*,' Steffie said indignantly. 'And I hadn't even done it.'

'True. And you have our most sincere apologies. But don't worry – we have our best man on the job.'

'Who?' Steffie demanded.

'Winston Churchill.'

THIRTY-THREE

Ailsa

'You're free to go, Miss MacIver.'

Ailsa looked up at the policeman, wondering if this was some sort of sick joke, but the cell door was wide open and he was waving her towards it as a butler might. Well, as she assumed a butler might.

'I'm free to go? Just like that?'

'Those are my orders, miss, yes.'

'And Ned as well?'

'Mr Robinson has already been released.'

'Ailsa?'

Suddenly there he was, stepping into the room, a little dishevelled and with the start of a beard on his usually clean-shaven chin, but with the same quiet smile.

'Ned!' Ailsa ran to him, falling into his outstretched arms as the policeman looked awkwardly at the floor. 'Are you well? They didn't hurt you, did they?'

He shook his head.

'This isn't the Gestapo, Ailsa. I'm fine, just cold and hungry – still, nothing new there, hey?'

The policeman coughed.

'I've been asked to tell you both that you're invited to dinner at the governor's house this evening.'

Ailsa frowned. 'No, thank you.'

'Ailsa!' Ned gasped. 'Did you not hear the word "dinner"?'

'It won't be grand,' the policeman warned. 'Sir William has been eating the same rations as everyone else on the island.'

'I should hope so too,' Ailsa snapped, and Ned looked curiously at her.

'Ailsa, what's wrong?'

'Did he not come and visit you, Ned?'

'Sir William? No!' He stared at her. 'He visited *you*?'

'He did, a couple of days ago, huffing and puffing about me endangering the whole island by "playing boarding-school games" with my "girlie chums". There's no way I'm having dinner with that patronising old fool.'

Ned grimaced at the policeman.

'We'd appreciate it if you didn't repeat that.'

'I wouldn't,' Ailsa said. 'I'm quite happy for you to repeat it because he was very rude and I don't see why he should get away with it just because he has a stupid Sir in front of his name.'

'She's Scottish,' Ned told the policeman, who was desperately trying to escape the room.

'So?' she said. 'We have lords too and lairds and mormaers and all sorts of other folk who think the world owes them something because of the family they were born into.'

The policeman looked mortified.

'Sir William interviewed you because he is governor of the island, miss, not because he's a lord.'

'But would he be governor if he wasn't a lord?'

'Erm. Well, I—'

'No, he would not. We won't have dinner, thank you. That is, Mr Robinson may – don't let me stop you, Ned – but I will not be accompanying him.'

The policeman looked to Ned, but he shook his head.

'Perhaps just tell him we're very tired.'

'From the cruel treatment and debilitating lack of trust,' Ailsa added, sailing past and out into the corridor, desperate to feel the sun on her face. She was turning into one of those hobbits in Mr Tolkien's book and, dearly as she'd loved reading about Bilbo Baggins, pallid and wrinkled wasn't a good look on a young woman.

'I've, er, been asked to escort you to the air commodore's office, miss.'

She stopped halfway to the stairs, and stared him down.

'We have to go back to work?'

'I don't know, miss.'

'You don't know much, do you?'

Ned slid an arm through hers.

'Give the poor lad a break, Ails, he's only doing his job.'

Ailsa sighed. Ned was right but she felt like a pressure cooker that had been filling with furious steam down here in the depths of the Lascaris caves, and she had to let it out somehow.

'Sorry,' she said to him. 'I'm a bit worked up.'

'I don't blame you, miss. I would be too. But at least you're out now and just in time too. Things are really heating up in Africa and we need all hands on deck.'

Ailsa's ears pricked up and she thought immediately of Steffie. Had they let her out too or would she be stuck in a prison in Cairo if the Germans took the city?

'What's happening?'

'Rommel's troops are encircling Tobruk and if they take that—'

'They have a port five hundred miles from Cairo and will be able to supply a full-scale attack with ease.'

'Exactly, miss. Here's the air commodore's office. Thank you for, er...'

He failed to find anything to thank her for and bowed himself hastily away, leaving them to knock on their boss's door.

'You will be polite?' Ned asked nervously.

Ailsa gave him a quick kiss.

'I'll try.'

'God help us!'

He rolled his eyes ceilingward but the commodore was whipping the door open, pumping both their hands and ushering them into chairs.

'Soup?' Hugh Lloyd offered. 'It's a bit watery but it has bacon in it – or so they claim.'

Ailsa half wanted to turn him down too as he must surely have been complicit in her arrest but she could smell the broth and, God help her, she was starving.

'Thank you,' she said, accepting a bowlful.

It was rough and greasy but, oh, it tasted good and she had to fight to eat it with something approaching decorum. *Don't slurp, Ailsa*, her ma's voice said in her head, and she automatically sat up straighter and sipped as delicately as she could.

'So, Ailsa,' Hugh was saying, 'I've been getting regular reports on this peculiar affair and I gather, after secret services got all hot under the collar about it, that there is no farm?'

'There *is*,' she retorted. 'It's a bairn's toy in the caravan I shared with two very good friends when I was working in Bletchley Park. We used it to represent the Mediterranean. A "girlie game", I think the governor called it.'

'Oh, don't worry about him. He's gruff with everyone. You would be too if you were running an island in danger of imminent surrender to the most brutal of enemies.'

Ailsa thought about that.

'I suppose I would.'

'*You'd* be ten times worse,' Ned muttered at her side, and

she gave him a hard stare before he sideswiped her with a cheeky wink.

'I'm just glad to have my name cleared,' she said primly to Lloyd. 'What changed everyone's mind?'

'Fresh evidence from BP.'

'Fran,' she breathed.

'I believe Miss Morgan was something to do with it,' Lloyd confirmed. 'She's free now, as is Miss Carmichael.'

'Thank God.' Ailsa felt tears prick but they were happy ones and fortified her even more than the soup. 'So what did they find? Who is Gute Quelle?'

Lloyd bit his lip.

'I'm not at liberty to tell you that but I think I can safely say that they proved the leak was not British.'

'So, it was...?'

'That's all I can say at the moment, I'm afraid. We appreciate your forbearance.'

'I didn't have much choice,' Ailsa pointed out. 'But I'd like to know I haven't gone through all this in vain.'

'It's diplomatically very sensitive.'

His careful wording roused her anger again.

'It's pretty damned sensitive for the people starving here on Malta,' she said sharply.

'Very true.'

'Not to mention those fighting Rommel's blitzkrieg in Africa.'

'Also true, but you appreciate the need for secrecy?'

Ailsa glanced at Ned, who looked very thoughtful.

'Clearly we do,' she told Lloyd crossly. 'That's why we alerted you to Gute Quelle before he could do more harm. Is he stopped now?'

'We're getting there.'

'Getting there?! Surely that's not good enough?'

At her side, Ned got to his feet. She looked nervously across to him, expecting him to shush her, but he was staring at Lloyd, his face alight with fury.

'It's the Americans, isn't it? It has to be the Americans.' Lloyd shifted in his chair. 'It *is*!'

'Sssh. Churchill is with Roosevelt. He'll sort it.'

'He'd better,' Ned shot back. 'It's all right for him dining in bloody Washington while we all turn quietly into skeletons out here in the heart of the battleground.'

'Yes,' Hugh agreed nervously. 'More soup?'

Ned shook his head. 'Never mind the soup – what are we going to do about the leak?'

Ailsa looked at him, standing next to her, bristling with indignation, and loved him even more than she had before.

'I think we have to trust the prime minister to sort that one, Ned,' Lloyd was saying.

'Fine, if we must, but he'd better get on with it.'

Ailsa stood up and slipped a hand into his, squeezing it.

'In the meantime, what can *we* do?' she asked.

Lloyd turned gratefully to her.

'I'm so glad you asked. I didn't want to push after your... ordeal, but as it happens, we would very much like to draw on your expertise.'

'Expertise?'

'The Germans are mounting an attack on Tobruk and messages are pouring in from across the Med. Marcia has picked up a faint signal that we believe may be Rommel's direct line to Kesselring, but they're operating on the highest frequency and we're struggling to pick up a clear signal.'

'Ailsa will find it,' Ned said confidently. 'She could pick up Hitler's farts on the airwaves.' He clapped his hand over his mouth. 'That is, erm, sorry, sir. I just meant...'

Hugh Lloyd didn't even bother to hide his amusement.

'I'm not sure we'll need *that*, Miss MacIver, but if you wouldn't mind having a go at tracking down this frequency...?'

'Of course,' she agreed. 'Lay on, MacDuff!'

The words reminded her with painful clarity of Fran the very first night she'd met her and Steffie on Bletchley station. Those girls had been her friends ever since and even on three separate land masses, she could feel their support.

Marching through to the Y-station offices, she made for her radio set but was stopped by a sudden round of applause. She glanced around to see everyone on their feet, clapping. For her? She gave them a shy smile, but felt rather ridiculous and waved them all back into their seats.

'Thank you very much and all that, but don't you lot have work to do? I hear there's a port to save.'

This was met with smiles and groans and everyone turned back to their radios as Lloyd ushered her to her own. It was like seeing an old friend and, picking up the headset that someone had very kindly padded with pretty petticoat fabric, she slipped it on and reached for the dials. God, she'd missed the airwaves! And they were alive today. She sat down, closing her eyes and tuning her whole self into the dial, letting her fingers rest lightly on it so she could feel the frequencies as she stalked them down. Marcia was right – there was one operating up on the highest bands. Adjusting the dial with the utmost care, she pinpointed the signal and suddenly the Morse was clear.

Picking up a pencil, Ailsa began swiftly writing down the message. It was long and, in a total breach of any radio protocol, was repeated almost immediately afterwards. The operator worked fast, as if excited, and Ailsa had to focus hard on the parade of dots and dashes but at last she had it all down in the usual five-letter batches. Lloyd took the slip himself and marched it across the office.

'Teleprint this to BP immediately,' he ordered and one of the girls bent to set up the Typex machine that would encode the enemy code, only for it to be decoded – hopefully twice over – back in boring old Buckinghamshire.

Would Fran see it? Ailsa wondered. And would she then send it on to Steffie? Surreptitiously she blew the Typex machine a kiss, as if her love might be transmitted with the sharp German letter-blocks. She felt desperately weary and longed to see them both, longed to be safe in a caravan at Bletchley Park, playing with toy animals over a glass of blackberry gin. Her head felt clogged and she stood uncertainly but just then the siren wailed out, loud and sharp. The Lascaris caves began to spin giddily around her and she felt dust clog her lungs and rubble send pain flowering across her foot.

'Help,' she choked, half-seeing a crack in the ceiling.

She pushed her chair away and heard it clatter behind her but then someone was taking her in his arms, and stroking her hair and kissing her flickering eyes.

'Hush, Ailsa,' a gentle voice said. 'I have you. I have you safe.'

'Ned,' she murmured and let herself drop into the endless comfort of his care.

THIRTY-FOUR

Fran

Fran stood over the stove making yet another round of coffees for Hut 3 as the clock hit 1 a.m. The drinks were disgusting but it was something to do while they willed Hut 6 to make a quick break on today's Red Code. The bombes had been put exclusively at their disposal as news filtered in of increased activity around Tobruk and all they needed was a lucky break.

'What about the Black Code?' she asked Peter, stirring the bitter chicory mix.

Word had spread about the American leak and no one could quite believe it was their diplomatic channels that had handed Gute Quelle to Hitler.

'What about it?'

'Has it been stopped yet?'

Peter coughed.

'I believe Churchill is "working up to it".'

'Right. Lovely. So, while he's sipping sherry with Roosevelt, this Bonner Fellers man is still transmitting his damned messages?'

Peter inclined his head and, behind him, Valérie tutted violently.

'It is ridiculous.'

'Worse than that,' Fran growled. 'It's dangerous. The whole fate of the war could turn on some damned president's sensitivities. If I was in the Whitehouse, I'd tell Roosevelt straight.'

'I don't doubt it,' Valérie muttered.

Fran paced in front of the stove, unable to believe that the authorities had been willing to throw three young women into jail over this but couldn't find the balls to tell the top brass. Then something occurred to her. She shot across to Peter.

'Travis said someone in Hut 6 broke the Black Code ages ago, Peter.'

'That's right.'

'So, we could read it?'

'In theory, yes. If we had authorisation to intercept the US traffic.'

'Then we should!' She grabbed his arm. 'If the higher-ups are allowing Gute Quelle to still send his bloody messages, could we not at least read what he's saying?'

Peter stared at her.

'Great idea, Fran. I'll get to Travis straight away.'

He slipped out of the hut as the kettle finally came to the boil and Fran distributed coffees to grunts of thanks. She sipped her own, trying not to gag as it coated the roof of her mouth, and was grateful when Valérie placed a tiny French truffle on her desk.

'Where did you get that?' she asked, her mouth watering as she unwrapped it, releasing the heady scent of cocoa.

'An uncle,' Valérie said with a wicked wink, and went back to her desk.

Fran shook her head, fascinated by Valérie's family, and for the first time she found herself wondering if she would ever meet them, if, once the war was over, they would... what? Live together? Was that possible? What would people think? And did that matter? Fran had a feeling that to Valérie it did not. The French girl seemed to revel in others' disapproval, but Fran wasn't like that. She already hated that her family didn't approve of her choice of occupation; could she bring herself to throw in an unconventional partner in life?

Time enough for all that, she told herself sternly, focusing on the huge map of the Med, criss-crossed with string. There were far more important things at stake than her own happiness, and she picked up the first of the unfiled messages and began systematically sorting for nuggets of information. Peter came back, saying he had Travis and Hut 6 hunting down Black, and together they plotted the new shipping.

'Why was there an American reporting on Allied movements anyway?' Fran asked him as the shift ground on.

Peter grimaced.

'Ridiculous, isn't it? They've had a military attaché out there for years and once he became PM, Churchill insisted on them being given access to our commands in the Med. He was concerned that the Americans didn't understand the importance of Africa to the overall war.'

'So he sent some bloke to transmit all our positions and tactics across the airwaves in a code we knew we could break?'

'I imagine we didn't know that at first.'

'But pretty soon after?'

'It does sound rather foolish like that.'

'Doesn't it just,' Fran agreed scornfully. 'All these ships sunk, Peter. All that oil poured into the sea, all those weapons and planes and foodstuffs sent to the fishes – not to mention all those lives.'

Peter ran a finger down the line of the next convoy proposed for Malta. They'd marked it out in string specially dyed yellow to indicate future routes and everyone knew it was vital. Far too vital to have some puffed-up Yank broadcasting it across the airwaves. And then there was Tobruk...

A loud bang on the message hatch made everyone jump. Fran ran to it, pulling on the string to guide the wooden tray with the precious decrypts into Hut 3. When she'd first had the carpenter build this tunnel there had been maybe twenty messages a shift coming across the primitive system. These days it was more like fifty and she eagerly watched the tray as it bumped towards her. When she drew it out, however, it had only one message in it.

'Oh,' she said, then she saw the heading:

PYRAMID to MONUMENT. REPORT ON BRITISH POSITIONS IN TOBRUK

'Black,' she said. 'This is the American. He's still transmitting and in some detail.'

She scanned the long document but her eyes weren't used to the five-letter formations and she was grateful when Peter took it from her and began reading it out in plain English. Well, American.

'New Gurkha regiments dug in at Tobruk and fresh. In reasonable order around the perimeter of the city, save in...' Peter hesitated, glanced disbelievingly around the room, and then read on, 'save in the SE where only the understaffed and inexperienced 5th Mahratta Light Infantry are stationed.' He stopped. 'Am I understanding this correctly?'

'That the American military attaché to Cairo has just told Rommel exactly where to concentrate his forces?' Fran supplied. 'I'm afraid you are.'

'We have to get this to Travis.'

'And, more importantly, to the troops,' Fran said. 'If we're quick, they can perhaps reinforce this south-east quarter before Rommel unleashes his guns.' She glanced to the clock. It was just gone 4 a.m. That would be 5 a.m. in Egypt and the sun would be starting to rise over poor Tobruk. 'When was the message sent?' she demanded.

Peter glanced at the preamble.

'Five hours ago.'

'Damn! That's ages for Rommel to prepare his troops. Is there an SLU in Tobruk?'

'I'm not sure. They're coordinated from Heliopolis.'

Fran thought of Steffie and prayed she'd been released and was back at her desk.

'We have to try and reach them,' she said. 'Gute Quelle has cost us more than enough in the Med without him costing us Africa too. Teleprinter – now!'

THIRTY-FIVE

Steffie

Steffie wiped sand from her eyes and cursed her damned conscience. She could be sleeping in the blissful comfort of a Shepheard's bed, luxuriating in the feel of Egyptian cotton against her freshly bathed skin and full of fine food and wine. Instead, she was in the Museum with a street-kebab at her side, frantically sorting through an influx of messages from BP as the sun rose over the tops of the pyramids. She didn't regret it for one moment.

'Where's the SLU?' she demanded.

'Transmitting from ten kilometres outside Tobruk,' someone supplied.

'That's good.'

'Not really. They can't get any closer. There's a mass of German troops in their way, poised for attack.'

'So we can't tell the poor buggers inside?'

'Oh yes,' Freddie Jacobs said. 'I've telephoned it through to General Ritchie on the direct line to Tobruk HQ.'

'Of course!' Steffie felt stupid. Communications between

cities within Egypt could run down the landlines instead of risking the airwaves. It was as easy as ringing your own mother.

'But we may be too late,' Freddie went on. 'We're getting reports of a panzer attack in—'

'The south-eastern corner,' Steffie finished wearily.

She couldn't believe this was happening. The terrible message had come through from BP in time to show them the impending tragedy just before it struck. What a disaster!

Steffie thought of Bonner Fellers and his kind, open face as he'd driven her to see Matteo in the hospital. Then she remembered him the night that Pearl Harbor had been attacked, six months ago. It was the very same day she'd spoken to Major Sansom about a possible spy and he'd condescendingly told her Cairo was rife with them. Then she'd gone swimming with the collaborators Francine and Maria Endozzi, and shared drinks with Bonner Fellers – Gute Quelle. She'd been consorting with the enemy far more that day than at any point in her conversations with Matteo.

What had Bonner said when the dreadful news of Pearl Harbor had come in? Something about not reporting back to Washington as bystanders any more but as full participants. She should have listened more carefully, thought about what that meant. But it seemed that no one else had been thinking about it either – and now look where they were.

'Keep working, Steffie,' she muttered to herself. She may not be manning a gun on the walls of Tobruk but she had a part to play in its defence, not to mention that of Cairo. If Rommel took Tobruk today, he would not stop there. He could be in the capital within days.

Messages were flooding into Heliopolis from BP. The terrible Black Code one had been first but now Hut 6 must have broken Red because the teleprinters had gone mad with commands between the various German units. This was a full blitzkrieg and the enemy operators were working at a speed they had to match. Occasionally, as she helped process the Sigint, she caught the initials FM in preambles and picturing Fran sat at a Typex in quiet old BP kept her calm. They weren't alone out here.

You'll be alone enough if Rommel comes, she thought and icy fear ran down her spine, but surely it wouldn't come to that? There would be escape routes into British territories, both down the Nile to Ethiopia and up the coast into Palestine. She would not be taken prisoner. She could not be. The imprint of her last two weeks in British cells was still marked in dirt on her skin and she knew with dark certainty that the Gestapo would be far less restrained in their questioning than the British – especially of intelligence officers.

Why on earth was I good at my bloody job? she wondered and then tutted at herself. They weren't defeated yet and if she really was good at her job, they would not be. She reached for the next message.

All morning they battled, their communications criss-crossing with German intercepts gleefully reporting advances and breaches, and increasingly panicked calls from HQ within Tobruk. Rommel's panzers broke through in the south-east within forty-five minutes of launching their brutal attack and by 8.30 a.m. the Germans had established a bridgehead nearly two kilometres wide. By noon, tanks were pouring through the perimeter and Allied troops were falling back into the streets, and at 4 p.m., General Ritchie called, saying he was moving to a new HQ in the north of the port. Steffie was close to Freddie Jacobs when he took that call and she could hear the bullets, grenades and shouts of battle echoing so clearly down the line that she almost ducked to avoid them.

She was exhausted but there was no way she was going to bed. At 7 p.m., the terrible news came that the town was taken and, with fifty thousand men stuck at the mercy of the invaders, finding escape routes was the new imperative. Steffie, with the rest of the team, combed the decrypts for clues as to the safest routes and it was only at midnight – when the Germans changed their Enigma key and the Red traffic went dead until Hut 6 figured out the new one – that she finally crawled out of the Museum to find her bunk.

Betty and the other girls welcomed her like a returning hero but even they were subdued and Betty's offer of gin was medicinal only.

'What's happening?' they asked grimly.

'They're coming,' was all Steffie could tell them. 'The Germans are coming.'

The next days were hell. A triumphant Rommel paraded into Tobruk on the morning of 21 June to receive news of his promotion to field marshal. German pride cut up the airwaves, both in code and in blatant, crowing, en clair messages. Some men had escaped and the South African garrison in the heart of the port had found time to broach all fuel and water tanks, but thirty-five thousand Allied troops had been taken prisoner in one of the biggest capitulations of the war.

'Churchill is furious,' Freddie reported, coming off the phone to GHQ.

'He's only got himself to blame,' Steffie said tartly. 'Pussy-footing around "diplomatic sensitivities" with the Americans while they let bloody Bonner carry on telling the Germans all about our battle lines. It's virtually treason.'

'Steffie!'

'What? It *is*.'

She wasn't alone in her view, though few knew the dark secret of Gute Quelle underpinning the terrible defeat. Morale in the troops strung out along the Gazala line was low and General Auchinleck flew in to take personal command as Rommel, after only the briefest of pauses for his victory celebra-

tion, began marching German and Italian troops west. Auchinleck drew the Allies back to a railway holding at a tiny place
called El Alamein on the main route to Cairo and everyone held
their breath. For a day or two, things seemed to stabilise but
then the high admiral removed most of the fleet from Alexandria, dividing them out between several other ports to avoid a
Pearl Harbor-style air attack, and it triggered panic among the
myriad diplomatic families in Egypt.

On the first day of July, Steffie was sent into Cairo with
urgent reports for GHQ and found the city in uproar. She
could barely get off the tram for the hordes of women and children crowding the platform, trying to get east. Many were
British families, but there were locals too, rushing to follow the
diplomatic crowd. Both groups were fighting tooth and nail for
places on the trams and trains and, as Steffie struggled past the
main station, she saw an elegant British woman scrapping with
an Egyptian mother, glossy nails out while her children
watched in disbelief.

'Stop that,' Steffie cried, grabbing her by the arm. 'Where's
your dignity?'

'Screw dignity,' was the near-hysterical reply. 'What use
will dignity be when the Germans get here?'

'Every use,' Steffie insisted. 'The Germans respect order.
And, besides, everyone will get onto the trains far more easily if
you are calm.'

'I don't want everyone to get on the trains,' the woman shot
back, eyes wild, 'I just want *us* to.'

Steffie stared at her, shocked, and the woman had the grace
to look ashamed, but then she stuck her chin up, grabbed a child
by each hand and made for the front of the vast crowd once
more. Steffie shook her head and turned away, pushing against
the human tide towards GHQ's offices, passing the KitKat
Club and Shepheard's Hotel and reflecting ruefully that their
studied opulence was little use to their spoiled patrons today.

Oh, she'd enjoyed both of them too, but those easy days were gone.

You're not as much fun now, Matteo's voice whispered and she tossed her head to send it packing. This was not a time for fun, but for action.

The GHQ offices were in a similar state of disarray to the streets beyond. Two large incinerators were burning in the yard and officials were throwing files out the windows to the men manning the flames. The air was filled with ash, like sick snow-fall, and with the wind getting up, half-burned scraps were flying everywhere. A peanut-seller came rushing up to Steffie offering a cone of nuts which, when she looked more closely, was wrapped in half of a typed report marked TOP SECRET. She bought them and headed inside.

'What's going on?' she demanded, spilling the peanuts onto Sansom's desk and smoothing out the report.

'We're burning all documents before the enemy get here.'

'Not very effectively. You might as well just make them into paper aeroplanes and fly them to Rommel.'

'Don't be facetious, Stefania. This is standard protocol in a tactical retreat.'

'You're running away?'

'Tactical retreat,' he repeated primly. 'We cannot afford for the Germans to get hold of either our material or our staff – they know too much. The same goes for you lot out at Heliopolis if you haven't worked it out already. We've got to escape to fight another day.'

'Why not just fight this one?'

'Because it's already lost, woman.'

She gave an exaggerated look round. 'Is Rommel here?'

'He will be. Auchinleck can't hold El Alamein for more than a day or two and once the panzers break through it will be fast.'

'You could go west and help fight,' Steffie suggested lightly.

Sansom shuddered.

'Orders from on high – no intelligence staff near the front line. I told you, we know too much. We're not retreating for our own safety but for the safety of all Allied personnel in Africa.'

Steffie could see his point but couldn't help thinking that the man had his own precious skin firmly at the top of his agenda.

'You know,' she tried again, 'that every message we pass on from Bletchley Park and our own codebreakers in Heliopolis can help Auchinleck fight. We're getting decrypts that tell us Rommel is low on supplies and his men are worn out. Don't we owe it to the soldiers on the front line to keep providing those?'

Sansom's eyes narrowed.

'Could you withstand Gestapo torture, Stefania?' A picture of her cell, below this very building, flashed into Steffie's mind and she cringed back. 'No. Didn't think so. Get out before Rommel is here, Musso too.'

Steffie stared at him.

'Mussolini is coming?'

'Flew into Derna yesterday to lead the charge into Cairo, complete with white horse for his triumphal entry.'

'He's brought a horse?'

Good Lord, that was so Mussolini, she thought. The man loved to cut a dash and what better way than on a white charger, like a medieval knight at the head of his tame tanks?

'Not only that but they've been sending messages to all sympathisers in Cairo telling them to get out their party frocks for the victory ball. The dressmakers have been inundated with requests as everyone clamours to suck up to the new bosses. They've hated the British for years over here and I think you'll find Rommel and Mussolini will be hailed like heroes – another damned reason to get out.'

Steffie thought of Mussolini waving to her and her sister on their way to school and wondered what his presence in Egypt might mean. He wouldn't hurt her, she was sure of it. He'd been friends with her father, he'd charmed her mother, he'd invited her into his bed! He wouldn't, for one minute, believe her capable of intelligence work and he wouldn't hurt her.

Much as it went against the grain, she supposed there was sense in evacuating the codebreakers and intelligence officers. They couldn't afford for the enemy to find out about Bletchley Park, or the entire war could be lost. She, though, the little debutante from Rome, might just have enough personal cover to hang in at Heliopolis and keep processing the messages that could give Auchinleck and his boys a tiny chance to hold.

And hold they did. When Steffie finally got back to the Museum, she found a calmer atmosphere than at GHQ. Staff were burning materials, but in a far more orderly way than in the heart of the hysterical city, and without cutting into the ongoing work of reading enemy transmissions.

'Rommel's not happy,' Freddie told Steffie. 'Our navy are covering the routes into Tobruk so he's still having to get his supplies from Tripoli and they're running very low. The planes off Malta just hit a convoy he was waiting for and his attack is faltering. If we can keep him back a little longer, he'll be forced to dig in.'

'Fantastic. Get every single panicking message up to the SLUs on the front line. The troops need to know the enemy are wavering – it will give them heart.'

And it certainly seemed to. The Allied troops fought with renewed vigour and then came more news.

'The Americans have committed to sending tanks and troops. Instant supplies are promised from Suez and a full-scale invasion is planned for the autumn. They'll come in from Tunisia and we'll catch Rommel in a pincer. All we have to do is hold.'

Steffie listened to that particular piece of news and felt the shimmer of Gute Quelle behind it. The Black Code had, finally, been stopped and Bonner had been recalled to Washington. He'd come briefly to Heliopolis in his shiny car but without any sort of smile on his round face.

'I'm sorry, Stefania,' he'd said, standing on the steps of the Museum, running his smart military cap round and round in his hands. 'I did ask them to check the security of the code on several occasions but they kept assuring me it was intact.'

She'd felt kind of sorry for him and she'd liked the man, but he'd still been hard to forgive.

'Quite specific in your reports, weren't you?'

'That's what Washington demanded.'

'But you were here, in the field. You could see the toll that fighting in a desert takes on men. You could see how ill-adapted some of our equipment is and how hard the climate has been on many of our lads, but you couldn't resist criticising.'

'There were many, many inadequacies.'

'Like the one on the south-eastern border of Tobruk?'

'I'm sorry.'

It wasn't enough.

'Washington needed to know that, did they? It helped Roosevelt did it, that particular, specific detail?'

'No. But at least the president is committed to Africa now. Operation Torch could save you.'

'Oh no!' She put up a hand. 'I'm not having that, Bonner. I can accept that you weren't deliberately sabotaging us, but sabotage us you did, so you don't get to ride in as saviours. This is an American mess and it's only right the Americans should help clean it up. I just hope they make it in time.'

He'd left looking cross and uncomfortable and that had made her feel the same. She felt very alone out here now but the messages kept coming, perhaps down Ailsa's headset and through Fran's hands into hers, and that thought kept her going.

And then, a few days later, Rommel signalled to Berlin that he could attack no more.

'He's retreating?' Steffie cried.

'He's digging in,' Freddie corrected her. 'But it's a start.'

And it certainly was. Mussolini flew his white horse sulkily back to Italy, the panicking people of Cairo returned to their homes and packed up their Nazi flags and ball gowns, and 'the flap' as they'd started self-consciously calling it, was over. At least for now.

THIRTY-SIX

AUGUST 1942

Ailsa

Ailsa stood on the office balcony, Ned's hand in hers, and the rest of her colleagues alongside them as they all craned out to sea. The usual pink light of dawn was tinged darker red with the sand that the sirocco had been blowing in from North Africa for the last two weeks but today something far more welcome was about to make it into Valletta's Grand Harbour from Egypt.

'Is that them?' Ailsa screwed up her eyes, trying to make out the detail of the strange shapes growing slowly larger at the harbour entrance. The sun, already hot, was in her eyes but it was clear enough that these were ships – three of them, lashed together, the central one listing horribly from a torpedo hole, but being propped up by the two either side. 'It *is* them!'

The vast crowds of Maltese people lining the harbourside below had come to the same conclusion and were cheering and waving flags and hats. Ailsa could see Filomena and Ruzar leaping up and down like twenty-year-olds, and smiled in relief. She and Ned had visited the old couple often since their night-

mare New Year's Eve together and they'd been getting dangerously frail without enough food. Pray God, these ships would
bring what they needed to live out their last years in comfort.

The crew of the supply ship *Rochester Castle*, moored to
one side, were cheering as well. They'd arrived yesterday – the
first ship to make it to the starving island in months – and had
been cheered in with frantic delight by the islanders. They'd all
been kept alive by the dogged supply subs carving their magic
carpet from Alexandria beneath the sea but it had been a hard
struggle and the sight of heavily laden vessels finally coming
into the harbour felt like a miracle.

The *Rochester Castle* had carried food so its arrival had
brought huge joy to the emaciated crowds, but they were out
again this morning to see the *Ohio* limping in with fuel to keep
the brave Spitfires in the air above Malta. The people here were
desperate for food, but they were desperate for victory too and
the oil was welcomed as rapturously as yesterday's tins and
dried goods.

'The tide is turning,' Ned said in Alisa's ear. 'I feel it.'

She looked at him and saw the intensity in his brown eyes.

'You think we're going to win?'

'I think we stand a chance. Rommel has got nowhere in
Africa and Kesselring has been called away from Malta to help
him out, but he can't do much without...'

He gestured to the *Ohio*.

'Oil,' Ailsa finished.

It was true. They'd known for a long, long time that the
battle in the Med would be one of supplies and for far too much
of that time they'd been on the losing side. German convoys had
managed to sneak through while their own were destroyed but
now, with Gute Quelle silenced and BP working overtime
reading enemy signals, the tide really did seem to be turning.

Last week Churchill had flown into Cairo and Lloyd had
let it slip to Ailsa that he was there to discuss Operation

Torch – an American invasion of Africa to back up the brave Allied defence. Plus, he'd ordered an exhausted General Auchinleck home and appointed the renowned General Montgomery to command in his place. 'Monty' had arrived two days ago and was reportedly already whipping his troops into new energy.

He was also, it seemed, very open to the sort of undercover intel BP could provide and the Y-station on Malta had been asked to give every last effort as Rommel's supply line grew longer and thinner. Everyone was more than willing and, with thousands of tonnes of supplies making it into Valletta, they might finally have the energy and the weaponry to give it their all. It would be a long road yet, but at least they could see it shimmering on the horizon.

The three ships were coming into the central harbour now and the crowd were going wild. A faint tune drifted in on the sand-filled air and everyone strained forward to hear it.

'What on earth are they playing?' Ailsa asked, watching the sailors on the top deck dancing a giddy jig.

Ned smiled.

'Can you not catch it on the airwaves, my favourite radio operator?'

She leaned as far over the balcony as she dared, straining to hear, and then, suddenly, the notes seemed to come into aural focus and she was smiling too.

'"Chattanooga Choo-Choo"!' she said incredulously.

The great American oil tanker was being nursed into Valletta Grand Harbour to the strains of 'Chattanooga Choo-Choo' from its own speakers. She laughed and let out only the faintest squeak of protest as Ned pulled her into a jive, sending colleagues scuttling backwards to make space for his lively movements.

'Ned! We're getting in the—'

'Oh, dance, girl!' Marcia shouted. 'The Lord knows, we've

had precious little to dance about for far too long, so kick up those heels and enjoy it.'

Ailsa needed no more urging and she let Ned swing her into what they could only pray was the start of a happier future.

The ships, it turned out, had not just brought food, weapons and fuel but something else – something almost as precious. The first Ailsa knew of it was when she saw sailors unloading large hessian sacks coarsely marked with one, short word: MAIL. She stopped, staring. Might there be...?

Hope sprang in her heart and she turned hastily away, not wanting the pain of having it dashed. It had been six months since any letters had got through to Malta. There would be thousands of them backing up to the many people on the island, so it would be foolish to think any of the sacks had anything for her. Even if Ma or Pa had actually bothered to write.

They know you're on Malta, a dark voice said in her head. *They know you're on Malta and they must know how badly it's been bombed and starved.* There was a news crew on the island and they sent reels back via the magic carpet so that the world didn't forget about them. Ailsa had seen a couple – shown on the island before being shipped home – and they were full of the sort of 'plucky locals digging in' rhetoric that would keep the Germans from knowing they were getting to them. But the pictures of the bombed-out streets and buildings must surely have struck the parents of someone stationed out here...?

'To work, Ailsa,' she told herself sternly, and headed down the Lascaris caves to plug into the airwaves just over the sea and fight Rommel through her petticoat-trimmed headphones.

So focused was she that she missed the arrival of the island postman and the clamour for his pile of mail. So deep into Morse had she dived that she didn't hear the squeals of colleagues who'd finally received word from loved ones, and it was only when someone tapped her on the shoulder that she surfaced to see Ned with a sheaf of envelopes in his hand.

'These are for you, Ails.'

She stared. There had to be fifteen letters.

'All of them?'

'Every single one.'

Ailsa reached slowly out, embarrassed to see that her hand was shaking, but Ned took it firmly in his own and folded her fingers over the little pile. Ailsa noted the writing across the front – small and laboured, as if the writer had been concentrating very hard.

'Ma,' she whispered.

Ned pressed a surreptitious kiss onto her forehead.

'I think you're owed a break, Ails – why not take these up to the castle?'

It seemed as good an idea as any and, still rather dazed, Ailsa let him lead her to the bottom of the stairs, but when he moved to escort her upwards, she put out a hand. What if these letters said harsh things? She didn't want Ned to see that. Didn't want him to think she was weird.

'You can't come, Ned.'

'I can't? Why?'

'We, er, can't leave two radios at the moment.'

'But...'

'And, besides, I want to do this alone.'

'Oh,' he said. Then, 'Right, fine, of course.'

He looked hurt but she hadn't time to worry about it. The letters were burning a hole in her hand and, after six months of waiting, she couldn't bear a moment more.

'Bye.'

She shot up the stairs, past the guard and into the heat of the castle courtyard. With the sun high in the sky, there was precious little shade which meant she had the square to herself. Cramming against the one wall with a modicum of shadow, she sank to the blockwork floor and untied the rough string binding the collection. The writing on every envelope was the same and the postmarks stretched back to January – shortly after she'd been stuck in the bomb shelter and written home. Suddenly impatient, she ripped open the first one.

Ailsa,

Please don't die. Truly, I could not bear it. Ever since you were born you've been everything to me and your pa and the thought of you trapped and suffering is beyond terrible – especially with us being so stupid and stubborn and foolish about you leaving the island. We were wrong, Ailsa, my dear, dear lassie. It would have been nice, of course, if you'd wanted to stay and marry Alasdair and have a family right here, where we could see you and any bairns every single day, but not if it wasn't what you wanted. We didn't listen. We just lectured and we hate ourselves for it. Please don't die, my beautiful wee girl. Please don't get bombed or shot or trapped, for you are everything to us.

Ma and Pa

Ailsa felt a sob tear through her at the awkward, anxious, glorious letter and could do nothing to stop it echoing around the castle walls. The guard on the doors stepped forward to peer at her in concern but, seeing her tears falling onto the letters in her lap, he retreated into his sentry box to leave her to her emotions. She would not, she suspected, be the only one on Malta weeping over her post and at least hers were happy tears. She tore open the next letter, then the next and the next. They were along similar lines but increasingly frantic as poor Ma had received no reply.

I fear I might be writing this into a void, Ailsa. I fear you might be a ghost already, though if you were, surely you would be here to haunt me? I would welcome that, my beautiful girl. I would welcome it even if you chose to come and berate me for all eternity for sending you away feeling unloved and unwanted, for at least it would be a piece of you.

Oh – honestly! Forgive a glaikit old woman her superstitions. Of course you are not dead, simply cut off like they show in the pictures. Pa and I go once a week now. It's a long trip to Skye and sometimes we miss the last ferry back and have to sleep in the port authority office, but it's worth it to see the newsreels.

This Malta place looks very beautiful, Ailsa – and very ruined. But the reels show people going about their business, some of them even smiling or waving. We scan the screen for a glimpse of you but have caught nothing yet. You will be one of the smiling ones though, Ailsa, I know it. You were always so bold and brave and ready for adventure. What on earth made us think you would ever be happy on North Uist? We should have been urging you to go, to see the world, to have fun. Then you might not have had to join the WAAFs to escape and you might not be stuck in that hell.

You will survive, Ailsa. Surely you will survive? I have to believe it or I will go mad and dash myself against the rocks like the poor demented selkies. I'm sorry, my sweet bairn, I'm so, so sorry that we let you go feeling sad. I know now that life on this earth is too short and precious to waste not being at one with those you love and I know we don't say it often, well, ever, but we love you, Ailsa. We love you so much.

Ma and Pa

Tears were streaming down Ailsa's face and she let them fall, feeling the Maltese sun steam them off her pale, Scottish cheeks. They loved her. They loved her and they were happy she was out in the world and they wanted to see her again. Sitting in the heat of the castle courtyard in far-off Valletta, Ailsa pictured the worn, serious, loving faces of her parents and wept for joy. Then, taking a deep breath and packaging the letters carefully back up, she pushed herself off the cobbles and made for her office. And for Ned.

Life on this earth is too short and precious to waste not being at one with those you love, her ma had said and she was absolutely right. Ailsa took the stairs down nearly as fast as she'd headed up and burst into the Y-station. Lifting one headset from Ned's right ear, she bent over him and whispered into his ear: 'I love you.'

He spun and grabbed her round the waist, pulling her onto his knee right there in front of everyone and kissing her. She wriggled self-consciously but then Ma's words came into her head and she thought, So what? – and kissed him right back.

'If I'm not disturbing here...?'

They leaped apart to see Hugh Lloyd looking down on them, a wide grin on his face. Ailsa sprang away from Ned.

'Sorry, sir. So sorry. It won't happen again. I mean, it doesn't usually happen. I just, well, I heard from my folks and they said you had to cherish those you love and I thought, I thought...'

'You thought you'd do so. Quite right, Miss MacIver.'

'Really?'

'Of course. Just this once. But if I may – I have news.'

'You do?'

'I do. You're being recalled.'

'Recalled?'

'To Britain. You've been here far longer than the twelve months recommended for work abroad and now that shipping is getting through, your recall has been issued.'

'But, but... Ned's been here longer than me.'

'Twelve months is the recommended limit for *women*.'

'Because, what, we're weaker? Do I look weaker? Do you think I've been weaker?'

'No! Of course not.'

'Quite the reverse,' Ned muttered, and she gave him a little kick.

'But rules are rules,' Lloyd said.

'You're sending me away? I'm your best operator.'

'I know and I have already put up a protest but there's no moving the cogs of bureaucracy once they start turning. Would you not like to see home?'

Ailsa thought of North Uist. She thought of the white beaches, of the fresh sea spray and the low cottages of the village, and she thought of her ma and pa.

'I would,' she agreed. 'It's just...'

She glanced to Ned, who looked as forlorn as she felt.

'It won't be for a few weeks,' Lloyd said kindly. 'And I believe Mr Robinson is due home leave at Christmas...'

'You are?' Ailsa asked him.

'I am?' Ned repeated.

Lloyd winked.

'You are now, young man. I'll make sure of it.'

Steffie glanced to the windows. With the Spitfires fuelled up and in bold action over the island, the Luftwaffe were restricting themselves to night raids so someone had opened up holes in the boards. Ailsa could see the Grand Harbour framed like a picture before her, the tops of the miraculous convoy ships poking into view. But she remembered the torpedo-damaged *Ohio* limping in this morning and nerves shot through her.

'Is it not just as dangerous heading out on the sea as staying here?' she asked Lloyd.

'A lot less so these days, thanks to all your hard work, but, yes, we need to be sure ships can get safely to Alexandria before we OK your departure.'

Ailsa's ears pricked up.

'Alexandria? In Egypt?'

'That's the one. I believe the plan is to ship you there for a short hop to Cairo and home via Palestine.'

'Cairo?' Ailsa stuttered. 'I know someone in Cairo.'

Lloyd smiled.

'One of your fellow farmers, right?' Ailsa flushed, but he patted her arm. 'Very good. Let's hope she gets time off to show you around. I hear it's a beautiful city, well worth protecting from bloody Rommel. So – back to work, hey, and I'll keep you abreast of plans as they unfold.'

'Right, sir. Thank you, sir.'

Lloyd gave them a quick salute and was gone. Ailsa turned back to Ned, stunned by all that had unfolded in the last hour, but he seemed to have gone.

'Ailsa MacIver,' he said from somewhere below. She looked down and there was Ned, dropped to one knee before her.

'Ned...'

'Ailsa MacIver,' he repeated, more firmly. 'I think you are the most stubborn, strong, caring, wonderful woman on this whole earth. I can't believe fate brought you to me here on Malta and I'm already dreading you going – and counting the days to joining you. When I do, I'd like to talk to your father but, first and far more importantly, I'm talking to you. Please, Ailsa, will you marry me?'

Ailsa stared down at him as the rest of the office, getting wind of what was going on, spun round to stare. She felt ridiculously self-conscious and wanted nothing more than to yank Ned to his feet and bury herself in the airwaves.

'Ned...'

Life on this earth is too short and precious to waste not being at one with those you love.

Her mother was right.

'Ned – it would be my absolute honour.'

And then he was up and sweeping her into his arms and the whole office was whooping in delight.

Goodness, Ailsa thought, as she lost herself in Ned's kisses. *Aren't I going to have a lot to tell Steffie when I see her!* She remembered that first postcard of the Sphinx that she and Fran had stuck to the side of the blinking 'big barn' in their funny little caravan, and smiled at the thought that she might actually see it for herself. Since storming off North Uist, she'd made amazing friends, travelled halfway across Europe and, it seemed, found a husband she could truly love. Ailsa felt absolutely certain that, despite the bombs and the hunger and the red-hot sand, she had never, ever been as happy as she was right now.

THIRTY-SEVEN

NOVEMBER 1942

Steffie

'Steffie!'

Steffie heard her name shrieked at a hundred decibels and was just in time to brace herself as a red-headed thunderbolt sprang through the crowds in Cairo railway station and flung itself at her.

'Ailsa!'

She hugged her friend tight, shocked at how skinny she was but relishing the warmth of her embrace. This was the girl who had stood just along Bletchley station that cold, March dusk two and a half years ago, refusing to acknowledge her wave. Steffie had thought perhaps she was uppity or cold but as soon as she'd got to know the quiet Scot, she'd realised she was simply shy. Or, at least, she *had* been.

'Oh Stef, it's so, so good to see you.' Ailsa finally pulled back and, holding Steffie by the shoulders, looked her up and down. 'You look so well.'

'And you.'

Ailsa tossed her hair back.

'I do not. I look a fright, though thanks for trying to pretend. There's not exactly been much to eat on Malta these last six months.'

'You poor thing.' Steffie took in the sharp angles of her friend's face, the thinness of her pale arms, and the way her WAAF uniform hung off her, and suspected she would never fully grasp what she'd been through. 'Was it awful?'

'Awful,' Ailsa confirmed. 'At least in some ways. Being permanently hungry was awful. Waiting for convoys and hearing they'd been blown out the water was awful. Being bombed day and night was awful. Oh, and the time I was trapped in an air-raid shelter and had to be dug out – that was pretty awful too.'

'Ailsa, no!'

She shrugged.

'I survived. It's more than many did.'

Steffie grabbed her in another hug.

'I'm so, so sorry.'

'For what?'

'For ever recommending you were sent out there. It was so stupid of me. I put you in the most terrible danger and—'

'Stop right there, Stefania Carmichael. First off, I could have said no, so I put *myself* in danger. And second off, it's been totally and utterly wonderful.'

'But you said...'

Ailsa waved an easy hand.

'The hunger and the bombs and la-di-la, I know.'

'La-di-la?' Steffie gasped. Goodness, Ailsa really had changed. She looked at her more closely and saw the glow across her freckled skin, the sparkle in her blue-grey eyes. 'Oh,' she said, grinning. 'Oh, I see.'

'What do you see?'

Ailsa's blush told her she was on exactly the right lines.

'What's his name? Come on, Ails, what's the name of the man who's turned a ravaged island under siege into paradise?'

'Steffie!' Ailsa protested, nudging her, but then she shyly added, 'Ned. He's called Ned Robinson and, and...'

Shyness finally got to her and she simply wiggled her left hand. There, sitting proudly on her ring finger was an unusual and very pretty sunshine-yellow stone set in simple silver.

'You're engaged?!'

Ailsa nodded, her eyes shining.

'Ned proposed to me the day the boss told me I was going to be posted home.'

'How romantic.'

'And he got me the ring a week later. Had it made specially. It's honey calcite – native to Malta.'

'It's lovely.'

Ailsa looked suddenly self-conscious.

'It's not a fancy diamond like yours but we—' Steffie held up her own hand to stop her and Ailsa stared at it in horror. 'Where's your ring, Steffie?'

'My *ex*-ring is who knows where with my *ex*-fiancé.'

'No! Oh Steffie, I'm so, so sorry. What happened?'

Steffie shivered. That was far too big a question for a bustling railway station and seeing Ailsa so glowing with love was bringing the hurt rushing back far too fast.

'I need a drink to answer that. Come on, Ails, I've wangled you a room in Shepheard's Hotel. It's the best in Cairo.'

'Just me?'

Steffie looked around.

'Oh, my goodness, is this Ned here too? Are you—'

'No, stupid! I meant, are you not staying with me?'

'I didn't want to presume...'

Ailsa shook her head and hugged her again.

'I've not seen you for a year and a half, Steffie. I want to make the most of every minute.'

Steffie grinned and picked up a neat bag at her side.

'Good job I packed in case then. Shall we?'

She ushered her towards the exit and Ailsa linked an arm through hers and nodded down at the bag.

'That's a tiny case for you, Stefania. Remember your grand luggage when we first arrived at BP?'

Steffie groaned.

'Do I ever? I thought my arms were going to drop off. And there was you with your smart duffel bag, looking every inch the pro traveller.'

'Ironic! And, if I'm honest, it was digging into my shoulder horribly.'

Steffie laughed.

'What a pair we were. At least Fran was sorted.'

'I wish she was here,' Ailsa said.

'Me too,' Steffie agreed, 'but we'll all be together again soon enough because...'

'Because?'

'Because I'm coming home with you. Some nonsense about women not being meant to work abroad for too long. No idea why but, to be honest, I'm glad. I love this city but with all that's gone on, I think I've had about enough of it for the moment.'

'I hope you can manage a couple more days.'

'With you here I can manage anything,' she agreed happily, leading the way out of the station onto the main road. 'Now... Ailsa?' Ailsa had stopped dead, staring around her. 'Is everything all right?'

'Oh, my lord!' Ailsa whispered as the noise and heat and stench of Cairo clamoured in on them.

Steffie tried to look at it through her friend's eyes and could sort of see why the Scottish girl was so shocked. Cairo was teeming with all the usual life. Right in front of them a woman with a cage of chickens on her head was arguing with a man leading a donkey laden with rolls of carpet. An irate Austin 7 was trying to get past and a rickety tram was bearing down on the whole scene at speed. Somehow, with the grace born of long experience, both woman and man managed to slide sideways, still arguing, in time to allow the Austin to zip away just before the tram collided with any of them and, as it went on its way, the street filled once more.

'It's so busy,' Ailsa said, her eyes as wide as moons.

'Welcome to Cairo. Come on, we'll get a trap.'

'A what?'

'A trap. Far cheaper than a taxi and easier to run because the only fuel they need is grass.'

'Grass?' Ailsa queried, but then gave a low 'oh!' as Steffie whistled to a passing donkey-trap and the driver swept to a halt and leaped down with a flourishing bow.

'Where to, lovely ladies? I take you wherever you want to go. Pyramids maybe? I do very good tour of pyramids. Very good.'

'The pyramids?' Ailsa gasped. 'Are they close enough to see?'

'Of course, lovely lady. With good driver they are very close. I take you?'

Ailsa looked as if she might say yes right there and then, and Steffie put a hand on her arm.

'Not today, thank you.'

'But—' Ailsa started and Steffie smiled at her. 'Maybe tomorrow.'

'I can call for you tomorrow,' the driver offered eagerly. 'Any time. Any time at all. I have good donkey – see.'

He indicated his beast which, to be fair to him, did look like one of the better-fed ones.

'What's her name?' Ailsa asked, stroking her nose.

'Frances,' the man said. Steffie and Ailsa both stared at him.

'Really?' Ailsa asked.

'Really. Was my mother's name.'

'You named your donkey after... Oh never mind. Wait till we tell Fran, Ailsa – it'll be hilarious.' She climbed into the trap, tugging Ailsa after her as the driver fussed around, delighted. 'To Shepheard's, please, and if Frances does a good job, we will most certainly hire her to take us to the pyramids tomorrow.'

'Oh, Frances will not let you down,' he said with another bow, then he leaped into the driver's seat in front of them and tugged on the reins. Frances did not budge. The driver muttered something furious to her in Egyptian but she'd found a tuft of grass at the side of the road and was not to be distracted. 'One minute. She very good donkey. Very good. She just...'

'Stubborn,' Steffie said. 'We know!'

And, to the driver's great bemusement, they both burst out laughing.

An hour later, after Ailsa had gawped anew at the opulence of Shepheard's and they'd taken turns luxuriating in a bubble bath, they settled on the terrace and Steffie ordered Martinis.

'I was meant to stay here the night after they finally let me out of prison,' she told Ailsa, 'but Rommel was encircling Tobruk and it didn't feel right lounging around drinking Martinis when I could be doing something to help.'

'Me too,' Ailsa agreed. 'Well, not the fancy hotel, obviously, but I went back to work. I remember wondering if the messages I was hearing down the airwaves were getting to you.'

'Via Fran.'

'Fran the donkey...?'

They giggled.

'Ironic, really, that that's one of the few animals we never had on the farm.'

Steffie groaned.

'That farm! Another of my stupid ideas – it nearly got us all in deep trouble.'

'Or it nearly got the whole world out of it. We were the ones going on about Gute Quelle. If we hadn't pushed it, this attaché chap might still be broadcasting to Washington and we might, might...'

She stopped and Steffie looked around Shepheard's, suddenly imagining Rommel and his Nazis living it up in here while she fled for her life. Gute Quelle had only been a part of Rommel's success but since he'd been silenced, things had certainly changed. The other day a German message had come in bemoaning the loss of their 'eyes' on the ground and there was no doubt the attacks were not as targeted as they'd been before. General Montgomery was claiming the credit, which was galling, but that was 'secret intelligence' for you and at least it had inspired confidence in the men. They'd seen Rommel off at the Al Halfa ridge and now they were storming all over the Germans at El Alamein.

The little railway siding that Sansom had confidently told her the Allies would not be able to hold for more than a few days, was fast becoming the site of a great victory. Yesterday, just hours before she'd been released to meet Ailsa, Steffie had been in the office when they'd decrypted a message from Rommel to high command in Berlin, asking permission to retreat. *Panzerarmee ist erschöpft* it had read. It hadn't taken much of Steffie's finishing school learning to interpret that one: The panzer army is exhausted.

Permission had been denied by Hitler – the man was a maniac – but BP's regular decoding of German supply lists told them that for once the Fuhrer was likely to be disobeyed. Rommel might still have men and tanks, but he had little ammunition or fuel and no choice but to back off or be annihilated. Not that backing off would help him much either as Operation

Torch was set for next week and he'd be trapped whichever way he turned. The Allies had won the supply war.

'It's bloody galling that the Americans are riding to the rescue,' Steffie confided to Ailsa, her voice low, though she really wanted to shout her indignation from the rooftops. 'They're not even needed, or they wouldn't be if Monty trusted our intel. Our decrypts showed the Germans were on their knees long before the *"erschöpft"* message and a determined strike could have secured victory without the need for any stars or stripes bounding in claiming glory.'

'When all they're truly doing is mopping up their own mess.'

'Exactly! I was so mad when I spoke to Bonner, Ails. He was a nice man, and a good general, I'm sure. He certainly had plenty of opinions about how we were running things out here.'

'Opinions he sent straight to Washington.'

'Via Hitler!'

They shook their heads at each other but now the waiter was coming with their Martinis and it was time to put it all behind them. Gute Quelle was silenced, Cairo was safe and they were together.

'Cheers!' Steffie said.

'Cheers.' They both drank deep then Ailsa looked into Steffie's eyes and said, 'And now, my sweet one, tell me about Matteo.'

It took a long time for Steffie to force the whole sorry story out, but it was good to finally speak about it to someone who understood. Betty had been kind enough but had taken an all-men-are-bastards approach to the problem, preferring to offer gin than chat. At the time, it had probably been better but now, with space to think, Steffie was glad to talk it over.

'Do you know what he's doing now?' Ailsa asked when she'd finally stuttered her way through the whole escape debacle.

Steffie shook her head.

'I don't know and I don't care.'

Ailsa leaned in.

'That's not true, is it?'

Steffie looked at her in surprise.

'It *is*. He's a bastard. The moment I said that I enjoyed my work, he decided he didn't want to marry me. That's shallow and callous and self-seeking and, and...'

What were the other words Betty had used? Steffie's head was hazy and they weren't finding their way to the surface.

'That's all true, but it doesn't stop you loving him.'

'Ailsa! How's that meant to help?'

She shrugged.

'Because, if you ask me, until you know what you feel you can't deal with it.' Steffie gaped at her and she looked suddenly self-conscious. 'Sorry. Martini talking. Forget it.'

'No. No, you're right.'

'I may not be. I'm hardly an expert. I just know that I was really, really angry with Ma and Pa for casting me off when I said I didn't want to marry Alasdair and I, you know, fuelled that when I was in Malta – did the whole "I hate them and don't want anything to do with them anyway" thing – but it didn't help. It just simmered inside me. It was only when I realised I loved them and didn't want to argue any more that I started dealing with it.'

'Right. And what's happened?'

Ailsa looked uncomfortable suddenly.

'Should we eat? I feel a bit unsteady.'

'In a minute. What's happened, Ailsa, with your parents?'

She fiddled with her pretty ring.

'They wrote to me saying they were sorry and they loved me.'

'Right. Nice.'

'Steffie, I didn't mean...'

'No, it really is nice. For you. I'm glad.'

'Maybe Matteo will come round too when he's had time to think. I bet he's really missing you, Steffie.'

'Yes, well, unlucky. He had his chance and he blew it. You're right though, Ails – I did love him and there's no point pretending otherwise. But I'll get over it. Especially with another one of these.'

She looked around for the waiter, but Ailsa grabbed her arm.

'Please, Stef – I really need to eat. There's not so much on me these days.'

Steffie shook herself.

'Of course. Sorry, Ails. Come on – if we're really lucky they'll have steak.'

'Steak?!' Ailsa's voice came out on a squeak.

'It's probably camel or something but they cook it pretty well.'

A waiter went past carrying two plates laden with chunky steaks, covered in a creamy sauce and Ailsa grabbed Steffie's arm.

'I think this place might actually be heaven,' she said weakly and hastened them to a table.

Steffie smiled softly.

'Pyramids tomorrow?' she suggested once Ailsa had ordered 'your two biggest, juiciest steaks' with supreme confidence and only a small slur.

'Pyramids tomorrow,' Ailsa agreed. 'With Frances.' They giggled. 'And we'll find a postcard to send to the real Fran to tell her we'll be back soon.'

'Hens returning to the farm...?' Steffie suggested but then they both sobered and looked at each other.

'Perhaps we won't mention the farm,' Ailsa said.

'Definitely not,' Steffie agreed.

They had both been through hard times out here in the

Med but perhaps, at last, they were coming to an end. Steffie pictured the caravan and, despite all the opulence of Shepheard's Hotel, she longed for it. Matteo was still a wound in her heart but, like all wounds, it would mend eventually. Having one friend with her was already proving a huge balm and it would be even better once all three of them were together again at last.

THIRTY-EIGHT

DECEMBER 1942

Fran

'Morning, Frances. Post for you.'

Fran gave Gloria a blurry smile. She'd never been great in the mornings and, Lordy, the cold didn't help. She ushered her landlady into the caravan, where the iron stove provided some warmth, and looked eagerly at the postcard.

Fran,

We're on our way home to the caravan. Make sure it's nice for us. Actually, it could be a terrible mess and we'd still love it. Journey back proving tiresome, though we're told we should get a boat in the next week. Really hope we're back for Christmas.

All our love,

Steffie and Ailsa

Fran sighed and turned it over to see a picture of Lisbon. Heavens – what were they doing there? She supposed that, with Spain and Portugal being neutral, it was a safe way to get passage home but it seemed an incredible detour from Egypt. She stuck the postcard on the wall next to the one of the pyramids that had arrived weeks ago and felt a deep pull of longing. Ridiculous really – these girls weren't her actual family, but somehow they'd come to feel like the sisters she'd never had and she was dying to see them again.

'Are they nearly here yet?' Gloria asked.

'Lisbon!' Fran said, though she knew Gloria would have read the card before she brought it across.

'What an adventure!'

'Isn't it? Ailsa will be thrilled. She was desperate to see the world.'

'Shame it's taken a war to do it, but, hey, that card was sent three weeks ago' – she *had* read it – 'so if that boat did come, they must surely be close. How far away can Portugal be?'

'Approximately fourteen hundred miles,' Fran said automatically.

With the Mediterranean more or less secured, she and Peter had been asked to start mapping the Atlantic waters where the German U-boats were wreaking havoc, so her geography had been expanded.

'That far! Gracious.'

Fran swallowed. Sometimes she hated knowing as much as she did. She'd assumed Steffie and Ailsa were coming home by plane, which had been worrying enough, but now she knew they were in the Atlantic... On the whole, the wolf packs were patrolling far higher up, in the shipping lanes between Britain and the USA, picking off convoys as they'd done for far too long in the Med, but who knew where one might stray. Surely, if her friends had left even two weeks ago, they'd be in the English

Channel by now? And if a boat had gone down, she'd know about it. It would be in her index.

Fran bit her lip and suddenly felt Gloria enfolding her in a hug, her woollen coat tickling her cheek in the exuberant embrace.

'They'll be here soon enough, love, you'll see, and you'll be eating turkey with them on Christmas Day for sure.'

Fran smiled.

'Thanks, Gloria, but I doubt it'll be turkey, even if they make it in time.'

'Oh, I wouldn't be so sure.' Gloria pulled back and gave her a broad wink. 'Amazing what you can fit into these barns.'

'You've got—'

'Ssh now. Mum's the word, hey?'

'Of course.'

Gloria gave her another quick hug and made for the door. As she pulled it open, an icy blast swept in but, to Fran's surprise, the older woman threw open her arms.

'You like the cold, Gloria?' Fran asked, pulling her cardigan closer. It was actually Steffie's – one of the many lovely items she'd left behind when she went to Egypt – and, although thin, quite wonderfully warm.

'Not the cold,' Gloria said, 'but look at those clouds!'

She gestured to the horizon and Fran squinted at the low, grey clouds squatting over the hills.

'Erm...'

'Snow,' Gloria chuckled. 'Those clouds mean snow. The grandkiddies will be very excited.'

Fran smiled. She rather liked snow herself and, as she looked at the decidedly heavy clouds again, she prayed it would fall while she was on leave. Growing up in Cambridge they'd been short of decent tobogganing hills, but there was a lovely one out at Old Woughton. She'd already promised Valérie she'd take her if the snows came.

'Tobogganing?' Valérie had said, stumbling cutely over the word. 'What is this tobogganing?'

'Going down the hill on a toboggan – you know, a sledge. Or a tray, if we can't find a proper one.'

'You want me to go down a mountain on a tray?!'

Fran had laughed and kissed her.

'It won't be a mountain.'

'Do you not have skis?'

Again, Fran had been struck by how different their upbringings had been, and longed to see Valérie's home – yet another reason to get this damned war won.

'You all set for Christmas?' Fran asked Gloria as she headed out into the yard.

'All set, love. Our Mary and the grandkiddies arrive tomorrow. Her Tom is stuck out in Africa but she had a letter yesterday and says he seems in good spirits.'

'He's at Tobruk, isn't he?' Fran asked.

Gloria's substantial chest puffed out in pride.

'He is that. His battalion were at the front of the charge to retake it, you know, or so he says. I wish they hadn't been. I'd much rather he was at the back but still – they made it and he's alive and well and holding the fort while others keep on chasing that Rommel down, so I'll take that. Won't be the same as having him round our own table, but at least he's safe for Mary and the littlies.'

'Amen to that,' Fran said.

The re-taking of Tobruk back in November had been huge cause for celebration and the church bells had been brought out of wartime retirement to ring across England on the Sunday after the victory. Rommel was on the run, Britain was rapidly gaining control of North Africa and there were murmurings in Hut 3 about an invasion of Italy. Churchill had been heard to call it the 'soft underbelly of Europe' and was preparing to stick an Allied bayonet right into it. With the Nazis struggling in

frozen Russia, the time was ripe and the mood in BP was
cautiously optimistic. Fran was praying that 1943 might see an
end to this horrible war, but, for now, it was Christmas. She
glanced at the clock.

'Heavens, I'd better get going. I'm off up to London today to
see my folks.'

'How lovely!' Gloria beamed.

'Yes,' Fran agreed because it would be, it really would be
lovely. They were important to her. She loved them. She just
hoped they didn't ask her to join the damned ambulance
brigade again.

Three hours later saw Fran and Valérie outside the smart
entrance of Oddenino's Hotel in Piccadilly. They both had
leave and, with Fran's family up, and Valérie claiming mysterious people to meet, they were grabbing the chance of a mini
holiday. Valérie had offered to sort a hotel and Fran had been
excited at the thought of being together, but she hadn't imagined anything quite like this.

'This can't be it,' Fran said, staring up at the grand building.

'Oh yes,' Valérie said, 'come on. It'll be far warmer inside.'

She made for the door, almost bumping into a very
elegantly dressed older couple, and Fran yanked her back.

'Valérie,' she hissed, 'there's no way we can afford to stay
here.'

Valérie spun round and dropped a whisper of a kiss on her
nose.

'We don't need to, darling. I have an—'

'Uncle?'

Valérie grinned.

'Correct. I have an uncle with a suite here. He's away for a
few days on, you know, business, so it's all ours tonight.'

Fran knew better, by now, than to ask about the nature of

the Rousseau family business and, really, who would turn down a room in this gorgeous place, not to mention a suite?

Think like Steffie, she told herself and tried to mimic her friend's easy swagger as she followed in Valérie's wake. She doubted she pulled it off, but Valérie had swagger enough for both of them and soon they were being shown to the top floor by an impeccable bellboy.

'Thank you,' Valérie said, slipping coins into his hand like a pro.

Fran stared around at the luxurious art-deco furniture, the rich, velvet curtains, the embossed wallpaper.

'Your uncle lives here?'

Valérie frowned.

'No, Frances. My uncle lives in Lyon but since the bastard greedy pig Nazis took the south of France as well as the north, he has been staying here.'

Fran swallowed. Vichy France had collapsed last month and the Germans were rampaging over the south, seemingly trying to make up for their failures in Russia. Valérie vacillated between fury and tears and if it ever got too much, Fran just tried to picture Nazis stamping their jackboots all over Cambridge and found new reserves of kindness for the girl she loved.

Now she grabbed Valérie's hand and pulled her down onto the elegant couch beneath the high windows, kissing her deeply.

'Well, it's lovely.'

She felt Valérie soften against her.

'It is. And for tonight, it is all ours. Our nest.'

Fran giggled.

'Our nest, yes.' She pulled away to look into Valérie's eyes. 'Do you think, Valérie, that after the war...'

She ran out of words. After the war was so hard to imagine. Her world had become dominated by BP and her exciting work

there, by life in the caravan, by Steffie and Ailsa and the battle
to keep them safe, by Valérie. She could scarce remember the
shy librarian she'd been before Peter's fateful visit to the university library nearly three years ago, and she certainly didn't want
to go back. But what *did* she want...?

'After the war...?' Valérie prompted, sounding unusually
nervous.

Fran swallowed. This was important. Being with Valérie
made her feel whole, real, complete, not to mention good old-
fashioned happy.

'Do you think that after the war, we might, you know, be
together?'

'Would you like that?' Valérie's voice was almost a whisper
and the usually sparky French girl looked uncharacteristically
afraid. But of what – of Fran pulling away, or of Fran getting too
close? There was only one way to find out.

Screwing up all her courage, Fran said, 'I would. Would,
er... would you?'

'Oh yes!'

Her heart lifted.

'Really? But could we? Would, you know, society let us?'

'Society – pah! What do they know?'

'Well, quite. I mean, absolutely. The only thing is that they
think they know a lot and...'

'And they are wrong. But it matters little. How many
women do you know who live together, Frances?'

Fran blinked.

'Oh, quite a few. We have this lovely pair of older ladies just
down the road from us. And Miss Mitchell, the senior librarian
at the UL lives with her, her...' She stared at Valérie. 'I've been
really stupid, haven't I?'

Valérie smiled and cuddled in close to kiss her.

'Not stupid, Frances, just innocent. It is very sweet.'

'So, we can...?'

'Live together as poor spinster friends, unable to find a husband with so many young men killed in the war...'

'I see. Yes! Poor us.'

Valérie's eyes sparkled wickedly and she jumped up and straddled Fran.

'Poor, poor us.'

And then she kissed her and Fran felt like the richest girl in the whole wide world.

'Would you like to come to dinner with my family, Valérie?' she asked when they finally pulled apart.

'I thought you'd never ask.'

'This is my friend, Valérie,' Fran said to her parents when they made it to Restaurant Frascati on nearby Oxford Street that evening. 'She's French.'

'Oh, you poor dear.' Anne Morgan clasped Valérie's hands. 'To have one's home invaded is such a terrible, terrible intrusion.'

'It is,' Valérie agreed. 'But we will win it back.'

'That's the spirit,' Fran's father said. 'The Germans have overstretched themselves in Russia and now we've got them on the ropes in the Med, the tide is turning. No idea what took us so long in Africa but I heard word there was a spy telling the Germans all our positions – bastard!'

'Really?' Fran said, not daring to look at Valérie for fear of laughing out loud.

'Yep. Some Bedouin probably. They're sneaky devils. Though I also heard something about a belly dancer. Wouldn't surprise me. I gather she didn't stop at belly dancing and you know what pillow talk is like...'

'Henry!' Anne admonished and now it was impossible for Fran to hide her laughter.

'Well, whoever it was, let's hope they've caught them.'

'Bound to have,' Henry said confidently. 'Good lot at the secret services, doing a top job.'

Under the table, Fran felt Valérie's hand rest lightly on her knee and glanced briefly over. She wished she could tell her father that she was a part of those services but Valérie knew and that was something. She surveyed the restaurant. It was a beautiful place, the huge room set out like a garden courtyard with elegant arches and potted trees providing lush greenery. It might not quite be Malta or Cairo or Lisbon but for tonight it felt exotic enough for Frances and she smiled at her parents.

'Is Robert coming?'

'Should be here any minute,' Anne said. 'Oh, and Frances, go gently with him.'

'Gently?' Fran frowned. 'But...'

'Mother, Father, little sis!'

Suddenly there he was, her elder brother, oozing bonhomie as always though, forewarned, Fran looked closely at him and could see the strain around his eyes and in the taut line of his shoulders.

'Rob. It's so good to see you.'

'You too, little sis. Really. You're a pain and all that but, well, I, you know, care about you. Quite a lot actually.'

Fran gaped at him. Her brother's usual means of showing care was to flick a tea towel at the back of her legs, so this was unexpected to say the least. At her side, she saw her mother looking anxiously up at them and so resisted her usual sarcastic response.

'I care about you too, Rob. Come and sit down.'

Robert took his place at the table and made ready small talk but it was clear this was the veneer of his bedside manner and not the real man beneath. Once they had ordered and he'd drunk – rather fast – two glasses of wine, Fran turned to him.

'What's it like out there, Rob?'

'Out, er, out there?' He gave a nod of his head in a vaguely southerly direction.

'On the front,' Fran agreed gently.

He shuddered.

'Vile. It's absolutely vile, Fran. I hate it. Men come into the hospital with all these horrific injuries – burns and cuts and limbs blown off in the most brutal of ways. And they're all so brave. They do the whole stiff-upper-lip thing and make jokes and tell me I'm wonderful as I dab bloody antiseptic onto a missing arm in the vague hope of saving them from septicaemia. It's only really at night that you hear them cry but then...'

He looked down, his fingers folding his napkin over and over in his lap. Fran reached out and placed her own around them, stilling him.

'It would be worse for them without you, Rob.'

'You think? Maybe not. Maybe if we just let them die that would be better. Sometimes this whole, grand medicine thing seems to be nothing more than a way to prolong suffering.' Everyone at the table drew in a deep breath. Robert looked at Fran. 'You got it right, Fran. Stay well away. Who needs to see blood and guts and the inside of a man's brains? We don't need people to stand around in white patching us up – we need people to finish this goddamned war. Are you doing that, Fran?'

Fran had no idea what to say but Valérie leaned over.

'She *is*, Robert,' she said with quiet calm. 'We can't say in what ways, but I promise you she is.'

'Then, thank you,' Robert said to Fran, looking calmer. 'Truly, thank you. And now, I'm on leave from all this mess, it's nearly Christmas and we're together. Let's celebrate while we can.'

And they did, from dinner through to cocktails back at Oddenino's and dancing to a wonderful swing band until the small hours. Fran danced with her brother, she danced with her father and she danced with Valérie and no one cared. As long as you were dancing, it little mattered who with. You just had to keep on kicking up your heels and praying that Fritz stayed off them until he could be sent packing. When they finally collapsed into bed, Fran cuddled into Valérie's arms and felt her world slide into place. It was a funny, sideways place – one she hadn't even known she could fit into – but it was hers and she loved it.

That afternoon, the train slid back into Bletchley and Fran woke from dozing on Valérie's shoulder.

'Are we back already?'

She felt as if she'd been in London for a week, not just one night, but it was curiously pleasant to see the tiny Bletchley station.

Home, she thought, as she scrambled to grab her bag from the overhead netting. If only Steffie and Ailsa were here too it would be perfect, but surely it couldn't be long. She flung open the door and the sweet sound of 'Ding Dong Merrily on High' wafted into the carriage.

'Look at those people!' Valérie exclaimed. 'They're singing.'

'Carol singers,' Fran told her delightedly, looking over to the group of scouts and guides huddled in the arched entrance, reading their carol sheets by the light of tissue-covered torches.

It was almost dark and the thick clouds were low over the station. The air was bright with frost and, as Fran stuck her hand out, snowflakes caught in her woollen gloves. She jumped down, her cold nose picking up the smell of mulling wine from the station canteen, and clapped her hands.

'Come on, Valérie, I'll treat you to... Oh.'

Fran stopped dead, for there, just down the platform, like the imprint of another evening almost three years ago, stood two young women.

'It can't be,' she breathed, but then they turned and she

knew that, like a perfect Christmas miracle, it was. 'Steffie? Ailsa?'

She glanced to Valérie, but the other girl was grinning broadly.

'Go!' she urged. 'Go, go, go. I'll see you later.'

Fran dropped a kiss on her lips and then she was turning and she was running and she was shouting their names: 'Steffie! Ailsa!'

'Fran!'

They dropped their bags and flung their arms wide and, as the carol singers hit the 'glorias' with quite impeccable timing, Fran fell into the embrace of her two best friends and knew that now she truly was home.

THIRTY-NINE

NEW YEAR'S EVE 1942-3

Steffie

Steffie looked around the shabby happiness of the Duncombe Arms, feeling simultaneously completely at home and utterly dislocated. The wooden floorboards felt unfamiliarly sticky, the wallpaper very dark, and the smell – a mix of cigarette smoke, beer and damp wool – suffocating.

Her year and a half in Cairo was still permeating her sunbrowned skin and every so often she would find herself reaching up to flick away a fly or brush sand from her hair and then remember that she was no longer in the desert but in a cold, damp, wooden hut in Buckinghamshire. Even the work here felt less urgent so far away from the front. Above all, though, there was one big contrast between the last time she'd worked in Hut 4 and now – Matteo.

'Selfish pig,' she muttered, because it seemed the right thing to do and he *had* been selfish. And a pig. Maybe.

Had he been right to be offended when she'd refused to escape with him? she sometimes wondered. It had been very romantic after all. He had lain himself on the line, told her that she was more important to him than his country, so was it any surprise that he'd been hurt when she hadn't been able to do the same? She sighed.

'Drink, Steffie?' Harry Hinsley asked, bouncing up. 'It's so good to have you working for me again, you know.'

She smiled gratefully

'Thanks, Harry.'

'What'll it be then – pint of the landlord's finest ale like your friend?'

He gestured to Ailsa, clutching a pint of peculiar, cloudy liquid.

Steffie wrinkled up her nose. 'No thank you!'

She wanted to ask for a Martini, served with an olive in a chilled glass, just like at Shepheard's, but she was hardly going to get that at the Drunken Arms. 'A gin and lime would be lovely, Harry.'

'Coming right up!'

He swung off to the bar, pausing on his way through the crowd to kiss a pretty girl Steffie thought worked in Hut 8. She sighed again. Everyone was in love around here and New Year's Eve was bringing out the soppiness in the lot of them.

Christmas had been fantastic. She, Fran and Ailsa had spent it together in the caravan. They'd invited Valérie along but she'd been in London with one of an apparent bevvy of uncles, so it had been just the three of them. They'd decorated their little home up to the nines, bringing in fir branches and holly sprigs and pasting toilet-paper snowflakes to all the windows. The police had sheepishly returned the farm and they'd hailed it gloriously then frosted it with Epsom salts and stuck tiny holly trees on the grass of Malta and in front of the big barn of Egypt before fashioning a mini caravan out of a matchbox to sit by the little barn of England. Home.

On Christmas Eve, shifts over, they'd sat with a bottle of Alfie's fig gin, making endless paper chains out of cut-up magazines, and then Ailsa had fallen over trying to put them up and the other two had caught her and they'd ended up in a giggling heap on the caravan floor. Eventually, they'd picked themselves up to head out to midnight mass in the local church – a service so packed with the BP incomers that they'd had to stand in the graveyard but, warmed by the gin, they hadn't cared a jot.

They'd been slow out of bed the next day but had shared stockings packed with tiny treats and home-made goodies before proceeding to a treat of a Christmas dinner – a huge leg from Alfie's illicit turkey, fresh stuffing, delicious roast potatoes and a bottle of real French wine that Fran had got from one of Valérie's ubiquitous uncles. It had snowed again, coating the ground in the finest of powders, and after lunch they'd all wrapped up and gone out for a snowball fight with Gloria, Alfie and their grandchildren. It had been a wonderful day.

And tonight was a wonderful night too, Steffie told herself, plastering on a smile as Harry returned with her drink. 1943 would be a good year. She'd work hard, have fun, maybe even date again. Her stomach clenched at the thought and took a big gulp of her gin and looked around for her friends.

Fran was up on the impromptu dance floor, bouncing around in a most un-Fran-like way, hand in hand with the beautiful French girl, Valérie. They were clearly a pair, glowing in the light reflected by each other, and Steffie thought it was wonderful. She hadn't talked to Fran about it yet but she would, soon. She'd tell her that love is very precious and that you should seize it when you get a chance and hold on for all you're worth. Just as she hadn't...

She pulled her eyes away but they landed instead on Ailsa, threading her way towards her with her young man, Ned, in tow. There was another perfect pair. Ailsa had been so excited when she'd heard that he was landing on 27 December and had rushed off to meet him and catch the overnight train up to Scotland to meet her parents. They'd only got back a couple of hours ago but she was shining with joy.

'So,' Steffie asked her, 'tell me how it went.'

'Amazing!' Ailsa said, her Scottish burr sounding more pronounced after her time back home. 'Ma and Pa were so pleased to see me. They kept hugging me. They never hug me.'

'They hugged me too,' Ned said.

'They did!' Ailsa looped her arm around his waist and Steffie battled not to envy them their ease. That had been her and Matteo once, unable to keep their hands off each other. 'They hugged him all the time.'

'And when I plucked up courage to ask Ailsa's father for her hand in marriage – which is a daunting task, let me tell you, when you're faced with a grizzled fisherman...'

'He is not grizzled!' Ailsa protested. Ned raised an eyebrow at her and she laughed. 'Well, maybe a bit.'

'A lot,' Ned said. 'And definitely scary. But I'd barely even got the words out before he was falling over himself to say yes and calling Ma and—'

'Ma?' Steffie queried.

Ned blushed sweetly.

'She told me to call her that.'

'Did she indeed? You'll be having to learn Scottish reels next, Ned.'

'Oh, he already has,' Ailsa told her. 'Pa was off round the village calling everyone to the pub the moment he'd said yes. Quite the night it was.'

'It was,' Ned agreed ruefully. 'I thought it was quiet up on that island – turns out, I was wrong.'

Ailsa giggled.

'You coped admirably. There's not many people have to face the whole village in one go like that.' She leaned in to Steffie. 'Even Alasdair came.'

'The man you ran away from?'

Ailsa pulled a face.

'Poor Alasdair. But, guess what, he's stepping out with a lovely widow and they seem very happy together so, you know, all's well that ends well.'

'Lovely,' Steffie managed.

'We're going to see my parents tomorrow,' Ned went on proudly. 'I can't wait for them to meet Ailsa. They're going to love her.'

'I don't doubt it.'

'And then, when we get back, we thought we might...' They looked at each other and burst into wide smiles. 'We might get married.'

Steffie gasped.

'Married? Here?'

'Why not?' Ned said. 'I have to go back to Malta in two weeks, so we thought, let's just get on with it. I've applied for a special licence.'

'And I've got Ma and Pa train tickets down. They're terrified, bless them. They've never been to England and they think it's full of big, blond Anglo-Saxons waiting to kill them.'

'That's Germany,' Steffie said darkly. They all sobered and she hated herself. 'Stupid thing to say. Forget it. That's amazing Ailsa, Ned. Wonderful news.'

Ailsa took her arm.

'You *will* be my bridesmaid, won't you, Stef? You and Fran?'

'It would be my honour,' Steffie forced out but the words stuck in her throat and she looked hastily away. She was glad Ailsa was happy, she really was. Fran too. It was just...

Ailsa leaned in.

'I'm sorry, Stef. I've been tactless.'

'No, you—'

'You'll find someone.'

'Oh, I wasn't—'

'Of course you were and I don't blame you, but you *will* find someone. You're bright and smart and beautiful. They'll be queuing up.'

Steffie felt tears prick at her eyes and brushed them hastily away before her mascara ran. It was one thing feeling like a fright and quite another looking like one.

'I don't want a queue, Ails,' she whispered. 'I just want Matteo.'

In reply, Ailsa wrapped her arms around her and held her, as her mother might – if she were that sort of mother. In reality, when she'd seen her mother in London last week, she'd taken her out for lunch, bought her two new dresses and some shoes – some rather lovely shoes to be fair – and offered to set her up with a 'divine little lieutenant from the Hussars'. She meant well, Steffie knew, but it didn't help.

Far better had been the quiet hug from her father and the whispered words, 'I hear you're doing amazing work, Stefania.' She'd glowed with pride and told him she was enjoying it and she *was*, but amazing work didn't hold you close at New Year.

'Come on,' Ailsa said, pulling back and grasping Steffie's shoulders, 'let's dance.'

She tenderly wiped away traces of her tears and Steffie gave her a brave smile.

'Perhaps. No reels though!'

Her protest was in vain. Hugh Fosse was up at the front shouting something about 'Hogmanay' and some 'Gay Gordons', whoever they were, and a jig of a tune was blasting from the gramophone in the corner. Steffie was pulled helplessly into the dance but luckily it didn't seem too complicated and most people had little idea what to do anyway. She found herself whirled and spun and passed around the circle of laughing people and her aching heart settled slightly.

She supposed she could have been in a villa in the Italian hills with the love of her life and that would have been magical, but she would have been in hiding and she would have had to give up this – these friends, these colleagues, this new Steffie who people admired not just for her fancy fashion and pretty pout but for what she could bring to the team. She would have had to give up Bletchley Park and that was one thing she was glad she had not done. She knew that she'd made a difference to the war effort and that was worth a little personal suffering. Wasn't it?

She smiled up at Frank Birch as he turned her around the pub in the funny walk thing that seemed to be a key part of this crazy dance, and he gave her a broad wink.

'We'll get Jerry next year, right, Stef?'

'Right,' Steffie agreed.

We – that's who she was now, part of a we, and it felt good.

'My turn, I believe.'

Steffie blinked, trying to orientate herself as someone cut in. He spun her and she caught a shock of dark hair, a flash of chocolate-brown eyes. Her heart thudded and she lost her step.

'I've got you.'

The arms went around her, warm and soft, and he was guiding her off the dance floor and into a quiet corner. She saw Fran look up, Ailsa gasp and it was their reactions more than her own swirling senses that confirmed she wasn't going mad.

'Matteo?'

'Stefania.' He spoke her name with such tenderness and she reached up to touch his cheek, unable to believe it was truly him.

'What are you doing here?'

'Looking for you, of course.'

'But...'

'I'm working for the British now. I went into Africa with Operation Torch, infiltrating the German lines.'

'Infiltrating?' Steffie felt faint. 'That's so dangerous.'

'Not as dangerous as walking away from the woman I love.'

'What?' The music had turned to something even faster than before and over on the dance floor Ailsa and Hugh were prancing around large kitchen knives on the floor in a dance that had everyone whooping and clapping. Steffie looked into her one-time fiancé's eyes. 'What are you saying, Matteo?'

'I am saying, Stefania, my beautiful, smart, clever, amazing Stefania, that I was a fool and a bigot and a, a...'

'Pig?'

'Pig, yes. A great big, stupid pig. I was so caught up in my escape plan that I didn't think of you, of what you were doing and that it might be important. I just wanted everything to be as it was before the war, but it can't, can it? Nothing can be the same. I hated that but I've done a lot of thinking since, and a lot of missing you, and I've realised – it can't be the same but it could, perhaps, be better.'

He took her left hand in his, stroking it gently.

'I would be so, so proud to have a wife who does more than keep house and raise children and run charity balls – if she wants to, that is. In fact, I don't care what you do, Steffie, as long as you do it with me, at my side – forever.'

'Forever?' she whispered.

Before, "forever" had seemed such an easy concept, such a glittering path into houses and babies and giddy social events, but the war had changed that. Forever was more fragile now. Steffie didn't know if any of them had a future yet, let alone what she wanted to do with it.

Matteo looked at her uncertainly and she felt bad. She so wanted to step into his arms and be happy as Ailsa and Ned, and Fran and Valérie, were clearly happy, but so much had changed and it was going to take more than turning up at a dance to ensure that.

'Forever feels like a long time, Matteo,' she said eventually.

He hung his head but then it was up again, his brown eyes sparkling irrepressibly.

'What about for a date tomorrow then?' he suggested.

Warmth surged through her. He wasn't going to give up easily and that gave her hope. Besides, a date, with a dashing, handsome, entertaining RAF officer, was definitely something she could grasp.

'I'd love to, Matteo,' she said and laughed as he clutched his hand to his heart in the dramatic Italian way she'd all but forgotten.

'Praise God! I will show you, Stefania Eleanor Carmichael – I will show you that I have changed, that I value you, that I can make you happy. We can, you know, shape forever however we wish it.'

Steffie grasped him, kissing him quiet, and prayed he was right. With the Nazis still threatening so many shores, it was going to take a lot of determination, effort and will to shape all their forevers but for now it was New Year's Eve, they had the rest of the night ahead of them, and it was enough. It was more than enough.

'Let's dance, Matteo!' she cried and pulled him, laughing, into the reel as the people of Bletchley Park – the people working, unseen, to fight the evil threatening the world – spun 1943 and whatever it might bring into existence.

FORTY

They married in Bletchley church a week later with the snow whirling around, and holly and ivy as bouquets. The bride was beautiful in simple ivory lace, looking more faerie than ever with her red hair loose down her back and her bear of a father escorting her up the aisle.

'My wee bairn,' Mirren MacIver whimpered from the front pew.

Hamish looked from his daughter to his wife, suspiciously close to tears himself.

'Dry air down here in England,' he muttered in gruff Scots.

The two bridesmaids, just behind, exchanged knowing smiles. It had been a big journey for Ailsa's parents to follow in the path their daughter had set out on three years ago. But sleepy little Bletchley – for all its secrets – was hopefully not the monster-filled land they'd been led to believe and there were wide smiles behind the tears.

The bridesmaids took their places to one side, Steffie whisking up the edge of Fran's skirt just in time to stop her catching her unaccustomed heels in it and sending the whole bridal party flying.

The luggage she'd dragged up the road to Bletchley Park on that first gloomy night had finally come into its own. The three of them had emptied it out across the caravan one gloriously happy evening, like kids with a dressing-up box. Steffie was wearing her favourite Mariano Fortuny evening gown, Gloria had skilfully turned her coming-out gown into Ailsa's bridal one, and they'd all talked Fran into a glorious scarlet sheath.

'Dashed impractical,' she'd muttered, struggling to get into the BP Rolls Royce, but the way Valérie's eyes had widened when she'd stepped inside the church had made BP's top indexer blush more perfectly than any make-up artist could achieve.

The bridal couple, for all their shyness, said their vows in ringing voices, hands tightly clasped, and if Steffie's eyes drifted to Matteo, handsome in his new RAF uniform, or if Fran and Valérie mouthed the words along with the official pair, no one noticed in the general happiness.

The party, in the new assembly hall just outside BP, went on long into the night. Hugh Fosse led the dancing, with the bridal couple taking to the floor in style and the only incident being the rip up the side hem of Fran's constricting dress that Steffie happily waved away as 'a stylish improvement'. Ailsa's parents, wide-eyed and quiet at first, rapidly found their feet and Ned's parents were whipped around the hall with unexpected, but very welcome vigour.

Had Hitler only known, as Edward Travis commented over a restorative breakfast the next day, he could have attacked wherever he wanted without anyone at BP being any the wiser. But then, as he happily added, Hitler didn't even know about BP so it was a secret within a secret and the longer it stayed that way, the sooner they would win the war.

The BP bride and her maids would doubtless have agreed, had they not all been far too busy being happy to even think about it. The war would claim them again soon enough, but for a few short days it was time for love and that, after all, was what they were all fighting for.

A LETTER FROM ANNA

Dear reader,

I want to say a huge thank you for choosing to read *The Bletchley Girls*. From the moment I read the true tale of a young woman at Bletchley hiring herself a caravan, I had the idea for the story of Steffie, Fran and Ailsa, and I really hope you enjoyed it. If you want to keep up to date with all my latest releases, just sign up at the following link. Your email address will never be shared and you can unsubscribe at any time.

www.bookouture.com/anna-stuart

I, along with many others, have been fascinated by the astonishing efforts of the codebreakers for a long time, but it was when I started reading about the Y-service plucking enemy messages out of the airwaves and the SLUs sending the decodes out to the front line, that this story was truly born. Then I came across Bonner Fellers and the true story of 'Gute Quelle' and I knew that was something I wanted to explore. While most of the details of this astonishing breach of signal security are true – including that it was discovered at BP – I had fun inserting my fictional characters into the tale and hope readers enjoyed the way that it impacted them all.

If you enjoyed this novel, I'd be very grateful if you could write a review. I'd love to hear what you think, and it makes such a difference helping new readers to discover one of my

books for the first time. I also love hearing from my readers –
you can get in touch on my Facebook page, through Twitter,
Goodreads or my website.

Thanks for reading,

Anna

www.annastuartbooks.com

 facebook.com/annastuartauthor
twitter.com/annastuartbooks

BLETCHLEY HISTORICAL NOTES

Thanks to a number of excellent books and films in recent years, many people know something about the amazing work of Bletchley Park, but often just about the codebreaking. Although that was brilliant, it was the scope of the overall operation – from radio operators across the globe, to the codebreakers, to the people making sense of the decrypts and getting them into the field – that actually helped the war effort. It is that complex and secret teamwork that I found fascinating and that has driven my novel. Here are a few notes on some key elements:

Why Bletchley Park?

This old manor house just outside Bletchley village near Milton Keynes was chosen because of its geographical location on the main roads and trainlines between Oxford, Cambridge and London for easy transport of key personnel from the universities and war ministries. It also, just as critically, had excellent telegraph lines, vital for passing messages into BP in code and out again once cracked. It was bought by Admiral Hugh Sinclair in 1938 when he became frustrated with how slow the

War Office were being to recognise the need for a major Sigint (signal intelligence) site for the approaching war, and the first workers moved in under the codename 'Captain Ridley's Shooting party' in August 1939.

Recruitment was mainly by word of mouth, via the university and military networks. Later it became far more professional, but initially it was all quite ad-hoc, leading to the atmosphere of civilised, cultured equality that characterised the early days in the Park. It made sense, therefore, for Steffie to be recruited via her father's nod to his military chums, Ailsa to be spotted for her work on the amateur airwaves, and Fran via a Cambridge don she'd met at the university library.

I could go into great detail about the history of BP but there are many excellent books for those who are interested and I highly recommend a visit to the site itself to get a real feel for life in this most fascinating of wartime institutions.

Women at Bletchley Park

There were women present at BP right from its initial inception. They were initially in administrative roles but many of them soon proved their worth in higher roles and Dilly Knox, in particular, believed that women made excellent codebreakers and employed them almost exclusively in his cottage section of BP.

As the operation expanded and the bombes were brought online, requiring many people to run them, thousands of WRENS were brought into BP at an almost entirely clerical level, but there were women at the heart of all sections. It would be a mistake to say that many of them gained positions of seniority, but BP had a very flat power structure, partly due to the intimate nature of the work and partly due to it being temporary, meaning that no one was really fighting for progression, so women could excel even without apparent status.

The atmosphere was that of a relaxed, open meritocracy, with first names being used in a time when this was unusual and everyone, including minorities like women and gay people, being largely accepted at face value. This gave them a chance to shine and changed their expectations of what was possible in their lives once the war was over.

The Official Secrets Act at Bletchley Park

Everyone working at Bletchley Park had to sign the Official Secrets Act and there are first-hand accounts of the authorities putting the fear of God into employees – as in the novel – to be sure this most valuable of secrets was kept. In today's world of social media, in which no one's secrets are their own for long, it may be impossible for many of us to conceive how totally this one was kept.

As far as we're aware, no one in BP breathed a word of their work to their closest family and friends or, indeed, to people working in other sections within the Park. Inevitably there would be speculation, but BP authorities kept people in pigeon-holes to minimise the risk of their codebreaking operations becoming known. And it worked. The Germans never found out that the Allies had cracked Enigma, and this was of inestimable value in fighting – and winning – the war.

Even once the war was over, workers at BP were sworn to continued secrecy. The authorities recognised that there were more wars to come and that Sigint would be even more involved – the Cold War proved them sadly right – so many never got to tell their families or even their spouses what they had done until the information was declassified in the 1970s. There is a lovely story of one woman discovering for the first time at a BP reunion in the 1990s that her work there helped avert the sinking of a ship on which the man who subsequently became her husband had served.

Bletchley's brilliant dissemination of information

Most people are aware of the genius of the codebreakers who, with a combination of early computing technology and their own brainwork and persistence, cracked the supposedly uncrackable Enigma codes to read German (and Italian and Japanese) communications. But, brilliant as codebreaking is, without the solid if rather more dull work of translating, emending (filling in gaps and misunderstandings) and sending out, it would have been nothing more than a mathematical puzzle – satisfying for the great minds involved but of little practical use. Bletchley Park's true genius was turning itself into a vast machine for processing those decrypts in a pragmatic and highly effective way to disseminate the information to those fighting on the front lines.

Much of the credit for this belongs to Gordon Welchman, who established the pairings of the codebreaking Huts 8 and 6, with their translation and communication partners Huts 4 and 3. The next big step was the creation of the SLUs – Special Liaison Units – that operated in the various theatres of war to get the vital intel to those making operational decisions.

An unsung hero of Bletchley Park is the indexing system, of which there were several in the different units. These, as shown with Fran's work in the novel, were a way of collating intelligence so that all available information could be cross-referenced and hunted down. The work of pulling key facts out of the thousands of messages going through BP and filing them in categories – all by hand, of course – was inherently dull but vital. Being able to quickly access it was genuinely critical to a number of code breaks and key turning points, such as the Battle of Cape Matapan.

One early obstacle in getting information out to the field, as shown in the (very real) disputes in Hut 3 in the novel, was the tricky and at times bitter relationship between the war ministries and the civilian workers in BP. The leaders of the naval, military and air ministries were fiercely conservative and very protective of their powers, especially over their own people. The idea of tweedy university boffins sending information direct into the field was anathema to them and they assumed that it would create catastrophic confusion if someone inexperienced in combat tried to make decisions about what information was important in the field.

To be fair, few knew the extent of what was going on at BP, but early mistrust of 'ultra' intelligence meant many missed opportunities and it was hugely frustrating for men like Harry Hinsley, whose efforts to warn the Admiralty were ignored for far too long. It's credit to the patience, tact and sheer determination of those running BP that they found ways to demonstrate their understanding of both the messages and the front-line situations, and were slowly trusted to communicate straight to the field – greatly reducing the lead times and therefore providing vital intelligence to the men on the ground.

The Y-Service

Clearly, even with brilliant codebreakers and an efficient system to get information to your commanders, nothing works without the raw intel – the enemy signals. This is where the Y-Service (short for Wireless Service) came in, and it is a vastly underrated part of our war effort. There were hundreds of listening stations in Britain and across the globe including, to name but a few, Ceylon, Hong Kong, India, Australia, Algiers and, of course, Malta. I am indebted to Sinclair McKay for his excellent book, *The Secret Listeners*, and it is from his many stories of men and women working in exotic locations across the globe that Ailsa was born.

Wireless technology was still relatively new. It was only at the very end of the nineteenth century that Marconi had first convinced the world that it could work, but luckily it fascinated enough clever people for it to be progressing fast, and never more so than during the war. As described in the novel, the German offensive technique of blitzkrieg – sending in tank and air units to devastate an area sufficiently for the infantry to pour in relatively unopposed – required a lot of communication, necessarily mobile, so wireless was the only way. The Nazis believed that their Enigma machines made their codes secure enough to send on what was a totally open network, and Britain and her allies soon had radio operators in every possible spot to capture them and send them to BP and its outposts (such as Heliopolis) to decode and disseminate.

Like much of the work in the Sigint war, it was hard and dull, requiring extreme patience. Listeners were often posted in remote places, working for hours on end, in shift rotations that included interminable nights, to listen to messages in both Morse and 'en clair' chat. They had to be precise and meticulous and to work in utter secrecy. Some were in the military, so at least had the honour of wearing uniform in public places. Others were civilians who faced criticism – like many at BP, especially the service-age men – for not doing war work when, in reality, they were waging a hard and vital fight for control of the airwaves.

The Siege of Malta

Malta is the only nation ever to have been awarded a British medal – and with good cause. The Siege of Malta was a time of huge suffering for the people of the island. The first bombardments came from the Italians immediately after their declaration of war on Britain on 10 June 1940, and around a hundred thousand Maltese fled Valletta for the countryside, although many returned to the city later.

Malta, despite its key strategic position in the heart of the

Mediterranean, was woefully undersupplied with defences, especially planes to see off enemy attacks. Their first squadron was made up of just twelve Fairey Swordfish bombers who'd escaped from Southern France after the French capitulation in June 1940 and put up a valiant but limited defence until Hurricanes began to arrive at the end of July and Wellington bombers in October. They, too, did their best, but a severe shortage of spare parts hampered their efforts.

Trouble really came to the island when the Luftwaffe moved to Sicily at the end of 1940 and began attacking Malta, making the Italian bombardments look half-hearted, especially once the lethal dive-bombing Messerschmitts arrived in March 1941. That spring, conscription was introduced on Malta and rationing began. Britain did attempt to send more planes to Malta, with Blenheim bombers arriving and thousands being recruited to keep the airfields operational, and there was some relief when the Luftwaffe was diverted to Greece. But by December they were back on Sicily and serious attacks resumed on New Year's Day 1942, as shown in the novel.

This was a period of terror and hardship for the islanders. In early 1942, there were 117 continuous days of raids with the sirens going off, on average, ten times a day – double anything suffered by London in the Blitz. The period 20 March–28 August 1942 saw 11,819 sorties over Malta by the Luftwaffe with 6557 tons of bombs dropped, over half on Valletta. Many people were killed and, with convoys also being hit and Malta having very limited natural resources of its own, people were starting to starve.

At the end of April, the island was awarded the George Cross, but with Hitler and Mussolini approving Kesselring's invasion plans, it was little use to them. Luckily, Rommel fought to have the air support for his efforts in North Africa, giving the island a reprieve, and Air Marshal Tedder finally authorised the delivery of Spitfires. These nippy planes could get above the enemy aircraft in the fifteen minutes it took them to make it to the island from their bases on Sicily, so dogfights could take place away from Valletta, saving much bombing.

The Allies gained air superiority over the island by the end of May 1942 and in June, Gute Quelle was discovered and eventually stopped (see below). The severing of the Germans' information system, along with increased air defences, meant that a 32-ship convoy finally – after drastic delays – set sail from Britain. It was badly hit across the Mediterranean but at least the *Rochester Castle* and the *Brisbane Star* made it, with the *Ohio* oil tanker limping in between the *Penn* and the *Bramham* as shown in the novel, genuinely playing 'Chattanooga Choo-Choo' over their PA system.

It was, thankfully, the start of the end for Malta and more Spitfires held off a renewed Luftwaffe attack in autumn, while the Allies gained the field in Africa. On 20 November 1942, a convoy made it intact from Alexandria with 35,000 tons of much-needed supplies and that is the accepted date of the end of the Siege of Malta. It was just in time – surrender date had been set for 3 December!

For readers who would like to know more, I recommend the excellent *Fortress Malta: An Island Under Siege* by James Holland.

Cairo in the Second World War

I loved reading about Cairo both before and during the Second World War as it seems to have genuinely been a last bastion of high-society elegance and indulgence, while also – at Heliopolis at least – working incredibly hard to help us win the seesawing battle for North Africa. The city came dangerously close to being taken around the discovery of Gute Quelle in June 1942, and the events of 'the flap', with people scrambling to leave and secret documents being burned in a blind panic (and providing peanut sellers with paper!) are all true.

It's easy, sometimes, to look back on the Second World War and assume that we were always going to win but there are many critical points where it could so easily have gone the other way. The non-invasion of Britain was an obvious one, but holding off Rommel at El Alamein is definitely another and was in a large part down to the intelligence provided by BP, via the outpost at Heliopolis, so I was delighted to be able to put Steffie to work there.

Matteo is a fictional character but many Italian POWs were kept in Egypt and could, under certain circumstances, be visited in hospital. It is true that here and elsewhere pilots were known to visit the enemy air crew they had shot down. This practice was, however, largely put a stop to as the war progressed due to an undoubtedly correct feeling that it would cut into the killer instinct!

The places in Cairo shown in the novel such as the Gezira Club, Shepheard's Hotel and the KitKat Club are real and described based on witness accounts. Also real are many of the characters – the Endozzi sisters really did collect a list of those likely to collaborate if the Germans took the city, Major Sansom was an openly known 'spy-hunter' who operated with considerable success, and Bonner Fellers really was the unwitting source of dangerous amounts of German intel for almost a year.

Gute Quelle

The story of 'Gute Quelle' is shockingly unknown. The Americans, with Churchill's collaboration, managed to cover up this huge and very damaging breach of Sigint security so that few people realise that, thanks to their highly insecure Black Code, the Germans were briefed on virtually every British battle station and tactic in North Africa in the first half of 1942.

Post-war reports from Berlin's Chiffrierabteilung (code department), state that through the first six months of 1942, Colonel Fellers unwittingly provided: 'all we needed to know, immediately, about virtually every enemy action'. In an oral history, Dr Herbert Schaedel, the director of Chiffrier-abteilung's main intercept station near Nuremburg, recalled: 'They went crazy at Supreme Headquarters to get all the telegrams from Cairo. Rommel, each day at lunch, knew exactly where the Allied troops were standing the evening before.' This, not surprisingly, made the Germans very smug, with Joseph Goebbels, their propaganda minister, writing in April 1942: 'If the British knew in detail about us everything we know about them [from signals interception] it could have very grave conse-quences.' The delicious irony of this of course is that, thanks to BP, the British *did* know increasing amounts about them and it ultimately *did* have very grave consequences, but in 1942 the Sigint war nearly went badly wrong for the Allies.

The codebook really was captured from the American embassy in Rome (and Mussolini really did have the keys to them all!), and the code was also broken by the Germans (and, indeed by us) but still the messages were sent. Bonner Fellers was given unprecedented access to British units to forward Churchill's bid to draw America into the war and sent long and very specific reports to Washington that the Germans gobbled up gleefully.

There were, of course, no girls writing messages to each other about a farm – that part is my own fiction – but Gute Quelle was picked up in Hut 3 of Bletchley Park who took the information to the top. There were no interrogations, but it took much toing and froing between Britain and America to get the US authorities to uncover and stop the Black Code, so that Fellers truly did broadcast vulnerabilities at Tobruk that led to its fall. The only good thing to come out of this was that Churchill, who was with Roosevelt at the time, was able to embarrass him into providing huge amounts of kit for North Africa and committing to Operation Torch to secure it once and for all.

With the final unveiling of Gute Quelle, the Allies dodged a huge Sigint bullet that could easily have cost us Africa and possibly the whole war. I will leave the final word on this to an intelligence officer on Rommel's staff who, in his memoir, said that once Gute Quelle was stopped: 'In intelligence terms, Rommel could be compared to a man accustomed to going around at will and in broad daylight but suddenly forced to grope around in the pitch dark.' Uncovering Gute Quelle was amazing work by the radio operators, codebreakers and information processors of Bletchley Park and I am delighted to have been able to create Steffie, Fran and Ailsa to represent this little-known victory.

ACKNOWLEDGEMENTS

The writing of a novel can seem a very singular achievement but in fact it takes a team of people to get one out into the world in anything approaching a readable state, and I am exceptionally lucky in mine.

First there is my tireless husband, prepared to listen to novel ideas and concerns at the strangest of hours, and my children who are, perhaps, less prepared to listen but always there to celebrate at a launch! Then there is my writing cohort – my support system and fellow sufferers in this strange business we call writing. For years I have leaned on Tracy Bloom and Julie Houston, but this year I was lucky enough to expand the group on a fantastic writing retreat with Debbie Rayner, Grace Sheehan, and Karen Storey. I finished this novel in their inspiring company and love having others around me who understand the ups and downs of creating a book. Thank you, ladies.

Then there are those who help with the historical research – a part of the process that I love! For this novel, I was lucky enough to be able to visit the fantastic museum at Bletchley Park and get a real feel for the place, and I thoroughly recommend a visit to anyone. I must thank Dr David Kenyon, the amazing in-house historian, who was kind enough to meet me and answer many of my most niggly questions. It's credit to the excellent set-up at Bletchley Park that they employ a historian, and credit to David that he is such a thorough, intelligent and helpful one. Thank you, David.

Next come the Beta-readers like my dad and my good

friends Brenda and Jamie – the first people to whom I entrust my new baby in its fledgling state. And then (though to be fair these two are also rather crucial in the early stages), my editor Natasha Harding and agent Kate Shaw, who are not just the people who get my books out to the public, but also the ones who help me hone the core ideas, characters and storylines as the book is born. They have wise heads and great imaginations and I'm indebted to them both.

Following swiftly from them, are the amazing team at Bookouture who do the cover design, test the titles, produce the audio book and handle the marketing and logistics – all things I would be lost trying to do myself and that they do brilliantly and with such good humour and passion. Thank you to you all.

Finally, the readers. I would really like to thank all the amazing bloggers who take the time to read early copies of my books and provide such thoughtful and caring reviews. It's so appreciated. And last, but very much not least, are all you wonderful people who invest your money and your time in my stories and who are what make the whole thing worthwhile. Thank you so much and do, please, continue to get in touch as I really love to hear from you.

Printed in Great Britain
by Amazon

54157932R00223